ENVIRONMENT AND NARRATIVE

THEORY AND INTERPRETATION OF NARRATIVE
James Phelan and Katra Byram, Series Editors

ENVIRONMENT AND NARRATIVE

NEW DIRECTIONS IN ECONARRATOLOGY

EDITED BY

Erin James

AND

Eric Morel

THE OHIO STATE UNIVERSITY PRESS

COLUMBUS

Library of Congress Cataloging-in-Publication Data

Names: James, Erin, editor. | Morel, Eric, editor.

Title: Environment and narrative : new directions in econarratology / edited by Erin James and Eric Morel.

Other titles: Theory and interpretation of narrative series.

Description: Columbus : The Ohio State University Press, [2020] | Series: Theory and interpretation of narrative | Includes bibliographical references and index. | Summary: "Collection of essays connecting ecocriticism and narrative theory to encourage constructive discourse on narrative's influence of real-world environmental perspectives and the challenges that necessitate revision to current narrative models"—Provided by publisher.

Identifiers: LCCN 2019034865 | ISBN 9780814214206 (cloth) | ISBN 0814214207 (cloth) | ISBN 9780814277546 (ebook) | ISBN 0814277543 (ebook)

Subjects: LCSH: Ecocriticism. | Environmental literature. | Narration (Rhetoric)

Classification: LCC PN98.E36 E55 2020 | DDC 809/.93355—dc23

LC record available at https://lccn.loc.gov/2019034865

Cover design by Andrew Brozyna
Text design by Juliet Williams
Type set in Adobe Minion Pro

for Ben and Freddie, my favorites
From Erin

for Grandmaman, an avid reader and
early recommender of books
From Eric

CONTENTS

Acknowledgments   ix

INTRODUCTION   Notes Toward New Econarratologies
                 ERIN JAMES AND ERIC MOREL   1

I. NARRATOLOGY AND THE NONHUMAN

CHAPTER 1   Unnatural Narratology and Weird Realism in Jeff
             VanderMeer's *Annihilation*
                 JON HEGGLUND   27

CHAPTER 2   Object-Oriented Plotting and Nonhuman Realities in
             DeLillo's *Underworld* and Iñárritu's *Babel*
                 MARCO CARACCIOLO   45

II. ECONARRATOLOGICAL RHETORIC AND ETHICS

CHAPTER 3   Readerly Dynamics in Dynamic Climatic Times: Cli-Fi and
             Rhetorical Narrative Theory
                 ERIC MOREL   67

CHAPTER 4   A Comedy of Survival: Narrative Progression and the
             Rhetoric of Climate Change in Ian McEwan's *Solar*
                   MARKKU LEHTIMÄKI   87

CHAPTER 5   Ecocriticism as Narrative Ethics: Triangulating
             Environmental Virtue in Richard Powers's *Gain*
                   GREG GARRARD   107

III. ANTHROPOCENE STORYWORLDS

CHAPTER 6   Feeling Nature: Narrative Environments and Character Empathy
                   ALEXA WEIK VON MOSSNER   129

CHAPTER 7   Finding a Practical Narratology in the Work of Restoration
             Ecology
                   MATTHEW M. LOW   147

CHAPTER 8   Worldmaking Environmental Crisis: Climate Fiction,
             Econarratology, and Genre
                   ASTRID BRACKE   165

CHAPTER 9   Narrative in the Anthropocene
                   ERIN JAMES   183

AFTERWORD   Econarratology for the Future
                   URSULA K. HEISE   203

Contributors   213
Index   217

ACKNOWLEDGMENTS

WE WOULD LIKE to thank all of the contributors who have been part of the project at various stages. The initial call for proposals received dozens of interested and interesting abstracts, and the culling from this was even still too large. As a result, a subset of fascinating essays originally intended for the collection had to be split off and published elsewhere, and we are pleased with the result: a special issue of *English Studies* focused on ecocriticism and narrative theory that complements this collection. We thank the contributors to that issue: Dana Philips, Bart Welling, David Rodriguez, Marta Puxan-Oliva, Taylor Egan, and Daniel Cryer. We also thank the journal's editor, Odin Dekkers, and the peer reviewers for that issue who helped bring that scholarship to its audience. We would also like to thank our colleagues who were part of conversations about this book at its earliest stages: Eric Heyne, Nancy Easterlin, Glenn Wilmott, and Anna Banks.

We are so pleased to be releasing this collection in this series with The Ohio State University Press. All of the editorial staff have been easy to work with and supportive: Lindsay Martin, Kristen Elias Rowley, and Ana M. Jimenez-Moreno. This collection would not be as strong if it were not for the insightful and targeted feedback of the anonymous reviewers and especially the series editors, Katra Byram and Jim Phelan, who read the chapters and offered their recommendations. Katra's meticulous reading and Jim's solution-oriented feedback have helped each of our contributors sharpen their chapters to make the whole even stronger than the inherent strength of its parts.

Erin would like to thank her colleagues at the University of Idaho who supported her through this project and listened to early versions of its arguments. She owes much to the friendship of Jennifer Ladino, Jodie Nicotra, Alexandra Teague, and Tara MacDonald. She would also like to thank the members of the Ecocriticism Reading Group, especially Scott Slovic, Peter Remien, Xinmin Liu, Anna Banks, Debbie Lee, Donna Potts, and Kota Inoue, for their vibrant monthly conversations. Kota's memory lives on in these pages that he helped to foster. Numerous graduate students have helped Erin appreciate potential new directions of econarratological scholarship, including students in the "Narrative and Environment" seminar: Dustin Purvis, Jake McGinnis, Jordan Clapper, Joseph Perreault, Megan Tribley, and Vanessa Hester. Erin is also thankful for the University of Idaho's Seed Grant program, which provided financial support for this project. She would like to thank Eric, her favorite collaborator and the best editor that she knows, for being such a great friend and colleague. Above all, she would like to thank her parents, and Ben, Freddie, Rudy, and Poppet for their unconditional love.

Eric is grateful for those who provided feedback on his chapter over the course of its various iterations, including Gary Handwerk, Jesse Oak Taylor, Nancy Easterlin, Greg Garrard, Eric Heyne, Sam Hushagen, and Ned Schaumberg. The final form benefited especially from the elegance of Jim Phelan's feedback on the manuscript draft. In addition to the financial support of teaching positions in the University of Washington's Department of English and Program on the Environment, he received invaluable moral support throughout his time working on this collection from Ned Schaumberg, Lydia Heberling, Lowell Wyse, and William Lombardi. Eric's family has heard him stress about this project for years, and he sends them love and appreciation. But perhaps above all, Eric would like to thank Erin for this opportunity to collaborate on this project; few scholars have the opportunity to work on such a boundary-pushing project from the get-go of their careers, and fewer still have the privilege to work with as gracious and supportive a mentor as Erin. That she saw merit enough in his work to bring him on not just as a contributor but as a collaborator has felt like a gift.

Notes Toward New Econarratologies

ERIN JAMES AND ERIC MOREL

TWO SIMPLE PREMISES lie at the heart of this edited collection of original essays: first, that stories about the environment significantly influence experiences of that environment, and vice versa, and second that scholars can do a much better job of understanding those stories and suggesting alternatives. Further, these essays acknowledge that understandings of narrative change as the environment changes—that the modern environmental crisis, in addition to being partly a crisis *of* narrative, also promises to have a strong effect *on* narrative and narrative theory.

As a forum for discussing the reciprocal relationship between environment and narrative, this collection explores what we call *econarratology,* or the paired consideration of material environments and their representations and narrative forms of understanding. This collection's contributors suggest methodological possibilities within econarratology by examining the mechanics of how narratives can convey environmental understanding via building blocks such as the organization of time and space, characterization, focalization, description, and narration. They position narratives as important occasions and repositories for the values, political and ethical ideas, and sets of behaviors that determine how we perceive and interact with ecological homes. They also query how readers emotionally and cognitively engage with such representations and how the process of encountering different environments in narratives might affect real-world attitudes and behaviors of those readers. They suggest that changing humans' interactions with the environment requires not only new stories but also a better understanding of the ones that have long been in circulation. Moreover, they contend that today's environmental challenges necessitate revisions to models of narrative. Overall, this collection explores the ways in which econarratology expands and enriches the theory and interpretation of narrative.

PAIRING NARRATIVE AND ENVIRONMENT

Narratives have become a touchstone for scholarship within the emerging field of the environmental humanities. Collecting work in and across fields such as literature, philosophy, sociology, geography, anthropology, history, and science and technology studies, research in the environmental humanities seeks to offer up an interdisciplinary and wide-ranging response to today's environmental challenges and emphasize the idea that these problems are not exclusively environmental, but also deeply cultural. As Sverker Sörlin states, work in the environmental humanities suggests that "in a world where cultural values, political or religious ideas, and deep-seated human behaviors still rule the way people lead their lives, produce, and consume, the idea of *environmentally relevant knowledge* must change" (788). Thus far, work in the environmental humanities has tended to focus on key influential ideas that such interdisciplinary scholarship raises, such as the Anthropocene and the questioning of meaning, value, responsibility, and purpose in light of environmental crisis. It also tends to foreground its commitment to an earth-centered ethics of care and imagine alternatives to the destructive behaviors and attitudes that underlie environmental damage.

Unsurprisingly to the contributors to this collection, narrative has become a key site of inquiry for such discussions, as many environmental humanities scholars recognize a crisis of narrative subtending today's environmental crisis. In their introduction to the inaugural issue of *Environmental Humanities,* a journal for that emerging field, the editors call for an "unsettling of dominant narratives" and a study of "new narratives that are calibrated to the realities of our changing world" (Rose et al. 3). In doing so, they pick up on Val Plumwood's earlier observations in *Environmental Culture: The Ecological Crisis of Reason* (2002), where she cites a "dominant narrative of reason" that culminates in "global economic regimes that threaten the biosphere" as the primary cause of the modern environmental crisis (5–6). Similarly, in their introduction to *Global Ecologies and the Environmental Humanities,* Elizabeth DeLoughrey, Jill Didur, and Anthony Carrigan cite as a major theme of the environmental humanities the role that narrative plays in "drawing attention to and shaping our ideas about catastrophic and long-term environmental challenges such as climate change, militarism, resource extraction, the pollution and management of the global commons, petrocapitalism, and the commodification and capitalization of nature" (2). They further suggest that "a critical study of narrative . . . is essential to determining how we interpret and mitigate environmental crisis" (25). Ursula Kluwick concurs, noting that public understandings of environmental problems are "intrinsically tied to narrative strategies" (503); her work thus focuses on calling attention to specific narratives embedded in climate change discourse. Foregrounding their ethical commitment to environmental care explicitly, Ursula K. Heise and Allison Carruth posit that a key question of environmental humanities scholarship is "which concepts of narratives from the environmental inventory will move environmentally oriented thought into the future, and which ones shackle environmentalism to outdated templates?" (3). These scholars all argue that we have told ourselves stories about the environment that permit and encourage destructive behavior and call for a better understanding of these narratives and the exploration of new, more environmentally responsible ones.

Ecocritics have hovered over the connection of narrative and environment for some time without explicitly reaching for narrative theory. Though what counts as ecocriticism remains open to discussion, ecocritics still frequently invoke some or all of Cheryll Glotfelty's statement that "simply put, ecocriticism is the study of the relationship between literature and the physical environment. Just as feminist criticism examines language and literature from a gender-conscious perspective, and Marxist criticism brings an awareness of modes of production and economic class to its reading of texts, ecocriticism takes an earth-centered approach to literary studies" (xviii). Strategically capacious, this framing of ecocriticism's scope does more to propose a field of inquiry than a set of tools for working in that field. That field's explicit attention to narrative has been diffuse and diverse,[1] but one recent gesture by ecocritics such as Serenella Iovino and Serpil Oppermann, inspired by new materialist scholarship that views the material world as possessing its own agency, has shifted the ecocritical conversation to read the earth *as* a text. Materialist ecocritics often write of the "narrative agency of matter" and speak of "storied matter," arguing that "the world's material phenomena are knots in a vast network of agencies, which can be 'read' and interpreted as forming narratives, stories" (8, 1). According to these scholars, today's environmental

1. See, for examples, Ursula Le Guin's "The Carrier Bag of Fiction," Lawrence Buell's *The Environmental Imagination* and *Writing for an Endangered World,* Terre Satterfield and Scott Slovic's *What's Nature Worth?,* Slovic's *Going Away to Think,* and Daniel Wildcat's *Red Alert!*

crisis is not only a crisis of narrative; today's environment is also capable of producing *its own* narratives.

Another set of voices has started paying attention to narrative with a more critical or skeptical stance, wondering whether narrative as a mode is irreparably thwarted by environmental problems. These include Timothy Morton, Claire Colebrook, and Timothy Clark, as well as the writer Amitav Ghosh. A major benefit to bringing narrative theory into conversation with such arguments has to do with the specificity of its terminology; econarratology allows for cross-examining more skeptical claims on the basis of what definition of "narrative" they deploy—revealing that they often use the word nebulously, or in ways postclassical narratologies have complicated, or sometimes in ways that conflate the category of narrative with the novel. If, as Stef Craps and Rick Crownshaw discuss in their introduction to a special issue of *Studies in the Novel,* a variety of new and old novels seem to afford valuable insights on the plots and futures of climate change, econarratologists have reason to be optimistic that the even broader mode of narrative has much still to contribute to crafting cultural responses to present and future environmental challenges.

Yet despite the prominent role that narrative plays in these environmental conversations, the perspective of narrative scholars is largely absent. Some have offered possible starting places. Heise, in her groundbreaking *Sense of Place, Sense of Planet* (2008), argues for attending to the "challenges" of "narrative patterns" entailed by refocusing the scale of environmental concern from the local to the global (21, 22). Narrative formats such as the ramble in the nearby wild, she contends, seldom rise to the challenge of addressing the risk scenarios posed by destabilization of geophysical forces and patterns. But while this study has garnered intense ecocritical focus, Heise's attention to narrative forms has been eclipsed by critics' interest in her broader project of shifting scale. Heise repeats her call for sensitivity to narrative structures in her afterword to Bonnie Roos and Alex Hunt's *Postcolonial Green: Environmental Politics and World Narrative* (2010), in which she urges ecocritical scholars to consider the "question of the aesthetic." She notes that ecocritical analyses "have often tended to assess creative works most centrally in terms of whether they portray the realities of social oppression and environmental devastation accurately, and what ideological perspectives they imply," and that such assessments are undoubtedly necessary. But she also states bluntly that "if factual accuracy, interesting political analysis, or wide public appeal is what we look for, there are better and more straightforward places to find them than novels and poems." Her primary interest thus lies in the "aesthetic transformation of the real," which she reminds readers has "a particular potential for reshaping the individual and collective ecosocial imaginary" (258).

Nancy Easterlin shares Heise's interest in what forms and media do. In her "biocultural" work, which brings together evolutionary history and cognitive science to bear on questions of literary theory, she admirably explains the misguidedness of much ecocriticism that tries to find the genre or form that will "palliate the soul" to "culminate in an environmentally friendly perspective" (96).[2] Instead, she explains the interest of narrative as an "agentive force," writing that "integrating the actions and purposes of human groups within their prescribed domain, narrative brings into relation and coordinates sequence, causality, physical place, knowledge of interaction with human others, and self-concept" (139). In these terms, the stakes proliferate for studying narrative workings more widely and not only specific narrative genres, especially as ecocritics mull over the complexities of nature-cultures and their networks.

Several of this book's contributors also have attempted to yoke together environment and narrative in their previous work. Markku Lehtimäki explicitly merges ecocriticism and narratology in his essay, "Natural Environments in Narrative Contexts: Cross-Pollinating Ecocriticism and Narrative Theory," which interrogates "the reciprocal relationship between conceptions of nature and modes of storytelling" (120). As for Easterlin and Brian Boyd before him, human evolution's deep history presents Lehtimäki a point of confluence between subfields since it naturalizes the practices of narrative making that otherwise seem artificial. Further, he draws from rhetorical narrative theory's terms to suggest that naturalizing narrative expands ecocritical attention to the aesthetic, "synthetic" concerns.

Most directly, this collection builds on Erin James's *The Storyworld Accord: Econarratology and Postcolonial Narratives,* which first put forward the term "econarratology" as part of her interest in developing a method for studying mutual intelligibility across distances and cultures. Although James's specific project draws in central ways from the work of cognitive narratologists generally and David Herman's concept of storyworld in particular, she advances broadly that "econarratology embraces the key concerns of each of its parent discourses—it maintains an interest in studying the relationship between literature and the physical environment, but does so with sensitivity to the literary structures and devices that we use to communicate representations of the physical environment to each other via narratives" (23). This articulation of econarratology usefully describes the various and sometimes conflicting combinations of ecocriticism and narrative theory. Whatever their differences, they follow James's study in advocating for holding together concerns of con-

---

2. Similarly, Brian Boyd's work on "evocriticism"—his preferred term for a Darwinist mode of reading that interprets literature as an adaptive behavior of the human species—makes an illuminating pairing of narrative forms and environmental ideas.

tent and form, and they point out the high environmental and social stakes for doing so.

NEW DIRECTIONS IN ECONARRATOLOGY

The essays in this collection recognize three key directions in which econarratology might develop beyond these promising origins. The first concerns the representation of the nonhuman in narratives. Narrative theory has tended to be deeply anthropogenic in its approach to narrative; see, for example, the emphasis on human communication and interaction in James Phelan's definition of narrative (developed with Peter J. Rabinowitz, among others) as "somebody telling somebody else on some occasion and for some purpose that something happened" (Phelan, *Somebody* ix). The rhetorical model's centralized "somebody" is only one of many approaches to narrative that assumes human speakers. While narrative scholars agree that narrators and/or characters do not necessarily need to *be* human, all acknowledge that at the foundation of narrative lies a rhetorical situation reliant upon human capacities for language. After all, narrators must narrate, and narratees must have the ability to receive a narrative. But two recent essays query how this anthropogenic genre can help readers better understand the relationship between humans and the organisms and material with which we share the world.

In "The Storied Lives of Non-human Narrators," Lars Bernaerts, Marco Caracciolo, Luc Herman, and Bart Vervaeck examine what they call the phenomenon of "nonhuman storytelling." Their interest lies in the paradoxical idea that "readers are invited to reflect upon aspects of human life when reading the fictional life stories of nonhuman narrators, whether they are animals, objects, or indefinable entities" (68). Drawing on a long and diverse tradition of narratives that feature such narrators—including those by Franz Kafka, Italo Calvino, Julian Barnes, and Julio Cortázar, and nineteenth-century children's stories, among others—Bernaerts et al. argue that narratives featuring nonhuman narrators highlight and even challenge readers' conceptions of what it is to be human. They thus introduce a new conceptual framework for the study of nonhuman narration that relies upon a "*double dialectic* of empathy and defamiliarization, human and nonhuman experientiality" (69).

Bernaerts et al. identify a basic contradiction in stories featuring nonhuman narrators: narratives that represent nonhuman experientiality in impossible ways (talking rats, narrating mathematical equations, etc.) task readers with thinking through the capacities and limitations of human experientiality. The writers thus argue that preexisting conceptual frameworks for interpreting narratives are not suitable for such texts. In particular, they push against Monika Fludernik's idea of "natural" narratology that links narrativity to representations of human experientiality and the corresponding categorization of "unnatural" narratives, or anti-mimetic texts, suggested by Jan Alber, Stefan Iversen, Henrik Skov Nielsen, and Brian Richardson that violate the physical laws and logic of human experience by representing scenarios, characters, temporalities, and spaces that cannot occur in the real world. As Bernaerts et al. write:

> "Natural" narratology stresses the importance of human experientiality, while "unnatural" narratology stresses the anti-mimetic aspects of nonhuman narration. Between these two poles, something else happens as well . . . namely the projection of *nonhuman* experientiality. Often, if not always, nonhuman narrators use techniques of focalization, characterization, and consciousness representation to evoke nonhuman experientiality. Thus, nonhuman narration cannot be reduced to the unnatural and the strange, since it is caught in a dialectic of empathy and defamiliarization, the familiar and the strange, human and nonhuman experience. (75)

According to Bernaerts et al., stories featuring nonhuman narrators are neither wholly "natural" nor "unnatural"; they exist in a liminal space in between, representing impossible scenarios and characters and yet calling attention to the experiences of humans. The slipperiness of these categories—human experience and nonhuman experience, "natural" and "unnatural"—provide scholars a productive set of terms and tools with which to investigate the relationship between the human and the nonhuman and its representation in narrative. In turn, environmental humanities and ecocritical ideas about the more-than-human, the "mesh," and material agency add important new insight to complicate and sophisticate such analyses.

In "Narratology Beyond the Human," David Herman's interest lies not in nonhuman narrators, specifically, but in the place of humans in broader ecological contexts. Situating his essay within recent work in cognitive science, evolutionary biology, and ecocriticism, Herman argues that fictional narratives can serve as important imaginative tools for critiquing, dismantling, or reconstructing ideas about human selfhood in a modern world in which it is impossible to conceive of the human "self" as isolated and unconnected to larger ecological and biotic communities. Using Lauren Groff's short story "Above and Below" as a case study, Herman argues that a "narratology beyond the human" can not only illuminate "how a given self-narrative locates the human agent in a transspecies constellation of selves" but also can "assist with the construction of new, more sustainable individual and collective self-narratives that situate the self within wider webs of creatural life" (131). Herman's reading of Groff's story—and his theorization of a narratology sensitive to sustainability and the survival of wider biotic communities—enacts the very ethics of environmental responsibility and care for which environmental humanities and ecocritical scholars call.

We find a second direction for the development of econarratology in discussions of narrative ethics. When Glotfelty made connections between ecocriticism, feminism, and Marxism in her definition of the field, she declared that ecocriticism, like its feminist and Marxist predecessors, has a pronounced ethical orientation. Her conceptualization of ecocriticism privileges the environment in its analysis of literary texts, celebrating those that foster a sense of environmental responsibility among readers and critiquing those that perpetuate damaging environmental attitudes and behaviors.

Narrative theory has not always shared this ethical stance. Indeed, early work in what narrative scholars now label "classical narratology" mostly *avoided* such ethical interests. Drawing heavily on Saussurean linguistics that separates *langue* (the abstract, semantic principles of language) and *parole* (an individual utterance of language), classical narratology attempts to characterize narrative *langue,* or the "code or set of principles governing the production of all and only narratives" (Prince 48). This early work—typified by Gérard Genette's *Narrative Discourse* (1980)—focused on categorizing and classifying common narrative structures and introduced an extensive new lexicon of terms for narrative analysis. But scholarship in subsequent "postclassical" narratology has broadened its perspective not only to consider narrative *langue* but also the effects of narratives on real-world readers. An important part of this postclassical shift has been rhetorical approaches to narrative that conceive of such texts as purposeful communicative acts, in which narrative tellers seek to engage and influence the emotions and values of their readers. According to scholars such as Phelan, a narrative is a motivated act. Phelan states explicitly that "in telling what happened, narrators give accounts of characters whose interactions with each other have an ethical dimension" and that "the acts of telling and receiving those accounts also have an ethical dimension" ("Rhetoric/Ethics" 203). Consequently, for many postclassical scholars of narrative,[3] a study of narrative must attend not only to narrative categories and classification but also to narrative as a multisided ethical interaction.

---

3. Phelan develops this interest across multiple successive publications; for an example, see *Living to Tell About It*. Moreover, his interest in narrative ethics carries forward the work of his mentor Wayne C. Booth, whose books *The Rhetoric of Fiction* and *The Company We Keep* remain widely cited arguments about literary ethics. Not all work in narrative ethics is explicitly

We can view work by rhetorical narrative theorists, such as Phelan and Rabinowitz,[4] in light of other postclassical narratological scholarship that studies the ethical and political dimensions of narrative, or the *work* that narratives do and the effects that they have on their audiences.[5] Prominent among this work are those approaches to narrative that emphasize narratives as tools of ideology. Scholars of feminist narratology such as Susan L. Lanser and Robyn Warhol[6] connect the structures of narratives to the social context of their writers to highlight that categories of sex, gender, and sexuality are relevant to the analysis of textual entities. While Lanser in "Toward a Feminist Narratology" acknowledges that the "technical, often neologistic, vocabulary of narratology has alienated critics of many persuasions and may seem particularly counterproductive to critics with political concerns," she argues that feminism and narrative theory can productively inform each other, especially in terms of the role of gender in the construction of narrative and the importance of historical and cultural context for determining meaning in narrative (343). Similarly, narrative theorists invested in postcolonial literature and theory such as Fludernik and Marion Gymnich explore how particular narrative structures can construct, perpetuate, or subvert categories of race, ethnicity, and class in a given narrative.

None of this work—rhetorical, feminist, or postcolonial narratology—is explicitly environmental. But by foregrounding the ethical and political dimensions of individual narratives, and by positioning narratives as persuasive acts that engage and influence the attitudes and behaviors of their readers, they provide useful models for econarratological modes of reading sensitive to the ideological messages that particular narratives and narrative structures can encode in their representations of environments. They also stress the need to consider wider contexts of production and reception when analyzing narratives, thus opening up econarratology to reflections on the cultural and

---

rhetorical, however. The work of Adam Zachary Newton and Martha Nussbaum put greater stress on the act of reading itself as ethically engaged through-and-through. For Nussbaum, see *Love's Knowledge*. Newton's *Narrative Ethics* lays the groundwork for his Levinasian take on narrative ethics, but his more recent books *The Elsewhere: On Belonging at Near Distance* and *To Make the Hands Impure* will perhaps be of greater interest to ecocritics for their emphases on place, corporeality, and materiality of books and speech.

4. See, for example, their collaborative entries in the volume by Herman, et al.: *Narrative Theory: Core Concepts & Critical Debates*.

5. Some narrative scholars, following the direction of Ansgar Nünning, label these approaches as "contextualist narratologies." See Nünning's "Surveying Contextualist and Cultural Narratologies."

6. Warhol represents feminist narratology broadly in her contribution to Herman et al.'s *Narrative Theory: Core Concepts and Critical Debates*.

historical contexts of narrative tellers and readers in its analysis of narrative environments.

We find a third direction for the development of econarratology in a turn toward cognitive science. While ecocritics such as Glen A. Love and Dana Phillips have long suggested ecological literacy must be a central core of ecocritical scholarship,[7] ecocritics have tended to shy away from other forms of scientific knowledge, especially those dealing with human perception and imagination.[8] Yet the ecocritical appeal of insights from embodied cognition (the idea that cognition is dependent upon the experience of the physical body in an environment) and enactivism (the idea that consciousness arises via a body's interaction with its environment) are clear. As Alexa Weik von Mossner argues, the combination of ecocriticism, narrative theory, and cognitive science "can give us a better understanding of how we interact with [environmental] narratives on the mental and affective level in ways that are both biologically universal and culturally specific" (3). Caracciolo agrees, stating that ecocritical approaches to narratives informed by cognitive science help to explain "how the production and interpretation of stories fit into the larger picture of our meaningful encounters with the world" ("Narrative, Meaning, Interpretation" 368).

A cognitive turn will push studies of environment and narrative in several directions, foremost among these being enriched analysis of literary space. Inspired by cognitive studies that suggest that readers must mentally model and emotionally inhabit the context of a narrative's characters to understand a narrative, narrative scholars such as Herman and Marie-Laure Ryan have introduced new categories of narrative space to consider alongside temporal categories of order, duration, and frequency. In the process, they add new terms to the narratological lexicon, including "deictic shift" (the process by which narrative interpreters relocate from the here and now of their reading environment to the alternative space-time coordinates of a narrative environment), "figures" and "grounds" (located and reference objects, respectively), and "topological" and "projective" locations (inherent or viewer-related representations of space, respectively).[9] The concept of "storyworld," or a reader's mental model of the context and environment within which a narrative's char-

---

7. See Love's *Practical Ecocriticism: Literature, Biology, and the Environment* and Phillips's *The Truth of Ecology: Nature, Culture, and Literature in America.*

8. A notable exception here is Nancy Easterlin's work on the imagination and perception of material environments. See especially chapter 3 of *A Biocultural Approach to Literary Theory and Interpretation.*

9. For a richer analysis of narrative space, see Herman's "Spatial Reference in Narrative Domains." See also Marie-Laure Ryan, Kenneth Foote, and Maoz Azaryahu's *Narrating Space/ Spatializing Narrative.*

acters function, is essential to these discussions of narrative space. Importantly for considerations of narrative environments, the concept of "storyworld" calls attention to the worldmaking power of narrative, or its potential to immerse or transport readers into virtual environments that differ from the physical environments in which they read.[10] The study of space and place has been long central to ecocritical scholarship; as Lawrence Buell argues, "environmental criticism arises within and against the history of human modification of planetary space" (*Future* 62). Indeed, a basic concern of ecocriticism is the process by which *space,* which connotes abstraction, is modified into *place,* which connotes value and meaning. The spatial turn in narrative theory, inspired by research into the cognitive processes of narrative interpretation, provides ecocritics with an invaluable vocabulary by which to better analyze human perceptions of spaces *and* places. Likewise, ecocritical considerations of the values of inhabited places introduces a useful cultural dimension to discussions of narrative spaces.

In addition to encouraging narrative scholars to think through the ways in which readers simulate narrative space, cognitive science also has led narrative theorists to develop their understanding of how narratives can affect the emotions, attitudes, and behaviors of readers by encouraging them to simulate the emotional states and experiences of characters and/or narrators. Through Theory of Mind (ToM) and cognitive simulation theory—respectively, Lisa Zunshine's and Blakey Vermeule's preferred terms for the mind-reading activity that they claim is essential to narrative comprehension—these scholars argue that narratives provide readers with safe spaces in which to "try on" the emotional states of others. They thus suggest that narratives help us improve our everyday interactions with real-life others, as they permit readers to project themselves into other consciousnesses and thus experience *what it is like* for others to move about the world. Suzanne Keen, in her work on narrative empathy, explores the potential of narratives to prompt the "spontaneous sharing of feelings, including physical sensations in the body, evoked by witnessing or hearing about another's condition," or encourage readers to feel "*with* another" (*Empathy* xx, xxi). As with rhetorical, feminist, and postcolonial approaches to narrative, scholarship in cognitive narratology and narrative empathy has not yet addressed environmental issues nor considered the uses of these models for analysis of narrative environments.[11] But as they query the potential for narratives to introduce readers

---

10. For further scholarship on narrative transportation/immersion, see Richard Gerrig's *Experiencing Narrative Worlds* and work by Melanie C. Green and Timothy C. Brock.

11. Two notable exceptions involve scholarship on animals and graphic novels: Keen's "Fast Tracks to Narrative Empathy" and Herman's "Storyworld/Umwelt." See below for further discussion of the latter.

to new experiences and emotional states—including those linked to perceptions of and interactions with particular environments—they provide literary scholars with insightful and illuminating models for reading environmental experiences in narratives and studying the emotional effects of engaging with virtual worlds.

Cognitive ecocritical approaches to narrative will also enrich studies of the body and literature. Stacy Alaimo's notion of trans-corporeality, "in which the human is always intermeshed with the more-than-human world," has encouraged ecocritics to consider "the extent to which the substance of the human is ultimately inseparable from 'the environment'" (2). Analysis of the intermeshing of the body and its environment and the role that literature can/does play in that intertwining has much to gain from embodied and enactivist understandings of narrative comprehension. On a basic level, embodied cognition helps literary scholars better understand the readers' emotional engagement with literary environments, as they foreground the ways in which reading narratives produce bodily, affective responses among readers. Scholars such as Caracciolo take this idea one step further, arguing that narrative comprehension demands that readers navigate the imagined environments of narratives via a virtual body and thus simulate or enact embodied engagements with environments in an "off-line" mode. Finally, cognitive approaches to narrative and environment will also boost the empirical research that ecocritical scholars increasingly call for—see, for example, Weik von Mossner's *Affective Ecologies* (2017) and Scott Slovic and Paul Slovic's *Nerves and Numbers: Information, Emotion, and Meaning in a World of Data* (2015). Cognitive scholars have amassed a rich corpus of empirical research via fMRI scans of the brains of individual readers and audience response studies, among other methods, that provides ecocritics with solid models for exploring how actual readers process and engage with narrative environments and how interaction with these virtual worlds may shape real-life attitudes, values, and behaviors.

We would like to flag two additional directions of new econarratological work that are rich veins of analysis of narrative and environment. As she indicates in the subtitle of *The Storyworld Accord: Econarratology and Postcolonial Narratives,* James's initial discussion of econarratology in that publication focuses explicitly on postcolonial narratives. She argues that while econarratology is applicable to a broad range of texts from different historical periods and geographical regions, econarratological readings of postcolonial narratives "stand to offer up particularly rich insights into how people around the world imagine and inhabit their environments" and thus can play "an important role in a more sensitive and sustainable response to today's environmental crisis" (xiii). We can view James's work in light of a growing cluster of texts that, although they don't use the term "econarratology," pair ecocritical and formal readings of postcolonial narratives, including Jens Martin Gurr's "Emplotting an Ecosystem: Amitav Ghosh's *The Hungry Tide* and the Question of Form in Ecocriticism," Kylie Crane's *Myths of Wilderness in Contemporary Narratives* (2012), and Roman Bartosch's *EnvironMentality: Ecocriticism and the Event of Postcolonial Fiction* (2013).[12] Indeed, in a reversal of the largely Anglo-European and American origins of both narratology and ecocriticism, econarratology's influences and early examples grow predominantly from analyses of postcolonial texts.

Non-Anglophone, indigenous, and postcolonial texts remain a crucial site of inquiry for econarratological scholarship. Environmental humanities scholars emphasize the importance of cultural context in their work; DeLoughrey, Didur, and Carrigan in their introduction to *Global Ecologies and the Environmental Humanities* forcefully argue that "a history of globalization and imperialism is integral to understanding contemporary environmental issues" (2). This work draws heavily on the distinction between the "full-stomach" environmentalism of the global North and the "empty-belly" environmentalism of the global South that historians Ramachandra Guha and J. Martinez-Alier draw in *Varieties of Environmentalism* (1997). The examples of environmental conflict that they discuss—including that of Project Tiger, the Indian national government's conservation program that has led to the displacement of the Chenchus community in the southern state of Andhara as their home forest is set aside for tiger reserves, and imprisonment of Indians that have been caught protecting their communities by injuring or killing tigers—offer a powerful corrective to the narrative that "the countries of the South . . . are too poor, too narrow-minded, or too relentlessly focused on the short term to be Green" (xvii). Guha and Martinez-Alier's work highlights not only the cultural and material contexts that produce environmental destruction and devastation, but also the idea that one's perception of and relationship to an environment is culturally coded. As a result, they argue that environmental ethos is also culturally coded and dependent upon local contexts. Closer attention to the narratives that inform such site- and culture-specific contexts illuminates cross-cultural blind spots and fosters the production of new environmentalisms sensitive to local attitudes, values, and behaviors. As language is one obvious example of such site- and culture-specific context, econarratology will benefit from expanding to consider the nuances of not only postcolonial and indigenous narratives written in English but also of non-Anglophone texts.

---

12. While not explicitly focused on postcolonial narratives, Raul Lejano, Mrill Ingram, and Helen Ingram's *The Power of Narrative in Environmental Networks* is an additional example of work that pairs environment and narrative, though chiefly in nonliterary contexts.

Future econarratological scholarship also must expand beyond written narratives. Orality, and especially aboriginal and indigenous oral storytelling traditions, is an especially rich direction for such work because of the ways in which it demands that scholars pair textual analysis with the study of the immediate environment in which the narrative both is told and received. Oral storytelling requires physical proximity of storyteller to audience; as Isidore Okpewho writes of African oral traditions, "most public performances of songs and tales are done in such a way that there is no physical separation between performer and audience members" (63). Oral storytelling is also a physical medium, in which the body of the storyteller (and the bodies of the listening audience with which it interacts) are vital components to the transmission and comprehension of narrative. These special components of oral narratives clearly connect traditions of orality to the interests of econarratological scholarship that we discuss above, including narrative spatialization and the focus on the body by new materialism scholars.

Future econarratological scholarship also will find much to discuss in visual narratives. As Marco Caracciolo's essay in this collection suggests, cinematic texts can be equally as creative in their representations of the nonhuman world as their purely literary counterparts. Other scholars have weighed in on the special potential of visual narratives to represent the nonhuman world in ways that purely literary narratives cannot. In "Storyworld/Umwelt: Nonhuman Experiences in Graphic Narratives," Herman explores how the medium-specific properties of graphic narratives can represent what it is like for nonhuman characters to experience events. Herman posits that because graphic narratives "recruit from more than one semiotic channel to evoke storyworlds," they stand to "emulate, with as much granularity or detail as possible, how other animals engage with their surrounding world" (160, 174). Herman does not argue that all graphic narratives represent nonhuman experiences with some degree of accuracy; he places such texts along a continuum of anthropomorphization, with *animal allegories* at one pole and *umwelt exploration*[13] at the other pole. Yet in his discussion of *umwelt exploration* graphic narratives such as Nick Abadzis's *Laika* and Grant Morrison and Frank Quietly's *We3*—texts that do not feature heavily anthropomorphized animals and that actively figure the "moment-by-moment experiences of nonhuman animals"—Herman suggests that visual narratives can not only represent animal

---

13. In using the term *umwelt,* Herman draws on German-Estonian philosopher-biologist Jakob von Uexküll's concept of the "lived, phenomenal worlds . . . of creatures whose organismic structure differs from our own" ("Storyworld/Umwelt" 159).

consciousness in ways impossible in purely literary narratives but also challenge basic anthropomorphic assumptions of narrativity itself as a representation of experiencing *human* consciousness (178).

In her discussion of narratives and transspecies empathy in *Affective Ecologies,* Weik von Mossner makes a similar claim about the potential of visual narratives. She focuses on the 2009 documentary *The Cove,* which bears witness in a pivotal scene to the slaughter of hundreds of dolphins by Japanese fisherman harvesting dolphin meat. Weik von Mossner observes that the scene contains "no commentary, no narration, just long minutes filled with images of relentless, brutal slaughter" as the fisherman "over and over again drive their spears into the bodies of the trapped animals" (105). For Weik von Mossner, the scene's visual and auditory cues are essential structures by which the narrative fosters empathy among viewers for the dolphins; she argues that scenes such as this are especially painful for human viewers to watch because of the tendency of those viewers to "empathize with nonhuman animals, feeling their joy, their fear, their terror and their pain" (106). She suggests that human viewers see the writhing bodies of the dolphins and hear the animals' anguished cries, and they develop a sense in turn of what it is like to be the subject of such animal cruelty. The film, according to Mossner, demonstrates that anthropomorphism "is not a necessary condition for our empathic responses to animals." This argument is testament to the powerful potential of narrative to shift the real-life attitudes, behaviors, and values of interpreters.

Yet the visual and auditory cues upon which this display of suffering depend are much more difficult to represent in written narratives because, in such texts, they would be always packaged by a narrator and thus always rendered in human terms to some degree, even if that narrator is nonhuman. This opens up a rich line of questioning for transmedial econarratological scholarship: what role do nonlinguistic cues in visual narratives—including both cinematic texts and graphic novels—play in encouraging empathy among readers for actual nonhuman subjects? Is transspecies empathy possible in written narratives that do not feature graphic images and sounds that are such effective conduits to cognitive and emotional sharing? Indeed, does an accurate portrayal of the "moment-by-moment experiences of nonhuman" lives depend upon semiotic channels *other than* the purely written? If transmedial narrative approaches open onto semiotic channels other than the purely written, then econarratology has many permutations ahead of it as it incorporates a wider array of ways to experience narrative.

IN THIS BOOK

Given these potential directions for the development of econarratology, we have grouped the essays in this collection into three thematic streams: 1) Narratology and the Nonhuman; 2) Econarratological Rhetoric and Ethics; and 3) Anthropocene Storyworlds. Together, these parts address ripe sites of connection and overlap between environment and narrative, including climate change fiction (or "cli-fi"), narratives of the Anthropocene, possible uses of narrative in environmental activism, representations of the nonhuman in narratives, and the influences that environmental crises stand to have on the *way* we tell stories. They also engage with a wide range of disciplines and academic interests beyond narrative theory, ecocriticism, and the environmental humanities, such as posthumanism, modernism, environmental conservation, the history of the novel, critical animal studies, environmental ethics, and restoration ecology.

The essays in the collection's first part, "Narratology and the Nonhuman," take cues from two conversations: 1) discussions of "unnatural narrative" and "unnatural narratology" by scholars such as Jan Alber, Stefan Iversen, Brian Richardson, and Henrik Skov Nielsen; and 2) posthumanist, new materialist, and material ecocritical scholarship by scholars such as Stacy Alaimo and Jane Bennett that grapples with the agency of humans and nonhuman matter. The essays pair these conversations in their analyses of representations of material agencies and intermeshings of human and nonhuman agents in narrative and, in doing so, encourage narrative theorists to rethink binary oppositions of "natural" and "unnatural." They also push narrative scholars to reassess the meaningfulness of human narrators and characters amid increasing attention to the seemingly "unnatural" agency of nonhuman materials, objects, and phenomena, and position various narrative structures as crucial and effective sources for understanding such agencies.

Jon Hegglund's essay "Unnatural Narratology and Weird Realism in Jeff VanderMeer's *Annihilation*" begins by charting the different uses of the term *nature* in ecocritical and narratological scholarship, most notably within materialist ecocriticism and unnatural narrative theory. Hegglund does not propose reconciling the two uses of the term but instead extends and critiques the foundational principles of unnatural narratology such that it might be adapted to better describe and interpret fictional narratives invested in the unpredictable and changing environments of the Anthropocene. Hegglund's primary interest is the fundamental division of unnatural text and natural world within unnatural narrative theory, which he argues does not admit narrative representations of the strange, transformative materialities of our current epoch. Yet he argues that scholars adapt unnatural narratology's emphasis on the anti-mimetic to read the drama of emergent, nonanthropomorphic agency from a "weird" materiality, such as that we find in VanderMeer's novel. Via his analysis of *Annihilation,* and drawing on object-oriented ontologist Graham Harman's notion of "weird realism," Hegglund fleshes out a "weird narratology" that analyzes nonhuman agency in narratives that foreground a blurring between human agents and material entities or environments in the Anthropocene.

In "Object-Oriented Plotting and Nonhuman Realities in DeLillo's *Under-world* and Iñárritu's *Babel,*" Marco Caracciolo considers how recent literary and cinematic narratives leverage the dynamics of plot to engage with the many threads tying together human and material worlds. Caracciolo argues that plot is biased toward human-scale temporality, social interaction, and psychological causation; as such, he sees it as inherently anthropocentric. But he also sees the potential for plot to stretch to represent forms of human and nonhuman intermeshings that are grounded in natural and physical phenomena. He reads DeLillo's novel and Iñárritu's film to highlight both texts' use of plot to represent the interrelatedness of reality: DeLillo by blending the fundamental forces of matter with human emotions and Iñárritu by tracing, through the film's disparate parts, a movement from the human to the nonhuman realm. Caracciolo's discussion of the plot dynamics of each text suggests that natural phenomena are an invaluable formal resource for storytelling itself.

The essays in our second part, Econarratological Rhetoric and Ethics, consider narrative as a transmission or transaction between storytellers and readers contextualized by today's environmental challenges. As such, they share an interest in rhetorical narrative theory as drawn from the work of Wayne C. Booth and James Phelan. The essays in this section explore the relevance of reading narratives in environmental activism and question what role reading narratives might play in our response to large-scale environmental problems such as global climate change.

In "Readerly Dynamics in Dynamic Climatic Times: Cli-Fi and Rhetorical Narrative Theory," Eric Morel examines recent conversations that imagine how fiction will influence how readers react to climate change. Morel argues that, while necessary and timely, this conversation curtails the second, also important question of whether and how climate change itself might come to influence reading. Morel suggests that the rhetorical narratological work of Phelan and Rabinowitz has much to offer environmental humanities scholars by way of lexicon and procedure when it comes to discussing climate conditions' relevance to readers' responses to narrative content, especially in terms of rhetorical narrative theory's framework of narrative audience and notions of narrative progression and rules of configuration. By bringing reception history into contact with rhetorical narrative theory, Morel suggests a direction for ongoing compatibility between rhetorical narrative poetics and contextualist narratologies.

In "A Comedy of Survival: Narrative Progression and the Rhetoric of Climate Change in Ian McEwan's *Solar*," Markku Lehtimäki explores two significant challenges that climate change poses to narrative: how do writers best approach a problem of such global proportions with the novelist's traditional toolbox? And, why should readers look to fictional narratives for answers to real environmental problems? Lehtimäki grapples with both of these questions in his analysis of the environmental rhetoric of *Solar*. He argues that, in *Solar*, the human race's struggle for survival takes the form of an environmental comedy in which the protagonist, a comical and obnoxious Everyman, tries to save the planet—and especially his own skin—by developing new technologies for using solar energy. Michael Beard may not be the protagonist we would like, but he may be the one we deserve. Drawing on the work of Phelan and Joseph Meeker, Lehtimäki argues that this narrative's comedy affords it metarhetorical potential, whereby narrative elements such as plot and character make visible some of the complexities about climate change.

Greg Garrard's "Ecocriticism as Narrative Ethics: Triangulating Environmental Virtue in Richard Powers's *Gain*" also makes use of Phelan's work to encourage environmental scholars to put the ethics of *telling*, rather than simply the politics of the *told*, at the center of their research and teaching. Garrard suggests that rhetorical narratology can help correct the tendency in much ecocritical work to consider questions of telling as secondary to the environmental implications of a text's content, such that this work has tended to focus on issues of plot, characterization, and setting at the expense of discussions of narration and focalization. He also is suspicious of arguments within ecopoetics that certain literary forms are inherently more "ecological" than others. As a corrective to such claims, Garrard stresses the need for analysis of the moral aspects of storytelling as a means of exploring a narrative's staging of environmental virtue and vice. Such staging, Garrard's argument suggests, broadens existing understandings of narrative ethics developed by scholars such as Adam Zachary Newton. Garrard illustrates his model of ecocritical narrative ethics with a formal analysis of Powers's novel about toxic consumerism and corporate personhood.

Our final part, Anthropocene Storyworlds, features essays explicitly concerned with the representation of modern environmental crises in narrative worlds. They thus take direction from Herman's work on storyworlds, as well as recent scholarship in cognitive narratology by Herman and Marie-Laure

Ryan, among others. These essays explore how the particular environments and natural phenomena associated with modernity challenge traditional narrative techniques and suggest new ones. They also question what conventions modern environmental narratives deploy, how a different set of representations may help readers better model storyworlds that appreciate the scale of problems such as global climate change, and what role such storyworlds may play in an environmental activism sensitive to the worldmaking power of narrative.

Alexa Weik von Mossner, in "Feeling Narrative Environments: Econarratology, Embodiment, and Emotion," investigates the link between narratives and "topophilia," or the affective bond between people and place. Her essay explores the underlying narrative strategies in the evocation and imaginary experience of literary topophilia through readings of Sanora Babb's memoir *An Owl at Every Post* and dust bowl novel *Whose Names Are Unknown*. Drawing on recent work in affective and embodied narratology, as well as on psychological and enactivist approaches to narrative, she argues that fiction and nonfiction texts engage not only their readers' minds but also readers' bodies in the affective evocation of literary environments, which potentially has further value when thinking about narratives of environmental injustice. Ultimately, she argues for a pairing of ecocritical modes of reading and cognitive and moderate enactivist approaches to narrative to focus better on how literary texts enable their readers to *feel* imaginary environments.

Matthew M. Low is similarly interested in readers' modeling of narrative worlds in his essay, "Finding a Practical Narratology in the Work of Restoration Ecology." Low draws on the work of cognitive narrative theorists such as Herman and Ryan to argue that narratives of the prairie have the potential to serve two purposes. On the one hand, narration of, on, or about the prairie can have the effect of "reconstructing" for readers an ecosystem that has been reduced, in many places throughout the North American midcontinent, to less than one-tenth of a percent of its historic, presettlement extent. On the other hand, Low suggests, the theorizing of storyworlds by cognitive narratologists—and especially their classification of storyworlds as "reconstructed" and "dynamic" models of evolving situations—mirrors how restoration ecologists view the work of reconstructing the prairie. Low's essay surveys how restoration ecologists such as Chris Helzer narrate the process of prairie reconstruction to assert that the acts of (re)modeling worlds on the ground and in the minds of readers can be concomitant and ought to be the dominant strategy for revitalizing our most neglected ecosystem. He thus explores the potential of a hands-on, applied cognitive narratology suited to environmental restoration.

Astrid Bracke turns the collection's readers to considerations of global climate change and genre by identifying the generic parameters of "cli-fi" in her essay "Worldmaking Environmental Crisis: Climate Fiction, Econarratology, and Genre." She surveys recent climate change novels to understand better how narratives can represent an environmental problem that stretches the limits of the imagination. Bracke argues that cli-fi narratives put readers through a two-step process: they first depict a textual world that is very close to the actual world in which readers read, and then extend this familiar world into the unfamiliar, without the narrator stepping in to explicitly guide readers into navigating this new space. Illustrating these claims via readings of Barbara Kingsolver's *Flight Behavior* and Nathaniel Rich's *Odds Against Tomorrow*, and drawing heavily on Ryan's principle of minimal departure, Bracke offers scholars a useful guide for discussing cli-fi in contrast to other genres, such as speculative or apocalyptic fiction.

Finally, in "Narrative in the Anthropocene," Erin James examines today's environment from a broad, geologic scale to imagine how specific narrative techniques might help readers better understand conceptualizations of agency, time, space, and narration demanded by the Anthropocene. Taking cues from Gerald Prince's imagining of a postcolonial narratology, she envisages a narratology sensitive to matters commonly associated with our new epoch, such as the agency of the material world, the extremely long durations affiliated with environmental slow violence, new categories of spatialization demanded by representations of rising sea waters, and the collective narration necessitated by a new conceptualization of humans acting together, as a species, to enact global change. Her discussion of an "Anthropocene narrative theory" also asks how our definition of narrative itself may change in an age in which humans literally "write" the earth.

Our collection ends with an afterword by renowned environmental humanities and narrative scholar Ursula K. Heise.

Taken as a whole, the essays in this collection assert that the stories that we tell each other about the environment play a significant role in our perception of and interaction with that environment. They also assert the importance of our ability to analyze and understand those stories. They suggest that the vocabulary developed by narratologists could benefit environmental humanities and ecocritical conversations, especially in helping environmental scholars better account for the formal aspects of representations of environment in various types of narratives (novels, short stories, films, etc.). And they propose that environmental insights could broaden narrative theory, particularly in helping narrative scholars become more sensitive to issues of space and place, strengthening the connection between text and extratextual worlds of interest to many narratologists, and expanding the repertoire of questions narrative theorists ask of narratives to include those that are explicitly and implicitly environmental.

Although the essays in this collection address a robust range of topics and methodologies for econarratological readings, we do not suggest that this range is complete; there remain significant issues to address. Additional growth areas for econarratology include, but are not limited to, the conventions and consumption of digital narratives, greater focus on questions of environmental justice and the potential for econarratology as a base for forms of structural critique, the uses of econarratology in creative writing pedagogy, synergies between environmental history and the history of the novel, the role of storytelling in anthropological and sociological environmental studies (as well as the role of narratology in the environmental humanities more generally), the role of incorporating scientific methods into the study of narrative and of environment and narrative poetry. Important future work also lies in additional scholarship on postcolonial and indigenous narratives, similar to that which was so important to early attempts to pair ecocriticism and narratology, and the visual narratives that dominate much of today's popular culture. We also see much more room to expand upon some of the key considerations at the heart of this cluster of essays, including questions of the human and nonhuman, analysis of narrative discourse and rhetoric in light of environmentalism, readings of narrative space and the worldmaking power of narratives, and explorations of new narrative structures and genres inspired by new environments. We present this collection to you as a conversation starter and invite you to join us.

WORKS CITED

Alaimo, Stacy. *Bodily Natures: Science, Environment, and the Material Self.* Indiana UP, 2010.

Alber, Jan, Stefan Iversen, Brian Richardson, and Henrik Slov Nielsen. "Unnatural Narratives, Unnatural Narratology: Beyond Mimetic Models." *Narrative,* vol. 18, no. 2, May 2010, pp. 113–36.

Bartosch, Roman. *EnvironMentality: Ecocriticism and the Event of Postcolonial Fiction.* Rodopi, 2013.

Bernaerts, Lars, Marco Caracciolo, Luc Herman, and Bart Vervaeck. "The Storied Lives of Nonhuman Narrators." *Narrative,* vol. 22, no. 1, Jan. 2014, pp. 68–93.

Booth, Wayne C. *The Company We Keep: An Ethics of Fiction.* U of California P, 1989.

———. *The Rhetoric of Fiction.* 2nd ed, U of Chicago P, 1983.

Boyd, Brian. *On the Origin of Stories: Evolution, Cognition, and Fiction.* Harvard UP, 2009.

Buell, Lawrence. *The Environmental Imagination: Thoreau, Nature Writing, and the Formation of American Culture.* Harvard U, 1995.

———. *The Future of Environmental Criticism: Environmental Crisis and Literary Imagination.* Blackwell, 2005.

———. *Writing for an Endangered World: Literature, Culture, and Environment in the U.S. and Beyond.* Harvard UP, 2001.

Caracciolo, Marco. "Narrative, Meaning, Interpretation: An Enactivist Approach." *Phenomenology and the Cognitive Sciences,* vol. 11, no. 3, Sept. 2012, pp. 367–84.

Clark, Timothy. *Ecocriticism on the Edge: The Anthropocene as a Threshold Concept.* Bloomsbury, 2015.

Colebrook, Claire. *Death of the Posthuman: Essays on Extinction, Vol. 1.* Open Humanities Press, 2014.

Crane, Kylie. *Myths of Wilderness in Contemporary Narratives: Environmental Postcolonialism in Australia and Canada.* Palgrave Macmillan, 2012.

Craps, Steph, and Rick Crownshaw. "Introduction: The Rising Tide of Climate Change Fiction." *Studies in the Novel,* vol. 50, no. 1, Spring 2018, pp. 1–8.

DeLoughrey, Elizabeth, Jill Didur, and Anthony Carrigan, eds. *Global Ecologies and the Environmental Humanities: Postcolonial Approaches.* Routledge, 2015.

Easterlin, Nancy. *A Biocultural Approach to Literary Theory and Interpretation.* Johns Hopkins UP, 2012.

Fludernik, Monika. *Towards a 'Natural' Narratology.* Routledge, 2001.

Garrard, Greg. *Ecocriticism.* Routledge, 2012.

Genette, Gérard. *Figures of Literary Discourse.* Translated by Alan Sheridan, Columbia UP, 1982.

———. *Narrative Discourse: An Essay in Method.* Translated by Jane E. Lewin, Cornell UP, 1980.

Gerrig, Richard. *Experiencing Narrative Worlds: On the Psychological Activities of Reading.* Yale UP, 1993.

Ghosh, Amitav. *The Great Derangement: Climate Change and the Unthinkable.* U of Chicago P, 2017.

Glotfelty, Cheryll. "Introduction: Literary Studies in an Age of Environmental Crisis." *The Ecocriticism Reader: Landmarks in Literary Ecology.* Edited by Cheryll Glotfelty and Harold Fromm, U of Georgia P, 1996, pp. xv–xxxvii.

Green, Melanie C., and Timothy C. Brock. "The Role of Transportation in the Persuasiveness of Public Narratives." *Journal of Personality and Social Psychology,* vol. 79, no. 5, Nov. 2000, pp. 701–21.

Guha, Ramachandra, and J. Martinez-Alier. *Varieties of Environmentalism: Essays North and South.* Earthscan, 1997.

Gurr, Jens Martin. "Emplotting an Ecosystem: Amitav Ghosh's *The Hungry Tide* and the Question of Form in Ecocriticism." *Local Natures, Global Responsibilities: Ecocritical Perspectives on the New English Literatures.* Edited by Laurenz Volkmann, Nancy Grimm, and Ines Detmers, Rodopi, 2010, pp. 69–80.

Gymnich, Marion. "Linguistics and Narratology: The Relevance of Linguistic Criteria to Postcolonial Narratology." *Literature and Linguistics: Approaches, Models, and Applications.* Edited by Marion Gymnich, Jon Erickson, Angsar Nünning, and Vera Nünning, Wissenschaftlicher Verlag Trier, 2002, pp. 61–76.

Heise, Ursula K. "Afterword: Postcolonial Ecocriticism and the Question of Literature." *Postco-lonial Green: Environmental Politics and World Narratives.* Edited by Bonnie Roos and Alex Hunt, U of Virginia P, 2010, pp. 251–58.

———. *Sense of Place, Sense of Planet: The Environmental Imagination of the Global.* Oxford UP, 2008.

Heise, Ursula K., and Allison Carruth. "Introduction to Focus: Environmental Humanities." *American Book Review,* vol. 32, no. 1, Nov./Dec. 2010, p. 3.

Herman, David. "Narratology Beyond the Human." *Diegesis,* vol. 32, no. 1, 2014, pp. 131–43.

———. "Spatial Reference in Narrative Domains." *Text,* vol. 21. no. 4, 2001, pp. 515–41.

———. "Storyworld/Umwelt: Nonhuman Experiences in Graphic Novels." *SubStance,* vol. 40, no. 1, iss. 124, 2011, pp. 156–81.

Herman, David, James Phelan and Peter J. Rabinowitz, Brian Richardson, and Robyn Warhol. *Narrative Theory: Core Concepts and Critical Debates.* The Ohio State UP, 2012.

Iovino, Serenella, and Serpil Oppermann. "Introduction: Stories Come to Matter." *Material Eco-criticism.* Edited by Serenella Iovino and Serpil Oppermann, Indiana UP, 2014, pp. 1–18.

James, Erin. *The Storyworld Accord: Econarratology and Postcolonial Narratives.* U of Nebraska P, 2015.

Keen, Suzanne. *Empathy and the Novel.* Oxford UP, 2007.

———. "Fast Tracks to Narrative Empathy: Anthropomorphism and Dehumanization in Graphic Novels." *SubStance,* vol. 40, no. 1, iss. 124, 2011, pp. 135–55.

Kluwick, Ursula. "Talking About Climate Change: The Ecological Crisis and Narrative Form." *Oxford Handbook of Ecocriticism.* Edited by Greg Garrard, Oxford UP, 2014, pp. 502–16.

Lanser, Susan. "Toward a Feminist Narratology." *Style,* vol. 20, no. 3, 1986, pp. 341–63.

Le Guin, Ursula. "The Carrier Bag Theory of Fiction." *The Ecocriticism Reader: Landmarks in Literary Ecology.* Edited by Cheryll Glotfelty and Harold Fromm, U of Georgia P, 1996, pp. 149–54.

Lehtimäki, Markku. "Natural Environments in Narrative Contexts: Cross-Pollinating Ecocriti-cism and Narrative Theory." *Storyworlds,* vol. 5, 2013, pp. 119–41.

Lejano, Raul, Mrill Ingram, and Helen Ingram. *The Power of Narrative in Environmental Net-works.* MIT Press, 2013.

Love, Glen A. *Practical Ecocriticism: Literature, Biology, and the Environment.* U of Virginia P, 2003.

Morton, Timothy. "Poisoned Ground: Art and Philosophy in the Time of Hyperobjects." *symplokē* vol. 21, no. 1–2, 2013, pp. 37–50.

Newton, Adam Zachary. *The Elsewhere: On Belonging at Near Distance.* U of Wisconsin P, 2005.

———. *Narrative Ethics.* Harvard UP, 1997.

———. *To Make the Hands Impure: Art, Ethical Adventure, the Difficult and the Holy.* Fordham UP, 2014.

Nünning, Ansgar. "Surveying Contextualist and Cultural Narratologies: Towards an Outline of Approaches, Concepts and Potentials." *Narratology in the Age of Cross-Disciplinary Research.* Edited by Sandra Heinen and Roy Sommers, de Gruyter, 2009, pp. 48–70.

Nussbaum, Martha. *Love's Knowledge: Essays on Philosophy and Literature.* Oxford UP, 1992.

Okpewho, Isidore. *African Oral Literature: Backgrounds, Character, and Continuity*. Indiana UP, 1992.

Phelan, James. *Living to Tell About It: A Rhetoric and Ethics of Character Narration*. Cornell UP, 2004.

———. "Rhetoric/Ethics." *The Cambridge Companion to Narrative*. Edited by David Herman. Cambridge UP, 2007, pp. 203–16.

———. *Somebody Telling Somebody Else: A Rhetorical Poetics of Narrative*. The Ohio State UP, 2017.

Phillips, Dana. *The Truth of Ecology: Nature, Culture, and Literature in America*. Oxford UP, 2003.

Plumwood, Val. *Environmental Culture: The Ecological Crisis of Reason*. Routledge, 2002.

Prince, Gerald. *A Dictionary of Narratology*. Revised edition, U of Nebraska P, 2003.

Rose, Deborah Bird, Thom van Dooren, Matthew Chrulew, Stuart Cooke, Matthew Kearnes, and Emily O'Gorman. "Thinking Through the Environment, Unsettling the Humanities." *Environmental Humanities*, vol. 1, 2012, pp. 1–5.

Ryan, Marie-Laure, Kenneth Foote, and Maoz Azaryahu. *Narrating Space/Spatializing Narrative: Where Narrative Theory and Geography Meet*. The Ohio State UP, 2016.

Satterfield, Terre, and Scott Slovic, eds. *What's Nature Worth: Narrative Expressions of Environmental Values*. U of Utah P, 2004.

Slovic, Paul, and Scott Slovic. *Numbers and Nerves: Information, Emotion, and Meaning in a World of Data*. Oregon State UP, 2015.

Slovic, Scott. *Going Away to Think: Engagement, Retreat, and Ecocritical Responsibility*. U of Nevada P, 2008.

Sörlin, Sverker. "Environmental Humanities: Why Should Biologists Interested in the Environment Take the Humanities Seriously?" *BioScience*, vol. 62, no. 9, Sept. 2012, pp. 788–89.

Vermeule, Blakey. *Why Do We Care About Literary Characters?* Johns Hopkins UP, 2010.

Weik von Mossner, Alexa. *Affective Ecologies: Empathy, Emotion, and Environmental Narrative*. The Ohio State UP, 2017.

Wildcat, Daniel. *Red Alert!: Saving the Planet with Indigenous Knowledge*. Fulcrum Publishing, 2009.

Zunshine, Lisa. *Why We Read Fiction: Theory of Mind and the Novel*. The Ohio State UP, 2006.

I

NARRATOLOGY AND THE NONHUMAN

CHAPTER 1

Unnatural Narratology and Weird Realism in Jeff VanderMeer's *Annihilation*

JON HEGGLUND

IN THE past few decades, *nature* has undergone a period of crisis in many disciplines and fields of inquiry, with narratology and ecocritical theory no exceptions. Though it is well beyond the scope of this essay to track these transformations exhaustively, I do wish to highlight their particular convergences within the realms of postclassical narratology and materialist ecology, as well as indicate some narrative features that align with recent trends in ecocritical philosophy. This focus is occasioned by the increasing attention to ecological approaches to narrative and, to a lesser but still meaningful extent, the concern within materialist environmental thought on the importance of narrative in understanding the planetary challenges of the Anthropocene epoch.

To begin with the adventures of *nature* in postclassical narratology, we need to go back to Monika Fludernik's *Toward a "Natural" Narratology* (1996), which approached the systematic study of narrative not from the basis of literary texts but rather from a linguistic conception of spontaneous, oral, conversational narratives as studied by William Labov, among others. Already realizing the connotative messiness of the term *natural,* Fludernik signals a very specific usage of the word (as implied by the quotes around it in the title) that opposes it to the artificial, aestheticized qualities of literary narratives. For Fludernik, the salient criterion for narrative is not plot or genre but "experientiality," that is, "the quasi-mimetic evocation of 'real-life experience,'" which "correlates with the evocation of consciousness" and "reflects a cognitive schema of embodiedness that relates to human existence and human concerns" (9). In response to the self-avowed "anthropomorphic bias" of Fludernik's model (9), several scholars, most notably Brian Richardson and Jan Alber, sought to highlight the many narratives in the world-historical corpus that seem to violate or contradict this normative notion of a mimesis based upon human experientiality, and in response, they adopted the provocative term "unnatural narratology." For these scholars, unnatural narratology represents myriad narrative modes and methods that violate or contradict what seems to be "natural" in storytelling scenarios, highlighting the "non- and anti-mimetic" (Richardson 2) and the representation of the "physically, logically, or humanly impossible" in narrative (Alber 3). Though the practice of unnatural narratology has many distinctions among its advocates, the movement as a whole encourages a methodology that resists the tendency to naturalize a tacit bias toward the mimeticism and anthropocentrism implied by Fludernik's notion of experientiality.

Meanwhile, *nature* has taken a longer, more complicated journey in ecocritical and environmental thought. Through the 1970s and 1980s, *nature* was the (often unspoken) foundation of environmentally oriented literary studies. Indeed, the primary task of this movement was to set an authentic *nature* or *wilderness* over and against the artificial, destructive processes of industrial capitalism, urbanization, and commodity culture. Early forays into environmental aesthetics, highly influenced by the nature writing of Henry David Thoreau, John Muir, Mary Austin, and Aldo Leopold, favored a mode of descriptive realism to render the particularity and intrinsic beauty of nature. In the last two decades, however, first with the rise of cultural studies and more recently with the awareness of the new geological epoch of the Anthropocene, environmental aesthetics has become a more complex, ambivalent discourse, now intersected by feminism, postcolonial theory, science studies, posthumanism, and vitalist and object-oriented philosophies. In the 1990s, *nature* was increasingly seen as a production of culture and no longer synonymous with the *real* or *material* substratum of the world. As William Cronon puts it in his seminal 1995 essay, "The Trouble with Wilderness": "As we gaze into the mirror it holds up for us, we too easily imagine that what we behold is Nature when in fact we see the reflection of our own unexamined longings and desires" (7). Recent materialist thought has questioned nature on an even more fundamental level, insisting that the material world is neither a purely ideological nor culturally variable construct. Thinkers as diverse as Bruno Latour, Donna Haraway, Karen Barad, Jane Bennett, and Timothy Morton have argued for an ontological model of *nature* that emphasizes its entangled, hybrid, and self-organizing aspects, in turn bringing the embodied human subject down from the lofty perch of Cartesian separation from the world. *Nature* is no longer a pure, idealized Other to a normative human Self but is rather composed of the endlessly complex material interactions in which individual and collective human and nonhuman life exists. Because both culturalists and materialists reject a conventional, pastoral model of *nature*, however, the unqualified use of the term has fallen out of favor within many current ecocritical conversations.

This essay does not aim to reconcile these distinct uses of *nature* (but I think it is worthwhile to note at the outset that both unnatural narratology and materialist ecocriticism are formed *in opposition to* a sense of nature as a normative concept). My goal here is more modest: to extend and critique the foundational principles of unnatural narratology in the hopes that its insights and orientations might be adapted to better describe and interpret fictional narratives particular to the geohistorical epoch of the Anthropocene. In particular, I focus on the articulation of unnatural narratology advanced by Jan Alber, whose succinct definition offers both a concrete touchstone and a useful bridge to the concerns of material ecocriticism. My contention is that, while Alber develops a complex and thoughtful taxonomy for unnatural narratology, its foundational division of unnatural text and natural world does not adequately admit narrative figurations of the strange, transformative materialities of the Anthropocene. Unnatural narratology is alive to the fundamental weirdness of narrative representation, but that attention has not yet been steered toward the very "unnaturalness" of the natural world itself. I would particularly like to press Alber's notion of the unnatural as the narrative projection of an impossible storyworld. The recognition of the Anthropocene has prompted a reexamination of what may be possible in the natural world. The human transformation of nature has yielded very strange things indeed: a Europe-sized patch of floating plastics in the Pacific, poison-resistant urban rats, post-Fukushima radioactive boars, the genetic "editing" of human embryos—the list could go on ad infinitum. Given that such actually existing weird materialities blur clear distinctions between the *natural* and the *unnatural*, implicating human agency along the way, it would seem that the ontological premises of unnatural narratology could stand for closer examination. The very notion of narrative mimesis (or anti-mimesis) becomes a moving target when the contours of reality can no longer be taken for granted as ontologically secure.

Through a reading of Jeff VanderMeer's 2014 novel, *Annihilation*, I propose that unnatural narratology's focus on the anti-mimetic might be mutated into considerations of how narrative dramatizes the uncanny nature of mimesis itself, based as it is on the shape-shifting materiality of the world. Borrowing from the philosopher Graham Harman's notion of "weird realism," I propose that unnatural narratology's emphasis on the anti-mimetic might be adapted to read the drama of emergent, nonanthropomorphic agency from a "weird" materiality—hence I offer the idea of the "weird" as an adaptation of the "unnatural." VanderMeer's tale of an unknowable, distributed entity that has mysteriously taken over and transformed a region (referred to as "Area X") meets Alber's basic criteria of the representation of an impossible storyworld, but this label is complicated by the circumstance of the narrator, a biologist whose own embodied subjectivity is infiltrated by the environment of Area X itself. The narratological analysis of VanderMeer's novel calls for an openness to the ways in which narrative actively and dynamically *constructs* distinctions between subjects and objects, figure and background, characters and storyworld. My reading focuses on two aspects of VanderMeer's narrative in particular: 1) the narrative rendering of nonanthropomorphic, distributed agency and 2) the first-person narration, which offers a contingent, performative sense of the human constructed *through* the act of narration rather than the assumption of an ontologically distinct human "character" who precedes and subtends the novel's storyworld.

FROM THE UNNATURAL TO THE WEIRD: NARRATOLOGY, MIMESIS, MATERIALITY

Unnatural narratology might be best described as a confederation of common interests rather than a strict methodological program. In a 2010 *Narrative* essay collectively authored by three of its most prominent advocates (Jan Alber, Stefan Iversen, and Henrik Skov Nielsen), the authors propose that "the study of unnatural narrative seeks to describe the ways in which projected storyworlds deviate from real-world frames [and] tries to interpret these 'deviations'" (116). Unnatural narratology presents itself in opposition to narrative theory's implicit bias toward mimesis. The mimetic model, in which narrative is presumed to be a form of representation that refers to a "possible world" and conforms to conventional physical and cognitive frameworks, has held an unspoken, even coercive, power over all narratological descriptions and theorizations of narrative. The villain in the unnaturalists' story is "'mimetic reductionism,' that is, the argument that each and every aspect of narrative can be explained on the basis of our real-world knowledge and resulting cognitive parameters" (115). Unnatural narratology thus involves a cognitive reframing of narratives that consciously reject mimetic models of storytelling and a consequent exploration of how frames are revised, rejected, or blended through the reader's encounter with anti- or non-mimetic elements of a narrative. In their reading of Robert Coover's short story, "The Babysitter," for example, they refuse any interpretive strategy that would assimilate the contradictory events of the narrative into an overarching frame of mimesis—for example, that the logical impossibility of events can be explained by the subjective fantasies of a character or narrator. Rather, they argue that "one way of responding to the interpretive challenges of unnatural narratives is to create new cognitive parameters by reshuffling and/or recombining existing frames" (118). The thrust of unnatural narratology, in this instance, is not to resolve contradictions in favor of real-world laws that mute or silence anti-mimetic elements; rather, it wishes to highlight and explore such contradictions as a productive challenge to mimetic and anthropomorphic models. Though it contains the word "nature" in its name, unnatural narratology is fundamentally about modes of representation rather than any putative connections between the text and the material world.

It is the critique of mimesis that offers a bridge from unnatural narratology to an ecocritical approach, as materialist ecocriticism likewise wishes to complicate and challenge naturalized ideas of "reality." Alber isolates the narrative presentation of "physically, logically, or humanly impossible" storyworlds as the criteria for unnatural narrative. For simplicity's sake, I group these three together under the rubric of "impossible storyworlds" (as a materialist approach would ultimately subsume the "logical" and the "human" into the realm of the "physical"). Alber claims that "the unnatural (or impossible) in such narratives is measured against the foil of 'natural' (real-world) cognitive frames and scripts that have to do with natural laws, logical principles, and standard human limitations of knowledge and ability" (3). Expanding the scope of such narratives beyond their common association with postmodernism, Alber "posit[s] a historically constant notion of the unnatural," claiming that "the world we inhabit is dominated by physical laws, logical principles, and anthropomorphic limitations that are *permanent and stable*" (6, my italics). To be fair, Alber acknowledges that his notion of the natural is a "foil," and one that makes claims primarily about "cognitive frames and scripts" rather than the materialities that subtend conventional understandings. Yet, I think it reasonable to challenge—given their use of the natural/unnatural distinction in the very name of their program—the nature of their "nature," as it were. Though Alber's goal is more pragmatically oriented toward narratology, he slips ontological premises into the program: the unnatural is clearly based on an accepted, stable, commonsense view of nature. Thus, while Alber's goal is the elevation and serious consideration of narrative examples that violate real-world cognitive frames, this dynamic exists in a closed circuit between the reader's cognition and the narrative text, and in fact needs the bedrock of a "permanent and stable" reality to distinguish the rule-breaking exceptions of the unnatural. Unnatural narratology, to my mind, cannot afford to be so blithe in the easy importation of foundational ontological distinctions into conventionalized cognitive frames.

As the author of the book that advances the idea of "natural narratology," Monica Fludernik makes perhaps the most obvious critique of the unnatural-ists. In her response to unnatural narratology, Fludernik points out that the program's basis in negation—of natural narratology, of mimesis—"ends up reinforcing the mimetic rather than escaping from its clutches" (Fludernik, "How Natural" 366). Maria Mäkelä extends this critique by arguing that, even if we take mimesis as a legitimate target of critique, the unnatural view reduces a complex, textured process into a one-dimensional straw man. Mäkelä insists that mimesis, as we understand it through realist fiction, is itself infused with the unnatural rather than diametrically opposed to it. Drawing upon Vik-tor Shklovsky's notion of defamiliarization, Mäkelä notes that "many realist conventions are peculiarly balanced between the cognitively familiar and the cognitively estranging." (145). In Mäkelä's view, mimesis is never a smooth, seamless process of reproducing a familiar, conventional "real world" through particular stylistic and narrative choices. Using Gustave Flaubert's *Madame Bovary* as her touchstone, Mäkelä concludes that "realism would seem to be an art more of distortion than of reproduction" (153). Even while we should acknowledge that realism and mimesis are not identical, both concepts func-tion as part of the same hegemony of narratology to which the unnaturalist approach takes exception. Thus Mäkelä's point stands: even in their most con-ventional forms, mimetic or realist narratives always carry their own cogni-tively disruptive and defamiliarizing elements.

Like narratology, ecocritical approaches have had their own difficulties with mimesis. Ecocritics through the 1990s tended to place special powers within the "environment" (typically settings associated with an organic, green conception of nature). While rarely being so naïve as to claim that texts can mimetically represent worlds in a direct way, critics such as Lawrence Buell claim that ecocritically rich texts embody "a certain kind of environmental referentiality as part of the overall work of the text" (32). Buell, and others, claim that, while mimesis is never an absolute, textual representations can be more or less mimetic in their environmental representation: "Language never replicates landscapes," Buell argues, "but it can be bent toward or away from them" (33). Dana Phillips takes on these claims of a "soft" mimesis of environmental writing, reminding us that, when it comes to "nature" or "envi-ronment," text and world are manifestly distinct. Phillips wonders "why environmental literature should be deputized to make the presence and reality of the natural world available to us by proxy, when that world lies waiting to be explored by bookworms and bold adventurers alike" (7). Buell and Phillips are caught in something of a cul-de-sac as they circle round the question of mimesis: the former insisting on a constitutive relation between text and world, the latter sundering the relation altogether. Econarratology, specifically a weird, materialist narratology as I outline it here, points toward an escape route by shifting the question slightly: what happens when a text evokes a storyworld that itself draws our attention to the ontological messiness that prevents a clear separation between the two? This is not to say that, for the most part, we don't approach and experience such texts as representations—just like unnatural narratology, an ecomaterialist approach is focused on specific genres and narrative modes rather than narrative *tout court*—but such representations do model relationships between human subjects and storyworlds that disrupt conceptual divisions of subject and object, human and nonhuman, active agent and passive object or environment.

A materialist ecocritical approach sees narrative as intimately tied with our understandings of material processes in the physical world, rejecting Cartesian dualisms that continue to structure such binary oppositions. Stacey Alaimo has approached these questions by theorizing that human embodiedness is a kind of "trans-corporeality, in which the human is always intermeshed with the more-than-human world" and "ultimately inseparable from 'the environment'" (2). Clearly, these trans-corporeal models of humanness challenge the normative Cartesianism of the narratological subject, and conversely, the teeming, vibrant, shapeshifting contours of the material world complicate notions of "setting" or "environment" as the passive, inert background for a drama of human or anthropomorphic action. Serenella Iovino and Serpil Opperman address the entanglement of human and material worlds in narrative (if not quite narratological) terms. Drawing on the example of cancer-causing wastes in Naples, Italy, which effect agency through human and animal bodies as well as the collective social fabric, they ask: "Who is the storyteller of these stories narrated through and across bodies by manifold material–discursive agents, such as toxic waste, sick cells, individual organisms, and social forces? Who is really 'the narrating subject' if things— collectives, assemblages, actants—are narrative agencies?" (459). Iovino and Opperman do not rigorously theorize a model of narrative but suggest that "the narrative potentialities of reality" can issue from an "intrinsic performativity of elements" (459). Narrative, in their view, need not be composed of anthropomorphic agents possessing something like a consciousness or subjectivity; rather, their focus on material cause-and-effect relations (within which human actions are a subset) "broadens the range of narrative agencies" (149). This has implications for our understanding of fundamental narrative categories such as "character," "setting," and "storyworld": characters need not be human, settings need not be backgrounds, and storyworlds need not be filed under "mimetic" or "impossible."

While such scenarios may be of interest to the anti-mimetic proclivities of unnatural narratology, a key difference should be noted. Unnatural narratology approaches the anti-mimetic in a somewhat black-and-white way: the narrative presence of, say, a talking chair, is *clearly* a "crossover" from one recognized frame of human experience to another, and so a blending of frames takes place in this particular narrative instance. The basic categories of "real world" and "impossible storyworld" remain fixed, however, and our ontological footing is unshaken. In narrative scenarios that I will refer to as "weird," there is no such reassurance. To put this in terms of cognitive theory, frames that are knocked askew are unable to be fully restored to a stable, conventionalized position. Weird narratology, as I envision it, is aimed at narratives that foreground a blurring between narrative agents and material entities or environments—whether this blurring is visible at the level of discourse, story, or in the case of more interesting examples, such as *Annihilation,* both. Although writing from the disciplinary perspective of philosophy, the object-oriented ontologist Graham Harman gives a name to this dynamic in his readings of H. P. Lovecraft: weird realism. In his book of the same name, Harman reframes "realism" at an ontological rather than a representational level: "Reality itself is weird," Harman writes, "because reality itself is incommensurable with any attempt to represent or measure it" (51). In addition to troubling a clear ontological divide between the solidity of the material world and unnatural experiments of representation, Harman reframes realism as a descriptive rather than aesthetic mode, with "weird" narratives attempting to render a real, if unaccountably bizarre and unstable, world. Where unnatural narratology begins its analyses from a normative notion of the human, and its distinction from nonhuman elements of a storyworld—even as it may blur or erase these distinctions in the analysis of an individual narrative—a weird reading enters a narrative with no such assumptions in place. Granted, most readers will bring normative cognitive frames to bear on a narrative, but the key difference here is that weird realist narratives have the power to transform those frames so that the assumed stability of "the world" is no longer a stable, normative point of reference. Weird narratology can thus be instrumental in accommodating a more flexible, emergent understanding of agency and causality that does not depend upon the primacy of human, or even strongly anthropomorphic, actors.

WEIRD STORYWORLDS

Narratology already has many tools that could be put to use for the reading of weird narratives. One such concept is Porter Abbott's articulation of emergence, which gives narratologically minded readers a way to think about how narratives such as *Annihilation* track the transformations of background into figure, or "setting" into "character." Abbott describes "emergent behavior" as "the coming into being of objects or patterns that are not the result of a centralized authority or plan or guiding hand or pacemaker or any other kind of overarching control, much less an intention, but instead are the result of innumerable local interactions" (228). This describes VanderMeer's storyworld more or less accurately. The novel scaffolds a relatively conventional narrative mode (first-person retrospective narration) onto a radically unstable and ultimately unknowable storyworld, which is presumed to have some form of agency and sentience that resists easy anthropomorphism or explanation by an agent of "overarching control." The narrator, a biologist who is one of four members of an expeditionary team assembled by a governmental agency known as the Southern Reach, recounts her experiences on the twelfth expedition into a region known as Area X, a wilderness that has been strangely transformed by a mysterious "event" decades earlier. Since that time, unaccountable things—sometimes benign, sometimes violent and catastrophic—have happened to both the ecology of the place and to the humans who have ventured into it. For example, each member of the previous expedition, one of whom was the narrator's husband, mysteriously disappeared within Area X, only to reappear months later and shortly thereafter develop "inoperable, systemic cancer" that proved fatal within months (38). Other reports of strange creatures and happenings within Area X have filtered through to the biologist, generating mysteries about the *nature* of Area X and the causes of its transformation—in short, the reader enters the novel focused on an ontological mystery of the storyworld: What *is* this place? Is it an environment, or an acting agent in its own right? How did it come to be transformed in such a way to upset fundamental laws of nature?[1] In contrast to a stable, referential, objective storyworld—what David Herman refers to in *Story Logic* as "topological space"—our sense of spatiality is undone at the outset. First, a landmark appears that is not commensurable with the putative topological space of the storyworld, as it doesn't appear on the expedition's "official" maps. Second, there is a semantic inconsistency or mistake: the narrator describes a hidden

---

1. Many early reviews of the novel highlight this blending through the use of terms such as "ecological uncanny" and "weird ecology." See Carroll, Rothman, and Tompkins.

structure that "plunges into the earth" as a "tower" (and to which other characters refer as a "tunnel"). VanderMeer begins with a hint of the instability to come, a vertiginous unhinging of figure, ground, and the relation between the two. While the narrative presents a plausible, realist spatiality on the sentence level, it undermines any notion of a normative "real world" from which mimetic representation may or may not be derived. There is nothing ostentatiously anti-mimetic in the early pages of the novel, but the background of Area X and the semantic ambiguity of the tower/tunnel distinction generate a sense of uncertainty poised between "real world" and "anti-mimetic" cognitive frames.

The early pages of *Annihilation* fold a logical impossibility into the laws of the storyworld itself: that Area X is itself is a massively distributed, sentient being akin to what Timothy Morton describes as a "hyperobject."[2] As such, it is both a backgrounded frame that we are likely to code as "environment" or "setting" as well as a narrative actant or figure—a character of sorts. When the explorers attempt to identify the underground tower, they are unable to ascribe its existence to any kind of anthropomorphic agency, as the anthropologist in the group remarks that its model is "hard to identify" and that "the materials are ambiguous, indicating local origin but not necessarily local construction" (5). VanderMeer opens up a narrative gap that we are increasingly invited to fill with the hypothesis that these unexplained phenomena issue from a massively distributed entity. This hypothesis is further supported by the biologist's observation of various animals in Area X, which seem on occasion to be "possessed" with an unseen agency at odds with their species-driven behavior. At one point, a wild boar charges the group, but as it comes closer, "its face became stranger and stranger. Its features where somehow contorted, as if the beast was dealing with an extreme of inner torment. . . . I had the startling impression of some presence in the way its gaze seemed turned inward and its head willfully pulled to the left as if there were an invisible bridle. . . . It veered abruptly leftward, with what I can only describe as a great cry of anguish, into the underbrush" (12). The boar acts not according to the traits of its species but is instead described as being manipulated by some other "will" at odds with the boar's natural behavior—an agency visibly

---

2. In fact, VanderMeer's fiction and Morton's theoretical work have been mutually sustaining. Morton has used VanderMeer's fiction as an imaginative evocation of hyperobjects, and VanderMeer in turn has retrospectively acknowledged the mutual resonance: "After I wrote *Annihilation*, I started seeing reviews that mentioned your work in connection with it; that's why I picked up *Hyperobjects*, and the thing that was fascinating to me is that it appealed to both the organic and the mechanical sides. The mechanical side made me understand what I had written better because the very term 'hyperobject' kind of encapsulated what was going on organically in *Annihilation*." See Hageman et al., "A Conversation."

emergent but in no way attached to a discrete, identifiable entity. Other animals—an unseen, unidentified creature that moans at night, a dolphin with human eyes—index an emergent nonhuman agency through a blending of anthropomorphism and unknowable difference, prompting the biologist (and the reader) to impute complex, if still unknown, agency to actions or traits that violate commonsense, mimetic understandings of animal behavior.

The centerpiece of nonhuman, emergent agency in the novel is an entity that resides deep within the aforementioned tower. The biologist dubs this creature "the Crawler," as it moves slowly up and down the spiral interior, shooting an incandescent "ink" of tiny, hand-shaped spores in cursive script along the inner walls of the structure. The uncanniness of the tower is suggested from the novel's opening lines, but its relation to the environment of Area X and the Crawler within is foregrounded by the biologist's attempts to identify the boundaries where environment gives way to agency, and vice versa. The first thing that the party notices when descending into the tower is the writing on the wall: it looks "oddly organic," which piques the curiosity of the biologist. Her instinct is to "parse the lingual meaning" of the script (which reads like a deranged adaptation of a Puritanical sermon),[3] when her companion asks what the letters are made of. The biologist reverts to a scientific way of seeing, noting that the words were made from a substance that looked "like rich green fernlike moss but in fact was probably a type of fungi or other eukaryotic organism" (17). Soon the words are no longer language but "a miniature ecosystem" populated by translucent creatures "shaped like tiny hands embedded by the base of the palm" (17). As she peers in for a closer look, a nodule bursts open and sprays her with "spores," which she inhales (17). This material incursion transgresses the separation between a Cartesian observer-narrator and a passive material environment, and from this point, we are cued to treat the narrator as *both* a human witness of events *and* an emergent agent whose actions and perceptions may be a function of the distributed entity at work in Area X. This hybridity is theorized by William Connolly, as he describes human agency in contrast to Cartesian self-possession; it is, rather, an "emergent phenomenon, with some nonhuman processes pos-

---

3. An excerpt of the writing that is revealed to biologist is as follows: "*Where lies the strangling fruit that came from the hand of the sinner I shall bring forth the seeds of the dead . . . to share with the worms that gather in the darkness and surround the world with the power of their lives while from the dim-lit halls of other places forms that never could be writhe for the impatience of the few who have never seen or been seen. . . . Why should I rest when wickedness exists in the world. . . . God's love shines on anyone who understands the limits of endurance, and allows forgiveness. . . . Chosen for the service of a higher power . . . in the black water with the sun shining at midnight, those fruit shall come ripe and in the darkness of that which is golden shall split open to reveal the revelation of the fatal softness in the earth . . .*" (31–33).

sessing attributes bearing family resemblances to human agency and with human agency understood by reference to its emergence from nonhuman processes of proto-agency" (23). To put this in the context of *Annihilation*: functionally, there is an anthropomorphic narrator within a projected story-world, but ontologically, there is no categorical, material distinction between the weird, nonhuman entities and the supposedly human itself. From this point on, the biologist self-consciously interrogates the boundaries between subject and object, human and environment, and the narrative takes on a ver-tiginous quality as the narrator tries to both understand the emergent agen-cies within Area X as well as within herself.

NARRATORIAL HUMANISM

One might reasonably counter: even if elements in the storyworld are invested with some agency, doesn't the first-person character-narration implicitly privilege a normative model of the human? Yes and no. From cognitive and rhetorical perspectives, we have little trouble placing our narrative in this frame: cognitively, as we default to the well-worn convention of first-person retrospective narration; rhetorically, as the communicative situation is fore-grounded by reference to the recording of observations in her field journal as well as the direct address of the reader as "you." After the initial establish-ment of these frames, however, the narrative works to erode our confidence in the category of the human through the narrative description of the sto-ryworld, and indeed, through the narrator's retrospective description of her own embodied experientiality within the storyworld. Just as the storyworld features entities in a constant state of morphism, so, too, does the biologist exist in a state of ontological uncertainty as one emergent agency among oth-ers. Yet, authorial readers still engage the narrative through an entirely anthro-pomorphic *frame*, even as the human *content* of the narrator is indeterminate or absent. Rather than give us a simulation of a narratorial perspective or consciousness from the point of view of "Area X," or the Crawler, or whatever other agency is at work, VanderMeer chooses to filter perception through the flimsy, uncertain, constantly transforming perspective of a human narrator who is herself constantly interrogating the production of boundaries between human and nonhuman entities.

It should be said at the outset that the narration in *Annihilation* is con-spicuously retrospective from the novel's opening; that is, it is not merely nar-rated in the past tense, but attention is drawn to this gap when the narrator comments at the end of the first paragraph: "Looking out over that untroubled landscape, I do not believe any of us could yet see the threat" (3). She also implies a catastrophic conflict when she remarks of her companions, "I would tell you the names of the other three if it mattered, but only the surveyor would last more than the next day or two" (6). While these retrospective pro-lepses alert the reader that the narrator speaks from the other side of signifi-cant story events, there are not initially any references to any change in *her* condition from the narrated-I to the narrating-I. In the novel's initial pages, the retrospective narration draws attention to the *story*, in that the reader is cued to anticipate important events in the storyworld rather than changes in the mode of narration or the reliability of the narrator herself. From the moment that she inhales the spores on the wall of the tower/tunnel, however, the biologist's entanglement with Area X begins to become more of a con-cern in her own narration. Eventually she focuses the act of observation on herself rather than directing the distanced gaze of science exclusively upon the environment of Area X, and the narration becomes more self-referential. Within about four pages after her initial contact, the biologist wonders at least ten times if the spores are having an effect on her, what those effects might be, and if she will be able to distinguish her own "self" from the agency of the spores, or indeed of the complex, distributed entity that comprises Area X. This presents a conundrum for the reader. It would seem that a narrative presented by a first-person narrator runs the risk of filtering the mysterious, emergent agencies of the storyworld through the anthropocentric mold of human consciousness, thus presenting a clear boundary between the human narrator and the nonhuman storyworld. Alternatively, the narrator could be presented as patently unreliable, leaving the reader to infer a "truth" through the gaps in the biologist's reading and/or reporting of events. *Annihilation* offers a more complex stance on its narrator, however, by both preserving her observational reliability while casting doubt upon her own identity as a nor-mative, embodied human subject.

The temporal distance between the narrated-I and the narrating-I, and the knowledge that the narrating-I may have been compromised or altered by contact with Area X opens up questions about reliability. I take Phelan's point in *Living to Tell About It* that reliability is not a binary state. As Phelan argues, "A given narrator can be unreliable in different ways at different points in his or her narration" (52). In the case of the biologist, this is not a merely formal question. The narration gives the authorial audience cause to trust the biologist's *observations* as a scientist even as we may doubt her *motivations* as a flesh-and-blood, psychologically realistic human character. While this dis-tinction may point toward a largely unreliable narrator, the particularly com-plex moments of unreliability are in fact essential in cultivating the reader's empathy in the absence of more conventional psychological traits of a mimetic character. For all of the *ontological* doubts cast upon the biologist-as-human, the typological category to which we refer—her role as scientist—gives her *account* a strong degree of reliability. Ralf Schneider, discussing the cognitive processes that go into our understanding of characters in literary narrative, posits that the reader conventionally "tries to apply top-down categorization as a preference rule" (617). That is, readers bring existing knowledge of social and cultural categories to a text as they "try to establish a holistic mental model of the character early on. . . . The model will possess a number of well-defined features from which expectations, hypotheses, and inferences as well as explanations concerning that character's behavior can be generated" (619). The biologist presents an unconventional example of this: because the narrative contains a paucity of individuating details, we stay at that top-level categorization throughout the narrative and think of her as a capital-S Scientist, thereby granting her a relative level of epistemological reliability when her role as a scientist is foregrounded. Importantly, as the novel proceeds, these scientific acts of observation, hypothesis, and experimentation are turned toward her own embodied self, so that a direct relationship is established between her doubts about the purity of her humanness *and* the degree to which we believe she is giving a reliable account of the storyworld, both in terms of what she observes in Area X and the ways in which she herself has been changed *by* Area X.

One area in which her reliability is patently in doubt, however, is in her motivations for volunteering for the expedition. Perhaps the most important piece of background information that we learn about the biologist is that her husband was a member of the previous expedition to Area X, and that he returned in a significantly altered state and subsequently died of cancer shortly thereafter. Although this is one of the only details that individuates the biologist, she is careful to assert that it does not cloud her objectivity as a narrator: "I have hoped that in reading this account, you might find me a credible, objective witness. Not someone who volunteered for Area X because of some other event unconnected to the purpose of the expeditions. And, in a sense, this is still true, and my husband's status as a member of an expedition is in many ways irrelevant to why I signed up" (37). Of James Phelan's six types of unreliability, this appeal by the narrator falls most strongly into the category of underreading—an instance, according to Phelan, "when the narrator's lack of knowledge, perceptiveness, or sophistication yields an insufficient interpretation of an event, character, or situation" (52).[4] The biologist under-

---

4. See Phelan's discussion of the six types (misreporting, underreporting, misreading, underreading, misregarding, underregarding) from *Living to Tell About It*, 49–53.

stands that her grief for her late husband is not irrelevant to her own desire to join an expedition, but she appears to deceive herself as to the extent of this reason. This repression, however, appears not to affect her "reporting" capability, the insufficiency of which would cast doubt on *all* of her observations about Area X. Her unreliability is centered on her interpretation of her own emotional life, which draws upon cultural biases ("scientists should not be emotional") that can even strengthen the reader's impression of her observational acumen. Moreover, even when she discusses her emotional life, her use of euphemism ("some other event") and qualification ("in many ways" and "in a sense") attest to her concern for empirical accuracy while understating the degree of emotional attachment to her husband. Given that we tend to trust her observations, the cracks in the facade that relate to her own emotional life do not damage her overall reliability as a narrator so much as they convey an involuntary emotional response all the more compelling for her attempts to suppress it. This complex rhetorical performance adds up to a degree of narrational humanness that satisfies conventional expectations even as the nature of her material being is thrown into ontological doubt.

While the act of narration—or, put rhetorically, the attempt to communicate—takes center stage through the climax, the novel concludes with a reminder of narrative's inescapable materiality. Toward the end of the novel, the biologist reveals that, while bunkered in the lighthouse, she has "spent four long days perfecting this account you are reading, for all its faults" (127). The material artifactuality of the narrative is given a deeper significance when the biologist discovers a secret room in the lighthouse, accessible through a trap door. She discovers "a huge mound" that occupies the space of the room, "a kind of insane midden" containing "hundreds of journals" written by previous explorers of Area X (which reveals that there have in fact been many more than twelve expeditions) (70). The biologist picks up and reads some of them, including her husband's, seeing them as so many unread communications—but ultimately regards them as physical artifacts involved in their own material transformations. She notes that "the walls of the room were rife with striations of mold, some of which formed dull stripes of red and green. From below, the way the midden spilled out in ripples and hillocks of paper became more apparent. Torn pages, crushed pages, journal covers warped and damp. Slowly the history of exploring Area X could be said to be turning into Area X" (74). This decomposing pile of journals comprises a narration that cannot escape its own vibrant, transforming, transitional materiality, as it slowly morphs from subjective human voices narrating their observations *about* Area X into objects that themselves become part of the uncanny ecology *of* Area X.

The biologist recognizes this in her last act of the novel, as she leaves her journal on top of the decomposing pile before departing up the coast, deeper into Area X. By leaving her narration with the others, she acknowledges that any subjective account cannot transcend or be detached from the material ecology of Area X. If it is a human narrative, it is also a transient one—a transience reflected by the biologist's continuing awareness of her transformation from a Cartesian subject of knowledge into something else entirely: "Observing all of this has quelled the last ashes of the burning compulsion I had to *know everything* . . . anything . . . and in its place remains the knowledge that the brightness is not done with me. . . . The thought of continually doing harm to myself to remain human seems somehow pathetic" (128). Interestingly, even as the biologist relinquishes her own hold on a categorical humanness, the novel concludes with a flurry of first-person statements—including eighteen uses of "I" in the final 195 words—reasserting a functionally human identity in her own narration. The novel's final sentence—"I am not returning home"— stands apart as a final one-line paragraph, encapsulating this uncanny persistence of the narrating subject forever alienated from a homologous space of self-identity. The novel ends with a character narrator in a transformation away from the human, increasingly animated by an agency that is both her and not-her, both "environment" and material actant. At the same time, we cannot forget the ecological materiality of the narration itself, the black-and-white, lined journal with its inked-in pages recording the narration we are reading, slowly rotting on top of a pile of other notebooks, turning her story, and the stories of her predecessors, into deliquescent, moldering pulp.

CONCLUSION

In my reading of *Annihilation*. I've outlined the narrative mechanics that render fundamental interpretive frames ambiguous at the most basic, conceptual level. This "weirdness all the way down" stands in contrast to the reliance on a "permanent and stable" real-world reference demanded by unnatural narratology. Of course, one could argue that, by reading a work of literature, my approach cannot but reinscribe a representational model that falls short of the materialism advocated by ecocritical thinkers. Even so, VanderMeer's narrative figuration of emergent agency demands that the reader actively consider the cognitive processes by which we separate figure from background, agent from environment, narrator from storyworld. To use Karen Barad's language in her discussion of entangled material phenomena under scientific observation, at some point the reader makes an "agential cut" between subject and object, even if that cut is provisional and contextual. In contrast to the "Cartesian cut," which takes the subject/object distinction "for granted," the agential cut acknowledges the presence of an apparatus (say, fictional narration) that "enacts a resolution within the phenomenon of the inherent ontological (and semantic) indeterminacy" (140). The "agential cut" is post hoc, arbitrary, *not* natural. That is, we have to proceed *as if* this subject/object divide describes the morphic qualities of the phenomena under consideration, even if we know the material realities are more complex than a narrative rendering can admit. Where Barad is concerned with the scientific practice of quantum physics, an analogous operation is at work in fictional representation: the sequential, nominative medium of language can only resolve into a communicative act if certain protocols and conventions are followed.

Unnatural narratology has been a useful corrective to a kind of creeping mimeticism adopted by much postclassical narratology. Yet, as it is presently constituted, it is not well suited to an econarratology that no longer accepts a transhistorical, unchanging, "backgrounded" model of physical reality. Perhaps a more robust dialogue can emerge around the very question of mimesis, material agency, and the contingency of the "human" as a narratological category. These questions, moreover, should be relevant not only to prose fictions but to other narrative mediums as well: film, serial television, videogames, to name a few. The age of the Anthropocene itself demands a reframing of agency, temporality, and futurity—and the more narratology can address these dimensions at the intersection of literary analysis and planetary, ecological concerns, the more relevant it will become to twenty-first-century intellectual culture.

WORKS CITED

Abbott, H. Porter. "Narrative and Emergent Behavior." *Poetics Today,* vol. 29, no. 2, Summer 2008, pp. 227–44.

Alaimo, Stacy. *Bodily Natures: Science, Environment, and the Material Self.* Indiana UP, 2010.

Alber, Jan. *Unnatural Narrative: Impossible Worlds in Fiction and Drama.* U of Nebraska P, 2016.

Alber, Jan, Stefan Iversen, and Henrik Skov Nielsen. "Unnatural Narratives, Unnatural Narratology: Beyond Mimetic Models." *Narrative* vol. 18, no. 2, May 2010, pp. 113–36.

Barad, Karen. *Meeting the Universe Halfway: Quantum Physics and the Entanglement of Matter and Meaning.* Duke UP, 2007.

Buell, Lawrence. *The Future of Environmental Criticism: Environmental Crisis and Literary Imagination.* Blackwell, 2005.

Carroll, Siobhan. "The Ecological Uncanny: On the 'Southern Reach' Trilogy." *Los Angeles Review of Books.* 5 October 2015. www.lareviewofbooks.org/review/the-ecological-uncanny-on-the-southern-reach-trilogy.

Connolly, William. *A World of Becoming.* Duke UP, 2011.

Cronon, William. *Uncommon Ground: Rethinking the Human Place in Nature.* Norton, 1996.

Fludernik, Monika. "How Natural Is 'Unnatural Narratology'; or, What Is Unnatural about Unnatural Narratology?" *Narrative,* vol. 20, no. 3, Oct. 2012, pp. 357–70.

———. *Toward a 'Natural' Narratology.* Routledge, 1996.

Hageman, Andrew, Timothy Morton, and Jeff VanderMeer. "A Conversation Between Timothy Morton and Jeff VanderMeer." *Los Angeles Review of Books.* 24 Dec. 2016. www.lareviewofbooks.org/article/a-conversation-between-timothy-morton-and-jeff-vandermeer/.

Harman, Graham. *Weird Realism: Lovecraft and Philosophy.* Zero Books, 2012.

Herman, David. *Story Logic: Problems and Possibilities of Narrative.* U of Nebraska P, 2002.

Iovino, Serenella, and Serpil Opperman. "Theorizing Material Ecocriticism: A Diptych." *Interdisciplinary Studies in Literature and Environment,* vol. 19, no. 3, Summer 2012, pp. 448–75.

Mäkelä, Maria. "Realism and the Unnatural." *A Poetics of Unnatural Narrative.* Edited by Jan Alber, Henrik Skov Nielsen, and Brian Richardson. The Ohio State UP, 2013, pp. 142–66.

Phelan, James. *Living to Tell About It: A Rhetoric and Ethics of Character Narration.* Cornell UP, 2005.

Phillips, Dana. *The Truth of Ecology: Nature, Culture, and Literature in America.* Oxford UP, 2003.

Richardson, Brian. *Unnatural Voices: Extreme Narration in Modern and Contemporary Fiction.* The Ohio State UP, 2006.

Rothman, Joshua. "The Weird Thoreau." *New Yorker.* 14 Jan. 2015. www.newyorker.com/culture/cultural-comment/weird-thoreau-jeff-vandermeer-southern-reach.

Schneider, Ralf. "Toward a Cognitive Theory of Literary Character: The Dynamics of Mental-Model Construction." *Style,* vol. 35, no. 4, Winter 2001, pp. 607–40.

Tompkins, David. "Weird Ecology: On the Southern Reach Trilogy." *Los Angeles Review of Books.* 30 September 2014. www.lareviewofbooks.org/review/weird-ecology-southern-reach-trilogy.

VanderMeer, Jeff. *Area X: The Southern Reach Trilogy.* Farrar, Straus and Giroux, 2014.

CHAPTER 2

Object-Oriented Plotting and Nonhuman Realities in DeLillo's *Underworld* and Iñárritu's *Babel*

MARCO CARACCIOLO

IT IS fairly uncontroversial to say that narrative is a human practice that reflects human beliefs, values, and even the cognitive and physical makeup of our species. As inherently social animals, we tend to use stories to model everyday interactions among human subjects. Indeed, as researchers in both narrative theory (Herman "Stories") and psychology (Mar and Oatley) argue, narrative is geared toward the representation of intersubjective experience—the complex blend of cultural knowledge and cognitive skills that constitutes our engagement with other subjects.

But how does narrative handle processes and realities that fall beyond this domain of human action? How does it represent what several theorists refer to as the "nonhuman" (Grusin)—for example, phenomena that resist reduction to anthropocentric terms and/or question culturally widespread conceptions of the human? Examples of these phenomena include the timeline of the universe or the evolution of life on Earth, the interactions among subatomic particles, but also socioeconomic or environmental dynamics that destabilize a certain conception of the human subject as dualistically separate from the material world. Such realities take us to the outer limit of narrativity, the place where story borders on other discourse types—for instance, description or scientific explanation. Within the field of ecocriticism, Lawrence Buell was among the first to identify this anthropocentric bias of narrative, which led him to focus on nature writing—a genre that lies on the borderline of narrativity. This essay explores two case studies that, unlike Buell's, do not relinquish narrative but rather use narrative *form* itself as an experimental probe into the nonhuman world. The narratives in question are Don DeLillo's novel *Underworld* (1999) and Alejandro González Iñárritu's film *Babel* (2006).

My emphasis on experimental narratives ties in with the movement of "unnatural narratology," which calls attention to texts that challenge conventional storytelling strategies (see Alber et al.; Alber, Nielsen, and Richardson). I don't completely endorse the claims of scholars working within this movement, and I find their concept of "unnatural" somewhat unwieldy, but I do admire their effort to expand the corpus of narratology. In that respect, my case studies have much in common with unnatural narratology. My focus is on the notion of plot, which I define—building on a long narratological tradition (discussed by Kukkonen)—as narrative's organizing principle. Synthesizing various lines of work in narrative theory, I discuss plot as the fourfold logic—at the same time temporal, causal, thematic, and affective—behind narrative composition. In particular, I investigate what I call "object-oriented plotting," or cases in which an object takes center stage in a narrative and partly pushes plot beyond its anthropocentric comfort zone. The adverb "partly" reflects the tentative nature of this process: object-oriented plots do not (and cannot) completely eradicate the human element in narrative. Yet these narratives are able to evoke a sense of what ecophilosopher Timothy Morton calls "the mesh," or the constitutive intertwining between human realities and nonhuman processes (*Ecological Thought* 30). Such object-oriented plots decenter the human by using, at the level of narrative structure, a stand-in or "material anchor"—to borrow a term introduced by cognitive scientist Edwin Hutchins (*Cognition in the Wild*; "Material Anchors")—for nonhuman phenomena. In both my case studies, these material anchors are human-made objects that transcend their everyday usage as mere tools and thus elude anthropocentric grasp, serving as a reminder of our embedding in a more-than-human world. In *Underworld*, the material anchor is a baseball hit into the stands during a famous game between the Giants and the Dodgers in 1951. The baseball ties together the novel's storylines, signifying the enmeshment of human history and physical realities. A similar role is played in *Babel* by a rifle, which sets off the plot through the accidental wounding of an American tourist in North Africa. This event will have consequences as far as Mexico and Japan, but it is presented as a mere accident, thus uncoupling the film's plot from any clear-cut sense of psychological causation.

The notion of causality is key to my argument, since—as I explain in the next section—it straddles the divide between the human and the physical world. Both my case studies are characterized by a loosening of the connection between causation and psychological notions such as agency and intentionality: the plot is symbolically driven by epistemological uncertainty (in DeLillo's *Underworld*) or chance (in *Babel*) as a strategy for displacing narrative's bias toward human interaction. This move, in turn, has ramifications for the other dimensions of plot: it complicates the narrative's temporality through nonlinear structures, it inflects the texts' overall thematic coherence, and it shapes their affective dynamic.

The term "object-oriented plotting" is inspired by the philosophical trend initiated by Graham Harman under the heading of "object-oriented philosophy" and developed in recent years by theorists such as Ian Bogost and Timothy Morton (*Hyperobjects*). While some of the assumptions and claims made by these thinkers are debatable, their rejection of anthropocentric models is stimulating, not least because of the important challenge this rejection poses to narrative theory. Material objects, of course, have always played a role in narrative through their symbolic association with wealth and power. In the terminology of A. J. Greimas's actantial theory, objects can serve either as (literal) "objects of desire" or as "helpers" in a protagonist's quest. But standard quest narratives would *not* be an instance of object-oriented plotting as I define it here, because the sought-for object is subordinated to human intentionality: it constitutes a desire to be fulfilled, or a means toward reaching a certain goal. The upshot is that a plot that revolves around material objects is not necessarily object-oriented. For instance, "it" or object narrators in eighteenth- and nineteenth-century literature (see Blackwell; Bernaerts et al. 82–88) mainly serve an ideological or didactic function; objects in the realist novel contribute to characterization or to authenticating a fictional representation, as Roland Barthes's well-known account of the "reality effect" suggests. In these and in many other cases throughout literary history, the foregrounding of objects instrumentalizes the nonhuman, and thus subordinates it to the human: these narratives confirm, rather than question, an anthropocentric understanding of the world.

On the contrary, a plot is object-oriented when it challenges the subject/object dualism that is at the heart of Greimas's model, revealing the fragility and permeability of the culturally drawn boundaries of the (human) subject.[1] Arguably, this destabilizing dynamic has become salient in—and distinctive of—contemporary narrative practices because of the influence of scientific worldviews and ecological thinking. This chapter should thus be seen as a pilot study, engaging with two contemporary narratives in different media

---

1. For futher discussion of Greimas and the subject/object divide, see also Caracciolo, "Notes."

(print and film) while paving the way for a broader examination of contemporary narrative's engagement with the nonhuman world. With its focus on experimental texts, my argument contributes to current narratological approaches in two areas: work on experimental narrative within the already mentioned field of unnatural narrative theory, and work investigating modes of narrative's engagement with realities beyond the human (Bernaerts et al.; Herman, "Narratology beyond the Human"). This chapter should thus be seen as an extension of the "econarratological" research program recently outlined by Erin James. But whereas James focuses on spatial references in narratives and how they may draw readers into the storyworld, I will devote my attention to the temporal progression of narrative and how it is sustained by plot.

PLOT AND MODES OF CAUSATION

Described in broad strokes, plot is narrative's organizing principle, the set of strategies through which the narrated events and existents are integrated into an emotionally meaningful whole. Plot is a complex notion, though, and a closer look at narratological work on plot—as surveyed recently by Karin Kukkonen—reveals that four distinct dimensions feed into narrative organization: temporal relations between events (i.e., what comes before what); causal relations between characters and events (i.e., who performs what action and for what purpose); thematic coherence (i.e., what the story is about and what function or "point" it has within a larger communicative act); and affective dynamics (i.e., why the story is interesting and emotionally satisfying). Narrative theorists tend to assign a different weight to these dimensions: for instance, E. M. Forster's classic account of plot foregrounds causation, while James Phelan's rhetorical approach privileges affective dynamics emerging in the interaction between authors and audiences. Emotion plays an even more significant role in Patrick Colm Hogan's "affective narratology." Here, however, I'm less interested in singling out *the* basic element of plot than in exploring the interrelation between temporality, causation, thematic coherence, and affectivity. I thus build on the assumption that plot is an emergent phenomenon and that choices at the level of any of these four factors will have implications for the others as well.

The anthropocentric bias of narrative examined in the previous section is a case in point, since it inflects each of these factors. Yet causality is in a particularly interesting position. In their treatment of causation (Richardson; Kafalenos), narratologists tend to subsume all cause-effect relations in narrative under a single model or understanding of causality. Emma Kafalenos, for instance, argues that "*meaning* is an interpretation of the relations between a given action (or happening or situation) and other actions (happenings, situations) in a causal sequence" (1). In this definition, "action"—which implies agency and intentionality—is used interchangeably with "happening," which does *not* imply agency or intentionality. Hence, Kafalenos builds on the assumption that causality is fundamentally the same whether it involves minded agents or nonhuman entities. Dannenberg (26–27) complicates this monolithic view of causation by introducing Mark Turner's distinction between causation as progeneration, causation as action, and causation as necessary and sufficient conditions. The first builds on the biological concept of "lineage" to understand causal relations, as if an event could generate another event; the second refers to causation as direct, embodied manipulation of objects; the third focuses on the external conditions that make an event possible. This conceptualization is an important step forward, but for the purposes of this essay, it is still not fine-grained enough: what is missing is a clearer distinction between psychological and nonpsychological modes of causation. Some cause-effect relations logically imply human or anthropomorphic agency and intentionality, whereas others don't. The former are typically more central to the dynamics of plot, but nonpsychological modes of causation can also come into play. As an example, consider the following passage from Don DeLillo's *Underworld*:

> My son used to believe that he could look at a plane in flight and make it explode in midair by simply thinking it. He believed, at thirteen, that the border between himself and the world was thin and porous enough to allow him to affect the course of events. An aircraft in flight was a provocation too strong to ignore. . . . All he had to do was wish the fiery image into his mind and the plane would ignite and shatter. (88)

The narrator's son looks at the plane and conjures up the image of its midair explosion. The gesture of looking implies psychological causation—a relation between a mental state (the child's destructive impulse) and real-world events (his pointing his eyes at the plane). The notion of action, of which the child's looking is an example, thus occupies the middle ground between the mental and the physical world: through actions, mental causes turn into observable effects. This much seems uncontroversial. What happens in this passage, however, is that the child's desire falls flat, and the plane does not explode. That this is unsurprising for the reader shows that another mode of causation underlies our interpretation of this passage: the knowledge that the action performed by the child (looking at the plane) is *not* sufficient to bring about the desired effect, because this fictional world—which operates under what Richardson (38) would call a "naturalistic" causal regime—is governed by physical laws similar to those at play in the real world. Such laws are central to our understanding of causal relations among objects and bodies: human agency is subject to the constraints and affordances of the physical world, and it has to take them into account in order to match desired effects and actual consequences. Psychologists use the term "naïve physics" to refer to people's intuitive understanding of the ways in which the world is likely to "behave" when we interact with it in certain ways (see Proffitt). Clearly, this child's desire goes against the grain of naïve physics—and its failure is unsurprising because of this.

We may want to unpack the notion of causation even further. There are many forms of causation that cannot be reduced to the psychological model. For instance, we have causal relations between natural phenomena, like humidity and fog. Further, we have causation in the domain of socioeconomic phenomena that emerge from a network of human cultural practices and material conditions (for instance, one can say that malnutrition causes an increase in infant mortality rates). Finally, some causal relations blur the dividing line between human intentionality and physical factors. Consider the case of a plane accident where the pilots did not respond appropriately to a system malfunction that would have been relatively harmless in itself. In the Air France 447 crash of June 2009, the autopilot disengaged at cruising altitude because ice crystals clogged the so-called "pitot tubes," leading to inconsistent airspeed measurements. According to the investigators, the pilots' decisions, and not this temporary malfunction, resulted in an aerodynamic stall and the fatal impact with the Atlantic Ocean (see Smith). Through its complex causal history, the accident exemplifies the interconnection between human action, technology (computer-assisted flight), and natural phenomena that operate beyond human intentionality (the ice crystals).

Because of how it extends on both sides of the divide between human and nonhuman realities, causality is an ideal place to start if one wants to theorize object-oriented plotting. Narrative may put pressure on the psychological model of causation, integrating into its workings causal elements that *do not* involve agency or intentionality. In turn, this is likely to have reverberations at the level of narrative's temporal organization, thematic coherence, and affective dynamics. Over the following pages, I examine how this process plays out concretely in my case studies. In the next section, I use the notion of "material anchor" to show how in *Underworld* and *Babel* physical objects underpin the plot's nonlinear temporality. I then turn to how, through material anchors, nonhuman realities begin emerging in, and affecting, the overall progression of narrative. In the final section, I look at the thematic meanings and affective dynamics generated by object-oriented narrative strategies.

MATERIAL ANCHORS AND NONLINEAR TEMPORALITY

In the wake of George Lakoff and Mark Johnson's work, one of the central tenets of cognitive linguistics has been that abstract ideas and relations are typically understood by mapping them onto more concrete objects and events. An interesting example—discussed by Edwin Hutchins ("Material Anchors")—is that of people lining up to order at a café or to buy theater tickets. The line uses the customers' bodies and physical position in space to encode an abstract relation of precedence. The action of lining up for something is thus the result of the blend between a state of affairs (bodies forming a line) and an abstract ordering principle (who comes before whom). Another way to put this is to say, following Hutchins, that the physical line is a material anchor for conceptual structure: it allows us to keep track of abstract relations in a convenient, human-scale way.

In narrative, objects can also function as material anchors, making manifest and at the same time *grounding* at the diegetic level the abstract pattern of plot. This strategy is reminiscent of T. S. Eliot's concept of "objective correlative," except that what is made material is not (or at least not exclusively) an emotional state—as in Eliot's account—but the overall organization of plot. This kind of narrative signposting becomes particularly important when the plot is uncoupled from a sense of overarching human intentionality and cannot be straightforwardly mapped onto the progression of characters' beliefs and desires (a notion central to Marie-Laure Ryan's account of plot). In this case, material anchors help readers keep track of the events and their chronology.

My case studies are a straightforward example of this use of material anchors. *Underworld*'s multiple storylines are presented in anti-chronological order: after a prologue set in 1951, the novel moves backward from 1992 (Part 1) to 1951–1952 (Part 6). This temporal arrangement can be seen as a metaphorical journey into the past of Nick Shay, the protagonist: his youth was marked by a criminal act whose exact nature is revealed only at the end of the novel. However, this is only one strand in the plot, and the text consistently undermines a Nick-centered reading by bombarding us with a multiplicity of characters and episodes that have little do with the protagonist's life trajectory. Further, the novel's six parts are interspersed with three "Interludes" set in 1951 and entitled *Manx Martin 1–3* (I say more about the function of these interludes below).

Babel, on the other hand, is divided into three storylines unfolding in different parts of the world (Morocco, the US–Mexican border, and Japan). Frequent chronological shifts mark the narrative in the form of strategically placed transitions from one setting to another; retrospectively, we understand that these transitions imply a flashback or flashforward. For instance, about eight minutes into the movie, we see a young Moroccan boy, Yussef, firing a rifle at a tourist bus in the desert (see Figure 1). This is only meant as a test shot, since the bus is quite far and both Yussef and his elder brother, Ahmed, are convinced that the rifle has a shorter range. (We find out in a later scene that the bullet does reach the bus, wounding Susan, an American tourist.) After Yussef and Ahmed have fired the rifle, a cut takes us to the interior of a house, where a Mexican nanny is taking care of two children (Susan's children, we will soon infer). The nanny is talking on the phone with what we understand to be the children's father. That phone conversation takes place much later than Susan's wounding in the film's chronology, after she has been taken to the hospital: we will see the same scene from the father's perspective at the end of the movie. The transition from one spatial setting to another is thus accompanied by an unacknowledged temporal shift, a flashforward.

One might expect the presence of various storylines and locales in both *Underworld* and *Babel* to complicate readers' understanding of the overall plot pattern. I suggest drawing here on Arnaud Schmitt's work on multilinear storytelling and the narratological challenges it poses. According to Schmitt, plots may bring together multiple storylines in two ways: through what he calls "knots," or places where different storylines merge (with previously separate characters coming together in the actuality of the fictional world), and through less specific "connectors," or clues suggesting the possible convergence between two storylines, even though this convergence may remain a purely "hermeneutical line," in Schmitt's terminology (i.e., a readerly hypothesis).

In both my case studies, there is an overabundance of connectors, but very few knots in the strict sense; even the metaphor of the "storyline" (to which the notion of knot is clearly related) fails to capture fully the plot's peculiar narrative logic. In *Underworld,* individual episodes often feature some of the same characters, but it is difficult to establish any sense of clear-cut linearity because of the many gaps in the sweeping temporal arc traced by the novel. *Babel* has more limited temporal scope, but its overall organization is similarly mosaic-like, with the individual subplots remaining separate: we never see Susan coming home to her children, and the Japanese section is tied to the rest of the film only by a thin thread (one of the characters was the previous owner of the rifle fired by Yussef).

FIGURE 1. Yussef takes aim at the bus in *Babel*

The scarcity of knots means that the narrative pattern becomes not just more complex but also more abstract, because it never coheres into one or more salient action sequences that can stitch together the various episodes. Importantly, this process shifts the emphasis from the goal-directedness of psychological causality—the traditional focus of plot—to a sense of thematic interrelatedness. As Schmitt himself puts it, "Diegetic connectors generate thematic connection" (85). This is what happens in both *Underworld* and *Babel*—two plots kept together more by the proliferation of thematic echoes than by a stringent teleology. To compensate for this uncoupling of plot from goal-oriented actions, both narratives use what we may see as "material anchors" in Hutchins's sense: a baseball in *Underworld*, a rifle in *Babel*. These material objects circulate in the fictional world, passing from one character to another and forming a network of connections (or rather connectors) that help the reader navigate the multiplicity of characters and situations. Just like the physical bodies standing in line signify an abstract relation of precedence, the material history of these objects reflects—and at the same time embodies—the plot's unifying principle. These material anchors may be human-made objects, but they resist being seen as mere tools, pointing instead to a complex network of interactions crisscrossing the divide between human-level and nonhuman realities. Indeed, the critique of human mastery implicit in these objects is made more forceful by their human origin. Hence, we have what I call "object-oriented plotting" when, first, diegetic objects are used as material anchors for plot; and, second, these objects become associated with thematic and affective meanings that challenge narrative's inherent anthropocentrism.

UNCERTAINTY, HYBRIDITY, CHANCE:
NONHUMAN CAUSAL HISTORIES

What kind of objects are the baseball and the rifle? First of all, they are human artifacts invested with emotions and associated with various networks of causation in the psychological sense. In *Underworld,* this seems to take the form of a classical quest narrative. In 1951, the Giants won the National League pennant in a historic baseball game against the Dodgers; however, the ball, hit into the stands on the decisive home run, has vanished. As the game enters collective memory and achieves quasi-mythical status, the missing baseball becomes an object of desire for many fans, including the novel's protagonist, Nick Shay. A memorabilia collector, Marvin Laundy, claims to have tracked down the ball in a search described as "hard, fierce, thorough and consuming" (DeLillo 175). But for all his efforts Marvin doesn't have definitive evidence that the ball in his possession is the real ball. He explains that he was able to reconstruct the ball's "line of ownership" up to a man named Charles Wainwright, but "not back to the game itself" (181). Marvin adds: "I don't have the last link that I can connect backwards from the Wainwright ball to the ball making contact with Bobby Thomson's bat" (181). Despite the uncertainty surrounding the authenticity of Marvin's ball, Nick decides to buy it for the hefty sum of $34,500. This economic investment reflects the ball's (causal) power to evoke a sense of personal resonance and even emotional attachment, as Nick himself acknowledges: "I didn't buy the object for the glory and drama attached to it. It's not about Thomson hitting the homer. It's about Branca making the pitch. It's all about losing" (97).

Yet, in the novel's narrative economy, the baseball becomes more than a simple fetish invested with emotional meanings. Because the characters cannot establish the ball's authenticity, the narrative template of the quest fails to capture the full significance of this object: it is as if the ball asserted its "thingness"—its incommensurability with human emotions and desires—through the uncertainty of its line of ownership. Toward the end of the novel, Nick thinks: "Sometimes I know exactly why I bought it and other times I don't" (809). This paradox is inscribed in the novel's own narrative structure through the interludes, which focus on Cotter Martin, a child cast by DeLillo in the role of the ball's first owner. Cotter was at the stadium during the game between the Giants and the Dodgers, and was able to seize the baseball while in the stands. However, the baseball was soon to be confiscated by Cotter's alcoholic father, who sold it to Charles Wainwright. This is the missing link in Marvin's reconstruction, and the "proof" of the authenticity of his ball.

But neither Marvin nor Nick will ever become privy to what we, as readers, learn from the interludes. Readers will, of course, be aware that this narrative strategy is the result of DeLillo's intentional choices, but those choices strongly hint at the more-than-human significance of the ball: by evading the characters' desire to control its causal history, a material object seems to take over the logic of the narrative itself. This object resists human attempts at knowing or mastering its existence, and yet it governs the novel's composition: it figures in the prelude (which narrates the 1951 baseball game), in all the interludes, and it is frequently referenced or discussed by the characters elsewhere. Seen from this symbolic perspective, the novel is uncoupled from a sense of goal-oriented directedness and consigned to the vagaries of an unconscious object.

Moreover, the baseball is fundamentally hybrid, since it cuts across the boundary between human life and nonhuman processes. In an important episode, we see Nick Shay holding the baseball and inspecting it closely:

> The ball was a deep sepia, veneered with dirt and turf and generational sweat—it was old, bunged up, it was bashed and tobacco-juiced and stained by natural processes and by the lives behind it, weather-spattered and charactered as a seafront house. And it was smudged green near the Spalding trademark, it was still wearing a small green bruise where it had struck a pillar according to the history that came with it—flaked paint from a bolted column in the left-field stands embedded in the surface of the ball. (131)

With the material traces inscribed on its surface, the ball embodies a history that is not only human but chemical as well. At the heart of this passage is a productive tension between these poles—a tension perhaps best exemplified by the simile comparing the ball to a "weather-spattered and charactered . . . seafront house." The analogy between two inanimate objects (the baseball and the house) is expressed through a psychologizing metaphor, that of the "charactered" house—a paradoxical back-and-forth pointing to the constitutive intertwining of human "lives" and "natural processes." The same idea is reiterated more succinctly at the end of the novel, when Nick describes the baseball as "a beautiful thing smudged green near the Spalding trademark and bronzed with nearly half a century of earth and sweat and chemical change" (809). Human sweat stands on the same footing as earth, and both appear tied together by "chemical change"—that is, by underlying physical processes. Through its uncertainty and hybridity, the baseball thus stands in for a more abstract idea: the enmeshment of the human lifeworld with nonhuman causation. As a material anchor, the baseball introduces notions of uncertainty and hybridity into the plot progression, partly displacing the more familiar logic of human intentionality and teleology that we have come to expect in a novel.

Something similar happens with the rifle in *Babel*—though here it is the idea of chance that comes to the forefront. One of the characters in the Japanese section of the film was the first owner of the weapon; after a hunting trip in Africa, he gave it to his Moroccan guide. The rifle was later sold to a shepherd and ended up in the hands of the man's two young sons, one of whom accidentally shoots Susan while testing the weapon. Due to Susan's hospitalization, she and her husband are unable to travel back to the US as they had initially planned. The Mexican nanny in charge of their children is thus forced to take them with her to her son's wedding in Mexico. This excursion goes awry when, on their way back to the States, the nanny is arrested by US border officers as an illegal immigrant. The children narrowly escape death by dehydration during a botched escape attempt.

The film's three geographically distinct subplots thus trace the tragic consequences of a Japanese tourist's well-meaning gift. The narrative explicitly foregrounds the role of chance in this event sequence: the impression is that nothing happens *because* the characters wanted it, but because the circumstances conspired as if against any human intentionality. Even Susan's wounding is framed as an accident, and it is difficult to assign full responsibility to Yussef as he seems genuinely convinced that the bullet cannot travel as far as the tourist bus. Eventually, that shot will quite literally backfire when Yussef's brother, Ahmed, is fatally wounded in a shootout with the Moroccan police. In the world of *Babel*, everything goes wrong for reasons that may be compounded by human negligence (a rifle ending up in the hands of two boys) and misunderstandings (the police's mistaking the boys for terrorists), but can ultimately be ascribed only to the sheer chance of the bullet hitting Susan. This device has something in common with the poetics of chance and coincidence explored by Richardson (chap. 4) and, more recently, Dannenberg (chap. 4). What is specific to *Babel*, however, is that the coincidence plot fuses two levels of nonpsychological causality: the nonhuman mechanics of physical causation—the strict but blind laws governing the bullet's trajectory—and the network of globalization, which makes it possible for a rifle bought in Japan to alter the lives of people located as far as Morocco and North America. *Babel*'s rifle dovetails with the indeterminate history of DeLillo's baseball, of course. Both objects challenge a purely anthropocentric conception of plot: their narratives move beyond human agency, calling attention to the mesh of human and nonhuman causation.

A FEEL FOR THE NETWORK

We have seen above that plot is a four-dimensional construct, with temporal relations, causality, thematic connectedness, and affective dynamics all contributing to a narrative's overall organization. My analysis of *Underworld* and *Babel* so far has focused on nonlinear temporality and nonpsychological causality, but the setup of both narratives has clear ramifications in thematic and affective terms as well. Let's start from the thematic level. Both the novel and the film foreground the fictional world's interconnectedness, even as they put this idea to significantly different uses. In *Babel,* the rifle is a symbol of a globalized reality in which a gift received from a Japanese tourist in North Africa can fire a bullet whose consequences are felt as far as Mexico. Neil Narine investigates this dimension of the narrative, aligning it with a larger trend of "global network" films that attempt to portray, and at the same time critique, the socioeconomic interrelatedness of today's reality: how the West relies on the exploitation of marginal subjects (the Mexican nanny) or on the commodification of developing countries as tourist destinations (the Moroccan desert visited by Susan and her husband). *Babel* reflects on the consequences of this increasing globalization at the level of individual experience. The reference to Babel shouldn't go unnoticed: the biblical tower is a symbol of human hubris but also, crucially, of fragmentation and lack of communication; the film suggests that the dizzying interconnectedness of globalization results, paradoxically, in a sense of personal isolation and trauma (another keyword of Narine's analysis). The Japanese subplot is perhaps the most explicit in this respect: it focuses on Chieko, the deaf daughter of the Japanese man who was the first owner of the rifle. Traumatized by the suicide of her mother, Chieko communicates using sign language and spends most of her time with her deaf friends, being largely ignored by the rest of society: her silence serves as a psychological equivalent of a distressed, dysfunctional globalized reality.

Following Narine, the fact that an object, the rifle, and not a human agent supplies the plot's underlying causal logic could be read as a symptom of the objectification and depersonalization brought about by today's world. Seen in this light, the film's unsettling object-oriented plotting could be reconnected with human—perhaps even humanitarian—concerns. For instance, Rita Barnard argues that in *Babel* what "enables us to connect the three stories and three social locales is ultimately an intense, overarching affect: a kind of globalization of compassion that arises from a profound sense of human isolation and physical vulnerability" (9). I agree with Barnard about the role of affective dynamics in bringing the plot strands together, but I think the resulting affect is likely to be more complex than Barnard's reference to compassion suggests. We do sympathize with the characters, of course. But because we are unable to assign blame for the film's dramatic events, it becomes difficult to rationalize the sense of tragic foreboding that accompanies the viewing. In *Babel*, everything seems to go wrong, and for no (human) reason in particular. No amount of compassion can cancel out the dehumanizing power of the plot's chance-driven logic. This tension is neatly summarized by the last scene, in which Chieko, naked, is embraced by her father on the balcony of their Tokyo apartment. The camera undermines the warmth and affection of this final gesture by zooming out to reveal a cold expanse of night sky and dark skyscrapers towering threateningly over the two characters—a symbol, perhaps, of human frailty in front of nonhuman realities (see Figure 2). The film thus builds on a complex blend of sympathy and unease toward the unforgiving logic of the world beyond the human. Through the affective structure it generates, *Babel*'s object-oriented plot can be said to put viewers—or at least willing viewers—in touch with the depersonalizing network of human/nonhuman interactions, of which globalization is an important manifestation.

Underworld brings to bear on its object-oriented plotting a different, and possibly even richer, understanding of "interconnectedness." Nick, the protagonist, works in the waste management business. Early on in the novel he explains that he "traveled to the coastal lowlands of Texas and watched men in moon suits bury drums of dangerous waste in subterranean salt beds many millions of years old, dried-out remnants of a Mesozoic ocean. It was a religious conviction in our business that these deposits of rock salt would not leak radiation. Waste is a religious thing" (88). But *Underworld*, a novel set for the most part during the Cold War, is also obsessed with nuclear power. In a key passage, Marvin—the memorabilia collector—draws a link between the baseball and the atomic bomb: "They make an atomic bomb, listen to this, they make the radioactive core the exact same size as a baseball" (172). The baseball, in itself nothing more than the human residue of a recent past, is thus associated with phenomena whose scale far exceeds the human (the "salt beds many millions of years old" in Nick's remark), or with the physical forces harnessed by the atomic bomb. In this way, the novel participates in what Mark McGurl calls a new "cultural geology"—namely, "a range of theoretical and other initiatives that position culture in a time-frame large enough to crack open the carapace of human self-concern, exposing it to the idea, and maybe even the fact, of its external ontological preconditions, its ground" (380).

A similar interest in geological history emerges in a comment made by an online reviewer of *Underworld*, which I find particularly telling. The anon-

FIGURE 2. Chieko and her father embrace on the balcony of their Tokyo apartment in *Babel*'s last scene

ymous commentator refers to the solid black pages that divide the novel's parts and remain clearly visible when the book is closed, resembling geological strata:

> [DeLillo] has plumbed the depths of a dangerously complex time and an equally convoluted place. . . . This archaeology is our history. It is symbolized by the strata lining the edges of the book. Much as we would read the history of rocks or trees through the lines indelibly etched into granite canyons or across sylvan boles, we can only trace our lives, our histories, through the lines we have inscribed, lines that intersect (somewhat arbitrarily) with friends, lovers, enemies, and the random face or fact that emerges, unbidden, at odd yet appropriate moments. (Customer 1998)

The baseball summarizes, and inscribes into the novel's own stratified narrative structure, this nexus between the human and the nonhuman world. As the online reviewer's comment implies, affect is crucial to the plot's dynamic. A sense of wonder at the sheer scale of reality runs through DeLillo's novel, from the prologue's statement that "[longing] on a large scale is what makes history" to the "word that spreads a longing through the raw sprawl of the city" in the very last paragraph (11, 827). This is the sublime of hyperconnectivity—a feeling of awe at the density and depth of the connections between human history (the baseball, the protagonist's past) and material processes (nuclear radiation, the waste left behind by past civilizations). This feeling operates at multiple levels: it infuses the protagonist's experiences while sustaining the reader's interest in DeLillo's handling of such a vast, and multifaceted, narrative material. Object-oriented plotting thus becomes bound up with an affective dynamic: through its narrative strands converging on the baseball, its hybrid causal history, and its symbolic connections with waste and the atomic bomb, *Underworld* is able to open up emotionally resonant perspectives on the nonhuman world.

CONCLUSION

This chapter makes a first and admittedly preliminary attempt at theorizing stories in which the pattern of what we call "plot" is attuned to nonhuman realities. Narrative is a human practice, of course, and as such it is inevitably geared toward human interests and values. Yet storytelling always participates in a broader "cultural ecology" (Zapf): by entering into dialogue with other areas of culture—for instance, scientific knowledge—it may engage in a reconceptualization of humanity's position vis-à-vis physical realities that transcend individual human existence, or even the existence of the human species. It is this kind of reconceptualization that takes place in contemporary narratives such as *Underworld* and *Babel*. In both cases, the plot progression is tied to a physical object crisscrossing multiple storylines and replacing, or at least complementing, narrative's traditional focus on human intentionality and agency. The tension that derives from this operation is highly productive in terms of both the thematic issues it raises (the network of globalization or the hybrid "mesh" of causality) and the affective dynamics it generates.

This attunement between narrative and nonhuman realities is, like everything else in narrative, the result of a complex interplay between textual cues and readers' interpretive interests and propensities. To some extent, just as narrative is always keyed to human characters and themes, nonhuman phenomena can never be completely extraneous to it: after all, we live in a world populated by nonhuman animals and objects that are often causally implicated in human endeavors. However, narratives differ in the degree to which they call attention to, and integrate into their own workings, this causal efficacy of nonhuman entities. My case studies in this chapter display a high level of attunement to the nonhuman, but other narratives may be more subtle and ambiguous, and still raise analogous questions. Nor is this phenomenon unique to the twentieth century: while various areas of contemporary science highlight the interrelatedness of human and nonhuman phenomena, other historical periods reached a partly similar insight via dialog with other cultural practices. In my essay "Naïve Physics," for example, I observed how the same narrative pattern underlies Italo Calvino's "posthuman" engagement with the Big Bang and Dante's religious cosmology.

The specific nature of the "object-oriented plotting" I investigate in this chapter shouldn't escape us. On the one hand, *Underworld*'s baseball and *Babel*'s rifle put us in touch with nonhuman realities through the meanings they take on in the course of the narrative. On the other hand, these objects are prototypical examples of human-scale entities that can be directly manipulated since they are geared toward the size and sensorimotor skills of the human body. In *Underworld*, the importance of Nick's physical handling of the baseball is repeatedly emphasized: it is when manipulating the ball that Nick hits upon the idea of the enmeshment of human and geological history. In his own words: "How the hand works memories out of the baseball that have nothing to do with games of the usual sort" (132). In *Babel* this embodied dimension is perhaps less explicitly thematized, but it is still hinted at by the rifle—an object that not only affords bodily interaction but dramatically wounds Susan's body.

This foregrounding of physical interaction with the world through material objects confirms intuitions about the centrality of embodied patterns in human meaning-making (Gibbs)—including narrative form (Kukkonen and Caracciolo). In the case of object-oriented plotting, the involvement of bodily experience—of characters, but also potentially of readers—poses something of a paradox: the same material entity appeals to the makeup of the human body while problematizing the anthropomorphic agency that we tend to associate with embodiment as an existential and cognitive condition. The body is thus used as a vehicle toward our understanding of realities that in some fundamental way challenges (a certain conception of) human embodiment. This pattern, which I have already observed in other contexts (Caracciolo "Naïve Physics"; "Bones in Outer Space"), deserves being explored more systematically than I do here. The account of object-oriented plotting I outline should also be significantly expanded, taking into consideration a wider range of contemporary narratives.[2]

WORKS CITED

Alber, Jan, Henrik Skov Nielsen, and Brian Richardson, eds. *A Poetics of Unnatural Narrative.* The Ohio State UP, 2013.

Alber, Jan, Stefan Iversen, Henrik Skov Nielsen, and Brian Richardson. "Unnatural Narratives, Unnatural Narratology: Beyond Mimetic Models." *Narrative,* vol. 18, no. 2, 2010, pp. 113–36.

Barnard, Rita. "Fictions of the Global." *Novel,* vol. 42, no. 2, 2009, pp. 207–15.

Barthes, Roland. "The Reality Effect." *The Rustle of Language.* Translated by Richard Howard. U of California P, 1986, pp. 141–48.

Bernaerts, Lars, Marco Caracciolo, Luc Herman, and Bart Vervaeck. "The Storied Lives of Non-Human Narrators." *Narrative,* vol. 22, no. 1, 2014, pp. 68–93.

Blackwell, Mark, ed. *The Secret Life of Things: Animals, Objects, and It-Narratives in Eighteenth-Century England.* Bucknell UP, 2007.

Bogost, Ian. *Alien Phenomenology, or What It's Like to Be a Thing.* U of Minnesota P, 2012.

Buell, Lawrence. *The Environmental Imagination: Thoreau, Nature Writing, and the Formation of American Culture.* Harvard UP, 1995.

Caracciolo, Marco. "Bones in Outer Space: Narrative and the Cosmos in 2001: A Space Odyssey and Its Remediations." *Image & Narrative,* vol. 16, no. 3, 2015, pp. 73–89.

———. "Naïve Physics and Cosmic Perspective-Taking in Dante's Commedia and Calvino's Cosmicomiche." *MLN,* vol. 130, no. 1, 2015, pp. 24–41.

2. This is the goal of my current research project, "Narrating the Mesh" (http://www.narmesh.ugent.be/), which builds on many of the ideas advanced in this essay. The project is funded by the European Research Council (ERC) under the European Union's Horizon 2020 research and innovation program (grant agreement no. 714166).

————. "Notes for an Econarratological Theory of Character." *Frontiers of Narrative Studies,* vol. 4, no. 1, 2018, pp. 172–89.

Customer. "Fiction Is (No Longer) Dead." *Amazon.com Customer Reviews: Underworld.* 29 October 1998. www.amazon.com/review/R31A154KFZ342J.

Dannenberg, Hilary P. *Coincidence and Counterfactuality: Plotting Time and Space in Narrative Fiction.* U of Nebraska P, 2008.

DeLillo, Don. *Underworld.* Picador, 1999.

Eliot, T. S. "Hamlet and His Problems." *The Sacred Wood and Major Early Essays.* Dover, 1997.

Forster, E. M. *Aspects of the Novel.* Harcourt, 1985.

Gibbs, Raymond W. *Embodiment and Cognitive Science.* Cambridge UP, 2005.

Greimas, Algirdas Julien. *Structural Semantics: An Attempt at a Method.* U of Nebraska P, 1966.

Grusin, Richard, ed. *The Nonhuman Turn.* U of Minnesota P, 2015.

Harman, Graham. *Tool-Being: Heidegger and the Metaphysics of Objects.* Open Court, 2002.

Herman, David. "Narratology beyond the Human." *DIEGESIS,* vol. 3, no. 2, 2014, pp. 131–43.

————. "Stories as a Tool for Thinking." *Narrative Theory and the Cognitive Sciences.* Edited by David Herman. CSLI Publications, 2003, pp. 163–92.

Hogan, Patrick Colm. *Affective Narratology: The Emotional Structure of Stories.* U of Nebraska P, 2011.

Hutchins, Edwin. *Cognition in the Wild.* MIT Press, 1995.

————. "Material Anchors for Conceptual Blends." *Journal of Pragmatics,* vol. 37, no. 10, 2005, pp. 1555–77.

Iñárritu, Alexandro Gonzáles. *Babel.* Paramount Pictures, 2006.

James, Erin. *The Storyworld Accord: Econarratology and Postcolonial Narratives.* U of Nebraska P, 2015.

Kafalenos, Emma. *Narrative Causalities.* The Ohio State UP, 2006.

Kukkonen, Karin. "Plot." Edited by Hühn Peter. *The Living Handbook of Narratology.* Hamburg: Hamburg University Press, 2014. www.lhn.unihamburg.de/article/plot.

Kukkonen, Karin, and Marco Caracciolo. "Introduction: What Is the 'Second Generation'?" *Style,* vol. 48, no. 3, 2014, pp. 261–74.

Lakoff, George, and Mark Johnson. *Metaphors We Live By.* U of Chicago P, 1980.

Mar, Raymond A., and Keith Oatley. "The Function of Fiction Is the Abstraction and Simulation of Social Experience." *Perspectives on Psychological Science,* vol. 3, no. 3, 2008, pp. 173–92.

McGurl, Mark. "The New Cultural Geology." *Twentieth-Century Literature,* vol. 57, no. 3–4, 2011, pp. 380–90.

Morton, Timothy. *The Ecological Thought.* Harvard UP, 2010.

————. *Hyperobjects: Philosophy and Ecology after the End of the World.* U of Minnesota P, 2013.

Narine, Neil. "Global Trauma and the Cinematic Network Society." *Critical Studies in Media Communication,* vol. 27, no. 3, 2010, pp. 209–34.

Phelan, James. *Experiencing Fiction: Judgments, Progressions, and the Rhetorical Theory of Narrative.* The Ohio State UP, 2007.

Proffitt, Dennis. "Naive Physics." *The MIT Encyclopedia of the Cognitive Sciences.* Edited by Robert A. Wilson and Frank C. Keil. MIT Press, 1999.

Richardson, Brian. *Unlikely Stories: Causality and the Nature of Modern Narrative.* U of Delaware P, 1997.

Ryan, Marie-Laure. *Possible Worlds, Artificial Intelligence and Narrative Theory.* Indiana UP, 1991.

Schmitt, Arnaud. "Knots, Story Lines, and Hermeneutical Lines: A Case Study." *Storyworlds*, vol. 6., no. 2, 2014, pp. 75–91.

Smith, Patrick. "Automation and Disaster." *Ask the Pilot.* 1 November 2014. www.askthepilot.com/automation-and-disaster/.

Turner, Mark. *Death Is the Mother of Beauty.* U of Chicago P, 1987.

Zapf, Hubert. "Literature as Cultural Ecology: Notes Towards a Functional Theory of Imaginative Texts, with Examples from American Literature." *REAL—Yearbook of Research in English and American Literature,* vol. 17, 2001, pp. 85–100.

II

ECONARRATOLOGICAL RHETORIC AND ETHICS

CHAPTER 3

Readerly Dynamics in Dynamic Climatic Times

Cli-Fi and Rhetorical Narrative Theory

ERIC MOREL

FROM THE *New Yorker,* to *TIME Magazine,* to the *New York Times,* commentators heralded the arrival of climate fiction, or cli-fi, in twenty-first-century popular print and visual culture with variants of the question suggested by Dan Bloom to himself and five others in a *New York Times* debate: "Will Fiction Influence How We React to Climate Change?" Bloom is advocating for a category of works he hopes can move minds and hearts. Such questions, unfortunately, often take forms that effectually underestimate both fiction and reading. Bloom's own question notably elides the activity of reading—though presumably it precedes the other action of reacting. And if the answer to Bloom's question were to turn out negative, then the value of these fictions (and presumably reading them) would become altogether uncertain, if not imperiled. When the debate dwells on the merits of individual works as political silver bullets (or, in its Mr. Hyde version, as ideological miseducation)— or on the appropriateness of fiction media as sources of ethical instruction, tout court—the assumption of reading's transparency curtails other thought-provoking and relevant questions. I depart from these existing conversations by pursuing these other questions, such as how different interpretive strategies influence what readers take away from cli-fi, and what the continuing publication of cli-fi might signal about expectations readers apply to narrative interpretation.

As other scholars have noted, there are "problems with the definition of climate change fiction" (Craps and Crownshaw 1). Though not coined by Dan Bloom, it was more widely disseminated by him to aggregate works especially suggestive of global warming. There are those who are skeptical of the term overall[1] and others like Adam Trexler who object that what is being named is not so new ("The Climate Change Novel"). Notwithstanding these skepticisms, others including Antonia Mehnert attempt to make the term more useful by narrowing its application. Mehnert writes of her interest "in works that explicitly engage with anthropogenic climate change. In these books, meteorological phenomena do not just provide the background setting against which the story unfolds; climate change significantly alters and is a prevalent issue for characters, plot, *and* setting" (38). As my argument elaborates, I am wary of background/foreground content distinctions. I propose to deal with cli-fi's problem of definition differently, using a two-step move. First, I think it is critical to maintain a record of "cli-fi" as a historical marker—as the aggregating term in twenty-first-century media for a variety of texts, usually but not exclusively involving climate change. But cli-fi can and will expand from this initial set, I argue, to describe other, even earlier, narratives that resonate for readers with the expectations of works formally designated as part of the genre.

My essay proceeds along the lines of what rhetorical narrative theorists James Phelan and Peter Rabinowitz call "theory-practice," "inquiries in which theory aids the work of interpretation even as that work allows for further developments in theory" (Phelan 4). First, I make the case that those debating the merits of cli-fi would benefit from incorporating rhetorical narrative theory's framework of narrative audience; I lay out that model using Mark Twain's *The American Claimant* (Mark Twain's lesser-read[2] 1892 sequel to the 1873 novel he coauthored with Charles Dudley Warner: *The Gilded Age, A Tale of To-Day*) as an example of the consequences for interpretation of the novel that follow from occupying (or failing to occupy) the model's positions. From there, I trace how actual readers' connections to climate change, recorded in popular and academic criticism, stand to shift norms in reader expectations during reading. Thus, while individual works of cli-fi may not reorient actual readers' thinking on climate change, the increased number of these works promulgates climate change's existing and emergent impact on reading.

---

1. For example, see Bradley and Forthomme.

2. Larzer Ziff's pronouncement of *The American Claimant* as "the weakest of [Twain's] novels" succinctly captures the prevailing critical devaluing that explains its obscurity (78). Most references to the novel in Twain criticism link it dismissively to Twain's personal struggles and monetary needs.

WHETHER TO READ WEATHER IN A NARRATIVE:
TWAIN'S READERS' CHOICES

Discussing cli-fi and its value as a binary between effective or ineffective polit-icization frames the genre reductively. For example, its existing criticisms do not distinguish between evaluating possible misreadings of cli-fi and read-ings that find a particular work uncompelling, which curtails further thinking about how readers reconcile cli-fi's fictionality with extratextual knowledge about climate change. By contrast, the lexicon of rhetorical narrative theory—specifically, the work of Phelan and Rabinowitz as developed over multiple successive publications—helps to convene and compare a wider array of read-ings. In addition to illustrating ways Rabinowitz's model of audiences allows for these, my reading of Twain's *American Claimant* brings out the significance of changing relationships of the audience positions across history in ways rhe-torical narrative theory has not explicitly developed.

Rabinowitz's model posits three main interpretive stances.[3] Readers oscil-late among participation in these audiences while reading and are often aware of more than one simultaneously. The first, participating in the authorial audience, involves reading with an eye toward what the implied author wants readers to assemble from the narrative. The second, actual audiences, is what it sounds like: any readers with whatever particularities or meaning-making practices they bring to a text. The third, the narrative audience, reads to go with the flow of the narrative—that is, this audience accepts the narrative on its terms. If characters in a narrative interact with an abominable snowman, the narrative audience goes along with it rather than assuming the characters are hallucinating, even though as actual readers they don't believe in abomina-ble snowmen and, as authorial audience members, they understand the author as also not believing in abominable snowmen. Although many readers focus on entering the authorial audience, the model is nonprescriptive; the model's purpose is to allow for the parsing and comparing of responses through these positions.

The bemusing paratextual note that opens *The American Claimant* (a trait the novel shares with its prequel, *The Gilded Age*, and Twain's *Adventures of Huckleberry Finn*) generates similar distinctions as Rabinowitz's model. Para-texts often hold extra weight in shaping actual audiences' deductions about the authorial audience, and signs of the authorial voice as distinct from the narrator's also tend to distinguish between authorial and narrative audiences.

---

3. In later work, the rhetorical model incorporated a fourth, the narratee, which desig-nates the narrator's direct listener, whether characterized or not, based on the work of Gerald Prince. See "Introduction à l'étude du narrataire" and "The Narratee Revisited."

More atypically, however, this note also foregrounds the variability of actual audiences:

The Weather in This Book

No weather will be found in this book. This is an attempt to pull a book through without weather. It being the first attempt of the kind in fictitious literature, it may prove a failure, but it seemed worth the while of some dare-devil person to try it, and the author was in just the mood.

Many a reader who wanted to read a tale through was not able to do it because of delays on account of the weather. Nothing breaks up an author's progress like having to stop every few pages to fuss-up the weather. Thus it is plain that persistent intrusions of weather are bad for both reader and author.

Of course weather is necessary to a narrative of human experience. That is conceded. But it ought to be put where it will not be in the way; where it will not interrupt the flow of the narrative. And it ought to be the ablest weather that can be had, not ignorant, poor-quality, amateur weather. Weather is a literary specialty, and no untrained hand can turn out a good article of it. The present author can do only a few trifling ordinary kinds of weather, and he cannot do those very good. So it has seemed wisest to bor-row such weather as is necessary for the book from qualified and recognized experts—giving credit, of course. This weather will be found over in the back part of the book, out of the way. *See Appendix.* The reader is requested to turn over and help himself from time to time as he goes along. (459)

Twain plays on the common gripe of the weather delay to joke about liter-ary aesthetics and reception, and in so doing disrupts the usual relationship between narration and narrated. Use of the mentioned appendix might break down along three lines: use within the authorial audience, trying to gauge where Twain might prompt such a reference; use within the narrative audi-ence, wherein someone might stay attuned to the setting and events to recog-nize when weather would contribute to the narrative instead of "interrupt[ing its] flow"; or use by actual audiences, suggested here by the "help himself," where weather description would come into narrative as a matter of idiosyn-cratic preference. Although this paratext from Twain makes these positions more explicit than usual, the plurality of interpretation invoked here is by no means unique to his novel, and I argue accounts of cli-fi will be well served by attending to it. *The American Claimant* makes a useful springboard for this leap, in part because it presents an unexpected record of the idea of climate change as it seemed prior to its scientific consensus, and before that consensus inspired the historical marking of genre, and partly also because of the ways that this paratext stages tricky questions germane to cli-fi about the relationship of weather, narrative, and reading.

To ground these theoretical propositions, it is helpful to turn to a sample interpretation; as it happens, the *New Yorker*'s Kathryn Schulz has scooped me by discussing Twain's novel in a trajectory with cli-fi. Apart from this shared connection, however, our interpretations diverge. She writes, referring to the opening note, "'No weather will be found in this book' now reads either as denialist—a refusal to face climatic reality—or, very simply, as sad" (Schulz n. pag.). That Schulz does not read the note as deadpan corresponds with her not mentioning the appendix of Twain's novel. As an actual reader, Schulz is at liberty to feel however she does about Twain's novel, but I use Rabinowitz's framework here to argue her statement nonetheless offers a misreading insofar as it does not reconcile points raised within the authorial and narrative audiences.

Schulz also includes Twain in her piece to exemplify historical difference of concern: "Meteorological activity, so long yoked to morality, finally has genuine ethical stakes." Times have moved past Twain (as she reads him), and cli-fi enters as their standard-bearer. Using Rabinowitz's model to elucidate Twain's commentary on weather in the narrative, I counter such a timeline and suggest Twain's novel prompts readers to recognize (if in this case through absence) the "stakes" of weather and thus complements any emergent account of cli-fi's narrative or thematic innovations. Stemming from these questions of Twain's historical position relative to cli-fi, the second half of this essay takes up Schulz's proposition that *The American Claimant* "now reads" differently.

While the narrative audience may take Twain's opening note at face value, as perhaps Schulz does, reading the novel within the authorial audience would attend to Twain's characteristic, multilayered humor and the genre of satire in which *The American Claimant*'s prequel participates. After all, the weather note is suspicious: the contrast between the dare-devil author and the other experts—which sets up a competition even as it gestures toward humble deferral—is probably the main clue that some game is afoot. Also, any reader familiar with Twain as the writer of *Life on the Mississippi* (1883) and as a steamboat pilot, who would have habitually observed weather closely for that reason, might also deduce before flipping to the appendix that something tongue-in-cheek is at play. True to its word, the novel describes no weather aside from the first chapter's characterization of a morning as "breezy fine." The plot of the novel revolves around switched identities and scheming gone awry. Nor does the novel prompt readers directly to "See appendix" anywhere outside the prefatory note. Twain really leaves his readers to "turn over" as they may.

If and when readers do flip back to the appendix, "Weather for Use in this Book, Selected from the Best Authorities," they find a handful of snippets from works as different as nineteenth-century novels and the Book of Genesis. The descriptions range from the improbable to the ridiculous, and thus how weather might intrude in a narrative becomes apparent. One example reads:

> Merciful heavens! The whole west, from right to left, blazes up with a fierce light, and next instant the earth reels and quivers with the awful shock of ten thousand batteries of artillery. It is the signal for the Fury to spring—for a thousand demons to scream and shriek—for innumerable serpents of fire to writhe and light up the blackness.
>
> Now the rain falls—now the wind is let loose with a terrible shriek— now the lightning is so constant that the eyes burn, and the thunder-claps merge into an awful roar, as did the 800 cannon at Gettysburg. Crash! Crash! Crash! It is the cottonwood trees falling to earth. Shriek! Shriek! Shriek! It is the Demon racing along the plain and uprooting even the blades of grass. Shock! Shock! Shock! It is the Fury flinging his fiery bolts into the bosom of the earth. —*The Demon and the Fury*, M. Quad. (Twain 644)

The passage's frenetic sequence of impressions, its multiple emphatic triple repetitions, and over-the-top notes like "the lightning is so constant that the eyes burn" are all overwrought. No moment in Twain's novel calls for readers to turn and find such calamity.

The appendix—in "giving credit" via the excerpted weather passages— completes at least a basic joke from the prefatory note cutting along similar lines as *The Gilded Age*, where Twain and Warner lampoon those who mask lack of substance by proliferating decorative cover. This continuity between the novels partly stems from their sharing the Sellers character, who repeatedly wins influence by spinning bad ideas to persuade the gullible. But the joke's reach extends beyond particular jabs at named writers. Obviously, other novels will not put their weather "out of the way" in appendices. And really, these passages were chosen because they brought attention to themselves in their respective stories of origin. So, the criticism's thrust, on one hand, is that weather is best hidden in plain sight, described sparingly and innocuously. But this leaves one proposition from the prefatory note unaccounted for: Is, then, weather "necessary to a narrative of human experience"? Out of the way in the appendix or barely noticeable, the implication here reverses the initial concession and reinforces the place of weather as background window-dressing and as slowing a narrative line.

Perhaps, at this point, the line of questioning deviates anachronistically from the purposes of *The American Claimant*'s implied author, and my own ecocritical interest as an actual audience in how texts might mediate understandings of weather and climate (and vice versa) takes over a simpler rhetorical gesture. But asking about weather's necessity to narrative follows the text's grain in two ways. For one, Twain's joke here does ask about realist aesthetics and what realist works are ethically responsible for including: how much of what is necessary to human experience is "necessary to a *narrative* of human experience," and at what point does inclusion or description spill into excess? Second, these questions also register formally by staging the content and context relationship as the problem of relating the text of *The American Claimant* to its paratexts, a relationship that turning to the novel's concluding pages elaborates.

The novel ends after the switch-ups of identity and matters of lineage that form the central plot are revealed and untangled, yet the literal end of the novel is in some ways no end at all. The inveterate good-hearted and delusional con-artist Sellers stands up his protégé Hawkins, leaving only a letter to explain his absence—the novel closes with this letter as an interpolated text, in which Sellers introduces his next new scheme to win wealth and influence:

> In brief, then, I have conceived the stupendous idea of reorganizing the climates of the earth according to the desire of the populations interested. That is to say, I will furnish climates to order, for cash or negotiable paper, taking the old climates in part payment, of course, at a fair discount, where they are in condition to be repaired at small cost and let out for hire to poor and remote communities not able to afford a good climate and not caring for an expensive one for mere display. My studies have convinced me that the regulation of climates and the breeding of new varieties at will from the old stock is a feasible thing. Indeed I am convinced that it has been done before: done in prehistoric times by now forgotten and unrecorded civilizations. Everywhere I find hoary evidences of artificial manipulation of climates in bygone times. Take the glacial period. Was that produced by accident? Not at all; it was done for money. I have a thousand proofs of it, and will some day reveal them. (641)

He also proceeds to assure Hawkins that he has the "plan all mapped out" on a global scale, including his "intention to move one of the tropics up [to the north pole] and transfer the frigid zone to the equator. I will have the entire Arctic Circle in the market as a summer resort next year." The absurd logistics for making these "billions of money" involve harnessing sunspots.

Even though Sellers's letter has a terrifying sort of prescience, down to the calculations of first-world power to rationalize worse climates for poorer countries and to profit in the process, it seems anachronistic to say he writes here about climate change in the twenty-first-century sense.[4] Though Sellers's climate-swapping scheme may seem to come as an odd departure from the types of social commentaries that preoccupy the plot—such as criticism of ideals of class mobility—the ending is less of a non sequitur if considered in relation to the novel's paratextual humor. In fact, it complicates the joke and its logic substantially. Swapping climates dissociates a thing from its context without consequence. Climate, of course, results from aggregate measurements of air, water, and heat's interaction *with/over* a particular geographical context. The novel's comic problems result from each character's presumption or pretension to leave his original context (a British aristocrat trying to live as a meritocratic American, another American then posing as the aristocrat, and Sellers's own potential claim to the title through a genealogic stroke of luck), playing on the word "place" to link social standing and geographic/national origins. As a result, Sellers's final proposal to swap climates reads as absurd or bound to failure by deductive extension. That the appendix immediately follows the closing letter reinforces this connection, though readers who fail to turn the page thinking the appendix is irrelevant after finishing the novel may not catch on.

Weather, then—as a manifestation of climate—is indeed another example of context that cannot simply be extracted or moved around at whim; readers who took the appendix up on its premise (for however long until they realized how little it would gain them) actually demonstrate their willingness to buy into Sellers's idea before its presentation and lose their moral or intellectual superiority to other victims of Sellers's flimflam, since they prove they, too, are susceptible to his duping, which would appear so easy to ridicule when more hollow characters take the bait within the text. To whatever extent readers are in on the paratexts' joke (and some might never catch on), they enact a complicated combination of ethical judgments in connection to their evaluation of the novel's value and its humor's workings.

So, returning to Rabinowitz's terms, the trick Twain masterfully plays on readers is that, while they may (within the narrative audience) correctly understand Sellers's schemes and will almost certainly (reading within the authorial audience) recognize the criticism of characters misled by those hoaxes, they may as actual audience members fail to recognize how the novel's

---

4. Twain's library suggests he was familiar with John Tyndall and George Perkins Marsh. For more on weather science in the nineteenth century, see Moore and Fleming. For more on Twain and science, see Cummings.

paratexts subject them to the very criticism they identified—another level to the authorial audience and the way the narrative's reach extends beyond its fictional storyworld. Whether they succeed or fail to engage with the authorial audience by linking the paratexts and the final letter will determine actual readers' judgments about the ending and the novel's merit overall.

This interpretation of Twain's novel delineates how the audience positions suggested by Rabinowitz allow for adjudicating among readings. Schulz's consideration of Twain's book as "denialist" or "sad" stands out as privileging an actual audience's concerns over an authorial one, with the particular misfortune of obscuring that Twain's text raises questions precisely concerned with weather's "genuine ethical stakes." After all, the way Twain's weather joke disrupts assumptions preempts gestures attributed to cli-fi well ahead of the genre's rise. For example, journalist and environmentalist Bill McKibben's proclaims in his introduction to the cli-fi short story volume *I'm With the Bears* that while "on a stable planet, nature provided a background against which the human drama took place," cli-fi spotlights that "on the unstable planet we're creating, the background becomes the highest drama" (4). Twain's note seems to participate strongly in the former line, even developing the spatial quality in McKibben's background metaphor by putting weather "where it will not be in the way." Furthermore, the characterization of weather description as distinct from narrative motion (here the "author's progress") or as mere "fuss-up" echoes the familiar dismissal that "nature" typically comes into narratives as description or background. Yet my reading of Twain's novel above shows that it substantially complicates McKibben's division of "background" and "drama" well before cli-fi. In doing so, Twain's novel pulls at the strings of a similar division in narrative theory going at least as far back as Gérard Genette, who writes of "the absolute slowness of the descriptive pause," and that persists, as Phelan and Rabinowitz recently acknowledged: "Blurring setting with description can turn setting (one element *within* narrative) into a discursive mode that is, from certain philosophical perspectives, *in opposition to* narrative" (Genette 93; Herman et al. 85). Like most satirists, Twain does not propose a solution to the problems he exposes. Yet a reading that takes seriously his skepticism of weather's insignificance yields insights that are hardly "denialist."

Lines of questioning like "Will Fiction Influence How We React to Climate Change?" stress participation in the authorial audience; in other words, did readers get it? How will they act upon the understanding of climate change given unto them? Yet, surely another interesting trait of cli-fi is its stipulation that readers participate in its narrative audience. For whatever page-count, readers participating in the narrative audience accept climate change as a working premise, or the narrative will seriously misfire for them. That is, the situation is not just that climate change is *in* the novel (and that the ham-fisted author wants actual audiences to think a certain way about it politically), it's that readers have to accept it within the narrative's confines. By refusing to believe in climate change, readers would interpret all the characters of a novel like Barbara Kingsolver's *Flight Behavior* as living in a mass delusion (or, to return to my earlier example, fail to recognize that their disbelief in an abominable snowman does not provide an operative constraint within the storyworld). Although this reading may seem validating to the climate denier whose stance it would match, it can importantly be identified as an unproductive misreading of the text and not just a disagreement with the author (or critic) regarding the truth value of scientific data because of features internal to the narrative with which it will not align. Reading a work of cli-fi, insofar as it allows readers to inhabit a world as the narrative audience where climate change is factual and relevant, presents for readers what making compelling choices in the context of climate change might be like, which is meaningful intellectual work. Acknowledging the work of reading, cli-fi teacher-scholars can turn their attention to what follows—the moment where readers must reconcile or reject their actual positions to their intellectual work within the stipulations of the narrative and authorial audiences.[5] At such a moment, actual readers negotiating among these positions are required to exercise their judgment, opening the door to potentially accepting different ideas (as environmental humanists have long sought).

THE WAY WE READ NOW: ENVIRONMENTAL HISTORY AND NARRATIVE CONFIGURATION

Having used the rhetorical model of audiences to interpret Twain's novel, I now make the turn to the second half of rhetorical narrative theory's theory-practice: making a case for how works of cli-fi speak back to the model. Although my argument above suggests Schulz made a critical mistake in authorial reading, I have attended to her reading because her situating Twain's novel within the orbit of cli-fi is nonetheless a move I find compelling and one that evinces a larger trend in criticism, especially through her phrasing that Twain's note "now reads" a certain way. My argument in this section is that criticism of cli-fi provides a basis for what some narrative theorists have already speculated, which is that climate change has begun influencing how

---

5. For additional ideas and practical tools, see Beach's "Imagining a Future for the Planet Through Literature, Writing, Images, and Drama."

actual readers read narratives. I locate this within the rhetorical framework by demonstrating how various "rules of configuration" stipulated by Rabinowitz face shifts amid the developing history of climate change. At stake in these shifts might be a way, I conclude, to bridge rhetorical narrative theory with other diverse approaches in narrative theory more broadly—for example, feminist and critical race approaches.[6]

Any attempt to "cross-pollinate" (to credit Markku Lehtimäki's metaphor) the bibliographies of ecocriticism and rhetorical narrative theory risks bumping up against a longstanding and valuable tenet of the rhetorical approach: its a posteriori method. As Phelan has explained it most recently, "Rather than declaring what narratives invariably do or how they invariably do it," rhetorical narrative theory tries "to reason back from the effects created by narratives to the causes of those effects in the authorial shaping of the narrative elements" (6). If this at first seems uncontroversial, it nonetheless operates differently from approaches seeking to build a theory from conceptual distinctions and definitions. However, it also runs up against another strand of narrative theory, as Phelan acknowledges: "Rhetorical theory does not preselect for analysis certain matters of content, such as gender, race, class, age, sexual orientation, or (dis)ability, though it recognizes both that such methods have yielded valuable work on narrative and that some narratives do foreground such matters" (6). Initially, econarratology would appear just as incommensurate since, as Erin James has described it, it "maintains an interest in studying the relationship between literature and the physical environment" (23).

Similar impasses between ecocritical interests and a posteriori method might be observed with two articles published in narrative theory's flagship journal, *Narrative,* by Nicholas Royle and Takayuki Tatsumi, that advocate attention to environmental challenges. Royle's "Even the Title: On the State of Narrative Theory" performs its claim about the crossing of environmental history and reading to help make it. The passage that joins two of the article's three terms, "nanoment" and "narratoid,"[7] presents Royle's most direct claim about reading in the context of climate change. Urging narrative theory to be cognizant of environmental issues, Royle writes that the nanoment

---

6. Nonetheless, I stop consciously short of suggesting an "ecocritical rhetorical narrative theory." Nothing seems imminently gained by subdividing rhetorical narrative theory as a project, and my argument here labors to work within the rhetorical model rather than to splice it.

7. Royle's terms are largely incidental to my argument here, but he defines "nanoment" as "at once a slowing down and expansion" and narratoid as "a striking word or phrase that illuminates the text in which it is observed," also as "an effect—and perhaps an event—of reading" (7, 8, 8).

opens on to other perspectives—narrative, environmental, temporal, and so on. It accommodates a thinking of deferral and deferred sense, especially as regards the experience of "event" (what happened? When did it begin? When will it have ended?). It is haunted and spectral, unstable and uncontrollable. It affirms its singularity in a thinking of deep time and, today, the reality of the anthropocene [*sic*]. (Parenthetically here you feel compelled to add: no one should pretend that climate change is not radically altering the world of narrative studies: even within a narrowly meteorological context, "the clouds" for Yeats or Beckett are no longer but "the clouds" for us; whether Irish or English, "autumn" is not what it used to be; we can no longer read Bowen's description of that season without registering that the very narrative assumptions organizing the passing and return of the seasons and their representation in fiction are in a process of major transformation.) (7)

Royle's characterization of climate change as intrusive here is made a priori, despite his gestures toward Yeats and Beckett; the argument is predominantly conceptual and supported obliquely by suggested examples.

Arguing at a much larger scale than Royle's attention to the nano-, Takayuki Tatsumi has responded to Wai Chee Dimock's exploration of Henry David Thoreau's use of frogs in *Walden* to connote deep time; Tatsumi takes this focus on frogs in a different direction, examining Paul Thomas Anderson's film *Magnolia* and short stories by Haruki Murakami for their representations of apocalyptic raining of frogs. Tatsumi argues these and similar events (actual and literary) where lifeforms FAll FROm The SKIES (from which he coins "fafrotskies") blur the categories of natural and unnatural. Partly informed by the compound disasters of the Fukushima tsunami and the TEPCO Daiichi nuclear reactor meltdown, where the dangers of either catastrophe increased exponentially as a result of their messy combination, his reflections on the blurring of the natural and unnatural lead Tatsumi to claim:

> What is at stake now is not exactly the distinction between nature and civilization, I would argue, but rather that between the imaginable and the unimaginable. Some of us will want only to try and imagine what should be done after the disasters. But perhaps it is just as important to deeply speculate upon the nature of the unimaginable already embedded, but unnoticed, in the works of the imagination in art and fiction all around us, both present and past. (349)

Tatsumi prompts a double-directional relationship between narrative and experience, or reading and context. More specifically, his advocated shift from reactive response to speculation poses, at the level of individual actual readers, questions about the forward-looking moves readers make while reading. To a certain extent, his choice of example's implicit risk component follows upon Ursula Heise's argument that "narrative genres . . . provide important cultural tools for organizing information about risks into intelligible and meaningful stories," which also concerns texts' blueprints for cultural futures (138). But Tatsumi's claim does not restrict itself to genre, proposing instead a much more expansive curiosity about tropes and other narrative components awaiting detection in literary archives broadly construed—and this curiosity is itself occasioned by unfolding events in the present. Though a resourceful and energizing claim, this, too, presents an a priori approach by preselecting what it looks for in the study of narratives.

Neither Royle nor Tatsumi explicitly situates his argument within an ecocritical framework, raising questions about how econarratology with a foothold in ecocritical bibliographies can contribute to questions about reading and narrative. Actually, such questions about relationships between reading practices and environmental history have long been present, if not always at the surface, within ecocriticism. Cheryll Glotfelty's definition of ecocriticism from her introduction to *The Ecocriticism Reader* garners frequent citation, but few attend to her essay's opening paragraphs, where she establishes the need for ecocriticism partly by comparing scholarly journals to a "scan [of] newspaper headlines": "In view of the discrepancy between current events and the preoccupations of the literary profession," she wrote before the ascendancy of ecocriticism within the discipline, "the claim that literary scholarship has responded to contemporary pressures becomes difficult to defend" (xvi). While ecocriticism in the wake of Glotfelty's landmark volume has been diverse in its aims and methods, what Scott Slovic has called ecocritical methods of "contextualization and synthesis" can be used to contrast Royle and Tatsumi in 2013 and 2014 and Rabinowitz in 1987 as actual readers, throwing into relief the interplay of environmental conditions and readers' expectations about narrative, whether or not, as Phelan put it, narratives place those conditions in the "foreground" (Slovic 34).

Although Rabinowitz's audience model is the most cited contribution from *Before Reading* (1987), he proposed four less-discussed rules (notice, signification, configuration, and coherence) that are part of rhetorical narrative theory's ongoing attention to how readers experience or think through the act of reading narrative—what Phelan has consolidated within narrative's "progression" as the unfolding of the narrative and readers' responses to that unfolding. Despite their name, Rabinowitz's "rules" are not hard-and-fast but instead describe patterns readers learn and deploy over the course of their experience with narratives. Readers continue to apply the rules that "work" for as long as they work, and in this way Rabinowitz's rules have always been, as Phelan describes the rhetorical approach broadly, a "perpetual work-in-progress" (Phelan xi). What cli-fi contributes to this work-in-progress is two-fold: first, it marks a context that shows how environmental conditions, so apparently stable in 1987 that Rabinowitz could posit a rule about their constancy, have changed, and second, its proliferation offers an emerging mass of texts that may habituate readers to alternative rules, which may then collide with the old ones as those readers engage earlier texts.

Given that Rabinowitz defines rules of configuration as "govern[ing] the activities by which readers determine probability" and "allow[ing them] to answer the question, 'How will this, in all probability, work out?,'" his choice to title the chapter "The Black Cloud on the Horizon: Rules of Configuration" strikes a surprising chord alongside Royle's emphasis on clouds as invoking climate change and the unpredicted turn in their significance. The title names the convention of foreshadowing that uses black clouds or stormy oncoming weather to signify dark times ahead by combination of the literal and figurative. As Rabinowitz makes clear, readers often learn such conventions early in simpler texts, where their use is straightforward, but also often find them applicable in more complicated and nuanced texts.

Another rule of configuration offered by Rabinowitz is even more suggestive when thinking about climate change's potential impacts on reading: "the rule of imminent cataclysm." The rule of imminent cataclysm suggests, "If a story begins at a specified moment right before a general upheaval . . . we are probably being asked to read with the expectation that that upheaval will influence the course" of the narrative (123). Rabinowitz's example cataclysms include the French Revolution, World War II, or the Stock Market crash of 1929 preceding the American Great Depression. But the etymology of cataclysm, which ties to biblical and other massive floods, fits climate change just as well or better, raising the possibility that climate change, too, could shape what actual readers expect in texts produced amid awareness of anthropogenic impact on climate. Rabinowitz does delimit that "the rule of imminent cataclysm, of course, applies only to works written after the cataclysm in question" (124). Yet Tatsumi's caution about the imperative not to wait until disasters have passed before thinking about available responses (perhaps particularly since anthropogenic impact on climate isn't a problem for which there is necessarily an "after"), destabilizes Rabinowitz's "of course." Though part of Rabinowitz's idea is that imminent cataclysm "works" for the purpose of configuration because it adds an element of predictability—authorial audiences knowledgeable about history recognize likely outcomes of certain events (especially when those events arise in a genre that does not signal their revision)—Tatsumi's observations about "fafrotskies" recall that present climate challenges endanger predictability itself. Climate change as "imminent cataclysm" involves predicting unpredictability, or predicting weather events with less predictable compound implications.

Regardless of whether cli-fi catches on as a generic term, works that have found their way onto cli-fi booklists share the "imminent cataclysm" of anthropogenic climate change as a narrative convention (indeed, as a raison-d'être). As an example, we can consider a passage from Nathaniel Rich's *Odds Against Tomorrow*. The driving cataclysm of the novel's plot has arrived, and raindrops "detonated in giant asterisks on the sidewalks"; then, "The sky had begun to darken. It looked enraged, a livid sky, full of eggplant colors, purple yielding to cast-iron black. There was something thrillingly exotic about the angry blackness of it, tense with intermittent electricity. The clouds were scowling" (145). The storm unfolds over several chapters, but this particular passage has the advantage of recalling both of Rabinowitz's tropes of configuration mentioned above, which readers trying to occupy the authorial audiences will recognize here as signaling imminent disaster for the characters—recognition borne out in the narrative audience. Where, in Rabinowitz's "black cloud" rule, the clouds mostly acted as metaphor for other perils, here the cloud is the trouble itself. And although readers of Rich's novel have been prepared for a cataclysm since the opening pages, the specific outcomes of this storm remain compound and unpredictable—as thematized by the protagonist Michael Zukor, a disaster scenario predictor and insurance salesman, getting blindsided by the hurricane.

But what is notable about commentaries on Rich's novel is that they provisionally exemplify Royle's and Tatsumi's arguments: *pace* Royle, the novel's hurricane wasn't just a hurricane for readers and *pace* Tatsumi, the novel was understood as source material for the previously unpredictable. References to Rich's take on environmental science, for example, take a backseat relative to the near-ubiquitous references to Hurricane Sandy. That the reception of this novel did not take agreement with the author as its center and focused instead on the shocking merge between narrative audience and actual audiences' worlds is notable in American National Public Radio's coverage of *Odds Against Tomorrow*'s release alongside the rise in usage of cli-fi as a new generic term. As its opening hook, the piece recounts an influential reader's moment of paratextual reckoning as he registers how a cataclysmic weather event (Hurricane Sandy) influenced his reception of Rich's novel on his desk:

When Superstorm Sandy hit New York City last fall, the publisher Farrar, Straus and Giroux, like most everything else, totally shut down. It was a week before power returned to FSG, according to Brian Gittis, a senior publicist. When he got back to his office, he began sorting through galleys—advance copies of books. And one of them caught him off guard.

Its cover had an illustration of the Manhattan skyline half-submerged in water.

"It was definitely sort of a Twilight Zone moment," Gittis recalls. (Evancie)

In microcosm, this incident starts the chain linking one actual reader's changed perspective on a book to a wider diffusion—the publicist shares his reading with Angela Evancie, who in turn publicizes the novel under the rubric of the new generic term, thus priming at least some of the novel's readers to understand it in a particular context.

For as long as anthropogenic climate change stayed a ridiculous premise, as in Twain's *The American Claimant,* it was unlikely to enter into readers' responses and expectations in significant ways, and no single novel (including Rich's) will likely change that. But increased conditioning from critics alongside the profusion and popularity of works where actual audiences' extratextual awareness of climate change turns out to be useful in guiding their experience of progression within the narrative audience might, over time, recalibrate expectations and affective responses. For some actual audiences, some words already register associations unanticipated in the authorial and narrative audience; my and Schulz's rereading Twain's *The American Claimant* alongside cli-fi's emergence exemplifies this, since its weather apparatus resonates differently for us in our context as more than a paratextual joke. While such responses will continually bump up against the limits of authorial reading in works where climate change does not, in fact, inform the text, those encounters will only reinforce the fact of the intervening changes in environmental history.[8] Ironically for a novel like Twain's, such historical differences may need to be signaled for future readers by additional paratexts like appendices.

---

8. My argument here has partial overlap with Vera Nünning's case for tracing reception history as a way of mitigating the ahistorical dimension of narratological work. But whereas Nünning does not reference Rabinowitz, my doing so has two purposes. First, it responds to the specific charges of ahistoricity leveled at rhetorical narrative theory for its a posteriori approach. Second, the audience model allows for distinguishing between what is a shift in normative cultural standards and what is misreading, which Nünning's argument leaves unaddressed.

My argument about cli-fi differs both from those who are optimistic about cli-fi's political efficacy on one hand[9] and the various commentators and critics lamenting that cli-fi may more-or-less offer a green spin on apocalyptic or postapocalyptic sci-fi narrative conventions rather than innovate narrative genres on the other.[10] That is, my argument is not necessarily about any single work but in the proliferation itself, echoing Adam Trexler's point that "broad reading enables patterns in climate fiction to be gathered" as part of his inquiry into how "climate change and all its *things* have changed the capacities of recent literature" (*Anthropocene Fictions* 15, 13). This calls to mind a shared irony about many of the pieces that survey the fledgling genre of cli-fi; although they often settle on one or a few preferred texts, these essays themselves exhibit the opposite impulse—namely, the productive judgments made available from the synthesis of reading more than one narrative.

By demonstrating how the accumulation of texts can shift readers' expectations through the new patterns it introduces, and by showing how dissemination of those patterns occurs through reception history in popular culture and criticism, I have made the case for the process by which reader interests and readerly dynamics can shift historically, and thereby come to impact reading of even texts that do not foreground those expectations. Of course, reading within the authorial audience—to the extent that readers still have that context available to them—will mollify anachronistic impositions by later actual audiences onto earlier literary works. But if one of the effects of narrative that rhetorical narrative theory studies, for example, is surprise, then the default

---

9. In one example, Lily Rothman writing for *TIME Magazine* situates the boom of cli-fi films reaching viewers in the summer of 2014 as "arriv[ing] on the crest of a new wave of optimism about the power of fiction" (52). But as Rothman's wave metaphor implies, this "power of fiction" is not new, but newly popular. Cli-fi gets cast here as the Intergovernmental Panel on Climate Change report with literary stylings and special effects, which uncomfortably connotes the desirability of getting past the literary to arrive at more important content; it uncritically redeploys the "conviction that [a genre's] capacity to palliate the soul will culminate in an environmentally friendly perspective" that Nancy Easterlin incisively unpacks in her ecocritically focused chapter from *A Biocultural Approach to Literary Theory and Interpretation* (96). *The Chronicle of Higher Education*, meanwhile, uses a terraforming metaphor that cli-fi courses are "Changing the Landscape of Literary Studies." I agree that including cli-fi in syllabi can be impactful, but Fernandes's piece celebrates new course offerings themselves as the impact, almost as though literature courses lacked means for engaging environmental issues prior to cli-fi's arrival.

10. For example, Gaard: "Cli-fi narratives remain confined within the apocalyptic failure of techno-science solutions, and uninformed by the global climate justice movement" (274); Trexler: "After 30 years spent imagining our possible futures, the limits of the genre are starting to bump up against the limits of our political imaginations" ("The Climate Change Novel"); and Forthomme: "In short, a not-so-new form of apocalyptic literature." However, remaining open to pushing back the historical frame of the genre's inception can qualify some of these criticisms.

assumptions readers bring to various aspects of narrative and the causes in shifts to that default in history surely matter to the broader project of rhetorical poetics in under-acknowledged ways. Econarratology, recognizing that neither the environment nor the reader are historical constants, can enrich rhetorical narrative theory's account then not just of new texts but even of the same text over time, across different readers, across different climatic norms.

WORKS CITED

Beach, Richard. "Commentary: Imagining a Future for the Planet Through Literature, Writing, Images, and Drama." *Journal of Adolescent and Adult Literacy,* vol. 59, no. 1, Jul. 2015, pp. 7–13.

Bloom, Dan, Heidi Cullen, Seán Ó Heigeartaigh, George Marshall, J. P. Telotte, and Sheree Renée Thomas. "Will Fiction Influence How We React to Climate Change?" *New York Times,* 29 Jul. 2014. www.nytimes.com/roomfordebate/2014/07/29/will-fiction-influence-how-we-react -to-climate-change.

Bradley, James. "The Rise of Cli-Fi." *Australian,* 24 Jan. 2015, p. 3.

Craps, Steph, and Rick Crownshaw. "Introduction: The Rising Tide of Climate Change Fiction." *Studies in the Novel,* vol. 50, no. 1, Spring 2018, pp. 1–8.

Cummings, Sherwood. "Science." *The Mark Twain Encyclopedia.* Edited by J. R. LeMaster and James D. Williams. Garland Publishing, 1993.

Easterlin, Nancy. *A Biocultural Approach to Literary Theory and Interpretation.* Johns Hopkins UP, 2009.

Evancie, Angela. "So Hot Right Now: Has Climate Change Created A New Literary Genre?" *NPR.org,* 20 Apr. 2013. www.npr.org/2013/04/20/176713022/so-hot-right-now-has-climate -change-created-a-new-literary-genre.

Fernandes, Rios. "The Subfield That Is Changing the Landscape of Literary Studies." *Chronicle of Higher Education,* 21 Mar. 2016. www.chronicle.com/article/The-Subfield-That-Is -Changing/235776.

Fleming, James Roger. *Fixing the Sky: The Checkered History of Weather and Climate Control.* Columbia UP, 2010.

Forthomme, Claude. "Climate Fiction, Why It Matters." *Impakter.com,* 16 Jun. 2014. impakter. com/climate-fiction-why-it-matters.

Gaard, Greta. "What's the Story? Competing Narratives of Climate Change and Climate Justice." *Forum for World Literature Studies,* vol. 6, no. 2, Jul. 2004, pp. 272–91.

Genette, Gérard. *Narrative Discourse: An Essay on Method.* Translated by Jane E. Lewin. Cornell UP, 1980.

Glotfelty, Cheryll. Introduction. *The Ecocriticism Reader: Landmarks in Literary Ecology.* Edited by Cheryll Glotfelty and Harold Fromm. U of Georgia P, 1996, pp. xv–xxxvii.

Heise, Ursula. *Sense of Place and Sense of Planet: The Environmental Imagination of the Global.* Oxford UP, 2008.

Herman, David, Robyn Warhol, James Phelan, and Peter J. Rabinowitz. *Narrative Theory: Core Concepts and Critical Debates.* The Ohio State UP, 2012.

James, Erin. *The Storyworld Accord: Econarratology and Postcolonial Narratives.* U of Nebraska P, 2015.

Lehtimäki, Markku. "Natural Environments in Narrative Contexts: Cross-Pollinating Ecocriticism and Narrative Theory." *Storyworlds,* vol. 5, 2013, pp. 119–41.

McKibben, Bill. Introduction. *I'm With the Bears: Short Stories from a Damaged Planet.* Edited by Mark Martin, Verso, 2011, pp. 1–5.

Mehnert, Antonia. *Climate Change Fictions: Representations of Global Warming in American Literature.* Palgrave MacMillan, 2016.

Moore, Peter. *The Weather Experiment: The Pioneers Who Sought to See the Future.* Farrar, Straus and Giroux, 2015.

Nünning, Vera. "Unreliable Narration and the Historical Variability of Values and Norms: *The Vicar of Wakefield* as a Test Case of a Cultural-Historical Narratology." *Style,* German Narratology Special Issue, vol. 38, no. 2, Summer 2004, pp. 236–52.

Phelan, James. *Somebody Telling Somebody Else: A Rhetorical Poetics of Narrative.* The Ohio State UP, 2017.

Prince, Gerald. "Introduction à l'étude du narrataire." *Poétique,* no. 14, 1973, pp. 173–92.

———. "The Narratee Revisited." *Style,* Readers and Authors Special Issue, vol. 19, no. 3, Fall 1985, pp. 299–303.

Rabinowitz, Peter, J. *Before Reading: Narrative Conventions and the Politics of Interpretation.* The Ohio State UP, 1998.

Rich, Nathaniel. *Odds Against Tomorrow: A Novel.* Farrar, Straus, and Giroux, 2011.

Rothman, Lily. "Nature Bites Back: *Godzilla* Leads a Surge of Summer Movies that Reflect Our Environmental Anxieties." *TIME Magazine,* 19 May 2014, pp. 50+.

Royle, Nicholas. "Even the Title: On the State of Narrative Theory." *Narrative,* vol. 22, no. 1, Jan. 2014, pp. 1–16.

Schulz, Kathryn. "Writers in the Storm: How Weather Went From Symbol to Science and Back Again." *New Yorker,* 23 Nov. 2015. www.newyorker.com/magazine/2015/11/23/writers-in-the-storm

Slovic, Scott. *Going Away to Think: Engagement, Retreat, and Ecocritical Responsibility.* U of Nevada P, 2008.

Tatsumi, Takayuki. "Planet of the Frogs: Thoreau, Anderson, and Murakami." *Narrative,* vol. 21, no. 3, Oct. 2013, pp. 346–56.

Trexler, Adam. *Anthropocene Fictions: The Novel in a Time of Climate Change.* U of Virginia P, 2015.

———. "The Climate Change Novel: A Faulty Simulator of Environmental Politics." *Policyinnovations.org,* 7 Nov. 2011. www.carnegiecouncil.org/publications/archive/policy_innovations/briefings/000230.

Twain, Mark (Samuel Langhorne Clemens). *The American Claimant. The Gilded Age and Later Novels.* Library of America, 2002, pp. 457–644.

Ziff, Larzer. *Mark Twain.* Oxford: Oxford UP, 2004.

CHAPTER 4

A Comedy of Survival

Narrative Progression and the Rhetoric of Climate Change in Ian McEwan's Solar

MARKKU LEHTIMÄKI

AS URSULA HEISE argues, perceptions of climate change and other environmental risks are shaped by narrative modes and rhetorical tropes, which serve as a means of "organizing information about risks into intelligible and meaningful stories" (138). Consequently, classical figures, tropes, and allegorical story models, such as pastoral, apocalypse, irony, tragedy, and comedy, retain their vitality when writers try to come to terms with climate change. Based on these premises, the rhetorical approach to narrative appears relevant when we are studying the ways in which fiction communicates ideas and values related to environmental phenomena. In this regard, the rhetorical emphasis in narrative studies can also be seen in the service of ecocritical or other politically engaged literary studies.

In this essay, I read Ian McEwan's climate change novel *Solar* (2010) as a fictional narrative taking part in the heated discussion about the problems and possibilities of narrative relative to large-scale environmental problems. In *Solar,* the human race's struggle for survival takes the form of an environmental comedy in which the protagonist, scientist Michael Beard, tries to save the planet—and especially his own skin—by developing new technologies for utilizing solar energy. The character's progression in the narrative is both negative and positive, just as the novel itself can be read either in a comic or in a tragic mode; Beard's body collapses while his ethical vision matures, and in the global discussion, climate change develops from an apocalyptic story into an aching reality. Indeed, McEwan's rhetorical narrative is built on complex negotiations, beginning with the challenging questions that the very topic of climate change poses: first, how does the novelist's traditional toolbox approach a problem of such global proportions, and second, should we even look to fictional narratives for answers to real environmental problems?

More specifically, I argue that despite being cast in a strongly mimetic mode in its plotting and characterization, *Solar* is a *metarhetorical* narrative about climate change, meaning that the novel extensively deals with the many-sided rhetorical dialogue associated with the climate-conscious talk. Just as the novel as a rhetorical and dialogical form complicates this talk, the ecocritical concern about the heating planet complicates the premises of a human-centered narrative. The novel also critically asks whether climate change is a *narrative* and whether the solution to this larger-than-human-life question is telling better and better *stories* that we can agree on—a contention that is sometimes voiced in literary-theoretical approaches to the Anthropocene. Some critics have found McEwan's comic and allegorical style somewhat disappointing, suggesting that environmental fictions were supposed to deal with environmental issues seriously. In my reading, Michael Beard, McEwan's ethically deficient protagonist, is a central part of the novel's rhetorical aim, as this mimetic-thematic-synthetic character holds up a mirror to human behavior in our age of the Anthropocene. After discussing the novel's style and some responses to it as well as Beard's character and its progression, I will focus on McEwan's way of using fictional narrative as a rhetorical form that can say something worthwhile about climate change. In this regard, my argument is related to the recent rhetorical conception of fictionality as a serious mode of discourse about the actual world.

When reading *Solar* in terms of its environmental rhetoric, I pay attention to the novel's narrative progression and its way of handling the complex issue of climate change through plot and characterization. As the narrative progresses, there are changes not only in the world's climate and global politics but in the protagonist's life as well. According to the rhetorical theory of narrative, this mimetic aspect of fiction—the life-like characters and their actions—is a central means of engaging the reader and addressing ethical issues. James Phelan employs the term *progression* to refer to "a narrative as a dynamic event, one that must move, in both its telling and its reception, through time," so that in examining progression "we are concerned with how authors generate, sustain, develop, and resolve readers' interests in narrative" (*Reading People, Reading Plots* 15). From the perspective of the rhetorical theory of narrative, readers' judgments of the narrative progression also depend on their individual ethical investments in characters and ideas.

While I focus on *Solar*'s narrative progression in my analysis, my overall aim is to merge narrative theory and ecocriticism in order to show how their methodological combination might help us read the rhetoric of climate change in fiction. In effect, I argue that ecocritics need to study specific rhetorical designs in fiction just as narratologists should consider the ways in which fiction communicates ideas and values about our living environment. In my view, the concepts of the rhetorical theory of narrative helpfully delineate the communicative designs and purposes of a fictional narrative such as *Solar*.

POET AND PHYSICIST: WORLDS OF ART AND SCIENCE IN IAN MCEWAN'S FICTION

Even before *Solar* was published, prominent ecocritic Greg Garrard made reference to Ian McEwan's forthcoming novel despite not having yet had a chance to read it. In these anticipatory remarks, Garrard mentions that McEwan's earlier work—*The Child in Time* (1987), for instance—provides "an implicit, and possibly deliberate, critique of many of the major ethical assumptions in ecocriticism" ("Ian McEwan's Next Novel" 696). In a subsequent essay on the published book, Garrard writes that *Solar* was "eagerly anticipated by those who hoped for a dramatic shift in public consciousness of the issue [i.e. climate change]" but that the finished product only confirms a widely held assumption about the realist novel as a mode ill-suited to this particular topic ("*Solar*: Apocalypse Not" 123). But the critic's disappointment perhaps stems more from execution than the novel as form. Garrard clarifies that the novel is "limited . . . by McEwan's choice of satirical allegory as a genre" (123). The rather unenthusiastic critical response to *Solar* among ecocritics and other readers appears to focus on McEwan's light-hearted approach to a grave issue. Another challenge for ecocritical and narratological readings alike involves the indeterminacy, even after examining the novel's narrative structure, rhetorical purpose, and aesthetic design, of the implied author's actual stance on climate change issues. In *Solar*, the implied author's views are refracted through the minds and discourse of characters and therefore remain elusive.

Apparently, McEwan's use of comedic, satiric, and allegorical story models is a choice rather unexpected from environmental fiction. Yet, instead of as theoretical "top-down" models, we should aim to judge individual works according to their specific purposes and achievements (Phelan, *Experiencing Fiction* 142). As Gary Johnson maintains, speaking of a rhetorically oriented approach to allegory, "rather than beginning with some ineffable standard of aesthetic merit to which a particular work either mysteriously (and sometimes inexplicably) rises or fails to [*sic*], the rhetorical critic starts by asking what an author's purpose in writing that work might have been" (21). Accordingly, I read *Solar*'s purpose as a kind of parody of environmental literary studies' overly pessimistic view of the human impact on nature as well as its overly optimistic notion that literary art can effect change. In this, I echo Astrid Bracke, who also notes McEwan's "satire of . . . ecocritical premises" (433). The novel is peopled with "merry" artists who are merry *because* they are "worried about global warming" (McEwan 67). Garrard argues, quite rightly to my mind, that "environmental literature and ecocriticism have typically embodied an unexamined moral idealism" ("Ian McEwan's Next Novel" 710). It has been a crucial part of ecocriticism not only to analyze literary texts but also—and even more so—to advocate for environmental awareness and social change. But the protagonist of *Solar*, a hardcore advocate of quantum physics, has doubts:

> Beard would not have believed it possible that he would be in a room drinking with so many seized by the same particular assumption, that it was art in its highest forms, poetry, sculpture, dance, abstract music, conceptual art, that would lift climate change as a subject, gild it, palpate it, reveal all the horror and lost beauty and awesome threat, and inspire the public to take thought, take action, or demand it of others. He sat in silent wonder. Idealism was so alien to his nature that he could not raise an objection. He was in new territory, among a friendly tribe of exotics. (77)

The Nobel Prize-winning scientist Michael Beard, who cares for neither art nor climate change and cares "even less for art about climate change," is happily ignorant of the fact that he is himself a character in a novel that is a modest piece of art about climate change (73). Even before this scene, Beard has been baffled by the suggestion that he consider art as one way of thinking about climate change: "There were novels Aldous wanted him to read—novels!—. . . and documentaries about climate change" (28–29). The space is now open for the politics and rhetoric of climate change, but as Dipesh Chakrabarty suggests, it is open "as much to science and technology as to rhetoric, art, media, and arguments and conflicts conducted through a variety of means" ("Postcolonial Studies" 9). In Beard's view, however, while fiction may have some rhetorical purpose of "lifting," "gilding," and "palpating" climate change, art is not serious enough to concern him.[1]

---

1. In an interview with *the Wall Street Journal*, McEwan maintains that the topic of climate change is "a subject impacted with hard science: physics, climate science, statistics, graphs, measurements—things that are fairly hostile to a novel" (Alter).

McEwan's novels often test and challenge clashing worldviews of science and poetry.[2] David Herman, using McEwan's novella *On Chesil Beach* (2007) as a test case, draws attention to narratives' role in wider discursive contexts; he writes that "narratives do not merely evoke worlds but also intervene in a field of discourses, a range of representational strategies, a constellation of ways of seeing—and sometimes a set of competing narratives" (Herman et al. 17). In McEwan's subsequent work, it is scientific (especially neuropsychological) explanations that have gained prominence; for example, the preference of science over poetry is a motif governing *Saturday* (2005).

In the course of Beard's lectures on solar energy to his academic audiences and his potential sponsors and investors, *Solar* becomes filled with discourses representing natural science, cognitive psychology, capitalism, and humanism. The floor is not occupied solely by Beard, for "the point of view of the audience" is also given voice (138). Obviously, we should be careful not to conflate this fictional and characterized audience's voice with the discourse-level communication between the implied author and the authorial audience—although it is possible that the fictional audience's views on climate change reflect those of the *actual* audience. The narrative, often using free indirect discourse and thus merging the narrator's voice with the character's viewpoint, explains that "Beard had heard rumours that strange ideas were commonplace among the liberal-arts departments" and that "humanities students were routinely taught that science was just one more belief system, no more or less truthful than religion or astrology" (132). Instead, Beard situates himself in another, "objectivist" camp that "could not accept that there was no reality without an observer" and that "believed the world existed independently of the language that described it" (65, 139). Beard remains skeptical of the postmodernist ideas espoused by cultural scholars—representing the abovementioned point of view of the audience—who dismiss facts of natural science as "socially constructed" and treat climate change and other worldwide environmental problems as only stories and narratives (131). He feels that "people who kept on about *narrative* tended to have a squiffy view of reality, believing all versions of it to be of equal value" (147; emphasis added). Whereas McEwan's previous work expresses skepticism about the explanatory power of poetry, in *Solar* he challenges literary scholars to reflect on unexamined celebration of narrative's possibilities. The text invites the actual audience of the novel—including the

---

2. McEwan suggests that science parallels literature as a means by which the world can be understood but that there are "insights which science has brought us and which literature could never equal," just as "there are many complex facets of experience for which science has no language and literature does" (Cook, Groes, and Sage 128).

literary theorist—to join debates about the validity of narrative approaches to nature.[3]

Skepticism notwithstanding, however, *Solar* itself is a thoroughly and self-consciously literary text. Even Beard's scientific work on light, space, and power actually goes back to his reading of John Milton. However, Beard does not realize Book One of *Paradise Lost* anticipates his doomed mission to harness sunlight in the verses beginning "A summer's day; and with the setting sun / Dropt from the zenith, like a falling star" despite quoting a fragment from them: "from morn / to noon he fell" (200). Ironically, Beard does not care for "the arty sort of people" who "intimidated him with literary references he did not understand" and who asked that he "synthesized [his] reading into some kind of aesthetic overview" (197, 202). Through this comical and rhetorical strategy, which makes Beard function as a foil for readers, the novel asks its reader to perform interpretive tasks that Beard himself is incapable of doing or unwilling to do because of his deep scorn for literary studies—that is, to read behind Beard's back for the implied author's views. I would argue that the implied author of *Solar* adopts, and encourages readers to adopt, an ironic and amused stance toward Beard's ethics—at least to a point. Beard also fails to recognize that his initial interest in "the redeeming power of the imagination," as exemplified by Milton's poetry, opens up his own mind, for a short while, to creative innovation of the kind that is needed to produce breakthroughs in the natural sciences (200). These are "daydreams," "manic moments," "episodes that braided the actual with the unreal" (116). Therefore, the celebrated "Beard–Einstein Conflation," which earns him the Nobel Prize in Physics, is the fruit of his youthful mind's imaginative power, almost Miltonic in its way of seeing.

In the narrative progression, Beard's scientific worldview repeatedly clashes with that of artists, as seen in his outraged response to a novelist called Meredith, who suggests that we should bring ethics into the realm of the natural sciences and vice versa: "Let's hear you apply [Heisenberg's Uncertainty Principle] to ethics. Right plus wrong over the square root of two. What the hell does it mean? Nothing!" (77). In Beard's view, physics is a realm purified of ethics and emotion, "Free of human taint, it described a world that

---

3. Beard, I think, would find the following theoretical assertion problematic: "[A]n essential ingredient of the process by which humans make sense of crises in public life—or feel inspired to work towards solutions—is *stories: narratives* we tell ourselves in order to find our bearings in a new situation. . . . Our success in developing a globally concerted response to the climate crisis, for instance, will depend on the degree to which we can tell *stories* that we can all agree on" (Chakrabarty, "Foreword" xiii–xiv; emphases added).

would still exist if men and women and all their sorrows did not" (9). Because Beard does not see any value in "human taint" and "sorrow," his mind is cold, detached, and reductive—and yet the reader mainly sees the narrative world through *his* limited viewpoint, which has "no language . . . for feelings" (197). Beard's scientific approach therefore intentionally excludes other minds. The reader's confinement to Beard's point of view may seem problematic, but it is absolutely essential to the novel's rhetoric and ethics. By making readers see the world through the protagonist's self-centered and objectifying vision, *Solar* makes its main move, asking us to reflect on our own ecological preconceptions and "unexamined assumptions" (155).

One easily concludes that Meredith speaks for McEwan, especially since this author-character is based on McEwan's own participation in the climate change conference at the North Pole in 2005. The text self-ironically presents Meredith to the reader through Beard's vision: a "gangling" and "spindly novelist," "this crop-haired fellow with rimless glasses," reading a "harsh, impenetrable fragment of a novel punctuated with expletives" (76, 77, 80)—supposedly the very narrative we are reading. Perhaps McEwan plays with self-parody here, even as his authorial persona splits in two: Beard embodies scientific skepticism, and Meredith represents the poetic approach. Even though Beard ridicules Meredith's ethics and art, the reader is nevertheless invited to view the fictional novelist's rhetoric as one among the serious discourses featured in *Solar.* According to one reading, McEwan defends poetry and the humanities in the age of economy and technology; according to another, equally valid reading, he exposes the limits of the arts, humanities, and especially religion in explaining the human mind and how it works in the natural world. It may be the case that Meredith, whom Beard boos, represents a novelist's weak position in the larger arena of climate change rhetoric.

SURVIVAL IN THE AGE OF THE ANTHROPOCENE

As mentioned, McEwan's use of comedy, satire, and allegory in his fictional approach to climate change has received mixed responses. While the rhetorical understanding of a work's specific purposes is one way to deal with this criticism, *Solar* also prompts me to revisit Joseph Meeker's argument in his pioneering work on environmental imagination, *The Comedy of Survival: Studies in Literary Ecology.* Meeker regards literature as an important resource of the human species—a means of its survival—since it offers insights "into human relationships with other species and with the world around us" (4).

For Meeker, *comedy* as a mode locates human beings in their natural environment, while *tragedy* is about humanity's doomed attempt to put ourselves above the world. Thus, whereas tragedy foregrounds the transcendent moral order, human supremacy over nature, and the importance of the human individual, the comic mode is fundamentally connected to human survival in the natural environment (52). Meeker seeks to determine whether literature contributes to the survival of the human species or to its extinction (25), and his emphasis on the comic mode as a model for ecological behavior may help us appreciate comedic elements of McEwan's novel.

However, in the Anthropocene, heroic, tragic, or comical stories of individual survival in the midst of wild nature may simply not suffice, and idealistic notions of narrative's all-encompassing powers have also become suspect—as Chakrabarty concludes, addressing the topic of survival in the climate change context, "It is precisely the 'survival of the species' on 'a world-wide scale' that is largely in question" ("Postcolonial Studies" 15). Climate change and its various environmental consequences are difficult to make sense of in human terms precisely because they radically exceed the human scale. Therefore stories focusing on human experience—such as *Solar*—have a necessarily limited grasp of environmental issues' global proportions. As I suggested above, McEwan employs both narrative comedy and allegorical satire to approach the experience of climate change, with a banal and failed scientist as his hero. For such a character, readers may question whether his conceptions about climate change should be taken seriously either:

> Beard was not wholly skeptical about climate change. . . . But he himself had other things to think about. And he was unimpressed by some of the wild commentary that suggested the world was in "peril," that humankind was drifting towards calamity, when coastal cities would disappear under the waves, crops fail, and hundreds of millions of refugees surge from one country, one continent, to another, driven by drought, floods, famine, tempests, unceasing wars for diminishing resources. (15–16)

As the narrative rhetoric discloses these alarming scenarios following from climate change, we are told that Beard does not believe in these alleged perils. He is annoyed by the apocalyptic rhetoric associated with climate-conscious talk about the planet, as well as sick of listening to the "familiar litany of shrinking glaciers, encroaching deserts, dissolving coral reefs, disrupted ocean currents, rising sea levels, disappearing this and that, on and on" (36). And yet, behind Beard's back, these global threats are conveyed to readers in a visually and emotionally evocative way, potentially raising their ecological awareness. While Beard believes he is dismissing these views, they in fact emerge as dialogical alternatives. McEwan's strategy here is effective both in terms of narrative rhetoric and in terms of environmental discourse.

What Beard does not recognize is that, in nine years and partly because of global warming, he will disappear, too. The narrative progresses from 2000 through 2005 to 2009, and there are changes in the climate: the Intergovernmental Panel on Climate Change (IPCC) gives its successive reports, and Al Gore challenges George W. Bush in the U. S. presidential election. At the beginning of the new millennium, the British government gets engaged with climate change "practically rather than merely rhetorically" (16). Yet Beard himself only "read about it" and "expected governments to . . . take action," and soon "the century had ended and climate change remained a marginal concern" (15, 75). The novel consists of three acts, each of which formulates a different viewpoint on the topic of climate change: first, Beard's skepticism about it (Part One, 2000), second, his rhetoric outlining the benefits of solar energy (Part Two, 2005), and third, his action of saving the planet and his own life (Part Three, 2009). Whereas the first part of the novel shows the protagonist's profound skepticism about global warming, the last part shows him convinced of its reality, much like Al Gore in his documentary film *An Inconvenient Truth* (2006). In fact, some pieces of Beard's rhetoric in front of his audience—such as his calculated expression in a staged theater performance that "the planet . . . is sick" (148)—parody Gore's populist phrasings. At the beginning of *Solar*, Beard's egotism strongly reflects humankind's self-centered attitude in the face of a crisis affecting the entire earth, but his subsequent conclusions—that in a crisis we understand "that it is not in other people or in the system or in the nature of things that the problem lies, but in ourselves, our own follies" (155)—signify his growing ethical vision.

Solar progresses from the "frozen shores" of the North Pole to the "savage heat" of the New Mexico deserts, so that human thinking and action are enveloped in the harsh and changing realities of the natural environment (79, 232).[4] The text depicts science, Beard's only and true religion, as practiced in sterile, lifeless sites, detached from human concerns. But the problem is achingly real; the changing climate—the freezing cold or the burning sun—affects everyday life. These effects make Beard seem like a comical figure and

---

4. Scott Slovic importantly notes that the popular phrase *global warming* does not quite describe the complexity of *climate change*, since what is happening globally is both extreme warming and extreme freezing. Therefore, for rhetorical reasons it makes sense to talk about the implications of "climate change" instead of "global warming" (119).

an egotist at the same time, for his fears about climate change are not really global but instead very local, concerning his own body.[5] As the narrative discourse and the story-time progress, climate change is written on Beard's body through extreme temperatures' influence upon his physical well-being:

> For when his business was done he discovered that his penis had attached itself to the zip of his snowmobile suit, had frozen in hard along its length, the way only living flesh can do on sub-zero metal. . . . And he was already in pain from the cold. (59)
>
> The instrument panel was showing an external temperature of one hundred and twelve degrees Fahrenheit, hotter than either man had ever known. . . . Beard was generally adept at avoiding inconvenient or troubling thoughts, but now that his spirits were low he was brooding about his health, and staring at the reddish-brown blotch, a map of unknown territory, on his wrist. (232, 238)

Beard's bodily experiences have consequences for his ethical thinking. He ponders, quite grudgingly, whether "climate change, radical warming above the Arctic Circle, was actually taking place and was not a figment of the activist imagination" (59). The world around him gives constant signs of its existence, so that Beard is forced to concede that not all were "abstract concerns," for some were "distinctly embodied" (184). Here McEwan utilizes Beard's bodily experiences for rhetorical purposes, foregrounding human experientiality as a way of dealing with issues as big and complex as climate change.

Beard's comical ventures around the globe are therefore firmly rooted in his physical experiences, while his questionable ethics are also emphasized. Beard steals his younger colleague Tom Aldous's pioneering work on artificial photosynthesis, the use of carbon dioxide, water, and sunlight as an endless resource for the solar energy industry.[6] It appears, however, that Beard is in it for commercial gain rather than the saving of the planet, so that, indeed,

---

5. Beard's banal situation is a kind of parody of the well-known environmental slogan "think globally, act locally," since his commercial ideas of saving the planet remain abstract compared to his comical actions on the physical and local level. Yet, as Timothy Clark, among others, suggests, "the issue of climate change also undermines the very possibility of acting only locally" (136).

6. As often in McEwan's fiction, the epilogue provides an ironic twist or reversal to the main narrative. In the appendix we are given the Nobel Prize Committee's presentation speech with its implication that Aldous's vision of artificial photosynthesis as a saving solution actually derives from Beard's initial work on "the complicated interactions between light and matter" (283).

climate change is something from which he *profits*. Compared to Aldous and his "deep interest in global warming, ecology, [and] sustainable development," Beard comes across as an opportunistic and selfish villain (270). This makes it difficult for readers to view him and his actions with sympathy. One of the most revealing conversations occurs in Part Three between the scheming Beard and his not-so-bright assistant Toby Hammer, who is worried about the possibility, mentioned on television, that the planet is *not* heating:

> "Here's the good news. The UN estimates that already a third of a million people a year are dying from climate change. Bangladesh is going down because the oceans are warming and expanding and rising. There's drought in the Amazonian rainforest. Methane is pouring out of the Siberian permafrost. There's a meltdown under the Greenland ice sheet that no one really wants to talk about. . . . Two years ago we lost forty per cent of the Arctic summer ice. Now the eastern Antarctic is going. The future has arrived, Toby." . . . Beard laid a hand on his friend's arm, a sure sign that he was well over his limit. "Toby, listen. It's a catastrophe. Relax!" (216–17)

There is clear irony here, for Beard needs the sun to get scorching hot in order to make his solar panels function more effectively. The very contradictoriness of Beard's practice occupies the core of *Solar*'s narrative rhetoric, for the novel dramatizes the potential dead ends to which even well-meaning individual or governmental practices may lead. Therefore, his telling Toby to "Relax"— because *it will remain* a catastrophe—is not very reassuring. We can view this white male physicist as an embodiment of a general refusal to think about the future of the planet. Beard's vices—gluttony, greediness, sexual promiscuity, opportunism, calculation, profit-seeking, and so on—hold up a mirror to humankind. His "grotesque body" is the very center of the novel's "satirical allegory" (Garrard, "*Solar*: Apocalypse Not" 125, 130). Beard consumes, steals, and exploits everything around him, whether it is food, women, or other scientists' research plans. As Beard's body starts to collapse and his ethics gradually deteriorates, he becomes a symbol of humankind's grossly exploitative way of treating the planet.

As we have seen, McEwan gives his main character pronouncedly physical attributes as well as allegorical dimensions—dimensions that Beard is unable to live up to precisely because of his physical shortcomings. Free indirect discourse at the narrative's beginning reveals that the "ethereal Beard of planetary renown" has "given up hopes of being the mortal chosen to find [the] grail," but near the end, Beard believes himself on a "quest to rescue humankind from self-destruction" (11, 66, 223). He thus aspires in vain to the role of his namesake, the Archangel Michael, who leads the heavenly forces against Satan in *Paradise Lost*; indeed, like Milton's god of fire, Hephaestus, he is "a falling star" in "the setting sun." Despite his allegorical dimensions, Beard is totally mundane; his "messy" life, filled with junk mail and empty bottles, mismatched socks and uncleared attics, never reaches "Eden, purged of clutter and distraction" (222, 226).

As a fictional figure, Beard fulfills the three character functions or dimensions outlined in rhetorical narrative theory: the *mimetic* component involves readers' interest in the narrative world as like our own and characters like ourselves; the *thematic* component involves readers' interest in the cultural, ideological, philosophical, or ethical issues the narrative addresses; and the *synthetic* component involves readers' close attention to the narrative as an artificial construct (Phelan, *Experiencing Fiction* 5–6). Beard's figure is, for good and ill, recognizably human and thus mimetic; his allegorical quality obviously serves thematic functions; and he is a useful narrative device for McEwan, enabling metafictional and intertextual commentary, and is therefore synthetic. Beard's developing skin cancer is an indexical sign of global warming, which is partially caused by short-sighted human actions, but Beard also symbolizes the planet's looming peril, even becoming an iconic image resembling the Earth: "an oily nausea at something monstrous and rotten from the sea stranded on the tidal mudflats of a stagnant estuary, decaying gaseously in his gut and welling up, contaminating his breath, his words, and suddenly his thoughts" (148). Indeed, the descriptions of his bodily features sometimes draw on geographic metaphors: "the archipelago of his disrupted selfhood" (142); "the northern hemisphere of his eyeball" (244). Beard's body therefore reads as a planetary metaphor for exploitation. The abstract dimensions of Beard's character are, however, converted into concrete functions of his character in the narrative progression (Phelan, *Reading People, Reading Plots,* 9), and the character's mimetic component comes to the foreground.

This is *Solar*'s greatest irony and the core of the narrative's difficult contradictions. Beard's selfishness is a symptom of humans' unsustainable treatment of their natural environment, yet he is the one who acts by thinking up solutions to save the planet. The ambivalence of Beard marks the novel's broader ethical indeterminacy. It is as if our future depended on Beard's growing self-reflexivity, precisely because in his greedy, selfish, and calculating mind he is "an average type" representing mankind (170).[7] Slovic writes that we are

---

7. As McEwan points out in an interview, "Global warming suddenly wasn't an abstract issue, because humans had to solve it—untrustworthy, venal, sweet, lovely humans" (qtd. in Garrard, "Ian McEwan's Next Novel" 718).

"an inventive, imaginative species—that is our nature," but we can "*apply* our minds or physical energy in sustaining or destructive ways" (6). Though, as some critics note, *Solar* reveals a pessimistic attitude about human behavior toward our planet (see Murphy 150), the novel also maintains some implicit hope about our ethical transformation. In Beard's case, while his bodily functions gradually collapse, there nevertheless remains some progression in his thinking and ethics.

NARRATIVE ART: A RHETORIC AND POLITICS OF CLIMATE CHANGE

Although some of the most challenging environmental problems have been popular topics in science fiction, fantasy, graphic novels, movies, and documentaries, *Solar,* together with Barbara Kingsolver's *Flight Behavior* (2012), is a rare example of climate change fiction in the mode of the traditional novel and psychological realism. In spite of their self-conscious employment of allegory and other rhetorical tropes, these two contemporary novels still fall into the category of the realist novel in the sense that they are "set in the here, the now, and the local" (Murphy 158). As Adam Trexler maintains, other modes and media "lack the novel's capacity to interrogate the emotional, aesthetic, and living experience of the Anthropocene" (6). However, following Trexler, we can ask what climate change does to conventional literary forms and what distortions and complications may occur in generic structures until they are better able to explore the Anthropocene's complexities and implications.

Solar thus raises a theoretical question about environmental imagination and the realist novel's limits in the age of anthropogenic climate change. Garrard maintains that "none of the traditional forms in literature, film, or television documentary is unproblematically suited to capturing the geographical and temporal scale, complexity, and uncertainty of climate change in particular" ("Ian McEwan's Next Novel" 709). Arguably, formulaic fictions will provide no sustainable solutions. Yet we may ask (together with Michael Beard) whether *any* kind of art will have the slightest influence on the future of the planet. Heise notes that climate change has begun to make its way into the cultural imagination and that it "poses a challenge for narrative and lyrical forms that have conventionally focused above all on individuals, families, or nations, since it requires the articulation of connections between events at vastly different scales" (205). Consequently, she argues that in their portrayal of climate change, some popular films rely on the conventions of "apocalyptic narrative" (206). These popular notions are also addressed by Beard with increasing cynicism: for him, "the end of the world" was a "fantasy," and when it comes to the special case of climate change, "the apocalyptic tendency had conjured yet another beast" (16). Thrillers and science fiction novels, Hollywood mega-films, and documentaries routinely utilize conventional, human-centered narrative strategies when dealing with something that both exceeds the human scale and presents a huge challenge to the future existence of the species. Also in *Solar*, McEwan seems to be unable to represent climate change except in the form of a conventional masculine narrative about a white male scientist trying to navigate his relationship with his several ex-wives and one daughter. Obviously, we can also read the novel as a parody of this clichéd plotline.

Instead of being a sympathetic and idealistic character with whom the readers can become friends, such as Dellarobia in Kingsolver's *Flight Behavior*, Michael Beard becomes more and more obnoxious as the narrative goes on, "a modern monster in the flesh" (138). He is tragically unable to follow the friendly advice of Jesus—a Spanish ice sculptor he meets at the North Pole conference—that "it was important never to lose faith in the possibility of profound inner change" (66). After all his misdeeds, Beard still wants to believe in his own redemption: "He would be redeemed. Let there be light!" (144). Finally, the very ending of the novel aims to restore some hope in the sense that there might still be love and happiness waiting for the protagonist after his five marriages and adulterous escapades. After Beard has lost everything (his solar power project and his reputation in the field of science), he still has his loving daughter Catriona, and the last word of the narrative is *love*: "As Beard rose to greet her, he felt in his heart an unfamiliar, swelling sensation, but he doubted as he opened his arms to her that anyone would ever believe him now if he tried to pass it off as love" (279). But the conclusion of the narrative also offers us another interpretation; the "unfamiliar, swelling sensation" in Beard's heart may actually be a sign of a coming heart attack, anticipated by his feelings of chest pain, exhaustion, and his being overweight. The ending can be alternatively interpreted as a happy one in the comic mode or as an unhappy one in the tragic mode—indeed, this moving back and forth between two (or more) possible interpretations is built in the novel's rhetorical design and purpose.

Regarding the rhetoric of climate change and its competing narratives, Chakrabarty notes an apparent preference for accounts neither purely scientific nor purely literary; thus, he argues, in order to bring the complex dimensions of climate change's "wicked problem" within the grasp of human experience, it is typical to use narrative practices ("Postcolonial Studies"

10–11, 17–18). While environmental problems are not texts, narratives (both scientific and poetic) offer the problem of climate change rhetorically to the larger public imagination—as McEwan does in *Solar*. This is also a view that Michael Beard, a staunch opponent of storied versions of the natural world, gradually adopts: he employs "narrative art" to make his case about climate change and solar power (180). Thus, in a conference on solar power energy Beard is trying to survive in front of a demanding audience: "He was warming to his tale, convinced that it had a useful conclusion that he would discover in the telling" (155). This may make Beard an unreliable storyteller and yet, at the same time, the most reliable there is: he is feeling the actual heat in the face of global warming, and this may result in his failure to tell the tale. Since he believes that climate change is not a narrative to be told and put away, he becomes a "kind of learned satyr" and "innocent fool" who has seen the light (137). One way to conceptualize this would be to say that Beard gradually moves closer to the ethical stance of the implied author.

In my view, there is both dialogue and discrepancy between the rhetorical theory of narrative and ecocriticism. Whereas, in rhetorical theory, narratives communicate ideas and values to audiences through textual designs, ecocriticism is interested in ways that literature can affect readers to act in sustainable ways in the real world. These two approaches and their interests can still be combined in order to develop a new, environmentally informed and engaged narrative theory. Seymour Chatman suggests that rhetoric in fiction should be seen as "end-oriented discourse," by which he means the way in which the novel "suades" its readers toward the investigation of some views of "how things are in the real world" (203). According to Phelan, the rhetorical approach emphasizes "narrative as a distinctive and powerful means for an author to communicate knowledge, feelings, values, and beliefs to an audience" (*Narrative as Rhetoric* 18). In ecocritical literary studies, there are likewise scholars who see the relationship between nature and literature as dialogical and crucially negotiated by rhetoric. Bonnie Costello suggests that "the ecocritical preference for referentiality over textuality, for real world over rhetorical and aesthetic concerns, seems misguided" (14). Defending the power of poetry, Costello argues that imagination and abstraction can draw us toward the natural world rather than away from it. She adds that "a rhetorically oriented criticism is aware of the text . . . as a series of motivated strategies and structures, which communicates something to an audience" (14). Here, in the idea of rhetorical community and transaction, might be the missing link between ecological and narrative poetics.

Recent developments in narrative theory also help us bridge narratology and ecocriticism. Henrik Skov Nielsen, James Phelan, and Richard Walsh argue that "the use of fictionality is not a turning away from the actual world but a specific communicative strategy within some context in that world" and that "rhetoric is prevalent wherever and whenever someone wants to move someone else to do or think or change something" (62–63). A conception of narrative and fiction as rhetoric is the key to making narrative theory relevant to environmental literary studies, since in rhetorical theory and ecocriticism, as voiced by Costello and others, there are shared ideas about strategies, values, and communication. From the combined vantage point of the rhetorical narrative theory and ecocriticism, fictional narrative is a powerful means for making various environmental issues palpable—although we are reminded of *Solar*'s rhetorical and open-ended questions about whether *art* would lift climate change as a subject, gild it, and palpate it.

Indeed it is a central tenet of ecocriticism that writing and reading literature should not be an end in itself but should lead to engagement, commitment, responsibility, and action in the real world (Slovic 3–5). Slovic also wonders how you can use "narrative language for this purpose, to tell the story of something as abstract and complicated as climate change?" (123). I would argue that McEwan's choice of comedy and allegory provides one possible solution and answer, as does his taking advantage of the distinctive features of fictional narrative as rhetoric.

However, *Solar* seems to speak back to idealistic notions of narrative and literary theory and their supposed power to affect the real world. What McEwan's fictional scientist would claim is that both ecocriticism and narrative theory are based on unchecked idealism. It is as if Beard, who feels that "greenery . . . was not to his taste," was not reconcilable with any kind of politically correct "green" reading (87). We could idealistically think that *Solar* proves Beard wrong, that art *can* "inspire" us to "take action" in the extratextual environment, but this kind of straightforward interpretation falls short of recognizing the rhetorical complexity of the implied author's call (77). Through Beard's slanted thoughts and other fictional voices, *Solar* asks its readers to reflect on the many sides of climate change discussion, including the question about the value of literary art and narrative theory in that discussion. As in the confrontation between Beard and Meredith, McEwan presents a many-layered approach to the climate change issue, weighing options and entertaining contesting versions, especially those provided by natural sciences and poetry in their respective visions of the world.

CONCLUSION: TOWARD A METARHETORICAL
NARRATIVE ABOUT CLIMATE CHANGE

Fictional narratives can obviously teach us values through their form, including complex characters, dialogic voices, many-layered viewpoints, and difficult human situations. All this makes novels and other narrative fictions a valuable means of communicating environmental themes deeply and persuasively to their audiences. In *Solar*, the various conflicting views inside the fiction invite the actual audience of the novel to take part in the heated discussion, to search for the implied author's design and intentions, and perhaps finally to conclude that some ethical problems resist easy solutions. It is this metarhetorical emphasis of *Solar* that, in my view, makes it a specific kind of rhetorical narrative. The novel exemplifies the idea that fiction can be a serious mode of discourse since it provides its readers with the possibility to think about narratives' rhetorical efficacy with regard to problems of the scale of climate change. Indeed, the ethical stakes of McEwan's novel prompt its readers to confront the idea that narrative as a rhetorical form can say something worthwhile about environmental issues. The novel's self-conscious rhetoric gives space to various conflicting views about our common world and shared realities without providing firm guidelines. The extremely complex issue— "the burning question" (149)—therefore remains open to further negotiation.

These open questions are reflected in the novel's narrative style, as Michael Beard's ceremonial confidence in front of a conference audience gradually gives way to disturbing inner thoughts: "'We pass through a mirror, everything is transformed, the old paradigm makes way for the new.' But the rhetorical flourish of these final phrases had a desperate air, his voice sounded thin in his ears, his conclusions were hollow after all. Where now?" (155–56). While Beard's project of providing a sustainable solution to the climate change problem is eventually doomed to fail, McEwan is ultimately successful with his chosen fictional approach. Apparently, following the rhetorical theory of narrative, we should trace a careful path across a complex site of textual meanings. Phelan writes that when reading fiction "we often come across narratives that do not seem to give sufficient signals for us to make clear and firm discriminations" (*Experiencing Fiction* 1–2). Despite his ambivalent role as Beard's antagonist, Meredith, the fictional novelist of *Solar*, does point the reader toward the ethical and rhetorical crux of the narrative, speaking of "the loss of a 'moral compass'" and the "difficulty of absolute judgments" (76). This kind of rhetoric inside the fiction—indeed, a kind of interpretative key to readers—mirrors the larger discursive and metarhetorical frame of the novel.

In conclusion, it may be suggested that through his rhetorical moves McEwan constructs an argument that real-world problems are not only narrative problems and that it is not only a question of different storied versions of climate change. Literary fictions can still contribute to the discussion about our global futures in concert or in clash with other discourses, either scientific, economic, technological, or philosophical. Finally, rather than reading *Solar* as a mimetic representation of the reality of climate change, we need to recognize another kind of design and intention: the novel is about the rhetoric associated with climate change.[8]

WORKS CITED

Alter, Alexandra. "Can Climate Change Be Funny?" *Wall Street Journal* [New York City], 25 Mar. 2010.

Bracke, Astrid. "The Contemporary English Novel and Its Challenges to Ecocriticism." *The Oxford Handbook of Ecocriticism*. Edited by Greg Garrard, Oxford UP, 2014, pp. 423–39.

Chakrabarty, Dipesh. "Foreword." *Global Ecologies and the Environmental Humanities: Postcolonial Approaches*. Edited by Elizabeth DeLoughrey, Jill Didur, and Anthony Carrigan, Routledge, 2015, pp. xiii–xv.

———. "Postcolonial Studies and the Challenge of Climate Change." *New Literary History*, vol. 43, no. 1, 2012, pp. 1–18.

Chatman, Seymour. *Coming to Terms: The Rhetoric of Narrative in Fiction and Film*. Cornell UP, 1990.

Clark, Timothy. *The Cambridge Introduction to Literature and the Environment*. Cambridge UP, 2011.

Cook, Jon, Sebastian Groes, and Victor Sage. "Journeys without Maps: An Interview with Ian McEwan." *Ian McEwan: Contemporary Critical Perspectives*. Edited by Sebastian Groes, Continuum, 2009, pp. 123–34.

Costello, Bonnie. *Shifting Ground: Reinventing Landscape in Modern American Poetry*. Harvard UP, 2003.

Garrard, Greg. "Ian McEwan's Next Novel and the Future of Ecocriticism." *Contemporary Literature*, vol. 50, no. 4, 2009, pp. 695–720.

———. "*Solar*: Apocalypse Not." *Ian McEwan: Contemporary Critical Perspectives*. Edited by Sebastian Groes, 2nd ed., Bloomsbury, 2013, pp. 123–35.

Heise, Ursula K. *Sense of Place and Sense of Planet: The Environmental Imagination of the Global*. Oxford UP, 2008.

Herman, David, James Phelan, Peter J. Rabinowitz, Brian Richardson, and Robyn Warhol. *Narrative Theory: Core Concepts and Critical Debates*. The Ohio State UP, 2012.

---

8. This essay is part of my research project *The Changing Environment of the North: Cultural Representations and Uses of Water* (SA 307840) funded by the Academy of Finland.

Johnson, Gary. *The Vitality of Allegory: Figural Narrative in Modern and Contemporary Fiction.* The Ohio State UP, 2012.

McEwan, Ian. *Solar.* Jonathan Cape, 2010.

Meeker, Joseph. *The Comedy of Survival: Studies in Literary Ecology.* Scribner's, 1972.

Murphy, Patrick D. "Pessimism, Optimism, Human Inertia, and Anthropogenic Climate Change." *ISLE: Interdisciplinary Studies in Literature and the Environment,* vol. 21, no. 1, 2014, pp. 149–63.

Nielsen, Henrik Skov, James Phelan, and Richard Walsh: "Ten Theses about Fictionality." *Narrative,* vol. 23, no. 1, 2015, pp. 61–73.

Phelan, James. *Experiencing Fiction: Judgments, Progressions, and the Rhetorical Theory of Narrative.* The Ohio State UP, 2007.

———. *Narrative as Rhetoric: Technique, Audiences, Ethics, Ideology.* The Ohio State UP, 1996.

———. *Reading People, Reading Plots: Character, Progression, and the Interpretation of Narrative.* U of Chicago P, 1989.

Slovic, Scott. *Going Away to Think: Engagement, Retreat, and Ecocritical Responsibility.* U of Nevada P, 2008.

Trexler, Adam. *Anthropocene Fictions: The Novel in a Time of Climate Change.* U of Virginia P, 2015.

CHAPTER 5

Ecocriticism as Narrative Ethics

Triangulating Environmental Virtue in Richard Powers's Gain

GREG GARRARD

ECOCRITICAL NARRATIVE ETHICS

Ecocriticism has most often been characterized as a form of political literary criticism, close kin to feminism and Marxism, albeit with a dramatically expanded sense of the relevant polity (Clark; Garrard; Glotfelty and Fromm; Feder). While I accept such characterizations in principle, I argue here for a shift to narrative ethics on two grounds. First, politicized ecocriticism often provides dishearteningly little insight into literature as such. At best, literary texts supply apt illustration of theoretical arguments developed prior to, and independent of, the reading encounter itself; at worst, the author's supposed exclusions and elisions are the pretext for unilluminating performances of scholarly self-righteousness. If literature can't surprise, enrage, and embarrass us—and not just our students—we have no business teaching it.

Second, politics is morality writ large, in any case. While publishing research and teaching and grading students are inherently political acts, *reading* remains a private, subjective, intensely emotive experience, to which the rubric of ethics applies more intuitively. As Adam Zachary Newton puts it, "Textual interpretation comprises both private responsibilities incurred in each singular act of reading and public responsibilities that follow from discussing and teaching works of fiction" (19). To think of literary criticism only as political is to forget the productive tensions—the wrinkles in the first reading; the jolts of reconceptualization as that reading goes public—between these distinct sets of responsibilities.

Jim Phelan has provided a useful schema with which to categorize the questions and concerns of narrative ethics:

> Investigations into narrative ethics have been diverse and wide-ranging, but they can be usefully understood as focused on one or more of four issues: (1) the ethics of the told; (2) the ethics of the telling; (3) the ethics of writing/producing; and (4) the ethics of reading/reception. (n. pag.)

Ecocritics have been interested in all four aspects of narrative ethics, but most attention has focused on (1) and (3). Questions of *telling* seem secondary within much ecocritical scholarship to the environmental implications of what is *told,* in terms of plot, setting and characterization. Many allusions have been made in ecocritical writings to the ethics of reading (4), although almost no systematic evidence has been collected about the actual responses of actual readers to environmental texts. Under the ethics of writing (3), Phelan lists several questions, one of which has come to predominate in politically *activist* ecocriticism: the ethics of *exclusion.* In practice, this amounts to a measure of the difference between what the author chose to write about and what the scholar thinks she *ought* to have written about.

I want to suggest that ecocritical scholars put the ethics of the *telling* (2) at the center of their research and teaching. It is the quality and significance of the telling, not the told, that justifies attention to great and singular literature, if anything does. This does not, though, imply any more than a strictly provisional distinction between the *form* of telling and the *content* that is told, especially if the distinction implies the former is abstract and generalizable (as in the more abstruse formulations of narratology) whereas the latter is the locus of a particularized meaning. As Derek Attridge argues:

> Meaning is . . . not something that appears in defining opposition or complementary apposition to form, as it is conceived in the aesthetic tradition, but as something already taken up within form; forms are made out of meanings quite as much as they are made out of sounds and shapes. Form and meaning both happen, and are part of the same happening. (loc.2251)

Newton points out that "Voice" possesses both a form and a content; "point of view" involves an "interdependence of percepts and concepts" (53). While it is accurate to categorize Richard Powers's *Gain* as a double-plotted novel narrated in the third person, with shifting though limited focalization, such a description risks the same violence of generalization as thematic categorization of, say, an "industrial novel." A responsible reading should, as Attridge suggests, bear witness to the novel's singularity, whilst striving toward singularity in its own right.

Moreover, I do not suggest that there could be such a thing as *ecological narrative form,* as such. Ecopoetics has long labored under the misapprehension that some poetic forms might be inherently more "ecological" than others:[1] William Rueckert argues in his seminal "Literature and Ecology" essay, "Properly understood, poems can be studied as models for energy flow, community building, and ecosystems" (qtd. in Glotfelty and Fromm 110), while Angus Fletcher claims an astonishing isomorphism of ecology, American democracy, and Walt Whitman's poems. According to Fletcher, it makes no difference whether or not the poems are *about* matters ecological, any more than it makes a difference whether or not the House of Representatives enacts pro- or antienvironmental legislation; it is the *form* that ensures the dissolution of the boundary between poem and environment. With specific reference to Whitman's exuberant catalogues, Fletcher celebrates

> the systemic character of the world or scene developed in the environment-poetic. For environments are a special kind of natural ensemble, where drama and story are not the issue, where emotion is subordinate to the presentation of the aggregate relations of all participants, rather than the striking enhancement of singular or single heroes or heroines. . . . Nature's economy calls not for a House of Burgesses, of Lords, of Commons, but more radically for "representatives" with whom we interact in a system of mutual co-representation. (123–24)

What could it mean to say that, in natural environments, "emotion is subordinate" to anything, even "the aggregate relations of all participants"? Such claims distort both ecology and poetics in order to posit a nontrivial relationship between them. As Nancy Easterlin points out, ecocritics have failed to learn from the history of literary theory:

> The history of Marxist attempts to align ideological commitments with specific textual practices attests to the inadvisability of pinpointing a correct aesthetics, for the simple fact of the matter is that the semantic content of

---

1. It is worth noting, though, that not all ecopoetry scholars subscribe to such mimetic theories. Other studies of ecopoetry have focused on the attitudes of prominent ecopoets (see Bryson), or the acts of attention to nature that ecopoetry fosters (see Felstiner; Bate).

an artwork cannot be discerned on the basis of something so general as a style or mode. (99)

The earliest ecocriticism was predominantly an ethics of the *told*: it looked to ecopoetry to convey deep ecological ethics by means of theme, imagery, and the foregrounding of the other-than-human world. Later theorists of ecopoetry looked instead for direct and persuasive articulations of poetic form with *scientific ecology* (albeit in a popularized and basically metaphorical sense). If this approach worked poorly with poetry, though, it flounders badly when applied to prose narratives, novels being even less like ecosystems than poems. Instead, I want to extend the attention to "form" by linking it differently to ecocriticism's ethical concerns.

The ecocritical version of narrative ethics I propose has more definite ambitions than those proposed by Attridge and Newton, both authors strongly influenced by Emmanuel Levinas. Neohumanist, Levinasian, and ecocritical narrative ethics concur in exempting literature from the burden of delivering specific moral lessons, but Newton's formulation is too remotely metaethical:

> "The ethics of reading"/"the ethics of fiction"/"the ethics of criticism": all such formulations sit precariously on an ambiguous genitive. By purposeful contrast, my proposal of a narrative ethics implies simply narrative *as* ethics: the ethical consequences of narrating story and fictionalizing person, and the reciprocal claims binding teller, listener, witness, and reader in that process. (10–11)

If the narrative relation *always* constitutes an encounter of/with the Other—a moment Newton considers inherently "ethical," following Levinas—it is hard to see how any normative distinctions can be made within or between narratives.

Even accepting Newton and Attridge's characterization of narration as always already ethical, environmental narrative ethics might still seek to elaborate more specific moral aspects of storytelling. It would abjure consequentialism, the ethics of the hospital administrator, and deontology, the ethics of constitutions and courtrooms, in favor of an ethical orientation more appropriate to the singularity of literature: environmental virtue ethics. As Ronald Sandler and Philip Cafaro propose, "An adequate environmental ethic . . . requires not only an ethic of action—one that provides guidance regarding what we ought and ought not to do to the environment—but also an ethic of character—one that provides guidance on what attitudes and dispositions we ought and ought not to have regarding the environment" (84). *Virtue* has acquired some horrible connotations: ankle-length dresses, lace doilies, nosy neighbors, and furiously repressed sexuality. *Environmental virtue* isn't much better: proudly driving a "clean diesel" (damn you, Volkswagen) past the F150s parked outside Tim Hortons, V8s idling, to buy some conspicuously grubby carrots from the farmers market. Yet in philosophy, virtue ethics represents the plausible view that morality is best seen as a matter of character, rather than the application of invariant objective rules or the outcome of a calculation of the pleasurable and painful consequences of our actions for innumerable moral patients.

Moreover, the serendipity that binds the notion of character from virtue ethics to the narratological concept of a fictional person reminds us that literature preeminently stages for us Sandler and Cafaro's question: "What sort of person would *do* that?" Literary fictions enmesh characters in plots that test them—this is the heart of a narrative ethics of the told—but they also narrate their fates in ways that imply judgment, or a range of possible judgments, upon them. As William Flesch shows in his brilliant *Comeuppance,* narrators are witnesses who employ focalizers as witnesses to the multifarious conclusions of characters who witness each others' words and actions, and who invite us, too, into the helplessly ethical relationship of bearing fascinated witness to the cooperation, defection, reward, and (especially) punishment of fictional people. Although Flesch does not use the term, his book outlines a kind of evolutionary narrative ethics that is closely aligned with my intentions here, by contrast with more familiar narrative theories that are primarily cognitive, such as Lisa Zunshine's "other minds" orientation, or affective, such as Suzanne Keen's study of narrative empathy.

In Flesch's sophisticated Darwinian account of literature, fictional narratives have a crucial role in monitoring and enforcing strong reciprocity:

> Fiction recruits [the] central capacity in human social cognition for taking pleasure in responding to the nonactual. It gratifies the proximal or psychological aim of our interest in what some have done and how others have responded. That aim is the pleasure we take in strong reciprocation, particularly punishment, a pleasure useful in nonliterary contexts as an incentive to altruistic punishment and presumably evolved for that reason. That pleasure is one of anticipation, and we take pleasure in anticipating altruistic punishment—enough so that we demand of others that they be altruistic punishers, and that we anticipate what will happen in ways that underlie our interest in seeing how things will turn out, our desire to follow events to their conclusion. (51)

The narrative ethics I propose, then, will take place at the point that a work of literature *stages environmental virtue and vice,* albeit not in relation to a preexisting set of precepts such as *environmental justice* or *deep ecology,* nor in relation to a predetermined set of abstracted narrative techniques designated as more or less *ecological.* In this ethical moment, the reader, allied with the narrator and focalizer in the desire to "see how things turn out" and form judgments about them, enjoys both the privileges and vulnerabilities of his place in the hierarchical organization of narrative and, at the same time, encounters the alterity that confounds too simple an alignment of his verdict with theirs. In the analysis that follows, I will seem to test this model of ecocritical narrative ethics on Richard Powers's novel *Gain,* although in truth it was the novel (teaching it, especially) that prompted me to account for its singularity in these terms. While the present essay does not attempt to narrate this reciprocal relationship as such, acknowledging it should challenge the reader to consider whether the model I propose can be generalized beyond the text that, in some measure, provoked it.

GAIN'S CHIASMIC PLOTS

The singularity of Richard Powers's novel *Gain* has two main sources in its narrative organization: a dual plot that juxtaposes the story of Laura Bodey, who ultimately dies of ovarian cancer, with the history of how J. Clare's Sons, a soap and candle manufacturer, became Clare, Inc., a multinational conglomerate; and a liberal sprinkling of what I will call *intratexts* (mostly advertisements and real or invented maxims about cleanliness) presented without comment in the gaps between the dual narratives. These narrative techniques inform environmental virtue in three ways: they portray, for our moral consideration, a growing corporation as a richly characterized protagonist; they make possible a reflective, critical relationship to the stereotypes about environmental risk dubbed "toxic discourse" by Lawrence Buell (35–45); and they foster a sense of ecological change as complex, contingent, and historical, rather than teleological and reductively deterministic. Clearly, virtue in this context precludes an authorial performance of self-righteousness for the reader's confident endorsement; it is a metacognitive, as much as a moral, ideal. Moreover, both Laura's and Clare's moral ambiguity can be used, reciprocally, to inform environmental virtue ethics, which otherwise tends to focus on individual heroism rather than struggle and compromise.

The dual narrative, Powers's most striking technique, has attracted the majority of the novel's commentary. A simplistic reading might be that Laura's story undermines the progressivism of the Clare story, turning *Gain* into a diatribe against industrial capitalism in the tradition of Dickens's *Hard Times* or Upton Sinclair's *The Jungle*. However, such readings generally minimize the narrator's enthusiasm as he conveys the rise of Clare International. The replacement of homemade liquid soap by industrially produced cakes was clearly a crucial factor in the most radical improvement in the conditions of life in human history. The narrator's own idiom is infected by the language of the humane optimism of early nineteenth-century America: "Dirt's duckling transformed to salve's swan, its rancid nosegay rearranged into aromatic garland. This waxy mass, arising from putrescence, became its hated parent's most potent anodyne" (37). First, alliteration reemphasizes the fairy-tale quality of the transformation of rendered animal fat into stearine soap; next, nineteenth-century diction such as "putrescence" and "anodyne" announces the corroboration of the Clare founders' hopes by narrative authority. Walter Kirn aptly summarizes the narrator's ethical orientation as "slightly skeptical but fundamentally awed" (Kirn). Deftly avoiding the usual novelistic clichés that portray the corporation as octopus or behemoth, Powers's sympathies are highly unusual for literary fiction, as Kirn acknowledges: "His wide-angle fatalism about commerce even glints at times with Bill Gates optimism. Powers plays down but doesn't rule out the chance that the wheel of invention, toil, and speculation just may land us all in heaven someday, virtual immortals with pensions fat enough to last through all eternity." If such connivance of a novel's narrator with the fate of a multinational corporation seems unethical, it is probably because environmentally oriented readers are the legatees of the 1960s anticorporate romanticism and skepticism that created new challenges for the company in a later period:

> The Clare brass failed to fight this collapse in reputation, because it couldn't comprehend it. The public had turned not just against Clare but against all industry and enterprise. Now that business had delivered people from far worse fates, people turned against the fate of business. Like the careless grantees in fairy tales, they forgot the force that freed them to complain in the first place. (383)

As elsewhere in the novel, free indirect discourse equivocates between the company's managers' perspective and the narrator's. Specifically, Powers ensures it remains unclear whether the simile that compares 1960s environmentalists to "careless grantees in fairy tales" is one the "Clare brass" actually used, or is the narrator's way of epitomizing their bafflement at the sudden switch in public attitudes. Assuming the balance is tilted toward the latter, we can say that the narrator's *gratitude* for the "force that freed" unprecedented millions of people from filth and want is a moral orientation evident at both levels of telling and told. As such, it challenges readers to consider whether a corporation can exhibit environmental virtue.

The Clare plot is, though, only half the story. Laura Bodey is an ordinary mother, divorcee, and realtor living in Lacewood, a Midwestern city dominated by a Clare agricultural products factory. With appalling rapidity, her narrative switches from the pleasures of gardening and the challenges of teenage children to the consequences of diagnosis with ovarian cancer: she seeks the most advanced medical treatment; the treatment devastates her body along with the disease; the treatment fails, and she dies. Despite Laura's lack of character development, though, the moral center of the novel gradually shifts toward her from the resistible rise of the Clare empire. As Jeffrey Williams writes, "In dramatic terms, the two plots take opposite trajectories, the Clare plot one of a bustling and entertaining ascent, Laura's a tragic and moving descent" (Williams).

While the fictive and legal personality of Clare gradually becomes more diffuse and less emotionally compelling, thanks first to incorporation and later to diversification, acquisition, and a stock market launch, Laura's is clarified for us by close, painful, near-exclusive focalization throughout her ordeal. Just as importantly, the temporality of the two narratives contrasts via an extended chiasmus: the compressed, elliptical telling required by Clare's century and a half of growth with the horribly distended temporality of Laura's suffering. Where the Clare narrative scurries through the decades like a visitor at the Chicago World's Fair, emphasizing diegesis, Laura's narrative evokes the intolerable, inescapable hours of chemotherapy treatment with mimetic immediacy and slowness. The narrator repeatedly draws attention to Laura's excruciating experience of time, as in this telling instance halfway through twenty-four hours of chemotherapy: "A day dripped out in microseconds outlasts the idea of time" (127). Elsewhere, the narrative parcels out her treatments in milligrams of poisonous cures and lists of medical brand names.

The juxtaposition of differentiated characterization, diction, and temporality generates a growing sense of irony, mostly at Clare's expense, although readers' own susceptibilities as historically conditioned consumers also garner some gentle mockery. For example, Clare early on learns to market "Nature" and its antithesis, cleanliness, in a single image: "Native Balm [the Clare soap brand] embodied all the natural wisdom lost to the onslaught of modern industrial chemistry, while each package remained immaculate, milled, dependable" (197). In case we were liable to miss the irony, the narrator has already primed us, channeling Laura with free indirect discourse, to suspect the slipperiness of "the natural." One of the chemotherapy agents transfused into her is taxol from yew tree bark: "How can tree bark hurt you? Tree bark is 100 percent natural. The Native Americans used to make all kinds of things out of tree bark. Canoes and houses. Mighty medicines. The completely natural toxin is set to drip into her for the next twenty-four hours" (126). Just as Clare once used the iconography of the Red Indian to sell industrially produced soap, so Laura sells herself chemotherapy with some reassurance from the "ecological Indian," that tenacious Western myth (Krech). More subtly, Powers challenges the dichotomy of nature and culture that underlies toxic discourse, according to which "artificial" toxins, carcinogens, and oestrogenic compounds are assumed to be more hazardous than those that occur "naturally" (Ames, Profet, and Gold).

Powers's refusal to collapse the chiasmic narrative into a satisfying conclusion likewise challenges toxic discourse. As Thomas Byers points out:

> In *Gain,* the expectation or assumption, conditioned by such popular corporate conspiracy thrillers as *Erin Brockovich* and *Michael Clayton,* is that the two plots are causally related—that the history of the corporation provides an explanation for the cancer, and that in the end the plots will converge in the exposure of the corporation's venal villainy, perhaps leading to its demise. (Byers)

The contrast between the plots draws its power in part through consistent, yet differentiated, use of free indirect discourse: in the Clare story, the technique simultaneously prompts and frustrates judgment (probably subconscious in most readers) of the unknowable complicity between the narrator and the company's corporate persona, while in the Laura story, free indirect discourse forces us into an emotionally draining proximity to the dying protagonist. Yet the relationship between the narratives is never quite resolved, and Powers rejects satisfying, moralistic closure in favor of their more ethically sophisticated and complex raveling.

TRIANGULATING INTRATEXTS

While Powers's chiasmic plots dominate both the novel and the critical responses to it, a narrative analysis must also account for the fragments of extraneous text that appear throughout, which I am calling intratexts[2] to sig-

---

2. 'Intratexts' refers to textual devices, including such embedded written artifacts as epitaphs or advertising slogans, that mark off internal subdivisions. The term is most frequently found in Classics scholarship (e.g., Alison Sharrock and Helen Morales, *Intratextuality*).

nify that they are distinct from the main dual narrative, while standing in a constructive internal relationship to it. They stick out in the text, partly because some employ unusual typography, but also because their variable narration and frequent extratextual reference contrasts with the erudite intimacy of the authorial persona. If free indirect discourse brings us uncomfortably close to *Gain*'s characters, human and corporate, provoking and complicating our moral response, the role of the intratexts is different but complementary.

There are, by my count, forty-one intratexts, ranging from the road sign welcoming visitors to Lacewood through an advert for Chicago's 1893 World's Fair to the epitaph to the words of Samuel Clare's daughter Elizabeth, inscribed to imitate a stonemason's hand:

> When we devote our Youth to God
>   'Tis Pleasing in his eyes
> A flour Offered in the bud
>   Is no vain saCrafiCe (86; [*sic*])

In this instance, the intratext conveys an event unrecorded in the main Clare narrative itself, as if in recognition of a boundary between worldly success and private loss.

Students tell me they skip over the intratexts and critics often ignore them, but they are vital to *Gain*'s narrative construction. I suggest above, drawing on Flesch's work, that focalization, narration, and reading can be seen as modes of witnessing, or gazing with attitude. For Flesch, the mystery of humans' distinctive altruism and cruelty is founded in the exigencies of ultra-sociality, which requires "altruistic punishment" (a perfectly apt paradox) in order to enforce "strong reciprocity." Its primitive form is revenge; its modern avatar is justice; spanning the two, historically, is the readerly interest in poetic justice. As we will see in more detail in the next section, though, *Gain* arouses an expectation of a just resolution, only to frustrate it. The intratexts not only inhabit the textual space between alternating passages of the two main plots; they also exist in an interstitial narrative and ethical location between the acts of witnessing that each of those plots invites. Yet the intratexts are not focalized in such a way as to offer unequivocal commentary on either of the chiasmic plots, even though a few are micronarratives with focalizers in their own right. Readers presumably read them *from the perspective of* whichever chiasmic plot attracts their moral sympathy, but cannot find unambiguous vindication there. Each intratext can also be read from the competing vantage point of the other plot, a narrative trick I should like to dub *triangulation*.

Some of the intratexts are intertextual quotations of real sources such as Ralph Waldo Emerson ("The greatest meliorator of the world is selfish, huckstering Trade" [7]) or Grace Hallock's 1928 publication *A Tale of Soap and Water: The Historical Progress of Cleanliness* (35, 100, 348). One intratext, a recipe for "Healthy Chinese Vegetables and Noodles" printed on the other side of an advertisement for Laura Bodey's realty business, reminds the reader that she, too, is a "selfish, huckstering" trader in her own right (61). At a later stage, when Laura starts looking for environmental causes for her cancer, there is a list of titles of scientific journal articles that clearly belongs to her narrative (233). Most intratexts, though, are advertisements for Clare products that form a potted history of American marketing, from bald nineteenth-century appeals to religiosity (48) to sepia-toned 1980s productions that repackage corporate history as environmental virtue (198).

Readers are likely to interpret Clare's marketing with varying degrees of individual cynicism, more or less according to taste and political orientation. Yet the positioning of many of the intratexts *in between* sections of the chiasmic plots means we are encouraged to read them from one or other of the points of view they provide. While *Gain*'s narrating persona is consistent and continuous,[3] the fictional or real intertextuality of the intratexts, together with their diverse narrative voices, constructs them as extrinsic. At the same time, though, they seem to allude internally to one or both main plots at a thematic level. For example, a micronarrative-style advertisement for Clare's Clarity blusher follows a woman in rapid sequence from mirror makeup retouch to risqué assignation in a fancy restaurant, then home, makeup redone and clothing miraculously transformed from "courtesan-spy white to hunter-green flannel" (107) during the drive home to her loving family. The ekphrastic narration of the TV advert concludes:

> *The whole story unfolds in just under thirty seconds. In their roughhouse clinch* [with her husband], *the flannel woman's purse falls open at her feet. With one hand . . . she reaches down and closes the clasp on a cake of blush hiding there.*
>
> *The voice-over returns, arch now, everything understood. "Some things you need never say at all.*
>
> **"Face by Clarity. For as many looks as you have lives."** (108)

We recognize this miracle of narrative compression, in outline, from innumerable similar thirty-second stories. We also, after a moment's reflection, under-

---

3. In the absence of overt personalizing features, and with the circumtextual knowledge of Powers's "egghead" reputation, we are likely to assume the narrator is an authorial persona.

stand it as selling the elusive fantasy that women can combine erotic allure with wholesome family life, with only a little smoothing over the boundary— which the advert reinforces rather than elides—in between.

Less obvious, though, is the intratext's position in between the narration of Julia Clare, the company's most effective booster in the nineteenth century, and Laura Bodey's dispiriting visit to a cancer specialist in Indianapolis. In the course of the former, Resolve Clare is led, with the help of his unstoppable wife, to the "gradual realization that what was good for soap was good for America. And better still, the other way round" (106). From the vantage point of the previous section of narrative, the Clarity advertisement embodies, at worst, the venal sin of igniting unachievable hopes in watching women; at best, it can be seen as an extension of Julia's own ambitious promotion of American industry, with female aspiration at its heart. Yet the section following the intratext returns to Laura's story as she seeks clarification of her prognosis without success: the specialist, who hasn't read her file, spouts jargon and figures that assert his expertise without enlightening his patient. Questioned as to the cause of her ovarian cancer, he replies obliquely, "There's . . . some evidence that provoking agents, either combined with or inducing an alteration in the immune system . . ." (111). If we infer—though Laura does not, at this stage—that Clare may be the source of such "provoking agents," the corporation's efforts to sell beauty products to women whom it is, simultaneously, condemning to death becomes a sick joke. By situating the advert in between the chiasmic plots, though, Powers forces the reader to decide, however unreflectively, whether to read it in the light of the one or the other, using a process of triangulation.

The triangulation effect need not imply that the Clare narrative suggests a sympathetic reading of the intratexts, whereas the Laura narrative necessarily requires a cynical reading. In this instance, an advertisement for asthma medicine, the contextual triangulation arguably involves a reversed effect:

BREATHING EASY

This year, Melissa blew out all her candles. In one breath. By herself. Last year, just humming along while the other kinds sang *Happy Birthday* left her gasping for air. Until Respulin appeared among the rest of her life's presents, each new candle taxed her lungs to the breaking point. She could not run, sing, shout, or even jump a rope. She lived in constant fear. A spring day felt like being buried alive.

Melissa turned nine today. Maybe she still can't spell oral leukotriene D_4 receptor antagonist. But she does know how to spell Happiness.

The Biological Materials Group
CLARE MATERIALS SOLUTIONS (130–31)

The genre is, again, recognizable: medicine marketing that tropes expensive pharmacological agents as "gifts" of modern science. It is another micronarrative of fear, hope, and gratitude, focalized through an imaginary beneficiary of Clare's products, and written in a confiding idiom that aligns her childish innocence and vulnerability with the company's protective, paternalistic expertise.

The intratext occurs just after one of the most painfully sustained narrations of Laura's chemotherapy, and is immediately followed by Benjamin Clare's development of a marketing strategy for Native Balm around the idea that "The Red Man never worried about his skin" (131). Laura is positioned, at this stage, as an adult equivalent of Melissa: an ailing recipient of miraculous medicines she cannot understand. Filled with nausea at the thought of food, she stashes her hospital lunch "As if she's a little child again, only now blessed with a handbag" (129). From this perspective, we might read the advert "innocently," as an emotionally heightened promotion of the real benefits of medical science. Triangulating from the Clare narrative, by contrast, suggests a cynical reading of the advert in which the corporation simply manipulates our parental emotions for commercial gain.

As the chiasmic plots seem set to converge in the latter part of the novel, the challenge of triangulation becomes more acute as the divergent interpretations available become more pointed. While Laura is the exclusive focalizer for most of her narrative, there is an odd passage where her ex-husband Don tries to glean information about Clare's toxic emissions from a friend in Clare's PR department. They are flirting and chatting when she suddenly realizes his real intentions: "And, in a syllable, everything changes. She misses no beat. Just as funny, just as warm, just as welcoming. But it's like a little layer of friendly gauze has come down between them" (296). Behind the welcoming demeanor we perceive ruthless corporate self-interest, just as we might expect. Indeed, the marketing image of Clare as your friendly neighborhood multinational is beginning to seem pretty threadbare by now, which primes us to read the next intratext—a press release reassuring the public in the wake of the publication of EPA Toxic Release figures—still more skeptically.

The statement seems perfectly rational: it acknowledges that "public concern over health is never unreasonable" and reminds readers that the EPA Toxic Release Inventory "makes no statement about any risks posed to health" by the substances it includes (297). It observes, correctly, that concentrations of trace substances matter far more than their mere existence and claims that "the levels of hazardous material coming from Clare's plants are negligible and pose no significant risk to anyone living in the vicinity" (297). Even given expectations shaped by classic toxic texts such as *Erin Brockovich,* we might have given Clare the benefit of the doubt, only now the chiasmic plots seem to be narrowing toward convergence. As readers naturally alert to proleptic hints of narrative resolution, we are likely to expect a lie's uncovering.

It never happens, as we have observed, and so the challenge—at once cognitive and ethical—of triangulation rests upon us until the end. The very last intratext occurs just after the Clare narrative tells us that the company "went green, inside and out," because "green, too, was a need, the same as any that has faced the species. And nothing met human need better than concerted human industry" (386). It occurs just before Laura's son Tim comes home to find her gasping: "In that shortness of breath, a waking dream of live burial" (388). In between the company's zenith and its human antagonist's nadir is the text engraved on a brass plaque in the hospital, which thanks "the Benjamin Clare Charitable Fund" for its generosity in renovating the hospital. Yet the narrative structure tends rather to undermine than underscore cynicism, most notably in the way the twin plot resolves into three tightly interwoven, persistently ambiguous, endings.

CAMERA, CORPSE, AND CORPORATION: *GAIN'S* THREE ENDINGS

Clare, at first sight, seems to emerge triumphant: the class action for allegedly producing carcinogens is resolved with a payoff, without admission of liability, to the plaintiffs, but Laura dies without seeing it. The troublesome agrichemicals division is sold off, and soon after, the Lacewood plant is closed down and moved to Mexico. There is never any proof of Clare's responsibility for Laura's illness, only attribution of guilt by (narrative) association.

Nor does Laura emerge as an environmentalist heroine. Her vague, wry skepticism toward consumerism is provoked repeatedly but quickly assuaged: "Peanut sheets. Laura is not sure what problem the sheeting of peanuts actually solves. What was wrong with yesterday's peanut concept? . . . Anyway, they make Ellen happy. No mean feat, these days" (29). She fends off her ex-husband Don's insistent demand that she seek the truth behind her illness, partly because she resists his annoying blend of paranoia and Mr. Fixit but also because she thinks affixing blame on Clare International is just too neat and simple: "The whole planet, a superfund site. Life causes cancer" (323).

Even when she summons up the will to oppose it, she is defeated by the ubiquity of Clare's products:

> She vows a consumer boycott, a full spring cleaning. But the house is full of them. It's as if the floor she walks on suddenly liquefies into a sheet of termites. They paper her cabinets. They perch on her microwave, camp out on her stove, hang from her shower head. Clare hiding under the sink, swarming her medicine chest, lining the shelves in the basement, parked out in the garage, piled up in the shed. (345)

The entemomorphic imagery conveys in a sinister key the very proliferation of household products that the Clare narrative had previously celebrated, but it also justifies Laura's ultimate fatalism. If it weren't this particular suite of products, it would be a slightly different one; if she threw out all the Clare stuff, it would only be replaced by Unilever or Johnson and Johnson.

In any case, as Ursula Heise's perceptive analysis demonstrates, *Gain* demonizes neither the company's *products* nor its *by-products*; rather, the Clare narrative questions the forms of legal personality the company assumes, which publicize risk and privatize profit. Heise observes:

> Part of the point in juxtaposing the two narrative strands, then, is to show how the corporate body and the individual body depend on each other, and how the corporate organism can become a lethal threat to the individual one. More than any single substance and more even that the whole array of products it delivers, it is the corporation as a social form that kills Laura Bodey. (loc.3745)

However, while Heise admires Powers's gestures toward a global perspective in the novel, she has reservations about its neorealist narrative voice:

> In *Gain*, . . . the self-assurance of the narrator's command of the global and his transparent (though complex) language remain in tension with the scenario of individual powerlessness vis-à-vis the global that the novel portrays. In this respect, the novel's formal accomplishment lags behind its conceptual sophistication. (loc.3860)

I dispute the powerlessness of the individual in the novel, although I admit Laura is deprived of options for unambiguously virtuous action. More debatable is Heise's assumption in *Sense of Place and Sense of Planet* that only the fractured and alienating language of the modernist narrative tradition, equated here with "formal accomplishment," will ruffle the reader's complacency and produce a critical, reflective response. This is the narrative ethics implied by the Russian Formalists' *ostranenie* and Brecht's *entfremdungseffekt,* and despite its still-widespread acceptance I'm not sure it has ever found empirical support. Moreover, as the Formalists knew, estrangement and automatization are moving targets; one can acclimatize to Beckett in time.

In fact, *Gain* ends with three fairly violent shifts in focalization. Immediately after Laura dies, the narration traces with astonishing detail the production of a disposable camera using parts from around the world but otherwise eliding the agency of its makers. Even though this camera is, far more than any other character in the novel, a global citizen, it turns out to be a "disposable miracle," inviting devastating comparisons to Laura's transient existence, extraordinariness, but also ultimate inconsequentiality—not least because the camera is used to photograph Laura on her deathbed, then thrown in the trash, undeveloped (397).

If the camera presents a dehumanized vision of Clare's global industry, the next section refocalizes through Franklin Kennibar, the first Clare CEO to be characterized to any depth since the firm went public in 1891. His reflections, looking down from his executive suite, are startlingly nihilistic:

> *We speak of bitter,* he thinks. *We speak of sweet.* We speak of bounce, we speak of body. Of hold and shine and non-stick and pine scent and quick-acting. In reality, there is no bitter, no sweet, no bounce or body. There is nothing but a series of chemicals, each distinctly shaped, stretching on forever into the void. (397)

His qualms go far beyond the delusive jargon of Clare's marketing to a fundamental questioning of the phenomena of subjective experience, what philosophers call "qualia." From this perspective, the corporation, itself a fictive personality, conjures the fiction of financial value from the fiction of subjective qualia. The Clare CEO appears to be experiencing existential angst, colored by industrial chemistry. At the same time, the shift from italicized direct discourse to free indirect discourse forces the reader to make subconscious judgments about the complicity of the authorial persona with Kennibar that are at once necessitated by the narration and rendered ethically undecidable by it. Whose nihilism is it, exactly?

Challenged by a journalist to explain the "purpose of business," Kennibar writes out a list of dozens of possible answers, from implausibly altruistic ("To improve the general welfare.") to wholly cynical ("To make things that people desire. To make people desire things.") (398). In any case, he is about to propose the breakup of the Clare behemoth as protection against a hostile takeover, yet another revolutionary transformation for the two-centuries-old company. Departing from that intimation of corporate mortality, the narration circles out, by means of erratically shifting focalization spanning Kennibar's network of employees. In a certain sense, all these people depend on the CEO—the focalization shifts out from him at the center—but then, as Kennibar reflects mordantly, his decision has itself been precipitated by the depression in the company's stock price thanks to a class action that included one recently deceased Laura Bodey. Thus, although the chiasmic plots are never definitively resolved—there is no smoking gun leading directly from the Clare Agrochemical Division to Laura's ovarian tumor—the reverberations from Laura's death nevertheless resonate globally.

The third ending shifts focalization once more, to Laura's son Tim, who has spent most of the novel shooting Nazis on his computer. He uses some of his mother's settlement to buy a more powerful machine, which he eventually puts to use as part of a research group at MIT working on "a computing solution to the protein folding problem" (404). After years protesting against Clare, "curiosity slowly got the better of bitterness." When his research group cracks the problem, he offers his mother's settlement money to help the company start up. Powers conjures a neat symmetry in the last paragraphs, imagining the software that functions as a "universal chemical assembly plant at the level of the human cell" in terms that specifically recall the chemical structure of soap: just as soap molecules are "ambidextrous," being water-soluble at one end and fat-soluble at the other, the protein-folding program "relied upon a chunk of code whose ambidextrous data structures looked out Janus-faced to mesh with both raw source and finished product" (405). More faintly, we might say that the intratexts, too, are Janus-faced, since they are always susceptible to reading alongside one or the other of the main narratives. The last line of the novel has Tim suggesting that "it might be time for the little group of them to incorporate." Thus the cycle of commerce begins all over again, only this time it proposes to intervene at a still-more intimate physical level than Clare's products.

GAIN: ETHICS AND NARRATIVE STRUCTURE

Given that Tim has challenged the company that may have killed his mother, his decision to imitate it has peculiar moral significance. Perhaps, as Joseph Dewey suggests, it should be seen as a failure on his part: "Though Powers surely cheers such medical research, its end logic is disquietingly familiar;

124 • GREG GARRARD

surely genetic engineering . . . represents a new century's unsettling version of Clare International, the nostalgic urge to flee the responsibility to die, to fix nature's 'flaws'" (127). Heise, too, argues that the ending is "curiously optimistic and pessimistic at the same time," because Tim's venture looks as much like repetition as progress (172).

To a large extent, any reading of the ending must follow from one's personal resolution of the chiasmic plot structure: any reader who has followed Clare's progress with dismay will view the emergence of the next generation as a new disaster-in-the-making. That said, Powers does not invite a moralistic response, having deftly avoided both the classic resolution of a tale of toxicity—the miasma is traced back to the source and the malefactor punished accordingly—and the more subtle temptation to depict the rise of a corporation as unequivocal moral decline. Thanks in large part to Romanticism, declensionist historiography is a pervasive structure of feeling in environmentalist thought that inverts narratives of progress with little or no attention to the astonishing gains in human welfare they celebrate. *Gain,* by contrast, commends to our moral attention the biography of a corporate character, as Bruce Bawer explains: "Clare's management acquires a concept of the corporate image and then consciously strives to establish the corporation as 'a person' not only 'in the eyes of the law' but 'in the minds of its customers.'" The legal "'person'" brought to life by incorporation is anthropomorphically elaborated by narration into a still-more complex fictive being. Having narrated Clare's life story over a century and a half, Powers asks us to consider, as do Sandler and Cafaro, "what sort of person would *do* that?"

Clare is unique in literary fiction, to my knowledge, as a corporate character whose environmental virtue is at least as complex a question as that of any merely human being. In this sense, it has the potential to extend our ethical sensibilities, rather than just being subjected to them. Even the company's ultimate dissolution, anticipated at the level of narration by the disorientating shifts of focalization away from Kennibar and back to him, can be read either as poetic justice for the company that killed Laura Bodey or as a further transmutation of an entity that has always had to adapt to survive. Declensionist historiography and reflexive hostility to corporate capitalism are morally and pragmatically debilitating because seven billion humans cannot live tolerable, sustainable existences without industrial production on a commensurate scale. When Powers's narrator compares environmentalists of the 1960s to "the careless grantees in fairy tales" who "forgot the force that freed them to complain in the first place," he is implicitly prodding us toward a more nuanced appreciation of Clare's moral character (383).

Our reliance on the products of industry for comforts we seldom fully appreciate need not enervate our judgment, just as climate activists' decision to drive to a protest site does not invalidate their argument. As environmentalists, we all abide in hypocrisy, and so we cannot accept it as a knockdown objection. Nonetheless, the narrative configuration of reader, narrator, and corporate character in *Gain* models an ethical relation that acknowledges that, by comparison with their ancestors, almost all the novel's readers are unimaginably privileged, even if, like Laura, they are also vulnerable to unprecedented risks. Key features of the novel's telling, notably the narrator's unknowable complicity with Clare and painful intimacy with Laura—both relayed by means of free indirect discourse—and the curious ambidextrous externality of the intratexts, demand ethical response even as they frustrate moralism. *Gain* challenges us—*requires* us, actually, by way of narrative—to weigh honest gratitude in the scales with the desire for justice and fear of personal and ecological harm, a moral quandary that is perhaps the central challenge for environmental ethics today.

WORKS CITED

Ames, Bruce N., Margie Profet, and Lois Swirsky Gold. "Dietary Pesticides (99.99% All Natural)." *Proceedings of the National Academy of Sciences*, vol. 87, Oct. 1990, pp. 7777–81, 14 Mar. 2016, www.pnas.org/content/87/19/7777.full.pdf.

Attridge, Derek. *The Singularity of Literature*. Routledge 2004, Kindle.

Bate, Jonathan. *The Song of the Earth*. Picador, 2000.

Bawer, Bruce. "Bad Company." *New York Times* [New York City], 21 Jun. 1998, www.nytimes.com/1998/06/21/books/bad-company.html?pagewanted=all.

Bryson, J. Scott. *The West Side of Any Mountain: Place, Space, and Ecopoetry*. U of Iowa P, 2005.

Buell, Lawrence. *Writing for an Endangered World: Literature, Culture, and Environment in the U.S. and Beyond*. Belknap, 2001.

Byers, Thomas B. "The Crumbling Two-Story Architecture of Richard Powers' Fictions." *Transatlantica*, vol. 2, 2009. www.transatlantica.revues.org/4510.

Clark, Timothy. *The Cambridge Introduction to Literature and the Environment*. 2011, www.assets.cambridge.org/97805218/96351/cover/9780521896351.jpg.

Dewey, Joseph. *Understanding Richard Powers*. U of South Carolina P, 2002.

Easterlin, Nancy. *A Biocultural Approach to Literary Theory and Interpretation*. Johns Hopkins UP, 2012.

Feder, Helena. *Ecocriticism and the Idea of Culture: Biology and the Bildungsroman*. Ashgate, 2014.

Felstiner, John. *Can Poetry Save the Earth?: A Field Guide to Nature Poems*. Yale UP, 2009.

Flesch, William. *Comeuppance: Costly Signaling, Altruistic Punishment, and Other Biological Components of Fiction*. Harvard UP, 2007.

Fletcher, Angus. *A New Theory for American Poetry: Democracy, the Environment, and the Future of Imagination*. Harvard UP, 2004.

Garrard, Greg. *Ecocriticism*. New Critical Idiom. Routledge, 2011.

Glotfelty, Cheryll, and Harold Fromm. *The Ecocriticism Reader: Landmarks in Literary Ecology*. U of Georgia P, 1996.

Heise, Ursula K. *Sense of Place and Sense of Planet: The Environmental Imagination of the Global*. Oxford UP 2008, Kindle.

Kirn, Walter. "Commercial Fiction." *New York Books* [New York City], 14 Mar. 2016 www.nymag. com/nymetro/arts/books/reviews/2754/.

Krech, Shepard. *The Ecological Indian: Myth and History*. W. W. Norton & Company, 1999.

Newton, Adam Zachary. *Narrative Ethics*. Harvard UP, 1995.

Phelan, James. "Narrative Ethics." *The Living Handbook of Narratology*, 2014. www.lhn.uni -hamburg.de/article/narrative-ethics.

Powers, Richard. *Gain*. Picador, 1998.

Sandler, Ronald D., and Philip Cafaro. *Environmental Virtue Ethics*. Rowman & Littlefield, 2005.

Sharrock, Alison, and Helen Morales. *Intratextuality: Greek and Roman Textual Relations*. Oxford UP, 2000.

Williams, Jeffrey. "The Issue of Corporations: Richard Powers' *Gain*." *Cultural Logic,* vol. 2, no. 2, 1999. www.clogic.eserver.org/2-2/williamsrev.html.

III

ANTHROPOCENE STORYWORLDS

CHAPTER 6

Feeling Nature

Narrative Environments and Character Empathy

ALEXA WEIK VON MOSSNER

NOT FAR into Sanora Babb's Dust Bowl novel *Whose Names Are Unknown* (2004), the Oklahoma homesteader Julia Dunne gets caught in a thunderstorm with her two young daughters. After spending a pleasant afternoon at a neighboring farm, the pregnant woman and her two girls are sent away before dinner, regardless of the fact that "it's looking stormy out" (34). Hoping that the sky might be "just threatening" (34), they embark on their long walk across open land. They do not get far before they realize that it was not a mere threat:

> They were almost a mile away, walking in the hollow, when the rain began in large slow drops, and the far horizon quivered with sheet lightening. Fork lightening snapped suddenly, splitting the moving clouds, flashing close to the wires. The whole flat world under an angry churning sky was miraculously lightened for a moment. A strange liquid clarity extended to the ends of the earth. Julia saw the trees along the creek and the animals grazing far away. The bleak farmyards with their stern buildings, scattered sparsely on the plains, stood out in naked lonely desolation. A sly delicate wind was rising. Their dresses moved ever so little. Thunder clapped and boomed. (35)

Written in realist style, this passage invites readers to imagine the sight of open land, heavy clouds, and sudden flashes of lightning. Much of the passage uses Julia as a focalizer, cueing readers to simulate *her* subjective experience of the situation as she imbues various features of the landscape with affective value to the point of personifying them: the buildings are stern, lonely, and desolate, and they are utterly exposed to the force of an "angry churning" sky that now proceeds to make its "threat" a reality. The sensory imagery in the passage is not solely visual but also includes the sensation of the "sly delicate wind" catching the women's dresses and the sound of thunder clapping and booming, foreboding the onslaught of rain that will soon follow.

What each of us imagines when reading this passage from Babb's novel will be quite different in terms of detail and appearance, depending on our personal experiences and cultural background. And yet—unless we for some reason exhibit an aberrant response—it will involve a swiftly approaching thunderstorm across an open, barren landscape and the movements, sensations, and feelings of the three desolate women as the "lightning crack[s] near them" and they run for shelter, "their breath cutting like knives in their lungs" (35). Narratologists have likened literary narratives to "instruction manuals" that contain "a set of instructions for mental composition" and invite readers to follow those instructions (Caracciolo 83; Scarry 244). The metaphor of the instruction manual is an interesting one because it stresses the active role of the reader as someone who *performs* the narrative in their minds, as psychologist Richard Gerrig has put it (*Experiencing* 17). Just like actors on a stage, Gerrig suggests, readers engage in acts of simulation during which "they must use their own experiences of the world to bridge the gaps in texts" and must invest their own emotions in order to "give substance to the psychological lives of characters" (17). But it is not only characters who are enlivened in that way. It is also the narrative environments that surround characters, the storyworlds that frame and enable their actions. "In trying to make sense of a narrative," explains narratologist David Herman, "interpreters attempt to reconstruct not just what happened but also the surrounding context or environment embedding storyworld existents, their attributes, and the actions and events in which they are involved. . . . Interpreters do not merely reconstruct a sequence of events and a set of existents, but imaginatively (emotionally, viscerally) inhabit a world in which things matter, agitate, exalt, repulse, provide grounds for laughter and grief, and so on—both for narrative participants and for interpreters of the story (570). Herman's narratological argument agrees with the theoretical assumptions of much of ecocriticism: that narrative environments are not only important to our understanding of a given narrative but they in fact play a central role in both character and plot development.

In this essay, I argue that the reverse is also true. Using a cognitive eco-narratological approach, I suggest that not only are narrative environments crucial for our understanding of characters, but characters are also central to our understanding of narrative environments.[1] The first section of the essay explores the role of embodied simulation and character empathy in this recip-rocal relationship. Using examples from Sanora Babb's memoir *An Owl on Every Post* (1994), it argues that while the evocative description of a narrative environment is what allows readers to imagine it, it is the narrative align-ment with *experiencing agents* that imbues that environment with vivacity and affective meaning. The second part of the essay returns to Babb's novel *Whose Names Are Unknown* to demonstrate that the same basic principles also apply to fiction and that the affectively charged experience of a narrative environ-ment can be an important feature of politically engaged novels such as Babb's.

EXPERIENCING NARRATIVE ENVIRONMENTS:
EMPATHY, EMOTION, AND EMBODIED SIMULATION

Econarratology, as Erin James defines and develops it in *The Storyworld Accord* (2015), is situated at the intersection of postclassical narratology and ecocriti-cism, thereby "pairing ecocriticism's interest in the relationship between lit-erature and the physical environment with narratology's focus on the literary structures and devices by which writers compose narratives" (3). More spe-cifically, James suggests that the combination of contextual approaches with cognitive narratology—which draws on the insights of cognitive science—is particularly well suited for an ecocritical exploration of the rich storyworlds within which literary characters function. All narrative texts, she observes, "even those that do not seem to be interested in the environment in and of itself, offer up virtual environments for their readers to model mentally and inhabit emotionally" (54). They are *virtual* environments because they only exist in the writer's mind and in those of individual readers, their only mate-rial form being that of black dots on a white page or that of pixels on some kind of electronic reading device. And yet they can be so vivid and engaging that readers feel strongly moved by them and even unwilling to (mentally) leave them by refocusing their attention on their actual environment.

How exactly the mental modeling and emotional inhabitation of literary environments comes to pass has been explained in a variety of ways. Gerrig suggests that it is, in part, an unconscious *mental performance* that involves

---

1. The notion of a "cognitive ecocriticism" was first introduced by Nancy Easterlin (257).

what he calls readers' "memory traces" ("Conscious," 42), but he does not spell out how exactly such a performative act plays out in readers' minds. Caracciolo offers an enactivist take on the subject, arguing that readers experience narrative space by "enacting a character's bodily-perceptual experience" of that space through what he calls a "fictionalization" of their own "virtual body" (160). I want to draw on another, neuroscientific account here, on one that does not require the theoretical construct of the reader's "virtual body" because it considers our imaginary experience of literary environments a case of *neuronal reuse*.[2] Like the enactivist approach, this approach draws on research in the interdisciplinary field of embodied cognition, but it relies on simulation theories, in particular on the notion of *embodied simulation* as it has been propagated by the Italian neuroscientist Vittorio Gallese.[3]

Embodied simulation theory is built on mirror neuron research and—at the most basic level—it must be understood as a "non-conscious, pre-reflective functional mechanism of the brain–body system, whose function is to model objects, agents and events" (Gallese, "Bodily Selves" 3–4). Neuroimaging research has shown that when we see another person act, we map those actions onto our premotor cortex, the part of the brain that is also active when we engage in actual movement. Remarkably, something related also happens when our brains process literary texts. As Gallese sums up the empirical results of several functional neuroimaging (fMRI) studies:

> Silent reading of words referring to face, arm, or leg actions, or listening to sentences expressing actions performed with the mouth, the hand, and the foot, both produce activation of different sectors of the premotor cortex. . . . These activated premotor sectors coarsely correspond to those active during the execution/observation of hand, mouth, and foot actions. Thus, it appears that the MNS [mirror neuron system] is involved not only in understanding visually presented actions, but also in mapping acoustically or visually presented action-related linguistic expressions. (457, "Mirror Neurons")

---

2. Neuronal reuse, also called neuronal recycling, postulates that "structures in the brain eventually adapt so well to their environment that culturally determined processes such as reading end up operating through them, even though they had not evolved for this purpose" (Jacobs and Schrott 130).

3. Embodied cognition is a vast and highly interdisciplinary and heterogeneous field that includes researchers in neuroscience, cognitive psychology, philosophy, and artificial intelligence. They are united by the belief that many features of cognition are shaped by aspects of the body beyond the brain, but there are substantial differences between subfields and individual researchers as to the exact role of the body and the surrounding environment in the emergence of mind and consciousness.

Whereas in the case of direct perception the premotor cortex "mirrors" the movements we see in other agents, in reading (or listening), the perception of movement thus plays out on the *imaginary* level with our brains reacting much in the same way they would respond to personally performed movement. This is what cognitive scientists call *neuronal reuse* since the same neurons that are active in performed movement also fire in response to perceived movement and imagined movement.

Importantly, the mirror neuron system not only helps us recognize the *actions* of others, real and imagined, but also in the attribution of *sensations, attitudes,* and *emotions.* "The perception of pain or grief, or of disgust experienced by others," explain neuroscientists Giacomo Rizzolatti and Corrado Sinigaglia, "activates the same areas of the cerebral cortex that are involved when we experience these emotions ourselves" (xii). Such "feeling with" is what we call empathy, and it can be triggered not only by our perception of actual people around us, but also by our imagined perception of a literary character. As I have argued elsewhere, we might feel along with a character even more fervently than with an actual person because a literary text can give us a degree of access to the emotions and sensations of another being that is rarely possible in real life (25). For econarratological readings, it is important to note that processes of embodied simulation are crucial not only for our empathetic engagement with characters but also for our experience of the narrative environments that surround these characters and that stand in complex relationships to them. Studies have shown that textual imagery relating to vision activates the visual cortex whereas textual imagery relating to sound, smell, taste, or touch activates other relevant brain regions through neuronal reuse (Keysers and Gazzola). That means that feeling along with a character is crucial in how readers experience and relate to a narrative environment.

Take the example of Sanora Babb's *An Owl on Every Post,* which chronicles her impoverished childhood in a dugout on the Colorado prairie during the second decade of the twentieth century. Babb's literary life was bounded by the Great Plains, where she was born in the Oklahoma Territory in 1907, and the coastal hills of California, where she died almost one hundred years later, in 2005. Although it has so far received little attention from ecocritics, her work shares in the inexhaustible delight in the natural world that marks the life and work of many American nature writers, a passion that she attributed to the five years she spent as a girl on the endless plains of Colorado. *An Owl on Every Post,* Babb makes clear in her afterword to the memoir, is her attempt to share the experience of those formative years in a way that helps readers understand what it meant to her, personally, to live "on a grand earth under a big sky, not just within walls" (251). In order to allow for such understanding, she not only offers descriptions of that open environment but also strives to convey a sense of *what it is like* to experience it by providing access to her younger self's qualia.

Qualia are most commonly used by psychologists and philosophers "to characterize the qualitative, experiential or felt properties of mental states" (Levin 693). First-person narrators tend to give readers a good deal of insight into the qualitative, experiential, or felt properties of their own mental states— what they think and how they feel about the people, things, and events they encounter in the storyworld. In the case of a memoir, it is suggested that this narrator is identical with the author, although critics and scholars of autobiography have long insisted that it would be a mistake to naively conflate the two, or to assume that the qualia of an autobiographical narrator are necessarily an accurate representation of the author's actual subjective experience of an event in the past. Rather, it must be seen as the author's attempt to bring to life for the reader their past subjective experience as they remember it at the time of writing. In Babb's case, it is the attempt to convey her changing emotional relationship to the harsh landscape of the Great Plains.

Babb was only seven years old when, in 1913, her mother sat her and her sisters down in a "slow mixed train of a handful of passengers and cars full of coal, flour, lard, canned food supplies, and other necessities" (*Owl* 7), leaving behind the city of Red Rock, Oklahoma, for an isolated broomcorn farm on the flat plains of Colorado, east of the Rocky Mountains. "The lackluster autumn landscape," as Babb remembers the sight from the train, "was like an old gray carpet spread to the far, far circling horizon. There was nothing more to see. This was an empty land" (7). Clearly, the writing of such sentences involves the embodied simulation of a remembered visual impression on the part of the author as well as an emotional engagement with that visual impression. Readers, in turn, must rely on the "instruction manual" of Babb's written account in order to recreate in their minds a version of the landscape that she remembered and then tried to transform into language during the writing process. Here and elsewhere, Babb relies on simile and metaphor in order to aid readers in that process of embodied simulation.[4] Calling the landscape "lackluster" and "empty," and comparing it to an "old gray carpet" may not provide readers with a lot of visual detail of the actual Colorado landscape, but it imbues the experience of that landscape with affective value. As George Lakoff and Mark Johnson have shown, newly created metaphors highlight a specific aspect of experience by mapping the unfamiliar—such as

---

4. On the activation of brain regions by metaphorical language, see Aziz-Zadeh and Damasio.

the subjective environmental perception of another person—onto the more familiar—such as one's own memory of the visional impression of an old gray carpet—on the grounds of structural similarity (152). Readers may or may not be personally familiar with the environment of the Great Plains, and that degree of familiarity will doubtlessly influence how they imagine it during the reading process. Regardless of their own experiences, however, the evocation of an old gray carpet gives them an immediate sense of how it looked and felt to that seven-year-old girl beholding it through the glass panes of a train. As Anežka Kuzmičová has pointed out, "There is no straightforward relation between the degree of detail in spatial description on the one hand, and the vividness of spatial imagery and presence on the other" (23). Instead, it is a process of sensorimotor resonance—and thus embodied simulation—that helps create in readers' minds an emotionally salient impression of a narrative environment that presents itself to the young girl as an endless expanse of "gray waste" (Babb, *Owl* 8) and that has a "primordial loneliness to it" (7).

The affectively laden perceptions of Babb's experiencing agent, then, are of central importance to readers' imagination of and emotional relationship to the environment she describes. As Elaine Scarry has pointed out, there are at least two features of narratives that enable readers to have what she calls "non-actual, mimetic perception" (9): one is the evocation of material conditions, the other is the evocation of characters' responses to those conditions that cue readers to empathetically share those responses. In first-person narration, both of these features depend on the narrator's qualia, but other characters can nevertheless be of importance in making the environment emotionally salient for readers. Babb remembers that her mother, who had "never [been] in a place without trees . . . was utterly unprepared for the desolation viewed from the train window. Even the companionship of her piano could not keep back the tears" (*Owl* 7). Readers do not have access to the mother's subjective experience, but the narrator attributes her tears to an emotional state of sadness that is triggered by the "desolation viewed from the train window." The mental image of the weeping woman therefore reinforces, for the reader, the impression of an environment that is harsh and hostile to human survival because it is lacking almost everything that is conducive to human survival: water, plant life, animal life, shelter.[5]

The interesting twist in Babb's memoir—one that resembles the expression of *xerophilia* that we find in the nature writing of Edward Abby, Mary Austin, Terry Tempest Williams, and others—is that she actually grows to *love* that

---

5. Humans are evolutionarily wired to perceive an "empty" environment as threatening because it offers little on which to live. On the perception of uncertain environments, see Kaplan and Easterlin.

inhospitable and harsh environment and that she wants to enable her readers to share that love.[6] The geographer Yi-Fu Tuan claims that familiarity with a certain place "breeds attachment when it doesn't breed contempt," and Babb remembers how despite the hardships she quickly developed a strong topophilic attachment to her new environment (99). This process begins to set in on the morning after her arrival. The first time the family gets up at dawn in their new home, they see

> the big sky turn pink and orange, then blue. The air was of such purity that we stood breathing deeply for the simple pleasure of breathing. Its fragrance was unlike the softer, leafy air we had known. Strong plants that lived in a land of little rain gave into the winds their pungent smells, sagebrush more powerful than all others. We turned around and around to see the full circle of horizon, the perfect meeting of earth and sky. (15)

Packed with vivid sensory imagery, this passage makes it easy for readers to imagine the material conditions of the prairie landscape as well as the family's sensory experience of it. Nothing is left here of the previously evoked "old gray carpet." Instead, readers are cued to imagine vivid colors such as pink, orange, and blue, accompanied by the strong scent of sage and other fragrant herbs. The narrative's primary experiencing agent—Babb's younger self—has completely changed her affective relationship to the prairie, experiencing "pleasure" when breathing in that strong herbal scent of the prairie. And since readers' imaginary experience of that ecological space is inevitably bound to the qualia of the first-person narrator, they are cued to imagine it in an entirely different way than they did before, invited to feel much more positive feelings in response to a large sky, vibrant colors, and invigorating scents. After all—it bears mentioning again—they have no direct access to an "objective" account of the environment or even to the qualia of another experiencer. Readers never get to know what it was truly *like* for Babb's mother to live far away from the city in this excessively simple and often extremely strenuous way. Nor do they get any direct insight into the qualia of Babb's father, who has been toiling on the land with her grandfather long before the women's arrival. Instead, readers are invited to simulate the qualia of a seven-year-old to whom this world is fascinating, not least because she finds out that it is not at all empty but filled with life.

---

6. Xerophilia is the ability of some "desert-loving" plants to survive in extreme conditions. Tom Lynch has extended the term to include the works of writers who love desert places.

Babb's memoir chronicles the challenges of growing up in a place where the crops are mostly doomed to failure, where beloved work animals die due to the harsh conditions and their human owners barely make it through another winter. And yet her narrative is brimming with evocative descriptions of "a world of liquid light, magnetic, overpowering" (33). Not only does the girl become enamored with the peculiar light that suffuses that world but she also feels "close to its animals and birds and sparse growing things, its silence, even its loneliness" (18). It is particularly the omnipresent owls that fascinate her, with their "great immobile star[ing], their heads swivel[ing]. They were watching for prey, the little field mice, no doubt, but to me they were curious, even ominous, an owl on every slender post like a night-blooming flower" (33–34). The girl's young and impressionable mind is awed by the rawness and sensual intensity of this world, "kept silent by a wondering stir of beauty, a longing of spirit asking a first and eternal question of the universe" (33). Readers are invited to share in this sense of awe, delight, and fascination which, in Babb's memory, outshines the hardships of the homesteader life.

Such imaginative sharing of an emotional experience prepares readers for Babb's afterword, and her affirmation that it was precisely this profound emotional experience that allowed her to know intuitively "that everything in the universe is connected, that all life is One," long before understanding the fact on an analytical level (251). The cognitive narratologist Patrick Colm Hogan has suggested that in narrative discourse "the implied author establishes a norm and in effect asks the reader to take up that norm to reflect" upon the elements of the discourse that have been made emotionally salient (*Narrative Discourse* 257). Through vivid sensory imagery, Babb's memoir invites readers to reflect on the interconnectedness of life and on the power of the prairie landscape to shape minds. As she explains in the afterword, she still "treasure[d] the deep influence of those years" (252) when, two decades later, she sat down to write a novel set in the same bioregion but at a time when everything she had cherished as a child had quite literally turned to dust.

EMPATHY, EMOTION, AND ENVIRONMENTAL INJUSTICE IN *WHOSE NAMES ARE UNKNOWN*

Following the destiny of a poor homesteader family from the airless expanse of the Dust Bowl to the flooded refugee camps of California, Babb's novel *Whose Names Are Unknown* could hardly have been titled more appropriately, not only because its fictional protagonists stand in for thousands of nameless "Okies" who fled the fatal Midwestern drought of the 1930s but also because the book itself was quite literally eclipsed by another one.[7] The novel was already under contract with Random House when its market was swept away by the publication of John Steinbeck's bestselling and Pulitzer Prize-winning *The Grapes of Wrath* (1939) whose devastatingly similar plot was in part based on Babb's very own notes about the California working camps (Rodgers x). After several unsuccessful queries at other presses, Babb was forced to shelve her manuscript and then lived just long enough to see its eventual publication by the University of Oklahoma Press in 2004. Now available to readers, *Whose Names Are Unknown* holds its ground regardless of its remarkable structural similarities to Steinbeck's masterpiece.

Robert DeMott has called *The Grapes of Wrath* "one of the most significant environmental novels of the century" because, from the dust storms that sweep the Oklahoma landscape at the beginning of the book to the floods that inundate California farm workers at the end of it, it foregrounds human-nature relationships (xix). The same could be said of *Whose Names Are Unknown*, only that a much larger proportion of its narrative is set in Oklahoma, following the daily lives of dryland farmers in the slow rhythm of the seasons, and that it shows much greater interest in these farmers' complex affective relationships to their environment.

Contemporary readers of Babb's manuscript were deeply touched by it. One of the editors who read it deemed the novel "more honest, moving, and human" than Steinbeck's book (53). Literary luminary Ralph Ellison was deeply impressed by Babb's evocation of place. "In re-reading your novel," he wrote in a letter to her, "I had the same feeling of an emotionally dense atmosphere I experienced during our first conversation (coming up Park Avenue in the dark) that was more of Kansas and the plains than of a taxi and New York" (qtd. in Battat 53). What Ellison describes here is the illusion of *narrative transportation*. Transportation, explain social psychologists Melanie Green et al., is the "psychological immersion into a story," a process that "entails imagery, emotionality, and attentional focus" (37). Regardless of whether we listen to a story (as seems to have been the case during the cab ride Ellison shared with Babb) or read it, we shift our attention away from our actual environment and, as Wojciehowski and Gallese put it, "suspend our grip on the world of our daily occupations" while engaging in processes of embodied simulation that allow us to vividly imagine the alternative world of the story and to react emotionally to it (n. pag.). As a result, we feel transported into that alternative

---

7. As Babb explains in her Author's Note to the novel, the title of the novel "is taken from a legal eviction note: *To John Doe and Mary Doe Whose True Names Are Unknown*" (xiii).

world. It is telling that Ellison singles out his *feeling* "of an emotionally dark dense atmosphere" rather than any particular detail of the landscape Babb described to him both personally and in her novel. We remember things best (though not necessarily most accurately) when they are charged with emotion (Hogan, *Affective* 164) and so it is no wonder that what Ellison associates with Babb's evocation of "Kansas and the plains" is how he *felt* about its "emotionally dark atmosphere" (Kensinger 241).

As in *An Owl on Every Post,* that affective charge results in part from Babb's tendency to channel literary environments through the subjective experience of characters. Unlike the memoir, however, the novel uses an omniscient third-person narrator and, on the surface at least, its characters are fictional. The novel tells the story of the Dunne family's harsh life in an underground dugout on their grandfather's barely subsistent broomcorn farm on the arid high plains of the Oklahoma panhandle, miles from the nearest town. Although it draws directly on Babb's childhood experiences, the fictional setting of the novel is transferred from Colorado to the state that, during the 1930s, would become the epicenter of the Dust Bowl, in the words of environmental historian Donald Worster, "the darkest moment in the twentieth-century history of the southern plains" (4). Babb was living far away from the disaster zone in Los Angeles when she wrote her novel, but she received letters from her mother who was witnessing the developments first-hand in Kansas. In addition, Babb's volunteer work for the Farm Security Administration in the San Joaquin and Imperial Valleys brought her in close contact with the dispossessed farmers who had already left the Midwest behind and now sought refuge in the quickly established camps in the hope that they would find work in California's orchards. Written during the nights that followed her long days in the camps, *Whose Names Are Unknown* is thus a fictional compound of Babb's remembered first-hand experiences and various second-hand accounts she received, a story that is at once fiction and nonfiction to the point of using the words of her mother's letters verbatim in one of the most dramatic moments of the narrative.

And yet, the pleasure, fascination, and delight that pervade Babb's memoir are still present in the early pages of the novel. The following passage is taken from a moment in the narrative after Julia Dunne has miscarried her baby as a result of her strenuous walk in the middle of the severe thunderstorm described at the beginning of this essay. Julia's husband Milt is deeply affected by the loss of what would have been his first son and close to despair over his inability to wrest a decent harvest from the land's meager soil. Despite his desperation, however, he feels a deep connection to that land:

> A deepening coolness and dusty smell of buffalo grass mingled with the freshness of the field, and now and then the disturbing smell of sagebrush blowing strongly made him turn from his thoughts to a pleasant awareness of the fragrant wind. This was a western wind, heavy with the pungent, lively smell of desert weeds and the dry earth filled with the sun. He felt the night around him, the great endless dark, and the intimate friendly feeling sprang up in him for the road that his feet followed by touch and familiarity. (60)

Once again, Babb foregrounds a character's qualia in her evocation of a natural environment. Instead of describing the physical features of the landscape, she focuses on Milt's subjective experience of it. As Erin Battat has pointed out, "Babb is at her best as a writer in her ability to find language that evokes a landscape characterized by the absence of physical features" (54). In the "deepening coolness" of the night, Milt is alert to the "dusty smell of the buffalo grass" and the freshness of the field," the "disturbing smell of sagebrush" and the "pungent, lively smell of desert weeds." It is too dark to see the physical features of the landscape and so Milt predominantly experiences it on the olfactory level. Readers are invited to emphatically share Milt's qualia through embodied simulation both in this nocturnal moment of pleasure and topophilic appreciation.

Only instants later, however, these positive emotions are overshadowed by "a mounting hulk of fear and doubt, ponderous with the question of the future uncertain" (60). This, too, is an emotional response to the environment, but one that is colored by Milt's understanding that the environmental conditions of the prairie determine the life of his family. As a farmer, he is given to searching the sky for signs of coming weather:

> He looked at the edges of the sky, hoping for clouds or the steely haze that might mean early snow. Off to the northwest a bank of clouds lay just darker than the sky, still like a great animal waiting to spring, showing the sleepy fire of its eyes when the faint autumn lightning winked. It was far away and would spend its strength on other land. His wheat and that of every prairie farm was waiting on the ground for rain. (60–61)

Whereas the previous passage limited readers' access to the narrative environment to his sense of smell, readers are here cued to simulate Milt's changing visual perception. Instead of a "great endless dark," he now can make out cloud formations, visual information that is not neutral but affectively charged by his hope for rain and his fear that it will not come. Like his wife Julia, Milt tends to personify nature, attributing not only material agency but also awareness to it. He believes that his land is "waiting" for rain, while the animal-like clouds seem to have eyes and the power to decide where they will pour their water. Babb's use of simile and metaphor suggests to readers on the cognitive level that the Dunne family is at nature's mercy. At the same time, the evocation of "a great animal waiting to spring"—an evolutionarily salient image that suggests immediate danger—allows them to empathize with Milt's feelings of fear through processes of embodied simulation.

The second passage that I want to consider is located near the middle of the novel, when the dust storms have reached the Oklahoma panhandle, burying everything in their way under heaps of dirt. Here, Babb once again takes pains to evoke the environmental conditions in a way that allows readers to experience not only how they look, taste, and feel, but also what emotions they evoke in those who are subjected to them. The dust is so all-pervasive that Julia can feel it "in her clothes and on her skin, in her mouth and nose, on everything she touched" (86). It is an unpleasant, suffocating physical sensation that amplifies the family's fear that the storm will take their crops. Milt picks up handfuls of dust and senses its "alien texture . . . fine and silky, with an oily feel" (87). His mind is spinning as it draws up multiple possible scenarios of how he might be able to save his crop or plant another one before the end of the season. Julia, for her part, begins to "keep a record of the strange phenomenon of the dust" (90). This is the part of the book that Babb took almost verbatim from her mother's letters, now transformed into Julia's first-person account as she tries to capture her subjective experience of the situation:

> *April 25.* Blew all night and still blowing almost black. It's a terrible feeling to be in this blackness. You don't know what is going on outside and imagine all kinds of things. It is so still, just blows and blows but as if there is no wind, just rolling clouds of dust. We haven't seen light for two days. I am worried about my chickens, some of them acting droopy. Dad is sleeping in the barn again, worrying about the horses. (94)

The sudden change in narrative voice and perspective allows for an even greater degree of immediacy and immersion as Julia shares her plight seemingly unfiltered by another narrating agency. Her voice is colored by anger, fear, exhaustion, and naked despair as the farm and everything that lives on it is submerged in dust for weeks and weeks on end. As a first-person narrator, she invites readers to empathetically feel along with her deeply negative emotions as they simulate in their minds what it is like for her to "hear the cattle bawling for water," sounding "so pitiful and helpless" and to lose her beloved neighbors to the horrible, suffocating dust (94).

Narratologist Howard Sklar has argued that readers' sympathy results from at least two basic components: "the heightened awareness of the suffering of another" and "a judgment of the explicit or implicit unfairness of that suffering" (28). Babb's novel aims to create such awareness by painting a vivid picture of the horrific environmental conditions of the Dust Bowl and by foregrounding how it affects her sympathetic, hard-working characters who do not deserve to suffer because they are not guilty of any deliberate wrongdoing. The Dunne's misery comes in many guises; it is emotional, physical, and deeply existential, and not all of it is weather-related. As Battat has noted, "The Dunnes and their neighbors bristle within a system of modern finance in which they are at the mercy of nameless, faceless institutional creditors" (52). Such institutions have no mercy, and neither does the environment care about the farmers' desperate struggle. "No use to keep on writing dust, dust, dust," decides Julia in her last journal entry, "Seems it will outlast us" (Babb, *Whose Names* 95). The narrative will prove her right, but instead of making it seem like an inevitable decision, it invites readers to share in the heartache involved in abandoning the place one is materially and emotionally attached to, the deeply felt sense that you simply "can't leave" and that circumstances nevertheless force you to do exactly that (120). It is this painful emotional struggle between place attachment and the need to survive that is at the heart of Babb's novel. As readers, we come to understand the desperation that comes with leaving behind what you love, whether it is a person or a place. The history of the United States has seen many forms of dispossession and displacement, and from the early days of the republic, the Sooner State has played a prominent role in some of the most notorious of them. As someone who grew up in "the Indian country of Oklahoma" and who, as a child, considered "the Oto Indians near Red Rock" her "other family," her "other home" (*Owl* 7), Babb was acutely aware of the economic, spiritual, and emotional consequences of Indian removal policies. And while her novel focuses on the plight of the poor white "Okie" farmers who we tend to associate with the Dirty Thirties, it also sheds a critical light on communities of color whose suffering is just as undeserved and unfair.

Like the Joads in *The Grapes of Wrath*, the Dunnes eventually give up their struggle and migrate west to work in the orchards of California, where they are subjected to different but equally unjust conditions of agricultural production. Unlike Steinbeck, however, Babb allows her characters to acknowledge the African American, Filipino, and Mexican migrant workers who toil next to them in the orchards "for the same reason we do" (*Whose Names* 180). Fueled by the understanding of a shared destiny and the recognition that "*I'm no better'n he is; he's no worse,*" Milt solidarizes with nonwhite workers in order to fight for higher wages and better living conditions (180). By the end of the novel, they all have been jailed for organizing strikes, but this has not changed their understanding that "all the men [who] had been standing alone in the wide valleys, dwarfed beneath the western sky" must be united by the "desperate need to stand together as one man" (222). Battat reminds us that Babb drew on her own first-hand experiences as Farm Security Administration employee in the migrant camps in her imagining of "interracial alliances among white, Filipino, and African American workers" against the exploitative practices of California farmers (12). It may very well have been these experiences that led her to develop "cross-racial empathy" (Battat 61), which she in turn tries to evoke in her readers as she expands the cast of characters on the final pages of her novel. Suzanne Keen has argued that character empathy can be used strategically by politically committed writers, since simulating the subjective experience of people whom we know to be fictitious may "disarm [us] of some of the protective layers of cautious reasoning that may inhibit empathy in the real world" (69). *Whose Names Are Unknown* was Babb's attempt to do such disarming by evoking sympathy and moral allegiance for a family of white dryland farmers and then inviting readers to extend those feelings to other, nonwhite families who work the land under similarly intolerable conditions. Perhaps it would have succeeded in engaging contemporary readers in such a critique of social and environmental injustice had it been published in its time.

CONCLUSION

Particularly important from the perspective of econarratology is that—in both of her books—Babb decided to give so much room to her protagonists' perception of the prairie environment and their complex emotional relationship to it. By giving access to these characters' qualia, Babb invites readers not only to see that environment through their eyes but to also smell it through their noses, listen to it through their ears, and feel it through their nerves. Arguably *all* narration involves some kind of experiencing consciousness that provides readers with information about the storyworld, but sensing and feeling along with the protagonist placed *within* that storyworld adds a different dimension. Detailed descriptions by an omniscient narrative voice may provide readers with a clear understanding of the physical properties of a storyworld, but the physical presence of an experiencing agent allows for the embodied simulation of personal exposure that adds an affective charge to that understanding. More important still, the feelings readers develop for characters in the course of a narrative will likely influence their imagined experience of environments that seem beneficial or threatening to those characters and therefore their emotional response to them.

Empirical studies have shown that "labeling a narrative as fact versus fiction does not affect the intensity of emotional response" (Green et al. 37) and yet we have to consider Keen's argument that labeling a story as fiction may have a liberating effect on readers that might lead to greater character empathy and thus to a somewhat different experience of the narrative environment. *Whose Names Are Unknown* invites readers to see the prairie through the eyes of a fictional family of farmers in order to understand the full emotional extent of what it means when everything you care for turns to dust, when you are uprooted, displaced, and disowned. Like *An Owl on Every Post,* the novel is a mental "instruction manual" that makes it easy for readers to simulate in their minds the sensory and sensual dimensions of the prairie environment as they present themselves to an experiencing agent. Unlike the memoir, however, the novel links the sensual evocation of the landscape to the tragic fate of the people who have become attached to such a difficult place and who are forced to leave it behind. "We ain't farmers anymore'n a man who works in a shoe factory is a custom boot-maker," declares Milt bitterly at the end of the novel to a racially and ethnically mixed group of migrant workers. "We're a lot of parts that can't stand alone because we haven't got an acre of our own to keep our feet on" (216). *Whose Names Are Unknown* is the story of this material and spiritual deprivation, a story that tries to give readers a sense of *what it is like* to experience it in order to allow for a fuller—and fully embodied—understanding of the migrant worker's situation.

What we may take away from these readings of Babb's little-known work is not only that cognitive econarratology can help us get a better sense of how exactly literary texts evoke virtual environments in emotionally salient ways but also, as I have shown, that such readings must not ignore the larger social, political, and ecological context of a given literary text. As James has suggested, an econarratological approach will also take "the extratextual world as a central concern," thereby considering "the relationship between the text, the reader, and the physical world that lies beyond the text" (14, 29). Given the current interest in the body and in the role of affect and emotion in our interaction both with the natural world itself and with cultural texts that represent that world, I believe that the insights of cognitive science and related narratological approaches can be highly productive for ecocritical analysis. As an emergent subfield of ecocriticsm, cognitive econarratology has the potential to open a new dimension in the analysis of environmental narratives of all kinds.

WORKS CITED

Aziz-Zadeh, Lisa, and Antonio Damasio. "Embodied Semantics for Actions: Findings from Functional Brain Imaging." *Journal of Physiology—Paris,* vol. 102, 2008, pp. 35–39.

Babb, Sanora. *An Owl on Every Post.* 1970. Muse Ink Press, 2012.

———. *Whose Names Are Unknown.* U of Oklahoma P, 2004.

Batatt, Erin Royston. *Ain't Got No Home: America's Great Migrations and the Making of an Inter-racial Left.* U of North Carolina P, 2014.

Caracciolo, Marco. *The Experientiality of Narrative: An Enactivist Approach.* De Gruyter, 2014.

DeMott, Robert. Introduction. *The Grapes of Wrath,* by John Steinbeck, Penguin, 2006.

Easterlin, Nancy. "Cognitive Ecocriticism: Human Wayfinding, Sociality, and Literary Interpretation." *Introduction to Cognitive Cultural Studies.* Edited by Lisa Zunshine, Johns Hopkins UP, 2010, pp. 257–75.

Gallese, Vittorio. "Bodily Selves in Relation: Embodied Simulation as Second-person Perspective on Intersubjectivity." *Philosophical Transactions of the Royal Society B,* vol. 369, 2014, pp. 1–10. doi.org/10.1098/rstb.2013.0177.

———. "Mirror Neurons and Art." *Art and the Senses.* Edited by Francesca Bacci and David Melcher, Oxford UP, 2011, pp. 455–63.

Gerrig, Richard J. "Conscious and Unconscious Processes in Readers' Narrative Experiences." *Current Trends in Narratology.* Edited by Greta Olson, De Gruyter, 2011, pp. 37–60.

———. *Experiencing Narrative Worlds: On the Psychological Activities of Reading.* Westview Press, 1998.

Green, Melanie C., Christopher Chatham, and Marc A. Sestir. "Emotion and Transportation into Fact and Fiction." *Scientific Study of Literature,* vol. 2, no. 1, 2012, pp. 37–59.

Herman, David. "Storyworld." *Routledge Encyclopedia of Narrative Theory.* Edited by David Herman, Manfred Jahn, and Marie-Laure Ryan, Routledge, 2005, pp. 569–70.

Hogan, Patrick Colm. *Affective Narratology.* U of Nebraska P, 2011.

———. *Narrative Discourse: Authors and Narrators in Literature, Film, and Art.* The Ohio State UP, 2013.

Jacobs, Arthur M., and Raoul Schrott. "Captivated by the Cinema of Mind." *Concentration.* Edited by Ingo Niermann. 2014, pp. 118–49.

James, Erin. *The Storyworld Accord: Econarratology and Postcolonial Narratives.* U of Nebraska P, 2015.

Kaplan, Stephen. "Perception of an Uncertain Environment." *Humanscape: Environments for People.* Edited by Stephen Kaplan and Rachel Kaplan, Ulrich's, 1978.

Keen, Suzanne. "Narrative Empathy." *Toward a Cognitive Theory of Narrative Acts.* Edited by Frederick Luis Aldama, U of Texas P, 2010, pp. 61–94.

Kensinger, Elizabeth A. "Remembering Emotional Experiences: The Contribution of Valence and Arousal." *Reviews in the Neurosciences,* vol. 15, no. 4, 2004, pp. 241–51.

Keysers, Christian, and Valeria Gazzola. "Expanding the Mirror: Vicarious Activity for Actions, Emotions, and Sensations." *Current Opinion in Neurobiology,* vol. 19, 2009, pp. 1–6.

Kuzmičová, Anežka. "Presence in the Reading of Literary Narrative: A Case for Motor Enactment." *Semiotica,* vol. 189, 2012, pp. 23–48.

Lakoff, George, and Mark Johnson. *Metaphors We Live By*. U of Chicago P, 2003.

Levin, Janet. "Qualia." *The MIT Encyclopedia of the Cognitive Sciences*. Edited by Robert E. Wilson and Frank C. Keil, MIT Press, 1999.

Lynch, Tom. *Xerophilia: Ecocritical Explorations of Southwestern Literature*. Texas Tech UP, 2008.

Rizzolatti, Giacomo, and Corrado Sinigaglia. *Mirrors in the Brain: How Our Minds Share Actions and Emotions,* Oxford UP, 2008.

Rodgers, Lawrence R. Foreword. *Whose Names Are Unknown,* by Sanora Babb, U of Oklahoma P, 2004, pp. vii–xii.

Scarry, Elaine. *Dreaming by the Book*. Princeton UP, 1999.

Sklar, Howard. *The Art of Sympathy in Fiction: Forms of Ethical and Emotional Persuasion*. John Benjamins Publishing Company, 2013.

Steinbeck, John. *The Grapes of Wrath*. Penguin, 2006.

Tuan, Yi-Fu. *Topophilia: A Study of Environmental Perception, Attitudes, and Values*. Prentice Hall, 1974.

Weik von Mossner, Alexa. *Affective Ecologies: Empathy, Emotion, and Environmental Narrative*. The Ohio State UP, 2017.

Wojciehowski, Hannah, and Vittorio Gallese. "How Stories Make Us Feel: Toward an Embodied Narratology." *California Italian Studies,* vol. 2, no. 1, 2011.

Worster, Donald. *Dust Bowl: The Southern Plains in the 1930s*. Oxford UP, 2004.

CHAPTER 7

Finding a Practical Narratology in the Work of Restoration Ecology

MATTHEW M. LOW

IN THE opening essay of *American Places* (1981), Wallace Stegner discerns that "when literally nothing is known, anything is possible," an observation he applies specifically to the fantastical visions and delusions of grandeur that characterized early explorations of the so-called New World, from passage-ways opening access to the riches of the East, to the cities of gold and foun-tains of youth that lay hidden within ("Inheritance" 4). "Inheritance" goes on to document the centuries-long process of acceptance—even resignation—that Europeans and, eventually, Euro-Americans had to undertake before "whatever authentic wonders of great rivers, mountains, plains, minerals, oil and coal, deep soil, fertile valleys . . . could be seen straight and inventoried in realistic terms" (14). Over half a millennium after those initial forays into and through North America, my work turns to Stegner's observation with a sense of irony, in part because a vast majority of us living on this very same ground, especially the midcontinent, find ourselves once again at a time when virtually nothing is known about the land that those earliest explorers passed over. Spe-cifically, with less than one-tenth of one percent of the native tallgrass prairie ecosystem remaining and only fractionally higher percentages remaining of the related mixed- and shortgrass prairie ecosystems, "knowledge," to borrow another observation from Stegner, has been "postponed" (7). The greed that preoccupied the earliest explorers from directly experiencing the bountiful resources of the prairie has been replaced by greed that strips the land of those same resources, thereby prohibiting direct experience of them in the present.

Writing from a strictly environmental perspective, the current status of the North American prairie as a largely unloved and unmissed landscape (but not "lost" or "vanished," as much recent coverage of this region has phrased it) is one of the great injustices of the "destructive infancy" of America's nationhood that Stegner describes in the latter paragraphs of "Inheritance." However, coupling an environmental—or ecocritical—response to the prairie's precarious position with some of the key components of narrative theory opens space for a more hopeful outcome. In fact, Stegner's quotation at the outset works so well because the second half of his antithesis, "anything is possible," is itself a foundational postulation of many subsets of narrative theory, including postclassical and cognitive narratologies, as well as studies of "unnatural" narrative. Take, for instance, Marie-Laure Ryan's explication of "possible worlds" in the *Living Handbook of Narratology*: "The foundation of [Possible Worlds] theory is the idea that reality—conceived as the sum of the imaginable rather than as the sum of what exists physically—is a universe composed of a plurality of distinct worlds" ("Possible Worlds"). In other words, when looking for a tool to make present what has been rendered absent—such as the North American prairie—one ought not overlook the capacity of narrative to imagine a world other than "the sum of what exists physically." This is not to say that narrative alone can bring the prairie back to its former prominence, but when "literally nothing is known" by those with the most to lose from its absence, what David Herman terms the "world-creating potential of stories" must be prioritized alongside land acquisition, reseeding, reintroduction of keystone animal species, and prescribed fire as necessary elements in the effort to rehabilitate the midcontinent's native grassland ecosystems (*Storytelling* 103).

The title of this essay uses the term "practical narratology" not so much out of the desire for a coinage but as an effort to interject an immensely useful and compelling theoretical field into the world-at-large. Those familiar with ecocritical discourse will no doubt recognize a reference, if not necessarily an homage, to Glen A. Love's influential work *Practical Ecocriticism* (2003), which he poses as a step forward for ecocriticism that looks to "test [ecocritical] ideas against the workings of physical reality," while also utilizing what he calls "the empirical spirit of the sciences" (7). Love's work has an important place in the evolution of ecocriticism as a critical field, but my goal here is not simply to mimic his work within the realm of narrative theory. Instead, my use of the term "practical" originates from the desire to address a single question. It has been my experience that the critical study of narrative is the most effective means for gleaning insights into various modes of media and communication, from canonical literature to mainstream political discourse. Thus, I cannot help but wonder: might this field also be applied to a more functional outreach or extension? If it can, which is the case I will make here, then given the dire consequences of our myriad looming environmental crises, perhaps such functionality could be used to reconstruct vibrant, thriving, healthy storyworlds and actual worlds simultaneously. In other words, a practical narratology with an environmental focus would look to combine the cognitive turn in narrative theory—for instance, immersion in the reconstructed storyworld of an ecocentric narrative—with direct, embodied experience of landscapes in the process of ecological restoration or reconstruction. Though having a more narrowly focused interest in how narratology intersects with environmental discourse, my term is deeply influenced by Herman's belief that "narratives can be used to make sense of what goes on in the world via accounts of the experiences of persons—experiences that crucially involve, without being wholly reducible to, sets of beliefs, motivations, and goals" (*Storytelling* 74). Being more firmly grounded in "the experience of persons," the concept of practical narratology can be put to use both on the prairie and throughout the world, overcoming a number of obstacles that are faced by any meaningful response to our ongoing environmental crises—a list that includes misunderstanding, ignorance (willful and otherwise), mistrust, and especially as it pertains to the prairie, insufficient opportunity for immersion in an ecosystem through either a fully developed prairie storyworld or an intact prairie in the actual world.

In recent years, scholarship has emerged looking to place narrative theory in dialogue with other fields and discourses once thought beyond the purview of work done traditionally in the humanities. Much of this work has been done to show that the scope and reach of narrative analysis is not limited to what can be found on a page or screen. For instance, Nancy Easterlin closes her chapter on "Minding Ecocriticism" from *A Biocultural Approach to Literary Theory and Interpretation* (2012) by posing a challenge to ecocritics who have the opportunity to "illuminate values, relationships, social networks, and traumatic events [that] affect our positive constructions and terrible devaluations of natural and built locales. [For them,] literature will be a profound resource, showing that the capacity to trust and love other humans makes it possible to love the world" (151). Though not stated outright, an essential component of Easterlin's vision is taking the lessons learned through ecocritical analysis of literary texts and putting them in practice in actual world scenarios of ecological restoration and reconstruction. Positioning her work more squarely in the domain of cognitive narratology, Erin James's *The Storyworld Accord: Econarratology and Postcolonial Narratives* (2015) uses the title phrase to advocate "for an environmental treaty sensitive to the cultural differences of environmental imaginations and experiences gleaned from the reading of narratives" (253). As with Easterlin, James desires to see the work of ecocriticism more actively engage "narratological taxonomies, neologisms, and traditions," especially those of cognitive narratology, in order to take advantage of advances made in understanding "the human intellectual and emotional *processing* of narratives to query how narratives and readers interact" (4, 16). Given the shifting landscape of all modes of academic discourse and the growing need for a wider range of inputs into every facet of environmental discourse, the intersections that Easterlin and James model in their work, be they "biocultural" or "econarratological," enable the type of analysis that I am pursuing here. Indeed, the work undertaken in this study owes a great deal to James's theorization of econarratology, in particular her observation that "narratives . . . allow readers to simulate and live in environments they would otherwise be denied and experience those environments from an alternative perspective" (24). There are even notable resonances between James's focus on postcolonial narratives and my own emphasis on prairie storyworlds, despite some obvious cultural and geographical distances. In particular, postcolonial narratives push back against hegemonic narratives perpetuated within dominant discourse by opening up "culturally diverse understandings and experiences of global environments" that might otherwise be missed without engaging narratives outside the traditional canon (24). Similarly, my effort to establish a practical narratology focuses on a North American ecosystem that has been subjected to close to two hundred years of steady and intensifying marginalization, beginning with some of the earliest and most enduring written depictions of the prairie as the "Great American Desert," and continuing with modern-day dismissals of the entire region as "flyover" country.[1]

Looking back briefly to my days as a graduate student, I recall that my specialization began with ecocriticism, which then led (as a lifelong Midwesterner completely ignorant of the region's native ecology) to an interest in the prairie and the associated concerns of restoration ecology, including participation in some hands-on fieldwork like seed harvesting and prescribed burning.

---

1. A glaring omission from the present study is the injustice brought upon the indigenous human communities that made their homes in this region for millennia prior to Euro-American settlement. Though this aspect of the topic is beyond the scope of this essay, it is a topic that I have written about extensively elsewhere, in particular in those places where I have advocated for "prairie survivance" based on the work of Anishinaabe writer and scholar Gerald Vizenor. My work on this topic has been heavily influenced by three texts he has written or edited: *Manifest Manners: Narratives on Postindian Survivance* (1994), *Fugitive Poses: Native American Indian Scenes of Absence and Presence* (1998), and *Survivance: Narratives of Native Presence* (2008).

Only later did the field of narrative theory present itself as an immensely useful way of conceptualizing the perpetuation of the prairie's image as barren, empty, and worthless—space, as Doreen Massey phrases it, "to be crossed and maybe conquered"—through travel narratives written by early visitors like Washington Irving and reinforced by the likes of Buffalo Bill Cody and others in the latter half of the nineteenth century (4). With few exceptions, this image of the prairie has predominated continuously among those residing in this region from the opening, and so-called "closing," of the frontier through today. It was only upon reading Adam Zachary Newton's *Narrative Ethics* (1995/2009) that an understanding of narrative's role in perpetuating this image of the prairie began to take shape, illuminated largely by the principal focus of Newton's inquiry: "narrative as claim, as risk, as responsibility, as gift, as price. Above all, as an ethics, narrative is performance or act—purgative . . . malignant . . . historically recuperative . . . erotic and redemptive . . . obsessive and coercive" (7). In other words, telling stories about the prairie certainly had a price, that price being the eventual removal of all but small remnants of the indigenous plant, animal, and human communities that thrived on the midcontinent prior to Euro-American settlement. Viewed more optimistically, however, Newton's identification of some ethical imperative within the telling of stories gives hope that narratives of the prairie might also be a "gift," or at the very least "recuperative," in the spirit of Thomas King's challenge in *The Truth about Stories* (2003): "Want a different ethic? Tell a different story" (164). The last couple of decades have indeed seen a small uptick in these "different" sorts of stories about the prairie, including in the fiction of Annie Proulx and Marilynne Robinson, nonfictional texts by John Price and Paul Johnsgard, the poetry of Ted Kooser, and the photography and film of Michael Forsberg, among others. Their work, taken together, represents a formidable advocacy for the ecology of the midcontinent, though still not formidable enough to overcome the prevailing, fatalistic narrative of the prairie as a place long gone and never much worth saving in the first place.

In searching for common ground among ecocriticism, restoration ecology, and narrative theory, the concept of "worlds" has emerged as central to utilizing narrative as a means for responding to the crises facing the prairie. Theorization of "possible worlds," "actual worlds," and especially "storyworlds"—a concept that has become increasingly prominent in studies working from within the cognitive turn of narrative studies—turns out to be particularly apt in looking into an ecosystem that has been subject to routine removal from both narratives and landscapes of the North American midcontinent over the last two centuries. Herman's definition of "storyworld" in the *Routledge Encyclopedia of Narrative Theory* (2010), for one, offers a clear delineation of the ways in which this term moves the study of narrative away from mere close reading or even exegesis, and into the lives and experiences of readers themselves:

> *Storyworld* better captures what might be called the ecology of narrative interpretation. In trying to make sense of a narrative, interpreters attempt to reconstruct not just what happened but also the surrounding context or environment embedding *storyworld* existents, their attributes, and the actions and events in which they are involved. Indeed, the grounding of stories in storyworlds goes a long way toward explaining narratives' immersiveness, their ability to "transport" interpreters into places and times that they must occupy for the purposes of narrative comprehension. Interpreters do not merely reconstruct a sequence of events and a set of existents, but imaginatively (emotionally, viscerally) inhabit a world in which things matter, agitate, exalt, repulse, provide grounds for laughter and grief, and so on—both for narrative participants and for interpreters of the story. More than reconstructed timelines and inventories of existents, then, storyworlds are mentally and emotionally projected environments in which interpreters are called upon to live out complex blends of cognitive and imaginative response. (570)

Herman's use of "ecology" at the opening of this quotation is not an effort to align his cognitive narratology with environmental or ecocritical discourse, but it is suggestive that he recognizes crossover of some terminology between these fields. Indeed, this whole quotation is filled with such concurrent terminology, including "reconstruct," "embedding," "environment," "immersiveness," and "inhabit." Such concurrence is found in Herman's other writing on this topic and particularly in *Story Logic* (2004), where he goes so far as to claim that "narrative comprehension" itself ought to be considered "a process of (re)constructing storyworlds on the basis of textual cues and the inferences that they make possible" (6). Ultimately, it is the word "reconstruction" that is repeatedly invoked in Herman's writing about storyworlds that brings narrative theory and restoration ecology in most direct dialogue with one another, as in both fields it expresses a means of bringing "worlds" into existence.

Looking at a brief literary example will help elucidate these points of connection that have been identified in the long quotation from Herman above, as well as show how practical narratology can be extended from a storyworld to an actual world. As noted above, some of the most complete and compelling descriptions of the prairie come from travel narratives written about the grasslands of the midcontinent by its earliest Euro-American visitors, a good number of whom would go on to miscast the region as barren and desolate, despite the vivid storyworlds created within their own accounts. This was not always the case, thankfully, and the journals produced by most members of the Corps of Discovery expedition—Lewis and Clark themselves, but also others who wrote extensively about their experiences along the Missouri River watershed—lack the same apathy or outright hostility toward the prairie that characterizes the accounts that came after. For instance, a short selection from Sergeant Patrick Gass's journal illustrates the prairie's unceasing involvement in all matters of life and death for the men who would spend the better part of two years immersed in the midcontinent's native ecology. This example concerns the only death of a member of the Corps of Discovery, Sergeant Charles Floyd, an event that is striking today not only for its singularity in the two-year expedition but also for its clear impact on his comrades as it happened:

> Here Sergeant Floyd died, notwithstanding every possible effort was made by the commanding officers, and other persons, to save his life. We went on about a mile to high prairie hills on the north side of the river, and there interred his remains in the most decent manner our circumstances would admit; we then proceeded a mile further to a small river on the same side and encamped. Our commanding officers gave it the name of Floyd's river; to perpetuate the memory of the first man who had fallen in this important expedition.

Gass's brief narration of Sergeant Floyd's death is worth thinking about in connection to Herman's definition of storyworld. On the one hand, this is an exemplary moment from the journals in which most readers will "imaginatively . . . inhabit a world in which things matter": the expedition is not just navigating an unfamiliar environment, but dealing with human tragedy in the face of so many unknowns. That they traveled with Floyd's body an additional mile from where he succumbed to his illness, to a place of "high prairie hills" in order to bury him "in the most decent manner our circumstances would admit," shows that the physical surroundings played a role in their conception of the solemnity of this event and are thereby an important component of the storyworld that later readers of the journals would "mentally and emotionally project."[2] On the other hand, the importance of the storyworld invoked by Gass's account is all the more striking to anyone who has visited,

---

2. George Catlin's 1832 painting *View from Floyd's Grave, 1300 Miles Above St. Louis,* currently held by the Smithsonian American Art Museum, provides a vivid depiction of this spot along the Missouri River as the Corps of Discovery would have encountered it prior to the settlement and development of what would become Sioux City, Iowa. An earlier sketch of the place can also be found in Plate 118 of Caitlin's *Letters and Notes on the Manners, Customs, and Condition of the North American Indian,* vol. 2.

or even driven past, the obelisk marking Floyd's actual world gravesite on the southern edge of Sioux City, Iowa. Twice moved because of fears of erosion and grave robbers, the current location of the Sergeant Floyd Monument no longer overlooks native tallgrass prairie or even the small tributary bearing his name; instead, its slightly elevated view encompasses a busy interstate, an industrial site, apartment complexes, a strip mall, and a narrow stretch of the Missouri River "tamed" by the Army Corps of Engineers nearly a century and a half after the Corps of Discovery's initial passage through it. This most certainly is not the only instance of a storyworld superseding the current physical status of an ugly locale or degraded ecosystem, examples of which abound in the journals from the Corps of Discovery themselves. Yet this example is notable, perhaps paradigmatic, for documenting the way in which every facet of the prairie has been subjected to removal, neglect, or abuse, even parts of it demarcated as sacred space by those considered among the most important Euro-Americans to transverse this region. The prairie's presence in Gass's account, and its revitalization in his storyworld, is made all the more urgent by its continued absence from the ground where it once thrived.

Returning to Herman's various efforts to define "storyworld" over the last two decades, of most importance to the present study is the recurrence of the verb "reconstruct"—sometimes also written as "(re)construct" or, as a nominalization, "reconstruction"—to describe the process undertaken by the reader/interpreter of a given narrative to piece together the "textual blueprint" that ultimately enables the existence of a storyworld. This verb is not used exclusively ("creation," "modification," "modeling," or "(re)modeling" all come up as well), but the consistency with which it is used by Herman, and thereby other theorists responding to or building upon his work, warrants further inquiry. Perhaps not incidentally, "reconstruct" shares a root with two prominent fields within literary studies that have influenced narrative theory at virtually all levels: first, the structuralisms that built upon Saussure's linguistic theory and served as a model for those at the forefront of the "narrative turn," like Genette, Greimas, and others; and second, the poststructuralism and deconstruction that emerged in the latter half of the twentieth century with the goal of destabilizing, if not upending entirely, more traditional approaches to interpreting a text or narrative. If structuralism deprived readers of meaningful contribution to the interpretive process by pinpointing inflexible universalities in any given narrative, it could also be said that no small number of adherents to the fields of poststructuralism and/or deconstruction undercut those universalities to such a degree as to render the interpretive process all but meaningless. Thus, giving readers an opportunity to "reconstruct" crucial elements of a narrative is an empowering gesture that revives the presence of human agency in the transmission of narratives: in other words, "storytelling practices are inextricably interlinked with ascriptions of intentions to persons" (Herman, *Storytelling* 23). In order for a practical narratology to be effective in any way, recognizing the role of human minds, and human bodies, in the creation, transmission, and interpretation of narrative is an essential first step.

Human agency, or "ascriptions of intentions to persons," also lies at the heart of how "reconstruction" is understood and practiced in the field of restoration ecology, though it should be noted that there is some fluidity in how this term and related terms are used. The Society for Ecological Restoration, for its part, sees the broader work undertaken by professionals in this field as "*ecocentric restoration,* which is restoration focused on the literal re-creation of a previously existing ecosystem, including not just some but all its parts and processes" (Jordan and Lubick 2). Based on this fairly straightforward definition, when applied generally to the process of rehabilitating compromised or damaged ecosystems worldwide—such as forest, coast, mountain, desert, and so on—"restoration" is an adaptable term that describes the sort of work undertaken to "restore" something that has been lost or removed. However, as one narrows in on the prairie, some distinction is made between the work of "restoration" and the work of "reconstruction," both of which are further contrasted with the work of "preservation."[3] Another recent publication in the field of restoration ecology, for example, names "reconstruction" as one of the activities that might be undertaken in the larger process of restoration, specifically as it concerns the prairie: "Landscape reconstruction involves its practitioners in actively shaping (or reshaping) the natural world, creating (or re-creating) communities of species that can live together in an ongoing, self-sustaining way . . . Prairie restoration is the best known example" (Baldwin et al. 9). Instead of clearly delineating that "restoration" is *this* and "reconstruction" is *that,* this definition places an emphasis on the hands-on, physical labor of reconstruction, which again points back to human agency. Carl Kurtz's *A Practical Guide to Prairie Reconstruction* (2001/2013) offers the most straightforward usage of this term, and is therefore most helpful in linking actual world ecology back to the use of "reconstruction" in the context of

---

3. "Preservation" generally refers to protecting remnant species (both plants and animals) and/or ecosystems from further development or degradation. For some, such as Chad Graeve at Hitchcock Nature Center in Pottawattamie County, Iowa, priority ought to be placed on preserving the remnant prairies and oak savannas still mostly intact in small patches throughout the midcontinent. For others, such as the contributors to the essay collection *Beyond Preservation* (see below), the idea of "preservation" is misguided because it assumes that certain parts of nature haven't been compromised by human activity, which they don't believe to be true. Instead, they advocate for restoration, or reconstruction, projects that come as close to historic ecosystems as possible. My own work is not picking a side in this debate, though I would generally refer to the work being done at a place like Rochester Cemetery, which is a pioneer cemetery in Cedar County, Iowa, that contains one of the most ecological diverse remnant prairies and oak savannas left intact in the State of Iowa, as "preservation."

narrative storyworlds: "The term 'reconstruction' means starting prairie from scratch in a bare crop field," a process that involves "restoring a diversity of native grasses, sedges, and forbs (a collective name for prairie flowers) and implementing a management plan" (2). Looking at these various definitions, a point of agreement is the fact that "reconstruction" involves hands-on labor, or is something that ecologists *do*. Moreover, in personal conversations that I have had with restoration ecologists and land managers, who use a fluidity of terms to describe rehabilitating prairie ecosystems, there is at least agreement that the work undertaken in reconstruction entails starting with less (if any) intact prairie and involves more time and resources to achieve the desired outcome of "not just some but all its parts and processes" (Jordan and Lubick 2).

Agreement is also found among these definitions in the fact that the reconstructions of prairie ecosystems undertaken by restoration ecologists and land managers are "intentional systems," in much the same way that Herman observes intentionality in narratives and the storyworlds they contain. A prairie reconstruction is not going to come about by accident, even in those areas with the most resilient seed banks.[4] Likewise, a storyworld in a given narrative, fiction or nonfiction, is not going to reconstruct itself in the reader's/interpreter's mind. In both instances, specific actions must be undertaken to bring the desired "world" into existence, whether it is a multiacre prairie exhibiting profuse species diversity, or a location in a narrative in which key elements of the plot take place. For the former, choices are made about the type and distribution of grasses, legumes, and forbs, preventative measures for invasive species (such as prescribed fire), and the reintroduction of animal species like bison and elk; for the latter, Herman has written in several places of the ways in which "particular textual cues prompt readers to *spatialize* storyworlds, that is, to build up mental representations of narrated domains as evolving configurations of participants, objects, and places" (*Basic* 183). A certain subjectivity must be acknowledged in both cases, as no two restoration ecologists will interpret the reconstruction process on a given patch of prairie

---

4. The Iowa Natural Heritage Foundation refers to a "seed bank" as "the community of viable seeds present in the soil." In essence, even with the introduction of intensive agriculture throughout the midcontinent, once fields are no longer plowed or tilled, crops are not planted, and chemical applications are curtailed, there is always a possibility that a small percentage of prairie plants that once resided in the soil will return, thanks to the presence of the seed bank. Again, it is somewhat beyond the scope of this study, but the seed bank affords a relevant connection to indigenous cultures from this region. Melissa K. Nelson, writing of Anishinaabeg responses to contemporary environmental crises, asserts that "stories can go dormant. They can lie fallow for decades or even centuries, buried in the land like winter seeds waiting for an ideal spring. When the conditions are right, the story seed can emerge with the signature of its origins, but with new shapes and colors given the latest conditions it finds life in" (214).

the same way, just as no two readers will reconstruct the storyworld "prompts" of a given narrative uniformly. Herman addresses this issue later by pointing to the "strategic, always only partial mapping of textual cues onto storyworld dimensions" that are unique to the "particular uses to which the narrative is being put" (*Storytelling* 48). Likewise, nearly all restoration ecologists and land managers with whom I have discussed this topic emphasize the fact that no reconstruction will ever be a complete replica or re-creation of what existed prior to Euro-American settlement, nor will most reconstructions become what Chris Helzer of the Nature Conservancy refers to as "calendar prairies," or an idealized image of what a prairie "should" be. Instead, as Helzer points out, a much more realistic goal is "reconstructing functional landscapes" that might, to borrow Herman's term, be best determined by the ecological "affordances" of the size and location of a given prairie reconstruction.

In making the move to more concrete examples of reconstruction at work, a final term of concurrence between narrative theory and restoration ecology is that of "immersion." In fact, the dearth of opportunities for modern-day residents of the North American midcontinent to immerse themselves fully in either actual world prairie ecosystems or prairie storyworlds (failures that go hand-in-hand) drives this call for a practical narratology of the prairie. Marie-Laure Ryan makes as strong a case as any why more emphasis needs to be placed on the immersive experience provided by narrative, stating, "At its best, immersion can be an adventurous and invigorating experience comparable to taking a swim in a cool ocean with powerful surf. The environment appears at first hostile, you enter it reluctantly, but once you get wet and entrust your body to the waves, you never want to leave. And when you finally do, you feel refreshed and full of energy" (*Narrative* 11). Nineteenth-century metaphors comparing the prairie to an ocean aside, the hesitancy of readers and residents of the North American midcontinent to become immersed in what has become an unfamiliar native ecosystem is precisely the concern that Ryan articulates in the first half of this quotation, and the hope is that more accessible opportunities for such immersion would result in the reinvigoration she describes in the latter half. For instance, in her examination of sixteenth-century English Romance, F. Elizabeth Hart offers a clear articulation of why immersion in narrative storyworlds is a phenomenon that has changed the way humans think about themselves and their relationship to all manners of "worlds," in part by "considering the likelihood that increased numbers of readers also meant that narrative immersion simply became a more widespread, commonly shared, and familiar experience whose effect, overall, was to focus cultural attention on the mind and the specialized worlds that minds create" (105). Whereas Hart theorizes that this increase in narrative immersion ultimately led early readers to deeper understandings of "human interiority," the insight she provides also opens up speculation about the positive results derived from richer and more frequent immersion in prairie storyworlds and actual worlds today.

To reinforce the importance of immersion to implementing a practical narratology of the prairie, I offer here two literary examples and one personal experience as a sort of case study of what such functional application of narrative theory might produce. Whereas Wallace Stegner's nonfiction enabled an entry point into this topic in the opening paragraphs, his fiction provides an excellent example of how these concepts can be put into practice—in particular, his fiction set in rural Saskatchewan, the western extent of the North American prairie, such as the semiautobiographical novel *Big Rock Candy Mountain* and some of his early short fiction that he incorporated into that novel. There is frequent reference to the prairie in these stories, both the real and the imagined. In the short story "Buglesong" (1938), for instance, the young protagonist Bruce Mason drifts in and out of sleep as he listens to a strong prairie wind blowing outside: "*In his mind* he had seen the prairie outside with its woolly grass and cactus white under the moon, and the wind, whining across the endless oceanic land, sang in the screens, and sang him back to sleep" (13; emphasis added). This description offers two notable insights into the concept of immersion. First, Stegner's wording in this passage obviously ties in well with propositions of cognitive narratology put forth by Herman and like-minded theorists, as Bruce is quite clearly "reconstructing" a "mentally projected [world]," one that he knows intimately from the time he spends exploring the prairies (and hunting weasels) in the area around his family's homestead (*Story Logic* 49). In other words, it is his physical immersion in the prairie that enables this cognitive emergence of the prairie back inside his home. Second, this is a small example of a narrative about the prairie in which important textual cues about this ecosystem—the "woolly grass," "cactus," and "wind" in particular—are provided to the reader to "reconstruct" a prairie storyworld of his or her own. Even for those readers without extensive experience of direct immersion in actual world prairie ecosystems, the details that Stegner provides enable "imaginatively . . . inhabit[ing] a world in which things matter," thereby potentially mattering to the reader as well.

A fruitful counterexample is Annie Proulx's novel *That Old Ace in the Hole* (2002), likewise set in the region of shortgrass prairie, though much farther south in the Texas panhandle. While somewhat older than Stegner's Bruce, Proulx's protagonist Bob Dollar is also a transplant to this region, by way of Denver. Unlike Bruce, however, Bob does not encounter an intact prairie ecosystem at the time of his arrival, in large part because his own entry into this region is separated from the experiences of Bruce in frontier Saskatchewan by nearly three-quarters of a century. Thus, even though the characters inhabit roughly the same type of grassland ecosystem—which would have been contiguous for millennia prior to Euro-American settlement—these differences in chronology and geography create a vastly different encounter with the native ecology of this region. At the opening of the novel, an interesting acknowledgement is made that Bob "knew he was on prairie" as he first drives into the panhandle, and at least some sense of the history of the region is provided as well. In the very next paragraph, a major shift takes place, as Bob is still shown to be among those for whom "nothing is known" about the implications of being part of the prairie ecosystem: "Bob Dollar had no idea that he was driving into a region of immeasurable natural complexity that some believe abused beyond saving. He saw only what others had seen—the bigness, pump jacks nodding pterodactyl heads, road alligators cast off from the big semi tires. . . . It seemed he was not so much in a place as confronting the raw material of human use" (3). So, just as Bruce in "Buglesong" is capable of being immersed in prairie "in his mind" because of direct experiences of immersion in the ecosystem itself, Bob, at least at the opening of *That Old Ace in the Hole,* is incapable of the same sort of immersion, both physical and mental: the former because the shortgrass prairie as he enters it no longer resembles a viable ecosystem of "immeasurable natural complexity," the latter because the absence of a physical prairie negates any ability to become immersed "in his mind."

Over the course of the novel, this changes to a certain degree as Bob encounters characters invested in reconstructing some semblance of the historic shortgrass prairie ecosystem in the Texas panhandle, and so his ignorance is at least transformed into a sort of ambivalence. Near the close of the novel, we are told, "*In his* [Bob's] *mind's eye* he saw the panhandle earth immemorially used and tumbled"; this is followed by a vision that moves from the "probing grass roots" and "hooves of bison" of the native prairie through to the "scrape of bulldozers, inundations of chemicals" that he has more directly experienced in his time there (358; emphasis added). Though the wording is quite similar, what is depicted at the close of Proulx's novel is a very different sort of immersion than Stegner describes in "Buglesong." Bruce's experiences of immersion in the prairie allow him to visualize its presence, confident that it will be there when he wakes in the morning; Bob's experiences leave no such confidence, only a belief that "ruined places could not be restored," and there was only a visualization of a "ghost ground, ephemeral yet enduring" where the prairie once had been (358–59). The main difference between the two is that Bob Dollar, like most people currently residing in the midcontinent, by the end of the novel still has not been fully immersed in a thriving prairie eco-system, and so is incapable "in his mind's eye" of reconstructing the prairie in the way that Bruce does so effortlessly.

If, as Marco Caracciolo contends, "experience is an activity; it is an embod-ied exploration of the world," and it therefore follows that "readers enact the storyworld by relying on the virtuality of their movements," the contradictory experiences of Bruce Mason and Bob Dollar on the shortgrass prairie come into sharper focus ("Blind Reading" 90, 91). Extrapolating from these two fictional characters, and positioning them as readers or interpreters of narra-tive—a move warranted by the respective descriptions of their mental activity in attempting to visualize the prairie—Bruce's immersion in the prairie makes him a sort of "ideal reader" in the enactivist model, because he is able to fol-low the "blueprint" and build the world of the prairie in his imagination. Bob, who lacks the same level of "active and embodied exploration of an environ-ment," is therefore incapable of reconstructing a similar sort of storyworld in his own mind ("Blind Reading" 99). Extending these literary examples to the prairie as it exists today, it is no stretch to say that hopes for reconstructing meaningful amounts of ecosystem ultimately rely on more people—children in particular—like Bruce, who grow up immersed in the prairie, both story-worlds and actual worlds, who can lie in bed and conjure images of the prairie as they drift to sleep, confident in the knowledge that it will be there for them to tramp and explore when they wake. Writing elsewhere, Caracciolo con-tends that "it is on the plane of our emotional engagement that the impact of stories becomes clearly evident. . . . Stories can trigger emotional reactions by bringing into play values and evaluations that are part of recipients' emotional background" ("Those Insane Dream Sequences" 235–36). It is no stretch to posit that there are currently more Bob Dollars than Bruce Masons inhabiting the American midcontinent, but a practical narratology, and narrative more broadly, can help invert that reality by facilitating more consistent and com-pelling "emotional reactions" to this ecosystem through routine experiences with both prairie storyworlds and actual worlds.[5]

An area of Herman's extensive explorations of storyworlds that has thus far received too little attention is what he labels "*exophoric* strategies for world-building," a term introduced in some of his more recent writing on cogni-tive narratology (*Storytelling* 109). What follows will only begin to scratch the

---

5. My analysis of Bruce Mason and Bob Dollar as diverting types of "readers" of the prairie ecosystems they inhabit is but a small sampling of Caracciolo's writing on the topics of experientiality, embodiment, enactment, and immersion. The way in which fictional characters and actual readers intersect is of particular interest, especially as considered in Caracciolo's essay "The Reader's Virtual Body: Narrative Space and It's Reconstruction."

surface of the importance of this term to a practical narratology, as it draws a clear link between the literary analysis of prairie storyworlds and the sort of "world building" that can occur in situ while immersed in prairie actual worlds. Specifically, in the personal account that follows, I hope to demonstrate the importance of the sorts of narrative situations that feature "a storyteller combining utterances and gestures while telling a narrative on-site . . . both semiotic channels—the visual one supporting gestural communication and the auditory one supporting verbal communication—enable the storyteller to evoke more than one reference world" (112). As will be exhibited in this example, it matters that the narrative is shared "on-site," and it is significant that multiple reference worlds—in this case, before and after prairie reconstruction has taken place—are included in the narration in order to call attention to the degraded status of the land prior to reconstruction, and the thriving prairie ecosystem that has taken its place.

Suzan Erem is the founder and codirector of the newly formed Sustainable Iowa Land Trust, an organization that seeks to keep, or place, farmland throughout the state in permanent sustainable agriculture. On her own property in eastern Iowa, more than eighty acres of hilly land overlooking and abutting the Cedar River, she is in the process of converting what was formerly terraced farmland planted to grow crops like corn and soybeans into native tallgrass prairie and woodland. During a recent tour of Erem's property, she made an unprompted reference to the work she and her husband are doing on the land as "reconstruction."[6] Throughout our long walk through her property, not only was I physically immersed in a reconstructed prairie, I was also audience to an oral history of this land as Erem told the narrative of its transformation from degraded farmland to thriving prairie and woodland. Because the prairie has so vigorously taken to the slopes and bottomland of this property, I first had to reconstruct the storyworld of the degraded farmland, aided by the "utterances and gestures" of Erem describing and pointing to sites where terraced rows of corn or soybeans gave way to eroding hills and washouts dumping into the adjoining river; most strikingly, I had to reconstruct a monocultural landscape of a single crop (or barren land from late fall to early summer) in place of the diverse array of native grasses and wildflowers—bluestem, indiangrass, switchgrass, goldenrod, wild bergamot, mountain mint, to name a few—that I was now walking through. As Erem continued describing the reconstruction process, the storyworld became one of transition, from neglected farmland to nascent prairie and woodland, with

---

6. In order to give credit where it is due, it was during our subsequent conversation about the concept of "reconstruction" that she pointed me to the revised edition of Kurtz's *Practical Guide to Prairie Reconstruction,* which offers the more elaborate definition quoted in this essay.

young native plants competing with stubborn invasive species (there remains an abundance of Queen Anne's Lace) and oak saplings routinely eaten to stubs by deer. The fluidity of the storyworld at this point in Erem's narration brings to life Ryan's observation that "if we conceive of storyworlds as mental representations built during the reading (viewing, playing, among others) of a narrative text, they are not static containers for the objects mentioned in a story but rather dynamic models of evolving situations. We could say that they are simulations of the development of the story" ("Transmedial" 364). Indeed, the presence of stubby oak saplings and Queen Anne's Lace shows that the story of this place is truly dynamic and still developing. Eventually, through patient land management and the hard work of thinning invaders so that native plants can thrive, the storyworld of Erem's narration became equivalent with the second reference world, namely the reconstructed prairie ecosystem that I was currently immersed in "on-site." In Ryan's words, I truly left this place "refreshed and full of energy."

Of course, I must recognize that most of what I have written here is meant to address the general lack of opportunities for the sort of dual immersion in reconstructed prairie ecosystem and prairie storyworld that I experienced over the course of a couple of hours on a cool late-summer day. Not only has most of the prairie been removed, as has been well covered, but there is also the problem of a relative absence of "story creators" capable of reconstructing the storyworld of a given prairie as it transitions from degraded, damaged, or neglected land to something approximating its former diversity and vitality. As part of my own research into this topic, I have sought out such "story creators" in eastern and western Iowa, and eastern and central Nebraska, in order to immerse myself in prairie and to hear these narratives of reconstruction firsthand. This fieldwork, coupled with extensive reading of fictional and nonfictional narratives of the prairie, has led me to concur wholeheartedly with James's observation, echoing psychologists Melanie C. Green and Timothy C. Brock, that "direct experience is a powerful means of forming attitudes—a process that narratives foster because of their ability to enable the mimicry, or simulation, of experience" (20). The residents of the North American midcontinent cannot be forced to visit a reconstructed prairie, or spend a couple of hours on site with an ecologist, or even read a narrative in which the prairie is prominently, and positively, featured. But as advocacy for the prairie becomes more pronounced and organized, these are the sorts of strategies that must be employed, preferably concomitant with one another. We have already reached a point where "literally nothing is known," and if narrative theory can contribute anything to this crisis, it is by showing that any "world" is possible.

WORKS CITED

Baldwin, A. Dwight, Jr., Judith de Luce, and Carl Pletsch, "Introduction: Ecological Preservation versus Restoration and Invention." *Beyond Preservation: Restoring and Inventing Landscapes.* Edited by A. Dwight Baldwin, Jr., Judith de Luce, and Carl Pletsch, U of Minnesota P, 1994, pp. 3–16.

Caracciolo, Marco. "Blind Reading: Toward an Enactivist Theory of the Reader's Imagination." *Stories and Minds: Cognitive Approaches to Literary Narrative.* Edited by Lars Bernaerts, Dirk De Geest, Luc Herman, and Bart Vervaeck, U of Nebraska P, 2013, pp. 81–105.

———. "The Reader's Virtual Body: Narrative Space and It's Reconstruction." *Storyworlds: A Journal of Narrative Studies,* vol. 3, 2011, pp. 117–38.

———. "Those Insane Dream Sequences: Experientiality and Distorted Experience in Literature and Video Games." *Storyworlds Across Media: Toward a Media-Conscious Narratology.* Edited by Marie-Laure Ryan and Jan-Noël Thon, U of Nebraska P, 2014, pp. 230–49.

Easterlin, Nancy. *A Biocultural Approach to Literature Theory and Interpretation.* Johns Hopkins UP, 2012.

Erem, Suzan (President Sustainable Iowa Land Trust [SILT]) in discussion with the author, 28 Aug. 2015.

Gass, Patrick. "August 20, 1804." *Journals of the Lewis and Clark Expedition.* Edited by Gary Moulton, U of Nebraska P, 2002.

Green, Melanie C., and Timothy C. Brock. "The Role of Transportation in the Persuasiveness of Public Narratives." *Journal of Personality and Social Psychology,* vol. 79, no. 5, 2000, pp. 701–21.

Hart, F. Elizabeth. "1500–1620: Reading, Consciousness, and Romance in the Sixteenth Century." *Emergence of Mind: Representations of Consciousness in Narrative Discourse in English.* Edited by David Herman, U of Nebraska P, 2011, pp. 103–31.

Helzer, Chris (Nature Conservancy Eastern Nebraska Program Director) in discussion with the author, 31 Jul. 2015.

Herman, David. *Basic Elements of Narrative.* Wiley-Blackwell, 2009.

———. *Story Logic: Problems and Possibilities of Narrative.* U of Nebraska P, 2004.

———. *Storytelling and the Sciences of the Mind.* Cambridge: MIT Press, 2013.

———. "Storyworlds." *Routledge Encyclopedia of Narrative Theory.* Edited by David Herman, Manfred Jahn, and Marie-Laure Ryan, Routledge, 2010, pp. 569–70.

Iowa Natural Heritage Foundation. *Secrets of the Seed Bank: Tiny Clues to a Landscape's Past and Future.* 2001.

James, Erin. *The Storyworld Accord: Econarratology and Postcolonial Narratives.* U of Nebraska P, 2015.

Jordan, William R., III, and George M. Lubick. *Making Nature Whole: A History of Ecological Restoration.* Island Press, 2011.

King, Thomas. *The Truth about Stories: A Native Narrative.* House of Anasi Press, 2003.

Kurtz, Carl. *A Practical Guide to Prairie Reconstruction.* 2nd ed., U of Iowa P, 2013.

Love, Glen A. *Practical Ecocriticism: Literature, Biology, and the Environment.* U of Virginia P, 2003.

Massey, Doreen. *For Space.* Sage Publications, 2005.

Nelson, Melissa K. "The Hydromythology of the Anishinaabeg: Will Mishipizhu Survive Climate Change, or is He Creating It?" *Centering Anishinaabeg Studies: Understanding the World Through Stories*. Edited by Jill Doerflier, Niigaanwewidam James Sinclair, and Heidi Kiiwetinepinesiik Stark, Michigan State UP, 2013, pp. 213–33.

Newton, Adam Zachary. *Narrative Ethics*. Harvard UP, 1995.

Proulx, Annie. *That Old Ace in the Hole*. Scribner, 2002.

Ryan, Marie-Laure. *Narrative as Virtual Reality: Immersion and Interactivity in Literature and Electronic Media*. Johns Hopkins UP, 2001.

———. "Possible Worlds." *The Living Handbook of Narratology*. Edited by Peter Hühn, John Pier, Wolf Schmid, and Jörg Schönert, Hamburg University, 27 Sept. 2013, http://www.lhn.uni-hamburg.de/article/possible-worlds. Accessed 11 Jun. 2019.

———. "Transmedial Storytelling and Transfictionality." *Poetics Today*, vol. 34, no. 3, 2013, pp. 361–88.

Stegner, Wallace. "Buglesong." *Collected Stories*. Penguin Books, 2006, pp. 13–20.

———. "Inheritance." *American Places*. Penguin Books, 2006.

Vizenor, Gerald. *Fugitive Poses: Native American Indian Scenes of Absence and Presence*. U of Nebraska P, 1998.

———. *Manifest Manners: Narratives on Postindian Survivance*. U of Nebraska P, 1994.

———. *Survivance: Narratives of Native Presence*. U of Nebraska P, 2008.

CHAPTER 8

Worldmaking Environmental Crisis

Climate Fiction, Econarratology, and Genre

ASTRID BRACKE

IN BARBARA KINGSOLVER'S 2012 novel *Flight Behavior,* a scientist suggests that the media will only report on environmental crisis if it is "sexed up" sufficiently: "Every environmental impact story has to be made into something else" (318). His critique of the media points to the important—and often difficult—matter of communicating climate change. How stories are told is central to our understanding of them and their effectiveness. Nonetheless, while ecocritics and environmental humanities scholars acknowledge the key role of narratives in this respect,[1] the mechanics of this process—for example, the function of genre in representing environmental crisis—have yet to be explored in depth. An econarratological[2] approach to genre provides a useful starting point for exploring which forms, registers, structures, and tropes tend to feature in narratives of environmental crisis. This chapter positions genre as a key site of econarratology and provides an understanding of the workings of genre as a significant element in narrating environmental crisis. As such, it

---

1. See for instance Heise and Carruth; Rose et al.
2. Throughout, I use the term "econarratology" as defined by Erin James. Econarratology, she proposes, "embraces the key concerns of each of its parent discourses—it maintains an interest in studying the relationship between literature and the physical environment, but does so with sensitivity to the literary structures and devices that we use to communicate representations of the physical environment to each other via narratives" (23).

continues emerging work on the intersection of narratology and the imagination of climate crisis. In particular I'll draw on the concept of worldmaking and Marie-Laure Ryan's typology of genres to define the genre of climate fiction. The principle of minimal departure, I'll show, is one of the key elements through which climate fiction creates an uncomfortable sense of proximity, confronting readers with a crisis that is present and imminent rather than at a comfortable distance.

In what follows, my focus is threefold: first, I briefly explore genre in relation to narratology and ecocriticism; second, I (further) define the genre of climate fiction, or cli-fi; and third, I provide a reading of cli-fi novels to demonstrate that worldmaking is a key generic and narratological characteristic of climate fiction. Given these three aims, I deliberately limit myself to a discussion of just two works of climate fiction, in order to leave enough space to both set out a framework and provide a further fleshing out of cli-fi's generic characteristics—characteristics which, I'll show, require an expansion of the existing narratological repertoire.[3] My reading has three implications for our understanding of climate fiction, in particular, and genre, in general. The first is that I make explicit the physical dimension of genres, an element generally neglected by genre scholars in favor of social contexts. As I show, the construction of physical worlds, or worldmaking, is central to not only making sense of social worlds outside of the text, but especially to coming to terms with changing physical contexts. The second implication of my reading is that I extend Ryan's typology of texts in several ways: by adding cli-fi to it, and, importantly, by further developing her definition of chronological compatibility between the fictional world and the real world. My application goes beyond mere chronological setting and shows how climate fiction uses chronology—and especially the blurring between the fictional world and the actual world—to depict the epistemological uncertainty that characterizes climate crisis. Finally, the third implication of my approach is that I foreground the role played by the principle of minimal departure in climate fiction. Cli-fi novels, I argue, do not just *depict* climate crisis, but play with the principle of minimal departure to recreate the experience of living through risk and uncertainty on the scale of individual novels.

---

3. A more extensive analysis of works that can be called climate fiction, though not in terms of econarratology, is provided by Adam Trexler in *Anthropocene Fictions* (2015). Other possible novels that could be explored in this context are Ian McEwan's *Solar* (2010), James Howard Kunstler's *World Made by Hand* (2008), and possibly Cormac McCarthy's *The Road* (2006).

GENRES AS "DISCURSIVE MAPS OF THE WORLD"[4]

Genres are generally understood to do two things: to guide readers in their understanding of a text, and to help them make sense of the world by framing their perceptions and experiences.[5] In the first sense, genres function as what Peter Seitel calls "frameworks of expectation," "established ways of creating and understanding that facilitate human interaction and the communication of meaning" (277). When someone says "I'll kill you!" it's good to know whether this is a comedic situation, or when someone is serious—like in a thriller or crime novel—and it's time to run. In addition to genre's ability to provide insight into individual works, Seitel also suggests that genres "bring into focus the social contexts that shape and are shaped by generic performances" (275). In this chapter, I'll focus on this second function of genres: the way in which genres enable us to capture, understand, and represent the world around us, social as well as physical.

Genres have come to be seen as reflections of the environments in which they originate: as Tzvetan Todorov argues, "[They] bring to light the constitutive features of the society to which they belong" (19). This leads to an understanding of genres as what Ralph Cohen calls "historical and social formations that undergo transformations that shape a society" (xv). The question asked by genre theory consequently is "What kind of world is brought into being here?" (Frow 1633). As a narratological category, genre provides an especially fruitful entry point into ecocritical and environmental humanities discussions about narratives suitable to a time of climate crisis. Indeed, an understanding of genres may enable us to get closer to understanding our position and challenges in such a time—as Seitel notes, "Genres are also *tools* for living in society, chunks of communication that do work, and are designed to do that work, be it to educate, to test, to open a channel of communication, to punish, or merely to amuse" (277, original emphasis).[6] Genres not only provide us with the parameters to understand communication and texts, they also provide the frameworks to help people make sense of the world around them, especially in a time of crisis and change. While in genre studies the emphasis is gener-

---

4. See Frow (1633).

5. As John Frow suggests, "Genres give schematic guidance . . . to the users of texts" (1633). A third function of genre is that it can be prescriptive, in that it can influence and determine the work of artists. As Heta Pyrhönen notes, "Generic conventions are normative, telling authors what they should and should not do" (109).

6. Similarly, Bakhtin argues that genres are, as Pyrhönen summarizes, "ways of seeing and interpreting particular aspects of the world, strategies for conceptualizing reality" because they function as what Bakhtin calls "transmission belts" between social history and linguistic history (121).

ally on the social contexts from which genres originate and which they might help navigate, my exploration of cli-fi in this chapter shows how genres also originate from and help readers navigate physical contexts, especially those changing due to climate crisis.

Considerable terrain is to be won for both narratology and ecocriticism—and econarratology—in respect to the effect of genre in the understanding of (fictional) worlds. While genre is arguably at the heart of the study of narratives and could be seen as a narrative macrodesign, it is also often, as Susan Keen notes, "left out of theoretical discussions of narrative form" (141). In fact, genre scholars themselves have noted that although genre has a central position in classroom discussions and on the shelves of bookstores, contemporary literary critics discuss it less and less. Genre studies, as Michael B. Prince puts it, seem to be "the B-movie of literary studies, a big frame-up where all the really relevant questions of political and economic praxis are held at bay in a merely 'literary' preoccupation with form" (453).[7] Most current narratological approaches to genre build on classical work, especially generic classification (Todorov), leaving considerable room for in-depth explorations of the effect of genre on narrative environments and worldmaking.[8] This dimension is explored particularly by Marie-Laure Ryan, whose work on genre and worldmaking is central to my discussion of climate fiction below.

Ecocritics tend to leave genre unexplored, which is remarkable given the central role of genre in ecocriticism's early stages. In her introduction to *The Ecocriticism Reader,* Cheryll Glotfelty notes that one of the primary aims of ecocriticism is to recuperate "the hitherto neglected genre of nature writing" (xxiii). Even today, a marked preference for environmental nonfiction characterizes ecocritical publications.[9] In those cases in which genre *is* explored, ecocritics are generally concerned not so much with the internal workings of a genre but—in line with ecocriticism's aims of affecting change—the effect that

---

7. See also Frow, who has suggested that genre studies is "just not one of the topics about which interesting discussions are happening these days" (1627) and Marie-Laure Ryan who notes, "The attitude toward the concept of genre which one finds most pervasive in contemporary literary studies is a skepticism that conceals uneasiness and even discouragement" ("Introduction" 109).

8. For narratological discussions of genre see the brief lemma on genre in Porter Abbott's *Cambridge Introduction to Narrative,* the entries on genre theory (Michael Kearns) and econarratives (Ursula Heise) in the *Routledge Encyclopedia of Narrative Theory (Herman and Ryan),* and Heta Pyrhönen's discussion of genre in *The Cambridge Companion to Narrative (Herman),* and Susan Keen's *Narrative Form.*

9. "Environmental non-fiction in the tradition of Thoreau remains a major if hardly exclusive concern of twenty-first-century ecocriticism" (Clark 35).

genres have on readers and, consequently, whether some genres are ecocritically or environmentally more sound than others. Such ecocritical approaches depict a more evaluative approach to literature, exemplified by Richard Kerridge's typology of genre in which he lists those genres best suited to representing climate crisis, including, for instance, Modernist cut-up and collage.[10] Yet such readings may be problematic: as Nancy Easterlin suggests, ecocritics might ask themselves "whether it is advisable to theorize aesthetics on the basis of ethics" (97). Another line of ecocritical engagement with genre and narrative also holds that literature can affect human perceptions but, as Pieter Vermeulen puts it, "draws on the resources of literary narrative *not* to shape ethical and political action, but rather to begin to come to terms with the finitude of human life" (870). Trexler's work on climate fiction fits this category, as does my own. My reading of climate fiction shows how genre-specific elements of worldmaking become a means of making sense of the changing social and physical worlds outside of the text. As I demonstrate in the remainder of this chapter, such an approach results in an extension of narratological understandings of genre. Most importantly, it demonstrates how the narrative's use of generic characteristics makes the epistemological uncertainty typical of climate crisis part of the reader's experience of the novel.

DEFINING CLIMATE FICTION

Climate fiction has come to the fore since the beginning of the twenty-first century and, through its explicit concern with human-nature relations, can be seen to reflect, and engage in, the cultural discourse of environmental crisis over the past two decades. At the same time, it taps into an older tradition of ecodystopian and apocalyptic literature.[11] The term "cli-fi" as shorthand for climate fiction gained widespread popularity in the spring of 2013, following a report on NPR that defined it as "novels and short stories in worlds, not unlike our own, where the Earth's systems are noticeably off-kilter" (Evancie

---

10. See Kerridge, "Ecocritical Approaches to Literary Form and Genre." An early example of evaluative ecocritical engagement with genre is Joseph Meeker, *The Comedy of Survival.* Meeker's argument for comedy rather than tragedy as an environmentally better genre influenced Kerridge's reading of Ian McEwan's *Solar* ("The Single Source"), as well as Ursula Heise's reading of Douglas Adams and Mark Carwardine's *Last Chance to See* ("Lost Dogs") and Nicole Seymour's "Towards an Irreverent Ecocriticism."

11. See Adam Trexler's introduction in *Anthropocene Fictions.* Frederick Buell provides a discussion of twentieth-century dystopian and apocalyptic fiction in *From Apocalypse to Way of Life.*

par. 6). The articles that followed the NPR report echo this definition: Husna Haq distinguishes cli-fi from science fiction by arguing that it "describes a dystopian present, as opposed to a dystopian future, and it isn't non-fiction or even science fiction: cli-fi is about literary fiction" (par. 9), and Carolyn Kormann suggests in the *New Yorker* that "novels that would once have been called science fiction can be read as social realism" (par. 6). While most of these articles—which, to date, make up the brunt of early criticism on climate fiction—celebrate the potentials of the genre, some critics fear that the name "cli-fi" makes the genre sound "marginal when, in fact, climate change is moving to the center of human experience" (Kormann par. 4), or that "cli-fi" has been coined "for squeamish writers and critics who dislike the box labelled 'science fiction'" (Glass par. 4).

Despite this flurry of attention to the genre in 2013, it took until 2015 and Adam Trexler's *Anthropocene Fictions* for the first in-depth critical analysis of climate fiction. He argues that "climate change necessarily transforms generic conventions" and that climate novels change "the parameters of storytelling" (14). Trexler's argument fits in with ecocritical and environmental humanities scholarship arguing that, as Greg Garrard puts it, "climate fiction ought to test the boundaries of narrative and genre, perhaps to breaking point" (300). A clear delineation of the terms "Anthropocene fiction" and "climate fiction," used interchangeably by Trexler, is lacking in his work. To prevent similar confusion, I, like Garrard, use only the terms "climate fiction" and "cli-fi" to refer to novels that depict climate change and crisis. The definition of climate fiction that I propose in this chapter is moreover narrower than that suggested by Trexler's "Anthropocene fictions," and one that places cli-fi apart from genres such as science fiction and postapocalyptic literature.[12] Science fiction tends to be set in the more distant future while the potential and strength of cli-fi is that the works are set more or less right now. Furthermore, unlike postapocalyptic novels such as Cormac McCarthy's *The Road*, cli-fi is not set after a big rupture, a seemingly sudden event that changed all.[13] Instead, cli-fi describes a risk society, a constant state of living in potential man-made dan-

---

12. While Trexler remains relatively vague about his definition, his emphasis on the Anthropocene as a shaping force on literature suggests that *all* fictions composed in the Anthropocene are Anthropocene fictions.

13. In relation to *The Road*, Trexler suggests that these kind of apocalyptic novels "fail to place climate change or create a meaningful connection between it and the reader" (79). While, as Kerridge remarks, George Monbiot has called the novel "the most important environmental book ever written," Kerridge doubts its suitability as an environmental novel because of its "strategy of insufferability" that says to the reader, "here is something that gives you no option of reacting just a little. You must either face the scenario, or turn away from it unable to pretend you are doing anything else" ("Ecocritical Approaches" 374).

ger, rather than sudden and cataclysmic apocalypse.[14] Climate fiction reflects that, as Frederick Buell notes, environmental crisis "has become more and more a place in which people dwell, a context in reference to which they represent themselves" (250). Consequently, literature and popular culture at large reflect environmental crisis as "part of people's daily, domestic experience . . . problems that people now cope with daily, not just nightmares the future will bring more fully out" (280). Other distinctions can be made between cli-fi and both what Kerridge calls "narratives of resignation" on the one hand, and Amy Patrick's "precautionary narratives" on the other. Narratives of resignation are fatalistic and offer hope "only in the form of sardonic poetic justice and apocalyptic survivalist fantasy" (Kerridge, "Narratives of Resignation" 87). Precautionary narratives, on the other hand, rely on the sense that all is not lost. Rather than emphasizing irreversible degradation, they imagine environmental crisis in terms of "potential yet avoidable consequences" (Patrick 142, 145). Such hopefulness is also deeply problematic: "hopefulness," Clive Hamilton suggests, "becomes a way of forestalling the truth" (211). In its attempt to address both the immediacy and importance of environmental crisis, cli-fi takes the middle ground between skepticism and defeatism, and a (misguided?) belief that crisis can yet be averted.

A number of generic elements of climate fiction can be distilled. Taking the somewhat rough definition that genre = content + form, these elements both capture the thematics explored by the genre, as well as their formal, narratological features. In terms of themes and topics, climate fiction is concerned with climate change and science, and it tends to depict characters living in a risk society. The tension between familiarity (cli-fi is set in the present or very near future) and defamiliarization (the effects of climate crisis) is a key theme. Another is the tension that Trexler identifies between widespread awareness of catastrophic global warming and the failed obligation to act. Yet all of these elements would not succeed in truly capturing climate crisis or successfully bringing across the immediacy of climate crisis without a number of formal and narratological elements, such as contrasting lay characters and scientist characters and an emphasis on storytelling and narrativity as (metafictional) components of the novel. The most significant of these is the technique of worldmaking. The rest of this chapter will consequently focus on narrative worlds and especially the use of the principle of minimal departure as central to depictions of life in a time of climate crisis. After exploring in some more depth the strategies of worldmaking in cli-fi, I provide brief readings of

---

14. For foundational work on the concept of risk society, see Ulrich Beck; Anthony Giddens.

two works of climate fiction: Barbara Kingsolver's *Flight Behavior* (2012) and Nathaniel Rich's *Odds Against Tomorrow* (2013).

CLIMATE FICTION WORLDS

Worldmaking refers to both the ways in which the textual world is created and, in turn, how readers are able to make sense of it. In David Herman's words, the term encapsulates both "how narrative designs prompt the construction—enable the exploration—of different sorts of storyworlds" and "how the process of building storyworlds in turn scaffolds a variety of sense-making activities" (*Storytelling* x). The worldmaking possibilities of narratives tie in with the concept of storyworlds, projected environments that enable readers to travel from the actual world to the textual world, to gain access to it, understand it, and even experience it to some extent. My analysis of cli-fi emphasizes the important role that genre plays in this process of worldmaking and in the creation of the storyworld. Moreover, the process of worldmaking reflects the social as well as the physical dimension of genres: as the reader follows along to construct a fictional physical environment, they also engage in an act of making sense of their own changing social and physical world.

Interpreting a text within the framework of genre is far less a matter of knowing in advance exactly what the narrative's world will look like and primarily a matter of picking up on and interpreting cues that, often subtly, tell readers what the world they are entering looks like. Ryan argues that readers use their own world and environment as a starting point for their understanding of the narrative's world. She terms this process the principle of minimal departure: "We construe the central world of a textual universe . . . as conforming as far as possible to our representation of AW [the actual or real world]. We will project upon these worlds everything we know about reality, and we will make only the adjustments dictated by the text" (*Possible Worlds, Artificial Intelligence and Narrative Theory* 51). Getting from the actual world to that of the storyworld can happen quickly (for instance, if the narrator mentions locations such as Mars or aliens in the first lines) or slowly, as when a storyworld corresponds closely to readers' actual world or they are led to believe so. The relationship between the actual world and the textual—often fictional—world is a defining element of genre, as Ryan notes: "To know that a text is a fairy tale or a legend, a science fiction story or a historical romance, is to know, at least approximately, which aspects of the real world will be shared by the fictional world" ("Fiction" 415). Decoding a text, even when readers already know partly what to expect, consequently depends on the workings of the principle of minimal departure and the cues readers receive from the text itself.

Yet genre, and the ways in which readers arrive at an understanding of storyworld, is also a matter of the accessibility relations employed by a narrative or genre. Accessibility relations, Ryan argues, are "trans-universe relations" that function as "the airline through which the sender reaches the world at the center of the textual universe" ("Possible Worlds" 558). She distinguishes nine possible relations that show how the textual actual world (TAW)—or storyworld in Herman's and James's words—is different from, or similar to, the actual world (AW):

A. Properties: TAW can be accessed from AW if the objects in both worlds have the same properties.

B. Inventory: TAW can be accessed from AW if they are furnished by the same objects.

C. Compatibility of inventory: TAW can be accessed from AW if TAW includes all features (or "members") of AW in addition to some "native members."

D. Chronological compatibility: TAW requires no temporal relocation for someone from AW in order to understand the entire history of TAW. This means that a TAW is still compatible with the AW if the textual world is set in the past (as in a historical novel), but not if the narrative is set in the future. In that case, readers cannot know the *entire* history of TAW, since they cannot look into the future.

E. Physical compatibility: TAW can be accessed from AW if they share the same natural laws.

F. Taxonomic compatibility: TAW can be accessed from AW if both worlds contain the same species, and these species have the same properties (i.e., dogs still act like dogs, and not suddenly like birds).

G. Logical compatibility: TAW can be accessed from AW if both worlds do not contradict themselves. A nonsense narrative, for instance, is not compatible in this sense.

H. Analytical compatibility: TAW can be accessed from AW "if objects designated by the same words have the same essential properties" (i.e., in both worlds, a table refers to the same object, with the same properties.)

I. Linguistic compatibility: TAW can be accessed from AW if the language of TAW—and in which it is described—can be understood by someone from AW.

(paraphrased from Ryan, "Possible Worlds" 558–59)

These nine types correspond to a typology of genres that Ryan provides, to which I add climate fiction to further define the genre and show which parameters play a part in its worldmaking. In order to illustrate the relation between climate fiction and a number of other genres, and to demonstrate how Ryan's typology works, I present the table she provides in abbreviated form.[15]

TABLE 1. Relationship between Climate Fiction and Genre (from Ryan, "Possible Worlds," 560; expanded with cli-fi)

	A: Properties	B: Inventory	C: Compatibility	D: Chronology	E: Physical	F: Taxonomy	G: Logical	H: Analytical	I: Linguistic
Accurate nonfiction	+	+	+	+	+	+	+	+	+
Realistic and historical fiction	+	−	+	+	+	+	+	+	+
Science fiction	+/*	−	+/*	−	+	+/*	+	+	+
Cli-fi	+	−	+	+	+/ −	+	+	+	+

+: compatible
−: incompatible
*: used by Ryan because of a "−" on C (When the inventory of TAW is not the same as AW, it is likely that the objects common to both worlds do not have the same properties.)

As table 1 illustrates, realistic and historical fiction score nearly the same as accurate nonfiction with the exception of B, inventory, as the textual actual world or storyworld of a realistic or historic narrative is not necessarily furnished with the same objects as the actual world. A historical novel set in 1800 may be completely faithful to its historical reality if it doesn't include iPads, even though the actual world does, which is why it scores negatively on element B. The difference between science fiction and climate fiction lies primarily in C, D, E, and F. While Ryan suggests that the textual actual world of science fiction *may be* (hence the +/−) incompatible with the actual world in terms of its inventory and taxonomic compatibility, climate fiction depends on both worlds being so close together that these elements *are* compatible. In respect to E—physical compatibility—Ryan proposes that science fiction functions according to the same natural laws as the actual world. Yet it is

15. In the full table she includes thirteen genres: accurate nonfiction, true fiction, realistic and historical fiction, historical confabulation, realistic ahistorical fiction, anticipation, science fiction, fairy tale, legend, fantastic realism, nonsense rhymes, jabberwockyism and concrete poetry ("Possible Worlds" 560).

precisely this aspect that climate fiction frequently plays on: climate crisis has circumstances that have worsened so much that old laws no longer apply or new ones kick in. As this is not necessarily always the case for a narrative to be defined as cli-fi, I accord this element the symbol +/– in the typology. Finally, the table shows the biggest difference between science fiction and climate fiction in element D, chronological compatibility. The textual actual world, Ryan argues, cannot be set in the future—i.e., be older than the actual world—and still be accessible from the actual world. If it is older, the narrative is science fiction. Climate fiction, however, is set as close as possible to the present. Cli-fi's textual actual worlds, I argue, are consequently compatible with the actual world, since "climate fiction *reflects on changes as they are in the process of occurring*" as Garrard suggests (302, original italics). Indeed, the genre relies on its proximity to the present actual world and, as my examples below show, on readers barely being able to distinguish between the near future and the present of the actual world.

Expanding on Ryan's principle of minimal departure, I propose that the genre of climate fiction puts the reader through a two-step process. Cli-fi depends on first depicting a textual actual world that is very close to readers' actual world, providing cues that give them little reason to suspect that circumstances and developments might be different. Next, however, the narrative extends this familiar world into the unfamiliar, generally without the narrator stepping in to explicitly guide readers in navigating this new space. Instead, what happens is something akin to the myth of the frog who, placed in cold water and slowly boiled, does not jump out as its environment changes so gradually and imperceptibly. The two-step process of cli-fi is most successful when readers can barely tell apart the first and second step: as I explore below, both *Flight Behavior* and *Odds Against Tomorrow* combine the actual world and the textual actual world in such a way that it becomes almost impossible to tell apart what is real in the actual world and what is happening in the textual actual world. Consequently, by playing with type D in Ryan's list of accessibility relations the narratives reflect something of the epistemological uncertainty that defines today's unpredictable climate crisis, full of known and unknown qualities.

The textual actual world of *Flight Behavior* depicts protagonist Dellarobia Turnbow living with her husband and two young children on a struggling farm in rural Tennessee. The narrative provides several clues to emphasize that *Flight Behavior* is set in a world very close, or identical, to readers' actual world in the early 2010s: Dellarobia's husband Cub makes a joke about Al Gore (360), characters make references to Iraq and terrorism (62), and toward the end of the novel Dellarobia listens to a radio report about "[s]omething beyond terrible in Japan, fire and flood" (591) that likely refers to the 2011 earthquake and tsunami. *Odds Against Tomorrow* provides similar cues. In this narrative, Mitchell Zukor, a disaster specialist, comes to work for Future-World, a company that calculates the risk of everything from disease to terrorism to large-scale environmental collapse, thus enabling other companies to prepare for these crises or, through a loophole in the law, even insure themselves. This novel as well is set in a textual actual world roughly contemporary to readers' actual world: the characters refer to the 9/11 attacks at the beginning of the century, recall that Hurricane Sandy (2012) happened just a few years ago and experience existing contemporary fears of disease, eruption of the Yellowstone volcano, and rising sea levels. Cultural references furthermore conflate the textual actual and actual worlds: Mitchell's father has seen the films *Wall Street* (1987), *Die Hard* (1988), and *The Wizard of Oz* (1939), and Bill McKibben's book *The End of Nature* (1989) sits on Mitchell's shelf.

Kingsolver's novel slowly expands the readers' actual world into a lesser known, yet still familiar, textual actual world. The narrator's repeated references to rain, for instance, are one of the first cues that tell readers that something is going on in the novel that goes beyond their known reality in the 2010s. When the rain starts to take on apocalyptic proportions, the actual world morphs into the textual actual world. For the characters, though, the arrival of the thousands of monarch butterflies is the clearest clue that something fundamental is changing in their world—or, as Ovid Byron, the novel's scientist, puts it, that they have entered a whole new world, a world in which, as Dellarobia ponders, "you could count on nothing you'd ever seen or trusted, that was no place you wanted to be" (449). Although monarch butterflies are increasingly threatened, the scale that is depicted in *Flight Behavior* has not yet occurred in the actual world of Kingsolver's readers.

While *Flight Behavior* may seem realistic fiction to some readers unaware of the details of climate change and the fate of monarch butterflies, the step between the actual world and the textual actual world is slightly bigger in *Odds Against Tomorrow*.[16] Yet it too blurs the boundaries between the actual and textual actual worlds in a number of ways. Moreover, the fictional events it depicts are generally close enough to real events in the actual world to be plausible and recognizable. The first disaster to happen in the novel is the Puget Sound Earthquake that devastates Seattle. The narrator notes that characters could have expected this event, since "[a] significant earthquake struck northwestern Washington every twenty years, and a megathrust earthquake—

---

16. Indeed, this gap is likely the reason why Garrard critiques *Odds Against Tomorrow* for not being climate fiction, but an apocalyptic narrative that "sacrifices nuanced representation of risk in favour of an emotive worst-case scenario" (301).

greater than 9.0 on the Richter scale—every three or four centuries" (14). While (still) fictional, the chances of an earthquake happening near Seattle in the actual world of the novel's first readers are considerable—experts believe that there is a 10 per cent chance of an earthquake with a magnitude of 8.7 to 9.2 striking the Cascadia Subduction Zone in the Pacific Northwest in the next fifty years (Schulz, "The Really Big One" par. 14).[17] FEMA officials predict that when this earthquake happens, nearly thirteen thousand people will die, twenty-seven thousand will be injured, and a million will be displaced (Schulz, "The Really Big One" par. 13). Some of the other possible disasters that Mitchell sketches in his job as a "futurologist" equally extend contemporary realities in the readers' actual world, with some new elements added. Rather than Middle Eastern terrorists, the narrative presents the Chinese as a threat (59), and Mitchell predicts a Sino-American military conflict in the immanent future—alongside conflicts between Iran and Israel, Pakistan and India, and the Koreas more familiar in the actual world of the early twenty-first century. Although Mitchell's predictions sometimes run into the slightly absurd,[18] the actual disaster that the novel revolves around, Hurricane Tammy, is eerily recognizable. Hurricane Tammy is a category 2 hurricane, described by the narrator in similar ways to Hurricane Sandy, a category 1 hurricane that hit the eastern United States in the readers' actual world in October 2012. Superstorms and floods are well-known features of cli-fi, but most interesting in respect to worldmaking is the way in which *Odds Against Tomorrow* creates epistemological uncertainty by blurring the boundaries between the actual and textual actual worlds. Such blurring, I'd argue, is central to the workings of the cli-fi genre and, importantly, the way in which the narratives enable readers to experience some of the epistemological uncertainty typical of climate crisis.

Odds Against Tomorrow demonstrates the workings of climate fiction particularly well when its readers are unsure whether what they are reading is part of their own actual world or of the novel's textual actual world, and hence, whether events like Hurricane Tammy are quite as much a part of fiction as they would like. Two instances illustrate this particularly well, both containing events from the actual world of the 2010s and the textual actual world of the novel that cannot be told apart unless readers have additional knowledge. In order to predict disasters as adequately as possible, Mitchell reads up

---

17. See Kathryn Schulz's articles on "the Big One," and this chart of activity on the Cascadia Subduction Zone: http://www.newyorker.com/wp-content/uploads/2015/07/Schulz-The-Big-One-Map-41.png

18. In one of his consultations, Mitchell sketches the scenario of people beginning to suffer from stigmata (78).

on reports and articles. One day he receives a report from the World Health Organization titled "Dengue and Hemorrhagic Fever: An Emerging Public Health Threat in the United States," a file containing new telemetric readings of unusual activity in the Yellowstone caldera, and an article from *Nature* titled "Recent Contributions of Glaciers and Ice Caps to Sea Level Rise" (65). While the first report does not exist in readers' actual world, and the alert level for the Yellowstone volcano was "normal" in readers' actual world at the time of writing this essay, the article on rising sea levels exists in readers' actual world and was published in 2012 in *Nature*.[19] A similar example is the heat wave that Mitchell mentions in the months before Hurricane Tammy strikes, with temperatures reaching 102F in New York City. Over the past years in the actual world, New York has experienced several very hot summers, including the one in July 2012, some months before Hurricane Sandy. While temperatures in the actual world New York remained below 100F,[20] readers may well confuse the fictional heat wave of the textual actual world with an actual heat wave in the actual world. These kinds of combinations, in which readers cannot determine at first glance what is true in the actual world and what only exists in the textual actual world, destabilize both the boundary between the two worlds as well as readers' knowledge and sense of certainty. By creating uncertainty about the chronology of the novel—relation D in Ryan's typology—and blurring the line between the textual actual world on the one hand, and the actual worlds of readers in the 2010s on the other, climate fictions reflect the uncertainty at the heart of climate crisis. Rather than merely describing this uncertainty, readers experience some level of it themselves when constructing the storyworld, and in trying to make sense of its temporal setting.

In *Flight Behavior,* this blurring between the actual world and the textual actual world is frequently less obvious than in Rich's novel. While this means that events of the scale depicted in *Odds Against Tomorrow* do not occur in the text, it also makes it more difficult for readers to gauge whether the world in the novel is really so different from the actual world, and whether they are not already experiencing the level of crisis that is fictionalized in the text. In other words, much like Dellarobia learns that she is living climate crisis, the ways in which the novel plays with its chronology also make the reader increasingly aware that they too might already be living it. This effect is achieved, for instance, when the novel presents a series of events that range

---

19. The Volcano Alert Level can be found on the website of the Yellowstone Volcano Observatory. https://volcanoes.usgs.gov/observatories/yvo/. Accessed 15 December 2016.

20. See Jacob et al. For temperatures in New York in 2012, see graph in "New York Central Park Daily Maximum/Minimum Temperatures for 2012": https://www.climatestations.com/images/stories/new-york/ny2012.gif.

from the fictional to the actual in the world of the 2010s—all of which are hard to pinpoint as either being real or not. One of these is Ovid Byron's description of droughts in Australia: "Walls of flames, Dellarobia. Traversing the land like freight trains, fed by dead trees and desiccated soil. In Victoria hundreds of people burned to death in one month, so many their prime minister called it hell on earth. This has not happened before. There is not an evacuation plan" (385). Although in readers' actual world between 1997 and 2009 Australia indeed faced the worst droughts in recorded history, the apocalyptic scenario sketched by Ovid has not (yet) taken place outside of the fictional context of the narrative. Earlier I referred to the radio report that Dellarobia hears toward the end of the novel that describes "[s]omething beyond terrible" happening in Japan (591). When Dellarobia subsequently looks out the window she sees that something has also happened to her own surroundings: the rain that has been falling for the past days has created a flood. Putting the 2011 earthquake and tsunami in Japan in the actual world side-by-side with the flood that devastates her home in the novel's textual actual world, and which forms the ending of the novel, makes both seem equally real, and equally plausible. In another instance, though, the actual world has—eerily—caught up with the textual actual world. Explaining to Dellarobia that the maximum of carbon molecules the atmosphere can hold while maintaining normal thermal balance is 350 parts per million, Ovid tells her that in the textual actual world of the novel, that figure has risen to 390. In May 2018, that number was up to 411.31 in readers' actual world—making life stranger than fiction.[21]

Climate fiction, then, is about more than *just* depictions of what a world in crisis looks like. Its force—and potential in terms of affecting cultural change—lies in the genre's mechanics, and especially, as I show in this chapter, its utilization of worldmaking strategies. Key to these is cli-fi's use of the principle of minimal departure to stretch the reader's actual world to encompass the possibilities the textual world suggests. An econarratological approach foregrounds the interplay of the texts' formal elements and the environment in crisis that they depict. It foregrounds the physical dimension of genres often overlooked by genre scholars, and moreover shows how an element central to both climate crisis and climate fiction—epistemological uncertainty—becomes part of the reader's experience of the novel through techniques such as the principle of minimal departure. At the same time, climate fictions also demonstrate to narratology the ways in which depictions of the environment and in particular climate crisis rely on, and extend, narratological categories, such as genre and matters of chronology. As such, my approach extends work

---

21. http://co2now.org/. Accessed 30 June 2018.

in narratology, particularly the typology of texts set out by Ryan. The possibilities of an econarratological approach to genre go beyond climate fiction, or indeed genre fiction in general. Environmental crisis is both one of the most pertinent problems and one of the most dominant narratives of the early twenty-first century. How we tell this story, which narratives and genres we choose, is a vital part of how we respond to it.

WORKS CITED

Abbott, H. Porter. *The Cambridge Introduction to Narrative.* 2nd ed. Cambridge UP, 2008.

Adams, Douglas, and Mark Carwardine. *Last Chance to See.* Ballantine, 1990.

Bakhtin, Mikhail. *The Dialogic Imagination: Four Essays by M. M. Bakhtin.* Edited by Michael Holquist, translated by Caryl Emerson and Michael Holquist, U of Texas P, 1981.

Beck, Ulrich. *Risk Society: Towards a New Modernity.* Sage, 1986.

Buell, Frederick. *From Apocalypse to Way of Life.* Routledge, 2003.

Clark, Timothy. *The Cambridge Introduction to Literature and the Environment.* Cambridge UP, 2011.

CO2Now.org. n.d. 30 Jun. 2018.

Cohen, Ralph. "Introduction: Notes Towards a Generic Reconstitution of Literary Study." *New Literary History,* vol. 34, no. 3, 2003, pp. v–xvi.

Easterlin, Nancy. *A Biocultural Approach to Literary Theory and Interpretation.* Johns Hopkins UP, 2012.

Evancie, Angela. "So Hot Right Now: Has Climate Change Created a New Literary Genre?" *NPR.* 20 Apr. 2013. www.npr.org/2013/04/20/176713022/so-hot-right-now-has-climate-change-created-a-new-literary-genre.

Frow, John. "'Reproducibles, Rubrics, and Everything You Need': Genre Theory Today." *PMLA,* vol. 122, no. 5, 2007, pp. 1626–34.

Garrard, Greg. "Conciliation and Consilience: Climate Change in Barbara Kingsolver's *Flight Behaviour.*" *De Gruyter Handbook of Ecocriticism and Cultural Ecology.* Edited by Hubert Zapf, De Gruyter, 2016, pp. 295–312.

Giddens, Anthony. "Risk and Responsibility." *Modern Law Review,* vol. 62, no. 1, 1999, pp. 1–10.

Glass, Rodge. "Global Warming: The Rise of 'Cli-Fi.'" *Guardian.* 31 May 2013. www.theguardian.com/books/2013/may/31/global-warning-rise-cli-fi

Glotfelty, Cheryll. Introduction. *The Ecocriticism Reader.* Edited by Cheryll Glotfelty and Harold Fromm. U of Georgia P, 1996, pp. xv–xxxvii.

Hamilton, Clive. *Requiem for a Species.* Routledge, 2010.

Haq, Husna. "Climate Change Inspires a New Literary Science." *Christian Science Monitor.* 26 Apr. 2013. www.csmonitor.com/Books/chapter-and-verse/2013/0426/Climate-change-inspires-a-new-literary-genre-cli-fi.

Heise, Ursula. "Eco-narratives." *Routledge Encyclopedia of Narrative Theory.* Edited by David Herman, Manfred Jahn, and Marie-Laure Ryan, Routledge, 2005, pp. 129–30.

———. "Lost Dogs, Last Birds, and Listed Species: Cultures of Extinction." *Configurations,* vol. 18, no. 1–2, Winter 2010, pp. 49–72.

Heise, Ursula K., and Allison Carruth. "Introduction to Focus: Environmental Humanities." *American Book Review,* vol. 32, no. 2, 2010, p. 3.

Herman, David, ed. *The Cambridge Companion to Narrative.* Cambridge UP, 2007.

———. *Storytelling and the Sciences of Mind.* MIT Press, 2013.

Herman, David, Manfred Jahn, and Marie-Laure Ryan, eds. *Routledge Encyclopedia of Narrative Theory.* Routledge, 2005.

Jacob, Thomas, John Wahr, W. Tad Pfeffer, and Sean Swenson. "Recent Contributions of Glaciers and Ice Caps to Sea Level Rise." *Nature,* vol. 482, 23 Feb. 2012, pp. 514–18.

James, Erin. *The Storyworld Accord: Econarratology and Postcolonial Narratives.* U of Nebraska P, 2015.

Kearns, Michael. "Genre Theory in Narrative Studies." *Routledge Encyclopedia of Narrative Theory.* Edited by David Herman, Manfred Jahn, and Marie-Laure Ryan. Routledge, 2005, pp. 201–05.

Keen, Susan. *Narrative Form.* Palgrave Macmillan, 2003.

Kerridge, Richard. "Ecocritical Approaches to Literary Form and Genre: Urgency, Depth, Provisionality, Temporality." *The Oxford Handbook of Ecocriticism.* Edited by Greg Garrard, Oxford UP, 2014, pp. 361–76.

———. "Narratives of Resignation: Environmentalism in Recent Fiction." *The Environmental Tradition in English Literature.* Edited by John Parham, Ashgate, 2002, pp. 87–99.

———. "The Single Source." *Ecozon@* vol. 1, no. 1, 2010, pp. 155–61. www.ecozona.eu/index.php/journal/article/view/36.

Kingsolver, Barbara. *Flight Behavior.* 2012. Faber and Faber, 2013.

Kormann, Carolyn. "Scenes from a Melting Planet: On the Climate Change Novel." *New Yorker.* 3 Jul. 2013. www.newyorker.com/books/page-turner/scenes-from-a-melting-planet-on-the-climate-change-novel.

Kunstler, James Howard. *World Made by Hand.* Atlantic Monthly Press, 2008.

McCartney, Cormac. *The Road.* Alfred A. Knopf, 2006.

McEwan, Ian. *Solar.* Random House, 2010.

Meeker, Joseph. *The Comedy of Survival: Literary Ecology and a Play Ethic.* U of Arizona P, 1974.

"New York Central Park Daily Maximum/Minimum Temperatures for 2012." *Climatestations. com.* n.d. www.climatestations.com/new-york-city/.

Patrick, Amy M. "Apocalyptic or Precautionary? Revisioning Texts in Environmental Literature." *Coming into Contact: Explorations in Ecocritical Theory and Practice.* Edited by Annie Merrill Ingram, Ian Marshall, Dan Philippon, and Adam Sweeting. U of Georgia P, 2007, pp. 141–53.

Prince, Michael. "Mauvais Genres." *New Literary History,* vol. 34, no. 3, 2003, pp. 452–79.

Pyrhönen, Heta. "Genre." *The Cambridge Companion to Narrative.* Edited by David Herman. Cambridge UP, 2007, pp. 109–24.

Rich, Nathaniel. *Odds Against Tomorrow.* Farrar, Straus and Giroux, 2013.

Rose, Deborah Bird, Thom van Dooren, Matthew Chrulew, Stuart Cooke, Matthew Kearnes, and Emily O'Gorman. "Thinking Through the Environment, Unsettling the Humanities." *Environmental Humanities,* vol. 1, 2012, pp. 1–5.

Ryan, Marie-Laure. "Fiction, Non-Factuals, and the Principle of Minimal Departure." *Poetics,* vol. 9, 1980, pp. 403–22.

———. "Introduction: On The Why, What and How of Generic Taxonomy." *Poetics,* vol. 10, 1981, pp. 109–26.

———. "Possible Worlds and Accessibility Relations: A Semantic Typology of Fiction." *Poetics Today,* vol. 12, no. 3, 1991, pp. 553–76.

———. *Possible Worlds, Artificial Intelligence and Narrative Theory.* Indiana UP, 1992.

Schulz, Kathryn. "How to Stay Safe When the Big One Comes." *New Yorker.* 28 Jul. 2015. www.newyorker.com/tech/annals-of-technology/how-to-stay-safe-when-the-big-one-comes.

———. "The Really Big One." *New Yorker.* 20 Jul. 2015. www.newyorker.com/magazine/2015/07/20/the-really-big-one.

Seitel, Peter. "Theorizing Genres—Interpreting Works." *New Literary History,* vol. 34, no. 2, 2003, pp. 275–97.

Seymour, Nicole. "Toward an Irreverent Ecocriticism." *Journal of Ecocriticism,* vol. 4, no. 2, 2012, pp. 56–71.

Todorov, Tzvetan. *Genres in Discourse.* Translated by Catherine Porter. Cambridge UP, 1990.

Trexler, Adam. *Anthropocene Fictions: The Novel in a Time of Climate Change.* U of Virginia P, 2015.

Vermeulen, Pieter. "Future Readers: Narrating the Human in the Anthropocene." *Textual Practice,* vol. 31, no. 5, 2017, pp. 867–85.

Yellowstone Volcano Observatory. https://volcanoes.usgs.gov/observatories/yvo/. Accessed 15 Dec. 2016.

CHAPTER 9

Narrative in the Anthropocene

ERIN JAMES

WHEN SCHOLARS speak of narrative and the Anthropocene, they tend to do so in one of two ways. The first is the conversation that dominates work in the environmental humanities and positions narrative as part of the problem of and solution to environmental crisis. Scholars such as Val Plumwood, Deborah Bird Rose, and Ursula Heise, among others, suggest that a key factor in today's environmental challenges are the types of stories that we tell each other about the environment.[1] The editors of the first issue of *Environmental Humanities* articulate this stance when they call for an "unsettling of dominant narratives" and the popularization of "new narratives that are calibrated to the realities of our changing world" (Rose et al. 3). Change the stories, these scholars suggest, and change the damaging attitudes and behaviors that have brought us to this point.

Notably missing from this discussion are scholars of narrative theory, who have largely ignored the Anthropocene in their work. Perhaps this neglect stems in part from the claims of a second group of critics who link narrative

---

1. See Plumwood's *Environmental Culture* and Heise's "The Environmental Humanities and the Futures of the Human." For further examples, see *Global Ecologies and the Environmental Humanities* (edited by Elizabeth DeLoughrey, Jill Didur, and Anthony Carrigan), Ursula Kluwick's "Talking About Climate Change," Meina Pereira Savi's "The Anthropocene (and) (in) the Humanities," and Roy Scranton's *Learning to Die in the Anthropocene*.

and the Anthropocene in a much less optimistic way. Cultural theorists and literary critics steeped in deconstructivist philosophy, such as Claire Cole-brook and Timothy Morton, suggest that narrative is a rhetorical mode deeply unsuited to our current epoch.[2] In *Death of the PostHuman,* Colebrook argues that narrative is intimately tied to human perspectives and, as such, cannot adequately represent the broader timescales and wider conception of nonhu-man lives that our current moment of environmental crisis demands. Stating that the climate change that defines the Anthropocene is "catastrophic for the human imaginary," she argues that it "should not require us to return to modes of reading, comprehension and narrative communication but should awaken us from our human-all-to-human narrative slumbers" (10, 25). Simi-larly, Morton's recent work states that "global warming is a manifestation of the Anthropocene, the moment at which human history has intersected deci-sively with geological time," and that "philosophy is now tasked with bringing human thinking up to speed with this new reality" ("Poisoned Ground" 37). Out for Morton are art forms such as narrative that rely on a stable world informed by human categories such as "here" and "there," "then" and "now." In are forms such as Jackson Pollack's drip paintings that call conceptualizations of stability into question to stress disjunctiveness and our inability to perceive the complete, stable whole.

My approach to narrative and the Anthropocene offers a third direction— one that questions what contribution the Anthropocene stands to make to narrative studies and vice versa. This approach asks what an Anthropocene narrative theory might look like, or imagines a theory of narrative sensitive to matters commonly associated with the epoch.[3] An Anthropocene narrative theory thus corrects two shortcomings: a lack of engagement with narrative theory within the environmental humanities, despite a keen interest in the role that narrative and storytelling might and should play in today's environ-mentalism, and the almost total absence of considerations of the environment in narrative studies, let alone more specific discussions of the Anthropocene and climate change. It also grapples with the contradiction, present in the conversation that I outline above, that the Anthropocene is both produced and mitigated by narratives and, at the same time, incapable of being nar-

---

2. See also Timothy Clark's *Ecocriticism on the Edge* and James J. Pulizzi's "Predicting the End of History."

3. My discussion of narrative in the Anthropocene is inspired by Gerald Prince's work in "On a Postcolonial Narratology," in which he "wear[s] a set of postcolonial lenses to look at narrative" with the goal of sketching out a narratology "sensitive to matters commonly, if not uncontroversially, associated with the postcolonial (e.g., hybridity, migrancy, otherness, frag-mentation, diversity, power relations)" (373).

rated. I do this by thinking through various ideas and issues that we associate with our new geological epoch—especially those relevant to representations of narrative time and space and the processes of narrative production and interpretation—and envisaging their possible narratological correspondents. My primary goal thus is not to analyze individual narratives about the Anthropocene or global climate change by pointing to their strengths and shortcomings, nor to identify the parameters (or lack thereof) of the genre of the "Anthropocene narrative" or "climate change fiction" ("cli-fi"). Instead, I bring together the until now disparate conversations of the environmental humanities and narrative studies to propose an "Anthropocene narrative theory," or a theory of narrative sensitive to matters commonly associated with the epoch, to explore how narrative and the Anthropocene inform and are influenced by each other.

Such an exploration of the connection between narrative and the Anthropocene poses the following questions: how does narrative help us think differently about the Anthropocene? How do narratives provide us with safe contexts in which to explore how humans make and inhabit worlds in their own image? How does the reading of geological strata, tree rings, and ice cores, which are themselves material representations of sequences of events, challenge our most basic definitions of narrative and narration? How do the new conceptions of time and space associated with the Anthropocene diversify models of narrative chronologies and spatializations? How does the awareness of collective agency associated with the Anthropocene shed new light on types of narration? Indeed, how does the Anthropocene help us think differently about narrative? How does it inspire new structures that push against traditional narrative forms?

An Anthropocene narrative theory explores various ideas and issues that we associate with our new geological epoch and envisages their possible narratological correspondents. It considers narrative modalities via an Anthropocene lens to better account for the ways in which narratives—all narratives, both existing and possible—make sense. Such an approach to narrative and the Anthropocene stands to enrich a universal model of narrative by incorporating ideas pertinent to this new epoch and developing a richer vocabulary for analyzing individual narratives in the age of the Anthropocene. It also makes a case *for* narrative in the Anthropocene—for narrative as *the* dominant rhetorical mode of this epoch—by tracing the similarities between the two. It thus argues that, contrary to what some suggest, we stand to understand better the current state of the world and our relationship to it by engaging with narrative.

NARRATIVE AND THE ANTHROPOCENE:
HUMANS WRITING WORLDS

An Anthropocene narrative theory begins by addressing head on the idea that narrative is incapable of representing the epoch. In addition to the disagreeing perspectives that I outline above, a separate group of scholars is debating the ability of one particular type of narrative—the novel—to represent the epoch. In *Anthropocene Fictions: The Novel in a Time of Climate Change*, Adam Trexler disagrees with Colebrook's and Morton's claim that the epoch cannot be narrated. At the heart of Trexler's project is a diachronic study of the novel that tracks how it is evolving in the Anthropocene to represent new material and social realities. He argues that the formal qualities of the novel make it "a privileged form to explore what it means to live in the Anthropocene moment," most notably because of its heteroglossia and its interest in "assembl[ing] heterogeneous characters and things into a narrative sequence" (27, 14). Similarly, Stephanie LeMenager sees the novel as the rhetorical mode well suited to representing the Anthropocene. She argues that climate change represents "among other things, an assault on the everyday" that lends itself to the novel because of the latter's investment in the everyday, in "probable, cyclical, and even trivial experience" (221). Furthermore, she turns to the novel because of its successful history of offering "opportunities for trying out and testing material and social relations" (236). Amitav Ghosh's consideration of climate change novels represents the flip side of these arguments. Indeed, for Ghosh, the very phrase "climate change novel" is oxymoronic. He argues that the climate changes of the Anthropocene are vicious and extreme and, as such, they pose a major problem for writers of "serious" fiction because the very form of the novel, in its interest in individual human lives, relies upon a certain predictability that conceals the "unheard-of and the improbable" (27). He states that modern changes in climate are "too powerful, too grotesque, too dangerous, and too accusatory to be written about in a lyrical, or elegiac, or romantic vein"; the Anthropocene "defies both literary fiction and contemporary common sense" via its "very high degree of improbability" (32–33, 26). Ghosh ultimately concludes that a successful climate change novel does not exist because it *cannot* exist. The novel, he argues, is too rigidly tied to predictable patterns to accommodate adequately the startling events of the Anthropocene.

An Anthropocene narrative theory weighs in on these disagreements by foregrounding the ability of narrative to shift and change as does the world in which it is produced. In particular, it highlights the ways in which narratives have grappled with precisely the unpredictable timelines, broad spatial scales, and nonhuman perspectives that concern scholars such as Colebrook, Morton, and Ghosh. Elana Gomel's work in *Narrative Space and Time: Representing Impossible Topologies in Literature* speaks to the ability of narrative to accommodate temporal and spatial scales beyond those familiar to human experience. Her interest lies in "textual topologies that defy the Newtonian-Euclidean paradigm of homogenous, uniform, three-dimensional spatiality," and she roots such representations in narratives dating back to the Victorian era, especially in the work of Charles Dickens (3). Furthermore, she argues that "in many ways, narrative is ahead of science, providing a semantic armature for imagining and representing new forms of space and time" (24). The discussion of nonhuman narrators by Lars Bernaerts, Marco Caracciolo, Luc Herman, and Bart Vervaeck suggests that narrative, while an anthropogenic rhetorical mode, is not blinded totally by human myopia. In "The Storied Lives of Nonhuman Narrators," Bernaerts and his colleagues argue that such narrators can encourage readers to empathize with fictional autobiographical nonhuman storytellers while they reflect on their own humanness. Likewise, David Herman's "Narratology Beyond the Human" suggests that narrative is an important imaginative tool for perceiving the interconnections between humans in wider biotic communities.[4] This work not only foregrounds the fluid nature of narrative—the way that it can adapt to changing real-world contexts—but also calls into question the claims of narrative rigidity that Colebrook, Morton, and Ghosh make.

Perhaps more powerfully, an Anthropocene narrative theory also illuminates similarities between narrative and the Anthropocene. The most striking similarity is that both narrative and the Anthropocene are products of *humans writing worlds*. Narrative theorists such as Herman have long celebrated the worldmaking power of narratives, such that his very definition of narrative relies heavily upon the concept of storyworlds, or "mental models of who did what to whom, when, where, why, and in what fashion in the world to which interpreters relocate . . . as they work to comprehend a narrative" ("Storyworld" 570). Herman argues that storyworlds are one of the four basic elements of narrative and, as such, narratives provide readers with essential blueprints for worldmaking (*Basic*). Likewise, we distinguish the Anthropocene from the Holocene by acknowledging the capability of humans to irre-

---

4. For a selection of further examples of narrative theory that grapples with environmental issues, see David Herman's "Animal Autobiography; Or, Narration Beyond the Human" and "Storyworld/Umwelt: Nonhuman Experiences in Graphic Novels," Suzanne Keen's "Fast Tracks to Narrative Empathy: Anthropomorphism and Dehumanization in Graphic Novels," Alexa Weik von Mossner's *Affective Ecologies*, and Nancy Easterlin's *A Biocultural Approach to Literary Theory and Interpretation*.

coverably change the world. Humans in this epoch have rewritten the world to reflect their own activities and attitudes toward themselves and other species and matter. We literally see the effects of this rewriting in the inscription of human activity in geological strata. A similar sense of worldmaking is fundamental to narrative. This is a mode by which humans write worlds in which to immerse themselves—a mode by which we create and then emotionally and cognitively inhabit new time- and spacescapes and experiences. Understanding that process will surely give us insight into the ways in which we enact similar processes of world-creation and inhabitation in material, nonnarrative realms in this epoch. Cognitive narrative scholars have long made the argument that narratives provide readers with safe contexts in which to simulate, or "try on," the emotional states of others. Blakey Vermuele is explicit about this feature of narratives when she speaks of narrative as "emotional prosthesis": "Narrative can be seen as a vehicle by which people test scenarios without risking too much" (41, 47).[5] Given their world-creating power, we can similarly position narratives as potent simulations of the processes that have created the Anthropocene. Just as they provide us with safe contexts within which to experience the emotional states of others, narratives also provide us with safe contexts in which to study the worldmaking processes that define this epoch. We thus stand to understand our destructive role in the latter by grappling with the worldmaking power of the former.

Viewing narrative as a worldmaking rhetorical mode in light of the special characteristics of the novel helps to explain the importance of this particular type of narrative in the Anthropocene. The fundamental role that the novel has played and does play in imaginations of the Anthropocene should not surprise us given the historical overlaps between this mode and the epoch. Although geologists are still debating the official "onset" of the Anthropocene, many date the epoch as beginning with the rise of industrialization and colonization—right around the time that Daniel Defoe first published *Robinson Crusoe* (1719).[6] Of course, the rise of the novel and the onset of the Anthro-

---

5. See similar arguments in Lisa Zunshine's *Why We Read Fiction*.

6. Since the introduction of the concept, geologists have debated the date of the beginning of the Anthropocene. Crutzen and Stoermer's original proposal looked to an important historical juncture such as the Industrial Revolution for the origin of the epoch. Simon L. Lewis and Mark A. Maslin, in their *Nature* article "Defining the Anthropocene," examine global synchronous geological marks on an annual or decadal scale to point to 1610 and 1964 as possible start dates. They prefer 1610 as the origin date because of its connection to nautical exploration and colonization, noting that "the transoceanic movement of species is a clear and permanent geological change to the Earth system" (177). This date, they suggest, also "mark[s] Earth's last globally synchronous cool period before the long-term global warmth of the Anthropocene Epoch" (177).

pocene result from the same set of conditions: early secularism, scientific enlightenment, empiricism, capitalism, materialism, national consolidation, and the rise of the middle class.[7]

The characteristics of the novel also suggest similarities between it and the Anthropocene. Ralph W. Rader's definition of the novel as "a work which offers the reader a focal illusion of characters acting autonomously as if in the world of real experience within a subsidiary awareness of an underlying constructive authorial purpose" echoes several hallmarks of the Anthropocene: this epoch is one in which we perceive the *illusion* of human agents as acting autonomously, and one in which the world is written by an underlying human agent (72). Novels offer readers worlds dominated by human agents as created by human agents, and thus simulate humans' real-life perspective of and relationship to the world around them in the Anthropocene. Catherine Gallagher's assertion that, unlike romances and allegories that "assume a correspondence between a proper name in the believable narrative and an embodied individual in the real world," the novel that is about no one in particular also stresses a common link between it and the Anthropocene. Gallagher argues that early novels referred to a whole class of people in general because their fictional names had no real-world counterparts. "The founding claim of the form," she states, "was a nonreferentiality that could be seen as a greater referentiality" (342). She cites Henry Fielding's *Joseph Andrews* (1742) as illustrative of this new form—a text in which the narrator states that his story describes "not men, but manners; not an individual, but a species" (qtd. in Gallagher 341). Obviously this narrator's notion of the human "species" is markedly more limited than the conceptualization of the human species as collective agent so fundamental to the Anthropocene that I discuss below in more detail. The characters in Fielding's novel are located culturally, economically, and geographically, and thus do not and cannot speak for the entirety of the human species. Yet Gallagher's argument that early novels placed emphasis on the general instead of the specific individual speaks to the notions of collectivity that are so integral to our understanding of the Anthropocene. Indeed, an Anthropocene narrative theory argues that *all* novels have built into their foundations the attitudes and ideologies that produced the Anthropocene and climate change and thus, in this sense, are all representative of the epoch in their form. It suggests that the novel does not just reflect the social and material changes that produce the Anthropocene, but offers a particu-

---

7. I list here the conditions in England that Ian Watt cites as leading to the popularization of the novel, or "formal realism" in *The Rise of the Novel*.

larly rich testing ground for imaginatively exploring the implications of these behaviors in the word.

MATERIAL

Although narrative theory does not often appear in environmental humanities scholarship, a significant vein of that scholarship does concern itself with narration. Posthumanism and new materialism scholars such as Jane Bennett and Karen Barad have long encouraged their readers to consider the experiences and agency of nonhuman forces and matter. Material ecocritics Serenella Iovino and Serpil Oppermann take this idea one step further, referring to the "narrative agency of matter" in their arguments that all matter is "storied" and thus capable of producing its own narratives (8). They state: "The world's material phenomena are knots in a vast network of agencies, which can be 'read' and interpreted as forming narratives, stories" ("Introduction" 8, 1). An Anthropocene narrative theory calls this claim into question, given the inherently anthropogenic nature of narrative as a rhetorical mode. Indeed, when we place the idea of matter's agency within the context of narrative theory, we recognize its incompatibility with a rhetorical mode that involves, to cite James Phelan's definition of narrative, "somebody telling someone else on some occasion and for some purpose(s) that something happened" (*Living* 18). Phelan's definition points to the fundamental anthropogenic nature of this mode of communication—the rhetorical situation of narrative demands not only a speaker capable of wielding language in such a way as to describe events, but also a receiver of this language that the speaker attempts to persuade. The narrator and narratee may not be human in a given text, but by definition they must be human enough to tell and comprehend a story, respectively.

Furthermore, an Anthropocene narrative theory draws upon scholarship on comparative cognition and the evolution of narrative to highlight the anthropogenic nature of this mode of communication. Cognitive anthropologist Merlin Donald argues that it is the capacity for narrative construction and interpretation that sets humans apart from their closest genetic relatives. "Our genes may be largely identical to those of a chimp or gorilla," he writes, "but our cognitive architecture is not. . . . Our minds function on several phylogenetically new representational planes, none of which are available to animals" (382). Social psychologist Jerome Bruner agrees, arguing that humans "enter into meaning" by making narrative sense of the world around them, and that the innate disposition to narrative organization is so essential to human cognition that it is a precursor to language acquisition (68). Narrative theorist H. Porter Abbott also sees narrative as essential to human cognition and argues that the development of narrative meaning-making has allowed humans to exist in their own constructed realities: "If hominids found themselves, like all other creatures, thrown into a world governed by the seemingly eternal regularities of days and seasons, they found in narrative a way to impose shapes of their own devising back on the universe" (250). Taken together, this work suggests that narrative not only foregrounds human communication but that the capacity for narrative thought is uniquely human and provides humans with a distinctive relationship to themselves and the world around them.[8]

But we need not necessarily understand narrative's emphasis on the human as running counter to the critique of human exceptionalism that is so essential to Anthropocene scholarship. As Iovino and Oppermann themselves argue, to be anthropo*genic* is not necessarily to be anthropo*centric* ("Material" 82). An Anthropocene narrative theory takes inspiration from the idea of matter's narrative agency to explore how the Anthropocene challenges the very definition of narrative itself, especially in terms of what narrative is and where we find it. It pays particular attention to environmental representations of sequences of events such as those we find in geological strata, ice cores, and tree rings to posit an alternative conceptualization of material narrative agency that positions matter not as narrating but as possessing a basic degree of narrativity. An Anthropocene narrative theory, while acknowledging the anthropogenic basis of narrative, is also sensitive to ways in which fragments of narrativity appear in nonhuman material and can, in turn, inspire human narratives.

An Anthropocene narrative theory suggests that geological strata, ice cores, and tree rings offer us a representation of a sequence of events and, as such, display a minimal amount of narrativity. It is inappropriate to classify the rocks, cores, and rings as full-blown narratives because on their own they lack other basic elements of narrative, such as a narrator and/or narratee, an occasion for telling, an articulation of qualia, and a representation of a storyworld that human readers can model mentally and inhabit emotionally. In other words, rocks, ice, and trees are capable of representing sequences of events, but rock, ice, and tree material is incapable of producing other hallmarks of narrativity, such as focalization, the representation of the consciousness and emotional state of characters, metalepsis, free indirect discourse, and heteroglossia, to name a but a few. They are also not capable of representing changes in chronology or temporality; geologic strata, ice core, and tree ring

---

8. For more on narrative and comparative cognition, see my essay "Nonhuman Fictional Characters and the Empathy-Altruism Hypothesis."

time sequences progress steadily, with no analepsis or prolepsis to complicate the annual recording of events. But they do suggest the possibility of collaboration between human storytellers and nonhuman material. We see this idea in light of actual geological strata, ice cores, and tree rings, and especially geologist Jan Zalasiewicz's argument in *The Earth After Us* that the strata "contain within themselves countless narrative possibilities of the histories of former oceans and rivers, of lakes and shorelines and arid deserts" (17–18). We also see this idea in narratives that use such material fragments of narrativity as blueprints, including the "Good Oak" chapter of Aldo Leopold's *A Sand County Almanac* and Richard Powers's novel *Overstory.*

TIME

When discussing time and narrative, narrative theorists tend to distinguish between the timeline of the told (story time, relating to the *fabula*) and the timeline of the telling (discourse time, relating to the *syuzhet*). In his seminal 1980 book *Narrative Discourse,* Gérard Genette outlines a model of discourse time that still dominates narratology today. Genette's model identifies and codifies three types of chronologies common in narratives—order, duration, and frequency—and introduces key terms to narratives studies, such as analepsis and prolepsis (order), acceleration, deceleration, stasis, and ellipses (duration), as well as singulative, repetitive, and iterative (frequency). Since then, Brian Richardson has expanded Genette's model to better account for discourse time in postmodern narratives. Admitting that in most cases order, duration, and frequency are "all that is required," Richardson cites narratives such as James Joyce's *Finnegan's Wake,* Virginia Woolf's *Orlando,* and John Fowles's *The French Lieutenant's Woman* to introduce six new temporal categories: circular (endings that return to beginnings), contradictory (incompatible and irreconcilable versions of the same story), antinomic (narratives that move backward in time), differential (one chronology is superimposed on another, larger one), conflated (apparently different temporal zones fail to remain distinct), and dual or multiple (different plotlines, though beginning and ending in the same moment, take different timelines to unfold) ("Beyond" 48–53). Richardson is eager to point out that, given the uncanny nature of such timelines, these temporalities are anti-mimetic and occur only in fictional narratives.

By definition, the Anthropocene relies upon an imagination of extremely long chronologies. An Anthropocene narrative theory takes on representations of these chronologies, both considering what they would look like in a narrative and exploring the challenges that they pose to popular models of narrative time. Of particular interest here is Rob Nixon's notion of slow violence, or a "violence that occurs gradually and out of sight, a violence of delayed destruction that is dispersed across time and space" that he argues is central to the environmental injustice of the Anthropocene (2). Nixon suggests that such durations tend to accompany specific narrative structures—the narratives that he sees as featuring slow violence are "slow paced and open ended" and "elud[e] . . . tidy closure . . . [and] containment" (6)—but does not himself identify these structures. We find an intriguing representation of slow violence in Cherie Dimaline's recent dystopian novel *The Marrow Thieves*. This narrative creatively confuses timelines of the past, present, and future to draw attention to the slow violence of the Canadian residential school system and its accompanying environmental racism, suggesting that there may be more ways to represent the slow violence of the Anthropocene than the slow paced and open-ended techniques to which Nixon points. Similarly, David Mitchell's *Cloud Atlas* features a circular timeline to highlight the slow violence of slavery and class oppression. The representation of slow violence in both of these narratives suggests that we can no longer think of Richardson's categories of narrative time as purely anti-mimetic. The timelines of slow violence function so that, à la Richardson, "apparently different temporal zones fail to remain distinct, and slide or spill into one another" ("Beyond" 50). Conflated temporalities are a part of our everyday, "natural," nonfictional reality in the Anthropocene.

It is difficult to situate slow violence within Genette's model of narrative temporality, as it exists between two of the categories that Genette uses to determine duration: "scene" and "ellipses." This violence does not occur in quick, catastrophic events, but accumulates quietly in the background over long periods of time. In appearing off the page or in the background, the extremely slow durations of slow violence challenge the basic separation of description and plot that is fundamental to narrative theory. In "Boundaries of Narrative," Genette makes a clear distinction between narration and description. He writes that every narrative contains two types of representations: "representations of actions and events, which constitute the narration properly speaking, and representations of objects or people, which make up the act of what we today call 'description'" (5). He continues to write that these two antithetical categories correspond largely to considerations of time and space. Narration is "more active" while description is "more contemplative"; narration "links itself to actions of events" and thus "puts emphasis on the temporal or dramatic aspects of narration," while description "lingers over objects" and thus "seems to suspend the flow of time and to contribute to the spreading out of narrative in space" (7). Various scholars have since complicated Genette's binary. Harold G. Mosher, Jr., introduces the categories of descriptivized narration and narrativized description to highlight the ways in which Genette's two categories are often intertwined and exist not as separate poles but along a continuum. Labelling description as "a neglected stepchild in a very large family of narratological concepts," Monika Fludernik and Suzanne Keen explore the complicated relationship between narrative *perspectives* and descriptions of interior spaces in literature in a special issue of *Style* ("Introduction" 454). For Fludernik and Keen, representations of houses, drawing rooms, and halls from the perspective of individual characters complicates the idea that description is the "*other* against which *narrative* proper [i]s defined by juxtaposition" (454). Narrative scholars have long been engaged in a project that surveys a continuum of narration and description, or time and space. But slow violence tasks us with doing away with the continuum altogether, such that we must now recognize plots that are so slow as to be imperceptible to human experience. An Anthropocene narrative theory would thus recognize the importance of descriptive plots in this epoch.

SPACE

Just as the Anthropocene suggests that we expand notions of narrative time, so does it encourage us to thicken our understanding of narrative space. Cognitive narrative theorists such as Herman and Marie-Laure Ryan make a case for the importance of spatialization in narrative by suggesting that a text's narrativity increases with an appropriate amount of spatializing information, as such details can help readers create mental models of a character's context. Building on former work, most notably Mikhail Bakhtin's notion of the chronotope, Herman's spatialization model in *Story Logic* offers us the most robust account of narrative space. The model establishes six categories of spatializing information: deictic shift (the relocation of readers from the here and now of their reading environment to the virtual world of a narrative); figures versus grounds (located objects versus reference objects, respectively); regions, landmarks, and paths; projective versus topological locations (inherent versus viewer-related locations, respectively); motion verbs, which exist along a continuum of "come" and "go"; and what linguists call the WHAT/WHERE systems (nouns versus spatial prepositions).

An Anthropocene narrative theory refines and adds to this model. None of Herman's categories are particularly useful for tracking the representation of unstable spaces, such as aquatic space. Water is essential to our understanding of the Anthropocene, whether it be via models of rising sea levels, concern for severe coral bleaching in the Great Barrier Reef, or the increasing frequency of extreme and violent water-based events on land, such as tsunamis, hurricanes, and floods. To understand the current status of our world and its potential future in the Anthropocene, we must become better at analyzing the way that we imagine and interact with the water that surrounds us. And yet water, in its instability and fluidity, doesn't easily fit into these categories. A cluster of recent scholarship on water by scholars interested in the Anthropocene stresses this instability by positioning water as spaceless. Stacy Alaimo's work notes that, because they largely exist beyond state borders, "open seas have long been considered empty space" (234). Furthermore, she suggests that many imaginations of water as spaceless are informed by perceptions of the disorienting deep sea. Such spaces, because of their lack of light and solid blackness, deny viewers "any sense of scale, perspective, or depth. The flat wall of blackness denies us any foundation, direction, or orientation toward a horizon" (241). As such, these "unnervingly violet-black seas . . . renounce mastery, transcendence, and stable, terrestrial frames of reference" (245). Astrid Neimanis's work on water and human bodies agrees. Drawing on the French feminist celebration of fluidity as an inherently female imagination, Neimanis argues that imaginations of water "torqu[e] many of our accepted cartographies of space . . . and implicate[ ] a specifically watery movement of difference and repetition" (6).

The instability of water poses significant problems for models of narrative space. Concepts such as regions, landmarks, and paths, as well as bird's-eye views vs. on-the-ground views are useful for analyzing representations of static or stable space, but less convenient for discussing spaces that constantly shift and change, such as those underwater. The old proverb that "you never step into the same river twice" illustrates just how difficult it is to speak of stable spaces within aquatic environments. In his writing on narrative time, Herman introduces the concept of fuzzy temporality, or temporal sequencing that is strategically inexact and thus difficult to chart along a clear timeline. An Anthropocene narrative theory sensitive to the changes brought about by rising sea levels and an abundance of water develops a corresponding category of "unspatialization," or spatializing information that is strategically unclear or unchartable. We find a fine example of unspatialization in Marina Vitaglione's short speculative narrative about rising sea levels in Venice, *Solastalgia*. In this text, narrated by the city itself, almost all spatializing cues produce confusion for readers because the narrator itself is confused about space: the submerged city unsuccessfully attempts to maintain its terranean identity while telling its story after being subsumed by the Adriatic Sea.

Unspatialization allows literary scholars to better read the aquatic environments so essential to the Anthropocene, and recognize the ways in which they often illustrate key Anthropocene ideas about change—that nothing is stable in a world that is changing unpredictably. But while inspired by the instability of water, unspatialization is an idea that is not restricted to watery environments alone. As the title of Vitaglione's narrative suggests, this category of narrative spatialization better equips narrative and environmental humanities scholars to discuss *all* of the unstable and changing environments in the Anthropocene, not just aquatic ones. Environmental philosopher Glenn Albrecht defines solastalgia as "the pain experienced when there is a recognition that the place where one resides and that one loves is under immediate assault . . . a form of homesickness one gets when one is still at 'home'" (96). For Albrecht, solastalgia is a new form of psychoterratic illness linked to a negative relationship between humans and their support environment. For the purposes of an Anthropocene narrative theory, solastalgia is a useful reminder that terrestrial environments in the Anthropocene have taken on the instability of their aquatic peers. We can no longer step into the same *anywhere* twice in this era defined by radical, total, and complete change. Richard McGuire's graphic novel *Here,* which represents the corner of one room over geologic time, illustrates this concept nicely.

NARRATION

New imaginations of the human species in the Anthropocene—of the collective agency of humans *as a species*—pose various challenges to our current understanding of narrative and narrative structures. Historian Dipesh Chakrabarty calls for the need for humans to perceive themselves as agents that have, collectively, created a new world in the Anthropocene. He discusses how humans have produced the climate crisis by becoming "a force of nature in the geological sense," and looks at the massive global changes that have resulted from industrialization to suggest that we best now think of humans as a collective agent, acting together and on a grand, planetary scale (207). He thus argues that it makes little sense to only think of divisions between humans—the inequalities that are the focus of much historical scholarship. He states that the Anthropocene demands that we must now also have a second notion of humans as having a collective history that registers at the level of species. Chakrabarty also acknowledges that this imagination is unattainable, given that "species" is an impossible ontological subject position for an individual human to hold. Yet he argues that various narratives and forms will produce the imaginative work that will help humans navigate the ecological crisis.

Like Nixon and slow violence, Chakrabarty does not specify which narrative structures will help readers come closer to imagining species agency. An Anthropocene narrative theory would take up his call for new structures and recognize the ways in which they challenge the agency of certain types of narrators—most notably omniscient narrators. Jonathan Culler defines omniscience via an analogy between God and the author: "The author creates the world of the novel as God created our world, and just as the world holds no secrets for God, so the novelist knows everything that is to be known about the world of the novel" ("Omniscience" 23). Omniscient narrators exhibit what Culler refers to as "Total Information Awareness"; in practice, they tend to tell their stories at one level removed from the action of the storyworld, accessing "a vast store of knowledge, in excess of what might be expressed" (22, 23). An Anthropocene narrative theory asks: is it possible, in this new epoch, to narrate a story from a singular, all-knowing subject position that is not also a participant in the storyworld? Is it possible for one person to author a world so completely in this epoch? Chakrabarty's work answers "no." The Anthropocene points to the impossibility of the omniscient narrator by calling attention to the difficulty with which one tells a story from a singular, all-knowing position. No one human acts as an individual at the species level. In addition, species agency calls into question the traditional omniscient narrator's godlike distance from the events they narrate. No one in this epoch cannot *not* experience the Anthropocene. It is impossible to tell a story of others that is also not the story of yourself.

An Anthropocene narrative theory thus develops an understanding of narrative structures that, unlike omniscience, represent the collective agency of larger groups to author or create new worlds. One type of collective action that illustrates Chakrabarty's notion of species agency is that of the "we" narrator. In her 2017 essay on "We-Narratives," Natalya Bekhta argues that the we-narrator "creates a holistic supraindividual level that supersedes a mere aggregation of individual characters and thus cannot be identified or reduced to an "I" speaking on behalf of such a group" (165). Her prime example of this we-narrator appears in Joshua Ferris's *Then We Came to the End,* in which an entire office of white-collar workers narrate their fear of being laid off. We find an even more apt representation of collective agency in the Anthropocene in Chang-Rae Lee's climate change novel *On Such a Full Sea,* in which the community of B-Mor (a future dystopic Baltimore populated only by the working-class descendants of Chinese immigrants) narrates the myth of one of their own members.

Indeed, "we" narration is particularly useful for illustrating species agency because of the way it not only represents the supraindividual level of collective agents but also foregrounds the incompleteness of that group and the existence of other, sometimes unacknowledged groups outside of this aggregate. In the wake of Chakrabarty's essay, environmental humanities scholars interested in social and environmental justice have called into question the totality of the "we" of species agency, noting that only *some* humans are agents in the destructive behaviors and industries driving climate change. In her writing on climate change fiction, LeMenager notes that discussions of the emerging genre too often assume an all-inclusive "we": "For now, 'we' is the European American subject, comfortable enough in wealth, contemplating not only the loss of self-sovereignty but also the end of a kind of culture that has exceeded its ecological carrying capacity" (231). In LeMenager's model of the human species in this epoch, the collective agency of some humans has done more than others to create our new world. Some human communities are agents of the activity that drives climate change, while others are witnesses to the changes their fellow humans produce. All ultimately live in this new world but, because of structural inequalities, only a privileged few write that world. It is their actions that masquerade as universal.

"We" narrators implicitly call attention to the limits of their collectives, or the incomplete nature of their narrating agent. Of course, by definition a "we" must exist within a context that also includes a "them." In Ferris's novel, the "them" are those coworkers that are not a part of the narrating "we." In Lee's novel, the "them" are anyone outside of B-Mor, including the rich residents of gated communities whose appetites drive the environmental devastation in which B-Mor residents must live. In *Unnatural Voices,* Richardson points out that "we" narrators are a powerful trope in many postcolonial novels, and in these texts, "we" is often a powerful collective identity that stands in contrast to "them" of imperial authority. He concludes that "we" narration most often appears in texts seeking to emphasize the construction and maintenance of a powerful collective identity, and argues that "the vast majority of 'we' texts valorize collective identity in no uncertain terms. . . . 'We' is almost always a favored term and a desirable subject position that is to be sought out and inhabited" (50). Within the context of the Anthropocene, "we" narrators call attention to the epoch's sociopolitical and material inequities by pointing to the fact that all collectives necessarily are defined by their difference to other groups. Furthermore, the prominent role that "we" narration plays in postcolonial and ethnic literature such as Lee's novel provides readers with essential correctives to the idea that the European American subject implied in Chakrabarty's notion of "we" is the only collective agent of the Anthropocene, and thus the only group who gets to tell the story of this epoch. In texts such as *On Such a Full Sea,* the "we" who narrates is not the "we" who has created the dystopic conditions in which the story unfolds. This "we" is thus able to offer a crucially important counternarrative to the "we" who typically narrates the world in the Anthropocene.

In this essay, I've identified several directions of an Anthropocene narrative theory. Other paths remain open. Such an approach to narrative in this epoch might also ask: How do the digital materials that we associate with the Great Acceleration of the Anthropocene, which media scholars such as Nicholas Carr argue literally are rewiring our brains, change the way that readers interact with narrative? How do notions of distant futures and the possible extinction of humans, often represented in narratives via far-future narratees, open up new possibilities for models of narrative audience? How do climate scientists use (or not) narratives in communicating their work with the public? And how might empirical research on the reading process shed light on the potential of environmental narratives in the Anthropocene to shift the real-life attitudes, behaviors, and values of readers? In pursuing these questions and those that I explore above in more detail, an Anthropocene narrative theory not only provides us with invaluable insight into how stories shape that world in which we live, but also into how the Anthropocene is changing the very nature of narrative today.

WORKS CITED

Abbott, H. Porter. "The Evolutionary Origins of the Storied Mind: Modeling the Prehistory of Narrative Consciousness and Its Discontents." *Narrative,* vol. 8, no. 3, 2000, pp. 247–56.

Alaimo, Stacy. "Violet-Black." *Prismatic Ecologies: Ecotheory Beyond Green.* Edited by Jefferey Jerome Cohen, U of Minnesota P, 2013, pp. 233–51.

Albrecht, Glenn. "'Solastalgia': A New Concept in Health and Identity." *PAN: Philosophy, Activism, Nature,* vol. 3, 2005, pp. 44–59.

Bekhta, Natalya. "We-Narratives: The Distinctiveness of Collective Narration." *Narrative,* vol. 25, no. 2, May 2017, pp. 164–81.

Bernaerts, Lars, Marco Caracciolo, Luc Herman, and Bart Vervaeck. "The Storied Lives of Non-Human Narrators." *Narrative,* vol. 22, no. 1, Jan. 2014, pp. 68–93.

Bruner, Jerome. *Acts of Meaning.* Harvard UP, 1990.

Carr, Nicholas. *The Shallows: What the Internet Is Doing to Our Brains.* Norton, 2011.

Chakrabarty, Dipesh. "The Climate of History: Four Theses." *Critical Inquiry,* vol. 35, no. 2, Winter 2009, pp. 197–222.

Clark, Timothy. *Ecocriticism on the Edge: The Anthropocene as a Threshold Concept.* Bloomsbury, 2015.

Colebrook, Claire. *Death of the Posthuman: Essays on Extinction, Vol. 1.* Open Humanities Press, 2014.

Crutzen, Paul J., and Eugene F. Stoermer. "The Anthropocene." *The International Geosphere-Biosphere Programme Newsletter,* vol. 41, May 2000, pp. 17–18.

Culler, Jonathan. "Omniscience." *Narrative,* vol. 12, no. 22, Jan. 2004, pp. 22–34.

DeLoughrey, Elizabeth, Jill Didur, and Anthony Carrigan, eds. *Global Ecologies and the Environmental Humanities: Postcolonial Approaches.* Routledge, 2015.

Dimaline, Cherie. *The Marrow Thieves.* DCB, 2017.

Donald, Merlin. *Origins of the Modern Mind: Three Stages in the Evolution of Culture and Cognition.* Harvard UP, 1991.

Easterlin, Nancy. *A Biocultural Approach to Literary Theory and Interpretation.* Johns Hopkins UP, 2012.

Ferris, Joshua. *Then We Came to An End: A Novel.* Little, Brown, and Company, 2007.

Fludernik, Monika, and Suzanne Keen. "Introduction: Narrative Perspectives and Interior Spaces in Literature Before 1850." *Style,* vol. 48, no. 4, Winter 2014, pp. 453–60.

Gallagher, Catherine. "The Rise of Fictionality." *The Novel, Vol. 1.* Edited by Franco Moretti, Princeton UP, 2006, pp. 336–63.

Genette, Gérard. "Boundaries of Narrative." *New Literary History,* vol. 8, no. 1, Autumn 1976, pp. 1–13.

———. *Narrative Discourse: An Essay in Method.* Translated by Jane E. Lewin, Cornell UP, 1980.

Ghosh, Amitav. *The Great Derangement: Climate Change and the Unthinkable.* U of Chicago P, 2017.

Gomel, Elana. *Narrative Space and Time: Representing Impossible Topologies in Literature.* Routledge, 2014.

Heise, Ursula K. "The Environmental Humanities and the Futures of the Human." *New German Critique,* vol. 128, no. 43, August 2016, pp. 21–31.

Herman, David. "Animal Autobiography; Or, Narration Beyond the Human." *Humanities* vol. 5, no. 4, 2016, p. 82.

———. *Basic Elements of Narrative.* Wiley-Blackwell, 2009.

———. "Narratology Beyond the Human." *Diegesis,* vol. 32, no. 1, 2014, pp. 131–43.

———. *Story Logic: Problems and Possibilities of Narrative.* U of Nebraska P, 2002.

———. "Storyworld." *Routledge Encyclopedia of Narrative Theory.* Edited by David Herman, Manfred Jahn, and Marie-Laure Ryan, Routledge, 2005, pp. 569–70.

———. "Storyworld/Umwelt: Nonhuman Experiences in Graphic Novels." *SubStance,* vol. 40, no. 1, iss. 124, 2011, pp. 156–81.

Iovino, Serenella, and Serpil Oppermann. "Introduction: Stories Come to Matter." *Material Ecocriticism.* Edited by Serenella Iovino and Serpil Oppermann, Indiana UP, 2014, pp. 1–18.

———. "Material Ecocriticism: Material, Agency, and Models of Narrativity." *Ecozon@,* vol. 3, no. 1, 2012, pp. 75–91.

James, Erin. "Nonhuman Fictional Characters and the Empathy-Altruism Hypothesis." *Poetics Today,* forthcoming.

Keen, Suanne. "Fast Tracks to Narrative Empathy: Anthropomorphism and Dehumanization in Graphic Novels." *SubStance,* vol. 40, no. 1, iss. 124, 2011, pp. 135–55.

Kluwick, Ursula. "Talking About Climate Change: The Ecological Crisis and Narrative Form." *Oxford Handbook of Ecocriticism.* Edited by Greg Garrard, Oxford UP, 2014, 502–16.

Lee, Chang-Rae. *On Such a Full Sea.* Riverhead, 2014.

LeMenager, Stephanie. "Climate Change and the Struggle for Genre." *Anthropocene Reading: Literary History in Geologic Times.* Edited by Tobias Menely and Jesse Oak Taylor, Pennsylvania State UP, 2017, pp. 220–38.

Leopold, Aldo. *A Sand County Almanac.* Oxford UP, 1949.

Lewis, Simon L., and Mark A. Maslin. "Defining the Anthropocene." *Nature,* vol. 519, 12 Mar. 2015, pp. 171–80.

McGuire, Richard. *Here.* Pantheon, 2014.

Mitchell, David. *Cloud Atlas: A Novel.* Random House, 2004.

Morton, Timothy. "Poisoned Ground: Art and Philosophy in the Time of Hyperobjects." *symplokē,* vol. 21, no. 1–2, 2013, pp. 37–50.

Mosher, Harold F., Jr. "Towards a Poetics of Descriptivized Narration." *Poetics Today,* vol. 12, no. 3, Autumn 1991, pp. 425–45.

Neimanis, Astrid. *Bodies of Water: Posthuman Feminist Phenomenology.* Bloomsbury, 2017.

Nixon, Rob. *Slow Violence and the Environmentalism of the Poor.* Harvard UP, 2011.

Phelan, James. *Living to Tell About It: A Rhetoric and Ethics of Character Narration.* Cornell UP, 2004.

Plumwood, Val. *Environmental Culture: The Ecological Crisis of Reason.* Routledge, 2002.

Powers, Richard. *The Overstory: A Novel.* Norton, 2018.

Prince, Gerald. "On a Postcolonial Narratology." *A Companion to Narrative Theory.* Edited by James Phelan and Peter J. Rabinowitz, Blackwell, 2008, pp. 372–81.

Pulizzi, James J. "Predicting the End of History: Mathematical Modeling and the Anthropocene." *minnesota review,* vol. 83, 2014, pp. 83–92.

Rader, Ralph W. "The Emergence of the Novel in England: Genre in History vs. History of Genre." *Narrative,* vol. 1, no. 1, Jan. 1993, pp. 69–83.

Richardson, Brian. "Beyond Story and Discourse: Narrative Time in Postmodern and Mimetic Fiction." *Narrative Dynamics: Essays on Time, Plot, Closure, and Frames.* Edited by Brian Richardson, The Ohio State UP, 2002, pp. 47–63.

———. *Unnatural Voices: Extreme Narration in Modern and Contemporary Fiction.* The Ohio State UP, 2006.

Rose, Deborah Bird, Thom van Dooren, Matthew Chrulew, Stuart Cooke, Matthew Kearnes, and Emily O'Gorman. "Thinking Through the Environment, Unsettling the Humanities." *Environmental Humanities,* vol. 1, 2012, pp. 1–5.

Savi, Meina Pereira. "The Anthropocene (and) (in) the Humanities: Possibilities for Literary Studies." *Estudos Feministas,* vol. 25, no. 2, May–Aug. 2017, pp. 945–59.

Scranton, Roy. *Learning to Die in the Anthropocene: Reflections on the End of a Civilization.* City Lights Open Media, 2015.

Trexler, Adam. *Anthropocene Fictions: The Novel in a Time of Climate Change.* U of Virginia P, 2015.

Vermeule, Blakey. *Why Do We Care About Literary Characters?* Johns Hopkins UP, 2010.

Vitaglione, Marina. *Solastalgia.* Overlapse, 2017.

Watt, Ian. *The Rise of the Novel: Studies in Defoe, Richardson, and Fielding.* Updated edition. U of California P, 2001.

Weik von Mossner, Alexa. *Affective Ecologies: Empathy, Emotion, and Environmental Narrative.* The Ohio UP, 2017.

Zalasiewicz, Jan. *The Earth After Us: What Legacy Will Humans Leave in the Rocks?* Oxford UP, 2008.

Zunshine, Lisa. *Why We Read Fiction: Theory of Mind and the Novel.* The Ohio State UP, 2006.

AFTERWORD

Econarratology for the Future

URSULA K. HEISE

IN 2015, I started teaching a new undergraduate course called "Environment and Narrative" at my home institution, UCLA. The idea for this class came out of three impulses. First, it seemed to me imperative to show undergraduates with an interest in environmental issues and activism how environmentalist discourse is underwritten by particular narrative patterns: for example, how ideas about ecological conservation and restoration are often associated with storylines from the pastoral tradition, or how debates about climate change have been shaped by the genre conventions of disaster movies and novels. Second, the class aimed to foreground the idea that these underlying story patterns differ historically and by cultural community, so that North American narratives are only part of the broad spectrum of stories about humans' interactions with nature. For instance, North American stories about the inevitable degradation that comes from human interference with a natural world that is at its best untouched clash with narratives from indigenous communities that cast nature as a kind of house or garden that will fall into disrepair if humans do not take care of it. And third, the course encouraged students to begin to tell their own stories about environmental issues: sometimes new stories and sometimes old stories in new media such as short videos or graphic novels, on the grounds that some environmental stories have been told so often that they have come to be taken for granted and lost much of their persuasive power, while many other environmental stories remain untold.

The course readings combined fiction and nonfiction across text, image, and film with narrative theory. In teaching narratology along with environmental thought, I ran into several of the challenges that the essays in this volume highlight. Sophisticated experiments with story and discourse were less crucial to most of the texts we discussed than their constructions of narrative spaces and more broadly of storyworlds. Narration and focalization strategies turned out to be important for both fictional and nonfictional works, and also raised the question of how nonhuman or even inanimate forms of agency should be theorized. Questions of factuality and fictionality raised intricate problems for works that sought to combine scientific, historical, or political data with narrative. Emotions, particularly empathy, melancholy, anger, outrage, and despair, loomed large in students' engagement with the readings as well as with the creative assignments that forced them to anticipate their intended audience's reactions. A collection of essays such as this one would have been enormously helpful—and certainly will be in the future—in discussing these issues, because it highlights where narrative theory needs to be revised and expanded to address the dimensions of storytelling that particularly matter for environmentalism. I'll briefly focus here on three dimensions: story templates, the concept of the actant, and the question of temporal and spatial scales.

Narrative theory has mostly focused on two types of storytelling: on one hand, conversational storytelling undertaken on a daily basis by most people, which has been analyzed by theorists ranging from William Labov in the 1970s to Monika Fludernik in the 1990s; on the other hand, highly elaborate fictional storytelling as it occurs in short stories, novels, and feature films, which has been theorized over the last half-century in accounts ranging from structuralism and feminism to affect theory and cognitive science. Neither of these modes of theorization works unproblematically with works such as John Muir's *My First Summer in the Sierra*, Rachel Carson's *Silent Spring*, Cherríe Moraga's *Heroes and Saints*, Davis Guggenheim's *An Inconvenient Truth*, or Zacharias Kunuk and Ian Mauro's *Qapirangajuq: Inuit Knowledge and Climate Change*. All of these works rely on powerful story templates about humans and natural environments, but these are only partly addressed by either conversational or literary/cinematic theories of narrative. In fact, I came to rely on the concept of "story templates," ready-made narratives that form part of the repertoire of a particular cultural community and are deployed particularly in the confrontation with new situations and crises: a twist on the concept of cultural "masterplots" that Porter Abbott discusses briefly in his *Cambridge Introduction to Narrative* (46–49).

Some story templates resemble the "genres" of literary theory, whose complicated relationship with narrative theory Astrid Bracke astutely outlines in this volume: Muir's use of pastoral or Carson's of apocalyptic narrative are cases in point. But the equally recognizable story template of the turn to a simple life in texts ranging from Henry David Thoreau's *Walden* to Colin Beavan's *No Impact Man* does not constitute a genre in the traditional sense. And stories about environmental justice often mobilize one of two divergent story templates, neither of which corresponds to a well-established genre: "What's good for the land is good for the people" narratives align the interests of environmentalism with the social struggles of disempowered communities, whereas "green imperialism" stories focus on the conflicting goals of affluent conservation communities in the global North and poor local communities in the global South. It is such story templates that cut across fiction and nonfiction in environmental texts and films, and their cultural specificity highlights different visions of desirable and undesirable ways of inhabiting natural environments on the part of different societies. Some of the most productive connections between narrative theory and ecocriticism, in other words, emerge from the combination of the analysis of plot structure with genre theory and with the more specific study of default narratives that are commonly mobilized in particular communities.

Such story templates do not always adhere to a realistic portrayal of the world, at least not as this phrase would be understood by average North Americans and West Europeans. Recent explorations of "unnatural narratives" whose cognitive and emotional impact relies on their divergence from realism—stories with mutually exclusive plot lines, reversed time lines, or nonhuman speakers, for example—have done much to highlight how far individual narratives as well as what I call story templates can deviate from a simple mirroring of the world outside the text. Yet the phrase "unnatural narrative" remains complicated for any connection with ecocriticism, as the analyses by Jon Hegglund and Marco Caracciolo in this volume highlight. Ideas about what is natural or realist are highly variable by culture and historical moment: whether a story told by the ghost of a deceased person, for example, as in Ryūnosuke Akutagawa's short story "In a Grove" (1922) and the film version *Rashōmon* by Akira Kurosawa (1950), defies the parameters of the natural is a question whose answer depends on the historical and cultural location of the storytelling. Many of the oldest narrative genres—myths, cosmologies, and folktales, including indigenous ones—do not conform to contemporary definitions of the natural and the real, so that "unnatural" narrative probably constitutes the bulk of human storytelling, with European-style realism (itself based on a highly artificial set of conventions, as Roland Barthes's *S/Z* demonstrated decades ago) the numerical exception rather than the rule.

In addition, some elements of "unnatural" narrative, such as speaking animals or natural forces with a will of their own, question conventional boundaries between nature and nonnature in ways that have been explored in a wave of posthumanist and new materialist theories over the last two decades, as Hegglund's essay highlights—and some of these theories have precisely aimed to redefine nature and the natural from an environmentalist perspective. This does not invalidate Jan Alber, Stefan Iversen, Brian Richardson, and Henrik Skov Nielsen's criticism of narratological approaches that privilege mimetic texts and models of reading that rely on the construction of correspondences between nontextual and textual worlds. But it does mean that the ideas of reality, nature, and mimesis that underlie this criticism have to be carefully nuanced by cultural context and varying moments of narrative production and reception. Hegglund, in this volume, foregrounds that the Anthropocene, as a concept that emphasizes comprehensive human interventions into the natural world, has over the last two decades highlighted the "weirdness" of the nature of which humans now form part, from genetically engineered animals and plastic particles that pervade the oceans to unprecedented weather events. In this sense, stable and shared assumptions about what constitutes the natural world outside the text and what might be unnatural in a particular storyworld can no longer be taken for granted, and the narrative substance and form of Jeff VanderMeer's Southern Reach trilogy foregrounds this ambiguity in Hegglund's perceptive and detailed analysis.

But in a different way, such slippage in assumptions about what constitutes the natural reality of the extratextual world has always accompanied narrative analysis across cultural or historical boundaries. Understandings of the ontological status of dead people, to name just one obvious example, has varied widely over the course of history and continues to vary culturally in the present, and determines whether ghosts, spirits, séances, or other communications with the dead are approached as parts of the normal order of nature or as deviations from it in storytelling. Similarly, reasoning about the resemblances and differences between human identity and the identity of animals and plants has varied and continues to vary across a wide spectrum, determining whether certain behaviors on the part of animal or tree characters in a narrative are understood as natural or unnatural. It would be useful, therefore, to broaden Hegglund's critique of unnatural narratology beyond the "weird realism" that the Anthropocene calls for so as to include such culturally and historically conditioned differences and slippages in the understanding of nature—including humans. The concept of unnatural narrative might be a useful tool in the analysis of environmental storytelling, in other words, but only if such differences are taken into account. Nature has certainly turned "weird" in the perception of many Europeans and North Americans in ways that the concept of the Anthropocene usefully summarizes. But nature has always been weird when readers from one historical or cultural community have encountered stories about nature from another.

The concept of the actant might be another useful analytical tool for eco-narratology in the Anthropocene, in that it goes beyond conventional distinctions between human and nonhuman or animate and inanimate types of agency. The term was coined in 1966 by the structuralist theorist Algirdas Julien Greimas, whose "actantial model" of narrative, based on earlier studies by Vladimir Propp and Etienne Souriau, was meant to capture the central roles that structure a particular type of narrative: for example, the roles of the hero, the villain as the hero's opponent, the object of the hero's quest, the hero's helper, and the sender who initiates the quest in a folktale ("Eléments"; "La structure"). Actants do not line up with characters, since several characters can occupy the role of the same actant (Rosencrantz and Guildenstern in Shakespeare's *Hamlet,* for example), and neither are they limited to humans: divinities, earthquakes, or machines can function as actants as much as human individuals in a narrative. Unlike the notion of character, the concept of the actant does not focus on human or human-like agents, but rather on the more abstract question of what forces and transformations move a narrative plot forward.

Today, the concept of the actant is more closely associated with Bruno Latour's Actor-Network-Theory than with Greimas's narratology. Actor-Network-Theory (ANT) analyzes semiotic and material processes in a social network and does not accept categorical distinctions between human and nonhuman or animate and inanimate actors. Latour has explicitly acknowledged that he borrowed the idea of the actant from narrative theory:

> To break away from the influence of what could be called "figurative sociology," ANT uses the technical word actant that comes from the study of literature. . . . Because they deal with fiction, literary theorists have been much freer in their enquiries about figuration than any social scientist, especially when they have used semiotics or the various narrative sciences. This is because, for instance in a fable, the same actant can be made to act through the agency of a magic wand, a dwarf, a thought in the fairy's mind, or a knight killing two dozen dragons. . . . It is not that sociology is fiction or because literary theorists would know more than sociologists, but because the diversity of the worlds of fiction invented on paper allow enquirers to

gain as much pliability and range as those they have to study in the real world. (53–54)

For Latour, then, the concept of the actant enables a clearer look at the underlying structures of semiotic and material interactions in the social realm. It becomes a way of identifying vectors of agency and causation without regard for intentionality, and of leveling the differences between human and nonhuman, individual and collective, concrete and abstract agents that are fundamental in other forms of anthropology and sociology. This way of looking at the social world as if it were a kind of narrative has made its way into other paradigms in philosophy and the social sciences, such as political ecology and new materialisms. It may also at this point be useful to reimport it into econarratology, less as a way of mapping the logical structure of plots than of understanding whose agency counts and whose does not in the story templates that different cultural communities use for communicating about nature, and how these story templates shift over time.

The clashing stories about the agency of tigers in Amitav Ghosh's well-known environmental novel *The Hungry Tide* are a case in point. Villagers living in the tidal mangrove forests on the Bay of Bengal burn a live tiger that has killed several residents; they see the animal as the manifestation of a demon hostile to humans who demonstrates his desire to die by visiting the village. Visiting American biologist Piyali Roy, by contrast, is outraged by what she sees as a pointless act of vengeance against an animal incapable of human or superhuman agency. Whether one construes the actant in this event to be a more-than-human spirit being or a less-than-human animal crucially shapes its narrative and ecological meaning. This example also highlights that attributing agency to nonhuman entities, as new materialists such as Serenella Iovino and Serpil Oppermann encourage us to do, does not inevitably lead to outcomes that environmentalists in the global North would embrace (see also Erin James's perceptive criticism of the attribution of "narrative agency" to nonhumans in this volume). An econarratological perspective needs to register these different actant structures in mapping such divergent stories about the more-than-human world.

Kate Rigby provides a different, historically oriented example in her book *Dancing with Disaster*. Natural occurrences such as droughts, floods, and plagues were considered divine punishments by European societies until the middle of the eighteenth century. The disastrous Lisbon earthquake in 1755, however, began to shift cultural perceptions from God's agency to that of Nature, which enabled the modern concept of "natural disaster" and legitimated helping disaster victims. But in the context of twenty-first-century disasters, Rigby argues, this concept may no longer do justice to the human actions that trigger natural disasters associated with climate change. This shift might usefully be envisioned as a change in who or what functions as actant in European and North American disaster story templates, and consequently in the cultural practices shaped by these default narratives.

Beyond questions of agency, climate change and the Anthropocene have loomed large in recent discussions of environmental stories because of the challenges they pose in terms of temporal and spatial scales, and several essays in this volume engage masterfully with these debates. Amitav Ghosh has recently contributed to them with a volume of three essays entitled *The Great Derangement: Climate Change and the Unthinkable* (2016), one of which focuses explicitly on storytelling. The realist novel as it emerged in Europe in the eighteenth century, he argues, is incapable of dealing with the realities of climate change: it is concerned with everyday people and ordinary affairs rather than the improbable and extraordinary events that climate change is likely to bring about; it is keyed to the scale of the individual, the family, and the nation, not the globe; and it is structured so as to separate human culture from nonhuman processes and forms of agency, which are relegated to the natural sciences. All of this, Ghosh argues, makes the mainstream novel unfit to deal with the new ecological realities of the Anthropocene. He also discards science fiction, a genre better equipped to deal with these realities, on the grounds that its worlds are always located in a temporal or spatial other realm, not the here and now.[1]

This is a curiously literal understanding of science fiction and speculative fiction, whose future or alternative times and spaces have always served as metaphors for the here and now, as theorists of science fiction such as Raymond Williams and Fredric Jameson have shown. In fact, science fiction understood as a perpetuation of elements of epic into the age of the novel (an argument that I have made in greater detail in *Imagining Extinction*) is precisely concerned with the present in the context of large spatial scales, long temporal durations, and extraordinary historical events. It often deals with planet Earth as a whole, or even planetary societies in the plural; it engages with groundbreaking technological and social innovations; and it has not shied away from plot lines that stretch over thousands or even millions of years, as narratives from Olaf Stapledon's *Last and First Men* (1930) and Isaac Asimov's *Foundation* series of novels (1950s-1980s) to Neal Stephenson's *Seveneves* (2015) show. I therefore share Erin James's contention that claims about

---

1. For a more detailed engagement with Ghosh's arguments, see Heise, "Climate Stories" and "Science Fiction and the Time Scales of the Anthropocene."

the inability of narrative to address the Anthropocene are premature, underestimating as they do the number and variety of narrative strategies and experiments beyond mainstream realist fiction. Stories about humans' multifarious entanglements with the more-than-human world, with species, places, and climates, will surely continue to proliferate, and as Alexa Weik von Mossner's exemplary analysis in this volume shows, how these stories mobilize affect is as crucial to their architecture and their real-world impacts as the way in which they present factual insights into the functioning of ecologies. Econarratology will have an important role to play in analyzing and mapping this universe of stories about nature, and this collection of essays marks an important first step in this exciting intellectual venture.

WORKS CITED

Abbott, H. Porter. *The Cambridge Introduction to Narrative.* 2nd ed. Cambridge UP, 2008.

Akutagawa, Ryūnosuke. "In a Grove." *Rashōmon and Other Stories.* Tuttle, 1952, pp. 15–30.

Alber, Jan, Stefan Iversen, Brian Richardson, and Henrik Skov Nielsen. "Unnatural Narratives, Unnatural Narratology: Beyond Mimetic Models." *Narrative,* vol. 18, no. 2, May 2010, pp. 113–36.

Asimov, Isaac. *Foundation.* Doubleday, 1951.

———. *Foundation and Empire.* Doubleday, 1952.

———. *Second Foundation.* Gnome Press, 1953.

———. *Foundation's Edge.* Doubleday, 1982.

———. *Foundation and Earth.* Doubleday, 1986.

Barthes, Roland. *S/Z.* Seuil, 1970.

Ghosh, Amitav. *The Great Derangement: Climate Change and the Unthinkable.* U of Chicago P, 2016.

———. *The Hungry Tide.* Houghton Mifflin Harcourt, 2006.

Greimas, Algirdas Julien. "Eléments d'une grammaire narrative." *Du sens: Essais sémiotiques.* Seuil, 1970, pp. 157–83.

———. "La structure des actants du récit." *Du sens: Essais sémiotiques.* Seuil, 1970, pp. 249–70.

Heise, Ursula K. "Climate Stories: Review of Amitav Ghosh's *The Great Derangement.*" *boundary 2,* 19 Feb. 2018. www.boundary2.org/2018/02/ursula-k-heise-climate-stories-review-of-amitav-ghoshs-the-great-derangement/.

———. *Imagining Extinction: The Cultural Meanings of Endangered Species.* U of Chicago P, 2016.

———. "Science Fiction and the Time Scales of the Anthropocene." *English Literary History,* vol. 86, 2019, pp. 275–304.

Latour, Bruno. *Reassembling the Social: An Introduction to Actor-Network-Theory.* Oxford UP, 2005.

Rigby, Kate. *Dancing with Disaster: Environmental Histories, Narratives, and Ethics for Perilous Times*. U of Virginia P, 2015.

Stapledon, Olaf. *Last and First Men: A Story of the Near and Far Future*. Methuen, 1930.

Stephenson, Neal. *Seveneves*. William Morrow, 2015.

CONTRIBUTORS

ASTRID BRACKE is a Lecturer in English Literature at HAN University of Applied Sciences (Nijmegen, The Netherlands). She published *Climate Crisis and the 21st-Century British Novel* with Bloomsbury in 2017. In addition, she has coedited special issues on ecocriticism *(English Studies)* and literature and the visual arts *(Image & Narrative)*; published articles in *English Studies, Alluvium,* and *ISLE*; and was invited to write a chapter for the *Oxford Handbook of Ecocriticism* (2014).

MARCO CARACCIOLO is Associate Professor of English and Literary Theory at Ghent University in Belgium, where he leads the European Research Council Starting Grant project "Narrating the Mesh." His work has been published in journals such as *Poetics Today, Narrative, Modern Fiction Studies,* and *Phenomenology and the Cognitive Sciences.* He is the author of *The Experientiality of Narrative: An Enactivist Approach* (De Gruyter 2014) and *Strangers in Contemporary Fiction: Explorations in Readers' Engagement with Characters* (University of Nebraska Press 2016), and the coauthor—with Marco Bernini—of an introduction to cognitive literary studies in Italian *(Letteratura e scienze cognitive;* Carocci 2013).

GREG GARRARD is the Associate Dean of Research and Graduate Studies and Sustainability Professor in Literary Studies at the University of British Columbia, a National Teaching Fellow of the British Higher Education Academy, and a founding member and former chair of the Association for the Study of Literature and the Environment (UK & Ireland). He is the author of *Ecocriticism* (Routledge 2004, 2011, 2nd ed.) as well as numerous essays on ecopedagogy, animal studies, and environmental criticism. He is the editor of *Teaching Ecocriticism and Green Cultural*

Studies (Palgrave Macmillan 2011), *The Oxford Handbook of Ecocriticism* (Oxford University Press 2014), and the journal *Green Letters: Studies in Ecocriticism*.

JON HEGGLUND is Associate Professor of English at Washington State University. He teaches courses in modernism, twentieth-century Anglophone fiction, post-colonial literature and theory, film narrative, and documentary film and, along with articles in *ISLE: Interdisciplinary Studies of Literature and Environment* and *Twentieth-Century Literature*, he published *World Views: Metageographies of Modernist Fiction* with Oxford University Press in 2012.

URSULA K. HEISE teaches in the Department of English and at the Institute of the Environment and Sustainability at UCLA. Her research and teaching focus on contemporary literature; environmental culture in the Americas, Western Europe, and Japan; narrative theory; media theory; literature and science; and science fiction. Her books include *Chronoschisms: Time, Narrative, and Postmodernism* (Cambridge University Press 1997), *Sense of Place and Sense of Planet: The Environmental Imagination of the Global* (Oxford University Press 2008), and *Imagining Extinction: The Cultural Meanings of Endangered Species* (University of Chicago Press 2016). Heise is the managing editor of *Futures of Comparative Literature: The ACLA Report on the State of the Discipline* (Routledge 2016), and coeditor, with Jon Christensen and Michelle Niemann, of *The Routledge Companion to the Environmental Humanities* (2016). She is editor of the book series, *Literatures, Cultures, and the Environment* with Palgrave Macmillan and coeditor of the series *Literature and Contemporary Thought* with Routledge. She is a 2011 Guggenheim Fellow and served as president of ASLE (Association for the Study of Literature and the Environment) in 2011.

ERIN JAMES is Associate Professor of English at the University of Idaho. In 2015 she published *The Storyworld Accord: Econarratology and Postcolonial Narratives* with the University of Nebraska Press. Her previous publications include essays in the *Journal of Commonwealth and Postcolonial Literature* and in the *Journal of Narrative Theory*, as well as *The Bioregional Imagination* (University of Georgia Press 2012), *Teaching Ecocriticism and Green Cultural Studies* (Palgrave Macmillan 2012), *The Language of Plants: Science, Philosophy, Literature* (University of Minnesota Press 2017).

MARKKU LEHTIMÄKI, Ph.D., is Lecturer of Literature at the University of Eastern Finland and Adjunct Professor (Docent) of Comparative Literature at the University of Tampere, Finland. He is the author of *The Poetics of Norman Mailer's Nonfiction* (Temple University Press 2005) and coeditor of several anthologies, including *Intertextuality and Intersemiosis* (Tartu University Press 2004), *Real Stories, Imagined Realities: Fictionality and Non-Fictionality in Literary Constructs and Historical Contexts* (Tampere University Press 2007), and *Narrative, Interrupted: the Plotless, the Disturbing, and the Trivial in Literature* (De Gruyter 2012). His fields of expertise are American literature, narrative theory, ecocriticism, and visual culture. One of his recent publications is "Natural Environments in Narrative Contexts: Cross-Pollinating Ecocriticism and Narrative Theory" (*Storyworlds: A Journal of Narrative Theory* 5 (2013), 119–141).

MATTHEW M. LOW teaches literature, composition, and environmental writing in eastern Nebraska and western Iowa. His writing and research span the environmental humanities, with an emphasis on narrative ethics and the role of story in restoring the degraded ecosystems of the American Midwest.

ERIC MOREL graduated from the Ph.D. program in the University of Washington Department of English in Spring 2019. He completed his M.A. at the University of Nevada, Reno in 2012. His dissertation research studies readership and response through a comparative history of reading for works of nature writing and literary fiction in the late nineteenth century. In addition to having published in *ISLE* (2014), *Western American Literature* (2013), and the *Encyclopedia of the Environment in American Literature* (2013), he has an essay on Henry James's *The Italian Hours* forthcoming in a special issue of *Viatica*.

ALEXA WEIK VON MOSSNER is Associate Professor of American Studies at the University of Klagenfurt, Austria, and an affiliate at the Rachel Carson Center for Environment and Society in Munich. She received her Ph.D. in Literature from the University of California, San Diego in 2008. Her ecocritical scholarship has been published in journals such as *ISLE: Interdisciplinary Studies in Literature and Environment, Environmental Communication,* and the *Journal of Commonwealth and Postcolonial Studies.* She is the author of *Cosmopolitan Minds: Literature, Emotion, and the Transnational Imagination* (University of Texas Press 2014) and *Affective Ecologies: Empathy, Emotion, and Environmental Narrative* (The Ohio State University Press 2017), the editor of *Moving Environments: Affect, Emotion, Ecology, and Film* (Wilfrid Laurier University Press 2014), and the coeditor of *The Anticipation of Catastrophe: Environmental Risk in North American Literature and Culture* (Universitätsverlag Winter 2014).

INDEX

Abadzis, Nick, 14

Abbott, H. Porter, 35, 168n8, 191, 204

Abby, Edward, 135

"Above and Below" (Groff), 7

actant, 204, 207–9

actantial theory, 47

Actor-Network Theory (ANT), 207–8

actual audience, 69–70, 73–76, 81–83, 91, 103

actual worlds, 151–61

Affective Ecologies (Weik von Mossner), 12, 15

affective narratology, 48

agency: causality and, 47; in *Annihilation*, 37, 42–43; meaning and, 48–49; narrative, 3, 190–91, 208; reconstruction and, 155; species, 196–97

Air France Flight 447 plane crash, 50

Akutagawa, Ryūnosuke, 205

Alaimo, Stacy, 12, 33, 195

Alber, Jan, 7, 28–32, 206

Albrecht, Glenn, 196

allegory, 89–90, 99, 102

American Claimant, The (Twain), 68, 68n2, 69–75, 82

American Places (Stegner), 147–48, 158

Anderson, Paul Thomas, 78

animals. *See* anthropomorphism; non-human

Annihilation (VanderMeer), 29–30, 34–42

ANT. *See* Actor-Network Theory (ANT)

Anthropocene, 2, 27–29, 43, 88, 93–99, 183–88, 188n6, 189–99, 209

Anthropocene Fictions (Trexler), 166n3, 170, 186

anthropocentrism, 45–46, 48–49

anthropomorphism, 28, 31, 33–38, 62, 124

apocalyptic narrative, 83, 99–100, 170n13, 176n16, 205

Asimov, Isaac, 209

Attridge, Derek, 108–10

audience: actual, 69–70, 73–76, 81–83, 91, 103; authorial, 39, 69–70, 74, 76, 80–81, 83, 91; narrative, 68–71, 74–76, 81–82, 199

Austin, Mary, 28, 135

authorial audience, 39, 69–70, 74, 76, 80–81, 83, 91

Babb, Sanora, 129–31, 133–44

Babel (film, Iñárritu), 46, 52–53, 53 fig. 1, 56–59, 58 fig. 2, 61

"Babysitter, The" (Coover), 31

Bader, Ralph W., 189

Bakhtin, Mikhail, 167n5, 194

Barad, Karen, 28, 42

Barnard, Rita, 57

Barthes, Roland, 47, 206

Bartosch, Roman, 13

Beard, Michael, 90. See also *Solar* (McEwan)

Beavan, Colin, 205

Before Reading (Rabinowitz), 79–80

Bekhta, Natalya, 197

Bennett, Jane, 28, 190

Bernaerts, Lars, 6, 187

Big Rock Candy Mountain (Stegner), 158

Biocultural Approach to Literary Theory and Interpretation (Easterlin), 149

Bloom, Dan, 67–68

Bogost, Ian, 47

Booth, Waybe C., 8n3

Boyd, Brian, 5, 5n2

Brock, Timothy C., 162

Bruner, Jerome, 190–91

Buell, Frederick, 169n11, 171

Buell, Lawrence, 11, 32–33, 45–46, 112

"Buglesong" (Stegner), 158–59

Byers, Thomas, 115

Cafaro, Philip, 110

Calvino, Italo, 61

Caracciolo, Marco, 6, 10, 14, 132, 160, 160n5, 187, 205

Carrigan, Anthony, 2–3, 13

Carruth, Allison, 3

Carson, Rachel, 204–5

cataclysm, rule of imminent, 80–81

Catlin, George, 153

causality, 46–50

Chakrabarty, Dipesh, 90, 94, 100–101, 196–97

Chatman, Seymour, 101

Child in Time, The (McEwan), 89

Clark, Timothy, 4, 96n5

cli-fi. *See* climate fiction

climate change, 67, 71, 75–76, 90n1, 94–95, 95n4, 96, 99–104, 209

climate fiction, 67–69, 76–77, 80–83, 83nn9–10, 166, 169–80, 174 table 1

Cloud Atlas (Mitchell), 193

cognitive ecocriticism, 131n1

cognitive science, 10, 12, 46, 131, 204. *See also* neuroscience

Cohen, Ralph, 167

Colebrook, Claire, 4, 184, 186–87

Comedy of Survival, The: Studies in Literary Ecology (Meeker), 93–94

Comeuppance (Flesch), 111

Company We Keep, The (Booth), 8n3

configuration: narrative, 76–83, 125; rules of, 79–80

Coover, Robert, 31

Costello, Bonnie, 101

Cove, The (documentary film), 15

Crane, Kylie, 13

Craps, Stef, 4

Cronon, William, 28

Crownshaw, Rick, 4

Culler, Jonathan, 197

Dancing with Disaster (Rigby), 208–9

Dannenberg, Hillary, 49

Death of the PostHuman (Colebrook), 184

deep ecology, 110, 112

Defoe, Daniel, 188

deictic shift, 10, 194

DeLillo, Don, 46, 49–56, 58–59, 61

DeLoughrey, Elizabeth, 2–3, 13

DeMott, Robert, 138

depersonalization, 57–58

Dewey, Joseph, 123–24

Dickens, Charles, 187

Didur, Jill, 2–3, 13

Dimaline, Cherie, 193

Dimock, Wai Chee, 78

Donald, Merlin, 190

dual narrative, 112–13, 116

Easterlin, Nancy, 5, 10n8, 83n9, 109–10, 149, 169

ecocentric restoration, 155

ecocritical narrative ethics, 107–12

ecocriticism, 31–34, 79, 101–2, 131, 148–50, 168; cognitive, 131n1; defined, 3; ethical orientation of, 8; genre in, 168, 205; idealism in, 90, 102; materialist, 29, 31, 33; mimesis and, 32–33; narratology and, 102; nature in, 28–29; plot and, 205; rhetorical narrative theory and, 102; rhetorical theory vs., 101; unnatural narrative and, 205; worlds and, as concept, 151–52

ecological narrative form, 109

econarratology: defined, 1, 131, 165n2; environment in, 77, 131; future of, 203–10; new directions in, 6–15

Eliot, T. S., 51

Elsewhere, The: On Belonging at Near Distance (Newton), 9n3

embodied cognition, 10, 12, 132, 132n3

embodied simulation theory, 131–35, 138, 140–41, 143

emergence, 35, 38

Emerson, Ralph Waldo, 117

empathy, narrative, 11–12, 111, 133, 187n4

environment: embodied cognition and, 10, 132n3; genre and, 167–68; in *An Owl on Every Post*, 133–35; in *Annihilation*, 36–38; in ecocriticism, 32; in econarratology, 77, 131; in materialist ecocriticism, 33; narrative, 10–12, 130–37; narrative and, 1–6

Environmental Culture: The Ecological Crisis of Reason (Plumwood), 2

environmental history, 76–83

Environmental Humanities (journal), 2

environmental justice, 21, 112, 137–43, 198, 205

environmental virtue, 111–12

environmentally relevant knowledge, 2

Erem, Suzan, 161–62

ethics. *See also* narrative ethics: in ecocriticism, 8; narrative structure and, 123–25; in *Solar*, 92–93, 96–97, 99

"Even the Title: On the State of Narrative Theory" (Royle), 77–78

evocriticism, 5n2

experientiality, 27–28, 149

feminism: configuration and, 77; environmental aesthetics and, 28; storytelling and, 204; water and, 195

feminist narratology, 9, 9n6

Ferris, Joshua, 197–98

Fielding, Henry, 189

first-person narration, 30, 38–39, 42, 134–36, 141

Flesch, William, 111

Fletcher, Angus, 109

Flight Behavior (Kingsolver), 76, 99–100, 165, 175–76, 178–79

Floyd, Charles, 153

Fludernik, Monika, 7, 9, 27–28, 32, 194, 204

Forsberg, Michael, 151

Foundation series (Asimov), 209

Frow, John, 167n5, 168n7

Gain (Powers), 108–9, 112–25

Gallagher, Catherine, 189

Gallese, Vittorio, 132

Garrard, Greg, 89–90, 99, 170, 175, 176n16

Gass, Patrick, 153

Genette, Gérard, 8, 192–94

genre, 79, 83, 83n9, 165–71, 174 table 1, 174n15

Gerrig, Richard, 130–32

Ghosh, Amitav, 4, 13, 186–87, 208–9

Gilded Age, The, A Tale of To-Day (Twain and Warner), 68, 72

Global Ecologies and the Environmental Humanities (DeLoughrey, Didur, and Carrigan), 2–3, 13

Glotfelty, Cheryll, 3, 8, 79, 168

Gomel, Elana, 187

Gore, Al, 95

Graeve, Chard, 155n3

Grapes of Wrath, The (Steinbeck), 138

Great Derangement, The: Climate Change and the Unthinkable (Ghosh), 209

Green, Melanie C., 162

Greimas, Algirdas Julien, 47, 207

Groff, Lauren, 7

Guggenheim, Davis, 204

Guha, Ramachandra, 13

Gurr, Jens Martin, 13

Gymnich, Marion, 9

Hallock, Grace, 117

Haq, Husna, 170

Haraway, Donna, 28

Harman, Graham, 30, 34, 47

Hart, F. Elizabeth, 157–58

Hegglund, Jon, 205–6

Heise, Ursula K., 3–4, 79, 87, 99–100, 121–22, 168n8, 183

Helzer, Chris, 157

Here (McGuire), 196

Herman, David, 5–10, 14–15, 14n13, 35, 91, 130, 149, 151–56, 160–61, 187, 194

Herman, Luc, 6, 187

Heroes and Saints (Moraga), 204

Hogan, Patrick Colm, 48

humanism, 38–42, 91. *See also* posthumanism

Hungry Tide, The (Ghosh), 208

Hunt, Alex, 4

Hutchins, Edwin, 46, 51

hybridity, 55

hyperobject, 36, 36n2

"In a Grove" (Akutagawa), 205

Iñárritu, Alejandro González, 46, 53 fig. 1, 56–59, 58 fig. 2, 61

Inconvenient Truth, An (film), 95

Inconvenient Truth, An (Guggenheim), 204

indigenous, 13, 14, 21, 150n1, 151, 156n4, 203, 205

Ingram, Helen, 13n12

Ingram, Mrill, 13n12

interconnectedness, 57–58, 137, 187

intratexts, 112, 115–20, 115n2, 123, 125

Iovino, Serenella, 3, 33, 191, 208

Iversen, Stefan, 7, 30, 206

James, Erin, 5–6, 12–13, 131, 149–50, 165n2

Jameson, Frederic, 209

Johnsgard, Paul, 151

Johnson, Gary, 89

Johnson, Mark, 51, 134–35

Joseph Andrews (Fielding), 189

justice, environmental, 21, 112, 137–43, 198, 205

Kafalenos, Emma, 48–49

Kearns, Michael, 168n8

Keen, Suzanne, 11, 194

Kerridge, Richard, 169, 170n13

King, Thomas, 151

Kingsolver, Barbara, 76, 99–100, 165, 175–76, 178–79

Kluwick, Ursula, 3

Kooser, Ted, 151

Kukkonen, Karin, 48

Kunstler, James Howard, 166n3

Kunuk, Zacharias, 204

Kurosawa, Akira, 205

Kurtz, Carl, 155–56, 161n6

Kuzmičová, Anežka, 135

Labov, William, 27, 204

Laika (Abadzis), 14

Lakoff, George, 51, 134–35

Lanser, Susan L., 9

Last and First Men (Stapledon), 209

Latour, Bruno, 28, 207–8

Lee, Chang-Rae, 197–99

Lehtimäki, Markku, 5, 77

Lejano, Raul, 13n12

LeMenager, Stephanie, 186, 198

Leopold, Aldo, 28, 192

Levinas, Emmanuel, 110

Lewis, Simon L., 188n6

Life on the Mississippi (Twain), 71

lineage, in causality, 49

"Literature and Ecology" (Rueckert), 109

Living Handbook of Narratology, The (Ryan), 148

Living to Tell About It (Phelan), 8n3, 39

Love, Glen A., 10, 148

Lovecraft, H. P., 34

Magnolia (film), 78

Mäkelä, Maria, 32

Marine, Neil, 57

Marrow Thieves, The (Dimaline), 193

Marsh, George Perkins, 74–75

Martinez-Alier, J., 13

Maslin, Mark A., 188n6

Massey, Doreen, 151

masterplots, 204

material anchor, 50–54

materialist ecocriticism, 29, 31, 33. *See also* new materialism

materialist ecology, 27

matter, narrative agency of, 3, 190–91, 208

Mauro, Ian, 204

McCarthy, Cormac, 166n3, 170, 170n12

McEwan, Ian, 87–104, 90n1, 91n2, 96n5, 166n3

McGuire, Richard, 196

McKibben, Bill, 75

meaning, 48–49, 62, 108, 190–91

media, 5, 15, 47, 67, 68, 99, 148, 199, 203

Meeker, Joseph, 93–94

Mehnert, Antonia, 68

memory traces, 131–32

mental modeling, 131–32

metaphor, 134–35

metarhetorical narrative, 88, 103–4

Milton, John, 92, 98

mimesis, 29–33, 43, 206

mirror neurons, 132–33

Mitchell, David, 193

modeling, mental, 131–32

models, story, 89–90

Monbiot, George, 170n13

Moraga, Cherríe, 204

Morrison, Grant, 14

Morton, Timothy, 4, 28, 36, 36n2, 46–47, 184, 186–87

Mosher, Harold G., Jr., 194

Muir, John, 28, 204–5

Murakami, Haruki, 78

My First Summer in the Sierra (Muir), 204

naïve physics, 50

nanomoment, 77n7

narratee, 6, 69n3, 190–91, 199

narration: first-person, 30, 38–39, 42, 134–36, 141; narrative and, 196–99; nonhuman, 6–7; omniscient, 139, 143, 197; retrospective, 38–39; storyworld and, 143

narrative: in *Annihilation,* 38–40; Anthropocene and, 186–90; anthropocentric bias of, 45–46, 48–49; anthropomorphism and, 33–34; apocalyptic, 99–100; causation and, 50; defined, 190; dual, 112–13; environment and, 2–6; experimental, 46; human experience and, 73; humanism and, 38–42; humanity and, 45; intersubjective experience and, 45; metarhetorical, 88, 103–4; narration and, 196–99; in rhetorical narrative theory, 77; space and, 194–96; time and, 192–94; unnatural, 205–7; "we," 197–99

narrative agency, 3, 190–91, 208

narrative audience, 68–71, 74–76, 81–82, 199

narrative configuration, 76–83, 125

Narrative Discourse (Genette), 8, 192

narrative empathy, 11–12, 111

narrative environment, 10–12, 130–37

Narrative Ethics (Newton), 9n3, 151

narrative ethics: ecocritical, 107–12; in Phelan, 8n3, 108

narrative progression, 88–89, 92–93, 95, 98

Narrative Space and Time: Representing Impossible Topologies in Literature (Gomel), 187

narrative temporality, 193

narratoid, 77n7

"Narratology Beyond the Human" (Herman), 7–8

"Natural Environments in Narrative Contexts: Cross-Pollinating Ecocriticism and Narrative Theory" (Lehtimäki), 5

Neimanis, Astrid, 195

Nelson, Melissa K., 156n4

Nerves and Numbers: Information, Emotion, and Meaning in a World of Data (Slovic and Slovic), 12

neuronal reuse, 132n2

neuroscience, 132–33

new materialism, 14, 190, 206, 208, 286

Newton, Adam Zachary, 9n3, 107–8, 151

Nielsen, Henrik Skov, 7, 30, 102, 206

Nixon, Rob, 193

No Impact Man (Beavan), 205

non-Anglophone texts, 13–14

non-human characters, 14–15

non-human narrators, 6–7, 187

nonlinear temporality, 51–54

novel, 186, 188–89. *See also specific novels*

Nünning, Ansgar, 9n5

Nünning, Vera, 82n8

Nussbaum, Martha, 9n3

object-oriented philosophy, 47

object-oriented plotting, 46–48, 53–54, 57, 60

objectification, 57

objective correlative, 51

Odds Against Tomorrow (Rich), 81–82, 175–76, 176n16, 177–78

Okpewho, Isidore, 14

omniscient narration, 139, 143, 197

"On a Postcolonial Narratology" (Prince), 184n3

On Chesil Beach (McEwan), 91

On Such a Full Sea (Lee), 197–99

Opperman, Serpil, 3, 33, 190–91, 208

orality, 14

Overstory (Powers), 192

Owl on Every Post, An (Babb), 131, 133–39

Paradise Lost (Milton), 98

Phelan, James, 6, 8, 8n3, 9, 39, 68–69, 77, 88, 101–2, 108, 190

Phillips, Dana, 10, 32–33

physics, naïve, 50

plot: and modes of causation, 48–50; and object-oriented plotting, 46–48, 53–54, 57, 60; defined, 46; ecocriticism and, 205; in *Gain*, 112–15; masterplots, 204

Plumwood, Val, 2, 183

possible worlds, 148, 151

postclassical narratology, 4, 8–9, 27–28, 43, 131, 148

Postcolonial Green: Environmental Politics and World Narrative (Roos and Hunt), 4

postcolonial narratology, 9, 12–13, 184n3

postcolonial theory, 28

posthumanism, 16, 28, 190, 206

poststructuralism, 154

Power of Narrative in Environmental Networks, The (Ingram and Ingram), 13n12

Powers, Richard, 108–9, 112–25, 192

Practical Ecocriticism (Love), 148

practical narratology: defined, 148–49; reconstruction and, 154–58, 160; storyworld and, 151–54, 156–58, 160–61

prairie, 147–48, 150–51, 150n1, 152–57, 156n4, 157–62

preservation, 155, 155n3

Price, John, 151

Prince, Gerald, 69n3, 184n3

Prince, Michael B., 168

progression, narrative, 88–89, 92–93, 95, 98

projective locations, 10

Propp, Vladimir, 207

Proulx, Annie, 151, 158–60

Pyrhönen, Heta, 167n5

Qapirangajuq: Inuit Knowledge and Climate Change (Kunuk and Mauro), 204

Quietly, Frank, 14

Rabinowitz, Peter J., 6, 9, 68–69, 71, 77, 79–80

race, 9, 77, 143–44

Rashōmon (film), 205

reading, 76, 79, 83, 107–8, 130, 132

reality effect, 47

reconstruction, 154–58, 160

reliability, of narrator, 39–41

restoration ecology, 150–52, 155–57

retrospective narration, 38–39

Rhetoric of Fiction, The (Booth), 8n3

rhetorical narrative theory, 77, 101–2

Rich, Nathaniel, 81–82, 175–78

Richardson, Brian, 7, 28, 49, 192, 206

Rigby, Kate, 208–9

Rizzolatti, Giacomo, 133

Road, The (McCarthy), 166n3, 170, 170n12

Robinson, Marilynne, 151

Robinson Crusoe (Defoe), 188

Roos, Bonnie, 4

Rose, Deborah Bird, 183

Rothman, Lily, 83n9

Roy, Piyali, 208

Royle, Nicholas, 77–78, 77n7

Rueckert, William, 109

rule of imminent cataclysm, 80–81

rules of configuration, 79–80

Ryan, Marie-Laure, 10, 51, 148, 157, 166, 168, 168n7, 174–75, 174n15, 194

Sand County Almanac, A (Leopold), 192

Sandler, Ronald, 110

Saturday (McEwan), 91

Scarry, Elaine, 135

Schmitt, Arnaud, 52

Schulz, Kathryn, 71, 75–76, 82

science fiction, 170, 172, 174, 174 table 1, 175, 209

seed bank, 156n4

Seitel, Peter, 167

Sense of Place, Sense of Planet (Heise), 4, 121–22

Seveneves (Stephenson), 209

Shklovsky, Viktor, 32

Silent Spring (Carson), 204

Sinigaglia, Corrado, 133

Slovic, Paul, 12

Slovic, Scott, 12, 79, 95n4

slow violence, 193

Solar (McEwan), 87–97, 96n5, 97–104, 166n3

solastalgia, 196

Solastalgia (Vitaglione), 195

Sörlin, Sverker, 2

Souriau, Etienne, 207

space, narrative and, 194–96

species, 196–97

speculative fiction, 209

Stapledon, Olaf, 209

Stegner, Wallace, 147–48, 158–59

Steinbeck, John, 138

Stephenson, Neal, 209

"Storied Lives of Non-human Narrators, The" (Bernaerts, Caracciolo, Herman, and Vervaeck), 6–7

Story Logic (Herman), 35, 152, 194

story models, 89–90

storyworld, 10–11, 35–38, 151–54, 156–58, 160–61

Storyworld Accord, The: Econarratology and Postcolonial Narratives (James), 5–6, 12–13, 149–50

"Storyworld/Umwelt: Nonhuman Experiences in Graphic Narratives" (Herman), 14

survival, 93–99

Tale of Soap and Water, A: The Historical Progress of Cleanliness (Hallock), 117

Tatsumi, Takayuki, 77–79

That Old Ace in the Hole (Proulx), 158–60, 160n5

Then We Came to the End (Ferris), 197–98

Theory of Mind (ToM), 11

theory-practice, 68

Thoreau, Henry David, 28, 78, 205

time, narrative and, 192–94

To Make the Hands Impure (Newton), 9n3

Todorov, Tzvetan, 167

ToM. *See* Theory of Mind (ToM)

topological locations, 10

topological space, 35

"Toward a Feminist Narratology" (Lanser), 9

Toward a Natural Narratology (Fludernik), 27–28

toxic discourse, 112

trans-corporeality, 12, 33

travel narratives, 152–53

Trexler, Adam, 68, 83, 99, 166n3, 169, 169n11, 170nn12–13, 170–71, 186

triangulation, 116–20

"Trouble with Wilderness, The" (Cronon), 28

Truth About Stories, The (King), 151

Tuan, Yi-Fu, 136

Turner, Mark, 49

Twain, Mark, 68–75, 82

Tyndall, John, 74n4

umwelt exploration, 14–15

Underworld (DeLillo), 46, 49–56, 58–59, 61

unnatural narrative, 205–7

unnatural narratology: defined, 28; ecocriticism and, 31–33; experimental narratives and, 46; mimesis and, 29–31, 43 unspatialization, 195–96

VanderMeer, Jeff, 29–30, 34–37, 36n2, 37–39, 41–42, 206
Vermeule, Blakey, 12, 188
Vermeulen, Pieter, 169
Vervaeck, Bart, 6, 187
violence, slow, 193
Vitaglione, Marina, 195
Vizenor, Gerald, 150n1
von Uexküll, Jakob, 14n13

Walden (Thoreau), 78, 205
Walsh, Richard, 102
Warhol, Robyn, 9, 9n6
Warner, Charles Dudley, 68
water, 194–96
"we" narratives, 197–99

"We-Narratives" (Bekhta), 197
We3 (Quietly), 14
Weik von Mossner, Alexa, 10, 12, 15, 210
weird realism, 30, 34
Whitman, Walt, 109
Whose Names Are Unknown (Babb), 129–30, 137–44
Williams, Raymond, 209
Williams, Terry Tempest, 135
World Made by Hand (Kunstler), 166n3
worldmaking, 166
worlds, 151–52, 172–80, 174 table 1

xerophilia, 135–36, 136n6

Zalasiewicz, Jan, 192
Ziff, Larzer, 68n2
Zunshine, Lisa, 12, 111

THEORY AND INTERPRETATION OF NARRATIVE

JAMES PHELAN, PETER J. RABINOWITZ, AND KATRA BYRAM, SERIES EDITORS

Because the series editors believe that the most significant work in narrative studies today contributes both to our knowledge of specific narratives and to our understanding of narrative in general, studies in the series typically offer interpretations of individual narratives and address significant theoretical issues underlying those interpretations. The series does not privilege one critical perspective but is open to work from any strong theoretical position.

Environment and Narrative: New Directions in Econarratology edited by Erin James and Eric Morel

Unnatural Narratology: Extensions, Revisions, and Challenges edited by Jan Alber and Brian Richardson

A Poetics of Plot for the Twenty-First Century: Theorizing Unruly Narratives by Brian Richardson

Playing at Narratology: Digital Media as Narrative Theory by Daniel Punday

Making Conversation in Modernist Fiction by Elizabeth Alsop

Narratology and Ideology: Negotiating Context, Form, and Theory in Postcolonial Narratives edited by Divya Dwivedi, Henrik Skov Nielsen, and Richard Walsh

Novelization: From Film to Novel by Jan Baetens

Reading Conrad by J. Hillis Miller, Edited by John G. Peters and Jakob Lothe

Narrative, Race, and Ethnicity in the United States edited by James J. Donahue, Jennifer Ann Ho, and Shaun Morgan

Somebody Telling Somebody Else: A Rhetorical Poetics of Narrative by James Phelan

Media of Serial Narrative edited by Frank Kelleter

Suture and Narrative: Deep Intersubjectivity in Fiction and Film by George Butte

The Writer in the Well: On Misreading and Rewriting Literature by Gary Weissman

Narrating Space / Spatializing Narrative: Where Narrative Theory and Geography Meet by Marie-Laure Ryan, Kenneth Foote, and Maoz Azaryahu

Narrative Sequence in Contemporary Narratology edited by Raphaël Baroni and Françoise Revaz

The Submerged Plot and the Mother's Pleasure from Jane Austen to Arundhati Roy by Kelly A. Marsh

Narrative Theory Unbound: Queer and Feminist Interventions edited by Robyn Warhol and Susan S. Lanser

Unnatural Narrative: Theory, History, and Practice by Brian Richardson

Ethics and the Dynamic Observer Narrator: Reckoning with Past and Present in German Literature by Katra A. Byram

Narrative Paths: African Travel in Modern Fiction and Nonfiction by Kai Mikkonen

The Reader as Peeping Tom: Nonreciprocal Gazing in Narrative Fiction and Film by Jeremy Hawthorn

Thomas Hardy's Brains: Psychology, Neurology, and Hardy's Imagination by Suzanne Keen

The Return of the Omniscient Narrator: Authorship and Authority in Twenty-First Century Fiction by Paul Dawson

Feminist Narrative Ethics: Tacit Persuasion in Modernist Form by Katherine Saunders Nash

Real Mysteries: Narrative and the Unknowable by H. Porter Abbott

A Poetics of Unnatural Narrative edited by Jan Alber, Henrik Skov Nielsen, and Brian Richardson

Narrative Discourse: Authors and Narrators in Literature, Film, and Art by Patrick Colm Hogan

An Aesthetics of Narrative Performance: Transnational Theater, Literature, and Film in Contemporary Germany by Claudia Breger

Literary Identification from Charlotte Brontë to Tsitsi Dangarembga by Laura Green

Narrative Theory: Core Concepts and Critical Debates by David Herman, James Phelan and Peter J. Rabinowitz, Brian Richardson, and Robyn Warhol

After Testimony: The Ethics and Aesthetics of Holocaust Narrative for the Future edited by Jakob Lothe, Susan Rubin Suleiman, and James Phelan

The Vitality of Allegory: Figural Narrative in Modern and Contemporary Fiction by Gary Johnson

Narrative Middles: Navigating the Nineteenth-Century British Novel edited by Caroline Levine and Mario Ortiz-Robles

Fact, Fiction, and Form: Selected Essays by Ralph W. Rader. Edited by James Phelan and David H. Richter.

The Real, the True, and the Told: Postmodern Historical Narrative and the Ethics of Representation by Eric L. Berlatsky

Franz Kafka: Narration, Rhetoric, and Reading edited by Jakob Lothe, Beatrice Sandberg, and Ronald Speirs

Social Minds in the Novel by Alan Palmer

Narrative Structures and the Language of the Self by Matthew Clark

Imagining Minds: The Neuro-Aesthetics of Austen, Eliot, and Hardy by Kay Young

Postclassical Narratology: Approaches and Analyses edited by Jan Alber and Monika Fludernik

Techniques for Living: Fiction and Theory in the Work of Christine Brooke-Rose by Karen R. Lawrence

Towards the Ethics of Form in Fiction: Narratives of Cultural Remission by Leona Toker

Tabloid, Inc.: Crimes, Newspapers, Narratives by V. Penelope Pelizzon and Nancy M. West

Narrative Means, Lyric Ends: Temporality in the Nineteenth-Century British Long Poem by Monique R. Morgan

Understanding Nationalism: On Narrative, Cognitive Science, and Identity by Patrick Colm Hogan

Joseph Conrad: Voice, Sequence, History, Genre edited by Jakob Lothe, Jeremy Hawthorn, James Phelan

The Rhetoric of Fictionality: Narrative Theory and the Idea of Fiction by Richard Walsh

Experiencing Fiction: Judgments, Progressions, and the Rhetorical Theory of Narrative by James Phelan

Unnatural Voices: Extreme Narration in Modern and Contemporary Fiction by Brian Richardson

Narrative Causalities by Emma Kafalenos

Why We Read Fiction: Theory of Mind and the Novel by Lisa Zunshine

I Know That You Know That I Know: Narrating Subjects from Moll Flanders *to* Marnie by George Butte

Bloodscripts: Writing the Violent Subject by Elana Gomel

Surprised by Shame: Dostoevsky's Liars and Narrative Exposure by Deborah A. Martinsen

Having a Good Cry: Effeminate Feelings and Pop-Culture Forms by Robyn R. Warhol

Politics, Persuasion, and Pragmatism: A Rhetoric of Feminist Utopian Fiction by Ellen Peel

Telling Tales: Gender and Narrative Form in Victorian Literature and Culture by Elizabeth Langland

Narrative Dynamics: Essays on Time, Plot, Closure, and Frames edited by Brian Richardson

Breaking the Frame: Metalepsis and the Construction of the Subject by Debra Malina

Invisible Author: Last Essays by Christine Brooke-Rose

Ordinary Pleasures: Couples, Conversation, and Comedy by Kay Young

Narratologies: New Perspectives on Narrative Analysis edited by David Herman

Before Reading: Narrative Conventions and the Politics of Interpretation by Peter J. Rabinowitz

Matters of Fact: Reading Nonfiction over the Edge by Daniel W. Lehman

The Progress of Romance: Literary Historiography and the Gothic Novel by David H. Richter

A Glance Beyond Doubt: Narration, Representation, Subjectivity by Shlomith Rimmon-Kenan

Narrative as Rhetoric: Technique, Audiences, Ethics, Ideology by James Phelan

Misreading Jane Eyre: *A Postformalist Paradigm* by Jerome Beaty

Psychological Politics of the American Dream: The Commodification of Subjectivity in Twentieth-Century American Literature by Lois Tyson

Understanding Narrative edited by James Phelan and Peter J. Rabinowitz

Framing Anna Karenina: Tolstoy, the Woman Question, and the Victorian Novel by Amy Mandelker

Gendered Interventions: Narrative Discourse in the Victorian Novel by Robyn R. Warhol

Reading People, Reading Plots: Character, Progression, and the Interpretation of Narrative by James Phelan

CPSIA information can be obtained
at www.ICGtesting.com
Printed in the USA
LVHW092019150120
643749LV00001B/5